ALSO BY CHUCK PFARRER

WARRIOR SOUL
The Memoir of a Navy SEAL

SAINT BRENDAN'S BOAT

Killing
Che

2008 Random House Trade Paperback Edition

Copyright © 2007 by Chuck Pfarrer
Maps copyright © 2007 by David Lindroth, Inc.

Published in the United States by Random House Trade Paperbacks,
an imprint of The Random House Publishing Group,
a division of Random House, Inc., New York.

RANDOM HOUSE TRADE PAPERBACKS and colophon
are trademarks of Random House, Inc.

ISBN 978-0-8129-7411-9

Printed in the United States of America

www.atrandom.com

2 4 6 8 9 7 5 3 1

Book design by Jo Anne Metsch

Killing

Che

A NOVEL

CHUCK PFARRER

Random House Trade Paperbacks

New York

FOR MY MOTHER AND FATHER

Juntos cincuenta años

Whosoever unceasingly strives upward . . .

him we can save.

—GOETHE

What follows is a novel. Some of its characters are real, and some are not. As a courtesy to the living, a few names have been altered; the names of others I have not changed, out of respect for their heroism.

I have drawn liberally from Che Guevara's own campaign diary, as well as the notes, letters, and accounts of the comrades who lived, fought, and perished along with him and his dream.

They alone know what really happened.

The rest of us are left to marvel.

The Republic of Bolivia
Showing the Guerrilla Area

0   miles   400

0   kilometers   400

BRAZIL

PERU

PANDO

LA PAZ

BENI

Lake Titicaca

Hotel Casino de la Selva

La Paz

Chapare

COCHABAMBA

Cochabamba

SANTA CRUZ

Samaipata

Santa Cruz

Vallegrande

ORURO

Catavi

Sucre

area of guerrilla operations
(see detail map)

Potosí

Lagunillas

Camiri

POTOSÍ

CHUQUISACA

CHILE

TARIJA

Tarija

PARAGUAY

N
W   E
S

Masetti's body discovered

ARGENTINA

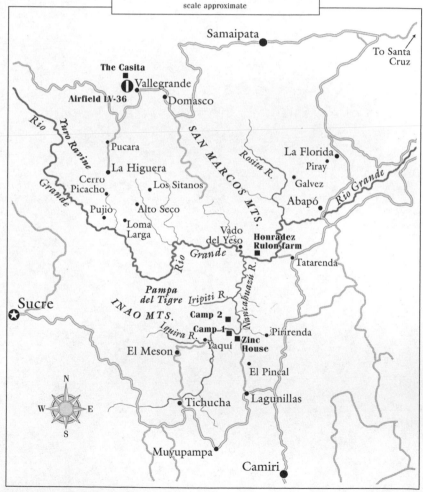

Ñancahuazú Valley
Central Bolivia, 1967

| 0 | miles | 60 |
| 0 | kilometers | 100 |

scale approximate

Samaipata

To Santa Cruz

The Casita

Vallegrande

Airfield LV-36

Domasco

Rio

Yuro Ravine

Pucara

SAN MARCOS MTS.

Rosita R.

La Florida

Piray

La Higuera

Los Sitanos

Galvez

Cerro Picacho

Abapó

Rio Grande

Grande

Pujio

Alto Seco

Loma Larga

Vado del Yeso

Honradez Rulon farm

Rio Grande

Tatarenda

Sucre

Pampa del Tigre

Iripiti R.

INAO MTS.

Camp 2

Nancahuazú R.

Iquira R.

Camp 1

Pirirenda

El Meson

Yaquí

Zinc House

El Pincal

N

W   E

S

Tichucha

Lagunillas

Muyupampa

Camiri

PART

I

Gathering

1

THE PLACE WAS not perfect. This was not where he'd wanted to fight, not on this road, and not on this hillside, which was mostly barren and lit fully by the afternoon sun. Che Guevara had not wished to ambush the truck in the first place, but the soldiers in it had seen the forward element as they were drawing water from the stream next to the road, and the engagement was sharp and fast. Guevara had cursed when the lead column blundered close to the road, and he was furious when he heard the *pop pop pop* of rifles firing ahead of him.

Guevara trotted past the burning truck, and the reek of flaming tires wafted over him, sharp and acrid. Some of the smoke was white, but most of it was black and rising in a dense, greasy pillar above the mountain road and into a vividly cloudless sky. By the time Guevara reached the place where the stream cut under the road, he guessed that perhaps a hundred bullets had been fired into the cab alone—a quarter blasted through the windshield—and as the driver lost control, the truck had lurched off the turn, smashing over a low guardrail but somehow remaining upright. Guevara had splashed out of the culvert in time to see the bodies of the driver and the passenger dragged from the cab. Their heads lolled, and the heels of their boots made white marks across the road as the corpses were hidden next to the stream. What had been fatal misfortune for the truck drivers would now become an opportunity for the guerrillas.

Guevara knew that from the valley the smoke could be seen for miles. As he crossed the road, he looked back at the burning hulk; inside the cab he could see the steering wheel ablaze in a perfect circle of flames. He was certain now that the army would come, and he was confident that at this distance, the Bolivian soldiers would not see him, his men, or the ambush put down on the last of the tight hairpin turns carved into the mountainside.

All he had to do was wait.

Cradling his rifle in the crook of his elbow, Guevara moved into cover behind a large boulder. His dark hair was shoulder-length, and his beard, thin as it was, covered his face from nose to chin. He was of medium height, and six weeks in the cordillera had made his features sharp and angular—he still looked younger than his thirty-eight years, but rather more haggard than he had looked in many months.

At the boulder, Guevara shifted the weight of his pack off his hips, then the straps from his shoulders. His back was wet where the pack had covered it, and his shirt stuck to his skin as he dropped the rucksack onto the gravel. Where Guevara took cover, there were two men, Joaquin and one of the Bolivian comrades, Willy. Joaquin calmly chewed a piece of grass as Guevara took a map from his pocket and unfolded it on the dirt. Resting his chin on his hand, Guevara looked at the map and then below, where the ribbon of oiled road switched back on itself in a series of tight hairpins. What was called the Camiri Highway was not much more than a two-lane dirt track. Often it was worse. Immediately before each of the hairpin corners was a rude wooden guardrail, and beyond the series of drop-offs, the road was thin and nearly straight as it traversed the valley nine or ten kilometers distant. In places, the road doubled on itself, trees clumped together, and on the valley floor, irregularly shaped plots of corn were bordered by clumps of brush and lavish stands of hardwood. As it paid off into the valley, the road shone almost white against the grass-covered hillsides.

Joaquin squinted down into the valley. On the road below, a truck and two jeeps appeared over a distant hill and slowly, slowly began the long climb.

"I'm guessing we have twenty minutes, maybe thirty," Joaquin said.

"Yes," Guevara answered.

"Do you think they'll send a patrol up first?"

"If they do, we'll see it."

Guevara took a pair of binoculars from his pack and studied the convoy. Behind the vehicles, ocher trails of dust blew off to the south. In each of two jeeps, a sergeant was behind the wheel, and beside him was an officer in a green field uniform and a gold-braided hat. Such hats. They were an amazement. Behind the jeeps, nearly invisible in the dust clouds, was a large American-made truck. A .30-caliber machine gun was mounted in a turret ring on the roof of the cab.

"How many men?" Joaquin asked.

"Enough to go around."

The soldiers in the convoy outnumbered the men he had on the slope, but that did not matter. Guevara watched for a few moments, then handed the glasses to Joaquin.

As he took the binoculars, Joaquin lifted himself on an elbow. Above the Ñancahuazú basin, the sun beat down, and glare burned from the windshields of the convoy. Joaquin counted thirty-eight Bolivian soldiers and two officers. Like Guevara, he wasn't worried by the numbers. Joaquin had learned long ago that a few men in ambush could kill many men on a road, and he was sure the comandante knew his business.

"Keep the center group out of sight in the ravine," Guevara said. "I'll initiate on the lead vehicle."

Joaquin glanced over the ambuscade; ten men were hidden along the outside of the turn, and another seventeen in a line with Joaquin and Guevara. They made roughly the shape of an L. Twenty more men were in cover just over the crest of the hill, backing up the main force—a surety against surprises on their flank or rear.

"You think they're ready for this?" Joaquin asked.

"Us or the army?"

Joaquin smiled tightly. Guevara took back his binoculars and placed them in his pack. "What's the matter, Joaquin? Got the butterflies?"

"Bats is more like it."

It was Guevara's turn to smile. Joaquin lifted himself to a crouch and trotted off toward a place among the second group.

Guevara adjusted his rifle strap and felt the slow, steady beating of his heart against the brown dirt. He breathed deeply and felt a twang of pain in his chest. He clenched his teeth hard. It was a tactic he had used since boyhood to hold off the asthma that was like an anvil pressing down on his lungs. He made his body rigid and inhaled deeply, imagining that he was drinking in air like water. He tried to make himself think of other things—to think of anything but the tightness around his heart and the wheezing in his throat. For an instant he considered having the men fall back, having them avoid this second contact, but he knew the convoy was too close. They were committed, and now the ambush must happen.

Guevara had not wanted contact with the enemy for several reasons. In the first place, the Bolivian comrades were green, and that was why they'd scattered after the first exchange of fire. A second and more tricky problem was that the contact had occurred too early in the day. There were still many hours of sun left, and in daylight the guerrillas could easily be pursued or spotted from the air. They were now only thirty miles from the garrison town of Abapó.

Guevara cursed again. At that manly art, he excelled—his favorite insult being "monkey-faced shit-eater"—and slowly, his mood lightened. In the first engagement, they had not lost a man, and two of the enemy were dead. Joaquin had told him that some of the Bolivian comrades had done well. They had dropped into covered positions and fired steadily. In every engagement, there are things to be learned, and now the Bolivian comrades would be taught to stand and fight. This was a start.

A fluttering of diesel exhaust pulled Guevara from his reverie. Creeping forward in low gear, the convoy came steadily up the twisting road. The Bolivian officer had kept his men in their vehicles—he'd been too stupid or too lazy to send a foot patrol first to investigate the burning truck. Guevara could see the major's jeep as it approached the start of the last hairpin. Standing on the passenger seat, the officer had one hand on the top of the windshield. As the convoy lurched around the turn, the major was looking at the burning wreck, staring at the only place around him where the guerrillas were not. The major was a paunchy man in a sateen uniform. There was a silver pip on each of his gold-braided shoulder boards. Guevara aimed carefully, the man's name tag positioned perfectly over the front sight. Several long seconds passed, and Guevara let the jeep roll slowly to the place he knew marked the end of the first squad.

When the lead jeep was just even with him, Guevara rocked the safety with his thumb and moved the muzzle of his rifle slightly to the right. He squeezed a long burst into the major's radio, an oblong box mounted on the rear of the jeep. Instantly, the guerrillas opened fire.

The ambush broke upon the Bolivian soldiers like a wave. The noise was astonishing, a cacophony of hammer strikes and screeching ricochets. Four bullet holes appeared in the windshield of the first jeep, and the driver jerked backward in a pink cloud of blood and brain matter. A bullet creased the visor of the major's hat, ripping it from his head and spinning it through the air like a pie tin. Although he had been missed, the major's knees buckled, and as he fell, he clutched at the uniform of the dead sergeant. Bullets kicked dust and gravel from the road, and the major pulled the sergeant's corpse on top of himself as a shield.

Bullets swept the turn in the road, striking everywhere. Riddled with fire, the truck slammed on its brakes, and the second jeep smashed into the rear of the burning truck. A young lieutenant spilled from the jeep, waving his pistol in the air and yelling for his men to advance. Some soldiers did jump down from the truck, but they fell where they landed in the road, crumpling like broken dolls. The lieutenant continued to rush forward and was cut down when he stumbled into the cross fire. He fell to his knees, then toppled over as three bullets drilled into him. He lay twitching in a widening puddle of blood that mixed with the dirt, rendering a pool black and thick as tar.

In forty-five seconds, all effective resistance had ceased. Several of the Bolivian soldiers threw down their weapons and started to run off downhill. Some made it. Some were shot down.

Guevara stood, placed his fingers in his mouth, and whistled loudly. The shooting stopped as if someone had turned off a tap. His ears were ringing, and the day seemed suddenly to have been made still. No birds sang. He could not hear the noise of the wind. For a long moment there was only the sound of the fire burning inside the cab of the wrecked truck.

In the shade of the first jeep, Major Gustavo Villa Lopez Buran curled himself against the tire and considered playing dead. The body of his driver was sprawled across his legs; blood from the sergeant's several wounds was soaking through the major's trousers. The major could hear the crunching of boots crossing the dirt road and he unsnapped the top flap on his leather holster, removed the pistol, an

American-made .45 automatic—and he tossed the gun under the jeep.
After this, Major Buran kept his head down and did not move. He
heard the moans of the wounded and commands being shouted. The
major kept his eyes closed and prayed not to be killed.

A boot pushed upon his shoulder.

"*Arriba, maricón.*"

Major Buran held his breath and did not move. The voice said again:
"Get up."

Major Buran slowly lifted his face from the dust. Above him stood a
bearded man wearing a green slouch cap like a cabdriver might wear.
The sun was directly behind the man's head, and looking up, the major
could see only a silhouette with a blinding corona behind it.

"Are you the ranking officer?" Guevara asked.

The major nodded, all at once aware that his mouth was dry as sand.
The man standing over him reached down and lifted the officer to his
feet.

"I'm prepared to accept your surrender."

"You have it," Buran stammered.

Next to the truck, the surviving Bolivian soldiers raised their hands.

"What's the name of your unit?" Guevara asked.

The major was silent, breathing like a man who had climbed a long
staircase.

"Come on, friend, let's do this the easy way," Joaquin said.

"We are the Second Company . . . Second of the Fourth Infantry
Division."

"Based in Abapó?"

The major took a second to answer. "That is correct."

The guerrillas herded together the unwounded soldiers, disarmed
them, and relieved them of their boots. Packs and crates of ammunition were handed down from the truck. The goods were quickly distributed among the guerrillas. The major was stunned, leaning against
the hood of his jeep, blinking like an idiot.

Guevara spoke in a measured tone. "We are going to patch up your
wounded, then your men are to be marched along the road back to
Abapó." Guevara slung his rifle and produced a well-chewed pipe. Despite his asthma, tobacco was his chief vice and muse. He reached into
the top pocket of the major's uniform and removed a silver Zippo
lighter. He flicked it open and applied the light to the bowl of his pipe.

The guerrillas heaped burning bundles of reeds into the two jeeps and the truck. The vehicles quickly started to burn.

Joaquin touched Guevara on the elbow. "We're ready, Comandante."

"Commence the withdrawal," Guevara said.

The guerrillas started off, one group moving uphill and following the stream. The second group ambled over the side of the embankment and plunge-stepped down into the canyon. Guevara removed a notebook from his pack and leaned against the hood of the wrecked jeep. As the major stood and panted, Guevara calmly composed a letter. He then tore the sheet from the notebook and handed it to Major Buran.

"This is a communiqué from the Army of National Liberation. Give it to your commanding general."

Buran took the paper, noticing for the first time that his fingers were black with blood and dirt. Guevara observed blandly that the major's hands were shaking. As Guevara put on his pack, he looked down at the body of the lieutenant sprawled next to the truck.

"Who was this man?" he asked.

"Cortazar," the major answered. "His name was Cortazar."

The lieutenant's head was turned, his pistol lying next to his outstretched hand, and his eyes were closed. He looked like a little boy, asleep forever.

"Tell his family he died bravely," Guevara said.

Trembling, Major Buran watched as Guevara and his band stepped off the road and vanished into the bush.

2

THERE WAS A map of Bolivia on the wall of the office at Avenida Camacho. Its frame was cracked and a gouge in the legend block seemed to indicate that there had been a collision with a flying object. The map was an amazing thing, not least because of its age, but because great portions of it were blank. The map dated from the period of the Chaco War in the mid-1930s, a trumped-up series of clashes between Bolivia, backed by Standard Oil, and Paraguay, backed with greater enthusiasm by Shell. Bolivia came out the loser, and the map was proof. On it, the nation was regularly interrupted by light-colored voids of parchment, huge swaths of countryside lost to its neighbor. In other places, the blanks were lands the Bolivians had managed to keep but had yet to survey. Some of this unexplored country was jungle, some was mountainous, and on the altiplano, some was almost lunar desert. Places that were blanks, truly. Often roads, or tracks that were reported to be roads, cut across stretches of empty paper, the vacuum seeming to indicate that no one thought enough of these places to even look right or left.

It was from one of these empty spaces, a vacant stretch of parchment south of the provincial seat of Tarija, that Paul Hoyle had just come.

From the street, the snarl of trucks and *minipolos* came up the stairs and reverberated in the empty waiting room. Hoyle sat in a straight-backed chair by the office door. His toes touched the unswept floor, and his weight tipped the chair back on two legs, leaning against the wall. Hoyle's jaw was strong, perhaps even undershot, his nose straight and thin. Under distinct brows, his deep-set green eyes were capable of great charm; they also might just as easily flash determination and passion. Hoyle's age was thirty-five and his build was angular; even under the drapery of a khaki jacket and trousers, his physique could be discerned as powerful. A pair of scars, one on his forehead over his right eye, and another tracing under his jaw, were the only things that advertised Hoyle as a man who might have secrets. In fact, he had many.

There was one other person in the waiting room with him: Miguel Castañeda, an eager young man who paced and smoked. Castañeda was decked in the garish uniform of a *tenente* in the Bolivian National Police—riding boots, jodhpurs, and peaked cap—the field-gray ensemble more than vaguely Nazi-looking.

"Not long now," Castañeda said. He exhaled, and smoke crawled into the yellow light slanting down from the transom.

Hoyle ignored him, as he had managed to do for most of the long, jangling ride from Potosí. His eyes went to the map.

Hoyle traced out the route they had traveled, from La Paz, south to Oruro on roads gouged through the Cordillera Central, on to Potosí, then Tarija, and into the southernmost part of that province: a V-shaped appendage jutting into Argentina. On the map, this, too, was void, though Hoyle knew the place to be a rugged huddle of mountains bound to the west by the headwaters of the Bermejo River and to the east by the Tarya.

It was there, at an intersection of trails above ten thousand feet, that Hoyle had found the bodies. Two men, or what was left of their corpses, the bodies three years in the elements and scavenged by condors. The skeletons were photographed in situ, and the bones were shoveled into a pair of military duffel bags to be trucked back to La Paz. Their papers and effects had identified them without question, but word had come by cable that forensic efforts should be undertaken to make certain. That errand brought Paul Hoyle and Lieutenant Castañeda into the small office off the Avenida Camacho and into the waiting room of Señor José Lempira de Murcia y Hernan, a onetime dental student whose livelihood was identifying skulls brought to him by the secret police.

As Hoyle stared at the map, his expression was unreadable, a perfect cipher. But he was, at this moment, disappointed, angry, and tired. The combination of these feelings imparted in him a gnawing sort of melancholy.

The trip from Tarija had been deadly long, made interminable by rain, Castañeda, and a broken drive shaft. The journey had also been astounding for the depth and wretchedness of poverty that it revealed. Bolivia had sometimes been called the Nepal of Latin America; the comparison was valid only as far as both countries were precipitous, isolated, and tragically beautiful. The nation through which Hoyle had traveled was the poorest in the Western Hemisphere, the most desperately backward place in the Americas, save Haiti. In the countryside, cholos, those of Indian descent, lived in almost Paleolithic squalor. There were places so far-flung and neglected that the camposinos had only the vaguest idea that there existed a thing called government, or that it was seated in a magic place called La Paz. Hoyle had seen poverty before, he was well traveled, but he had lately become used to the smiling, tropical kind of want. Privation under the palms. He was unprepared for the cold and damp, the long gazes of the Indian women, the appalling deformities of their children, or an existence where a bundle of reeds was considered tolerable shelter from driving snow.

Inasmuch as any task could be completed on time in Bolivia, Hoyle had located the bodies with remarkable alacrity. But it had still taken eight weeks, a month longer than he had been paid, and there was the gnawing question of what would happen now. Hoyle worried about his standing with his employers, a thing that was extremely tenuous. He thought of his disappointment at his present assignment, the half promises that had been made to him and broken, the plans he had made and built up on artificial foundations. He was lucky, he knew, to have a job at all.

Paul Hoyle had been a CIA paramilitary officer for eight years, serving in Latin America, Europe, and, most recently, in Southeast Asia. And it was in Laos ten months ago that Hoyle and the agency had parted company. There had been the death of an English journalist— some would not hesitate to use the word "murder"—but Hoyle saw the death as an operational necessity. His superiors did not fully share his views on the matter. Following a reprimand and suspension, Hoyle had resigned. The resignation he soon came to regret; it was a gesture he had made in a fit of pride, and in the months that followed, he had come to think less of this most costly of sentiments.

There followed a lotus time back in the United States, where he was unemployed and his marriage unraveled. His divorce, which had finally concluded at Thanksgiving, was still a raw thing in his heart. He owed money on a house he did not live in and another that he rarely if ever saw. He owed no money to his ex-wife, but he had taken personal loans from a friend who was a mortgage broker. Hoyle had borrowed in order to pay the divorce settlement, an amount roughly three times his annual salary, a lump sum his ex-wife preferred to alimony and any sort of continuing association with him.

This bit of extortion strangled a lifestyle that was already frugal, if not spartan. Although it nearly broke him, this arrangement, too, had been urged upon him by the CIA, chiefly because Hoyle's ex-wife knew what he did for a living.

The money, it was hoped, would shut her up.

Friends in the agency followed his decline, and he was offered a job—the task of recovering the two bodies in Tarija. Hoyle worked now in a diminished capacity, that of contractor, the word having malignant, shabby connotations within the intelligence community. The nomenclature was used for assassins, poisoners, and prostitutes: dispensable people with objectionable skills. The term also applied to ad hoc employees like Hoyle, onetime intelligence officers, cashiered, retired, or marginalized. Fallen angels.

The recovery operation was a make-work assignment, one granted to him out of pity, he knew, but without other prospects, he could do little but accept. Bolivia was not just a backwater. It was a dumping ground—a place of pencil pushers who had no careers, no prospects, and no friends in Washington. Hoyle knew this well, for he had served in La Paz as a junior officer and done his level best to get out. The land of Bolívar was thousands of miles from action, adventure, or any sort of real work. For the Company, Bolivia was a penalty tour, but Hoyle had no choice when the offer was put to him.

To locate the bodies Hoyle had spent his entire advance, overstayed four weeks, and now could only hope that the agency would pay his invoice. This was no certainty. If Langley said no, there would be damn little he could do about it.

There was a scraping at the door, and Señor Lempira shuffled into the waiting room. Bug-eyed, frumpy, he was dressed in a yellowing laboratory coat and carried two hatboxes. Each box contained a human skull.

"Absolutamente," Señor Lempira said. "Both are identified." He placed the hatboxes on the table, and Castañeda opened one and lifted out a skull by the eye sockets.

Bored with the skulls and bored with Castañeda, Hoyle stood. "You're certain?"

"Bridgework, fillings, and crowns. Also the roots." Thrusting out his lip, Señor Lempira took the skull away from Castañeda and placed it back in its box. "You can change the dental work, but not the anatomy. These are the people you were looking for."

Lempira handed Hoyle a manila envelope filled with dental X-rays as Castañeda counted out three hundred-dollar bills. Lempira took the money, Castañeda the hatboxes.

"This has ended well for us, Mr. Hoyle." The lieutenant grinned.

"It's been a pleasure working with you, *Tenente.*" Hoyle's lie was smoothly delivered. It was a talent that came easily to him.

THAT EVENING IN the safe house at the Plaza España, Hoyle gathered the dossiers and maps, opened a bottle of bourbon, and prepared to draft his message to Langley. The story of the skulls, of Jorge Ricardo Masetti and Héctor Atilio, was one of romance, fanaticism, and catastrophe.

Masetti had been a journalist, an Argentine, and the first to interview Che Guevara and Fidel Castro during the Cuban revolution. Eventually befriending Guevara, Masetti was converted to the cause and underwent extensive military training in Cuba. He assembled a force of Argentine leftists, and together with Cuban intelligence officers and members of Guevara's personal bodyguard, his group was infiltrated into Bolivia.

The guerrillas purchased a remote farm in the *departamento* of Tarija, across the Bermejo River from Argentina. Their goal was the establishment of a guerrilla *foco,* a revolutionary nucleus, in Argentina. Their plans were grandiose, their methods amateur, and their fate inevitable.

Masetti led his twenty-man force across the border into Argentina and established a series of camps in the mountains of Salta Province. Calling himself Comandante Segundo, Masetti vaingloriously announced their presence in a press communiqué, calling his band the People's Guerrilla Army. A steady stream of visitors and resupply trips to their base soon garnered the attention of the Argentinean *gendarmería*. In a matter of weeks their major supply camp was taken and six guerrillas captured. One by one, his men died of starvation, fell from cliffs, perished in firefights, or were captured. Only Comandante Segundo and Héctor Atilio were to escape the pursuing Argentine forces.

Hoyle's job had been to ascertain if the survivors had returned to Bolivia or had perished. Arriving in Tarija, he studied the terrain on both sides of the frontier, imagining the route Masetti would choose. Pursued by a superior force, Hoyle knew Masetti would be compelled to move along ridgelines, avoiding places of ambush, water supplies, villages, and roads, and to travel mostly at night. Masetti's only hope was to get his diminished command back across the frontier into Bolivia. Following a final clash below the headwaters of the Bermejo, Masetti left his casualties to fend for themselves, turned east, and made a final lunge for the border. Masetti and Atilio crossed into Bolivia but went no farther. Hoyle found their bodies on a south-facing slope, little more than rags and bones, tangled together under a cliff face jutting back toward Argentina. Their career as guerrillas had lasted barely thirty-six weeks.

Hoyle placed the dossiers of Atilio and Masetti in the kitchen sink and put a match to them. He watched as the flames crept across the faces, stirred the ashes, and then sat down to write: *Forensic identification positive of Masetti, Jorge, and Atilio, Héctor.*

Hoyle crossed out the names and above them wrote their CIA cryptoglyphs: SL/MALICE and SL/UPSTART. SL demarked their national affiliation, Argentine; this was followed by their operational handles, code names used in routine traffic. Hoyle continued to write, the pencil scratching over paper:

Bodies recovered inside Bolivian territory at grid reference XS 2381 2254. Condition of remains suggests time of death March–May 1963. SL/MALICE succumbed unk causes. SL/UPSTART of self-inflicted gun-

shot to head. Confirmed with Argentine and Bolivian liaison services
that remaining members PGA captured/killed within Argentina. Recovery accounts for last two members of Cuban-sponsored revolutionary group inserted Argentina. Regret efforts took longer than
expected.

He reread the message, encoded it by hand, replacing each word
with a five-digit number from his codebook, then sent the message on
the high-frequency radio concealed in the false bottom of his suitcase.
After the message was acknowledged, Hoyle recoiled the antenna and
listened for an hour to the Voice of America on the shortwave.

There were several stories of interest. Four hundred members of the
faculty of Yale University had signed a petition calling for the end of
the bombing of North Vietnam, and Cassius Clay had appealed to the
Louisville draft board to request a deferment from military service.
There was a piece on the Red Guards in China, and a last news item
from Latin America. The announcer blithely noted that twenty-four
hours ago, guerrillas had attacked a Bolivian army unit on the Camiri
Highway in Santa Cruz. Details were evolving, but a number of soldiers and one officer had been reported killed in the ambush. Further
details were promised by the Bolivian minister of information as they
became available.

Hoyle was dumbstruck. His report had been sent and could not be
pulled back from the ether. Could Señor Lempira have been mistaken?
Had Masetti and Atilio survived, moved north into Bolivia, and struck
the convoy?

The ambush had taken place two hundred miles north of where he'd
found the bodies. Had some members of the PGA survived? At thirty
minutes past the hour, a song was played between news items, "Inde-
scribably Blue" by Elvis Presley. This song was in Hoyle's communication plan, a signal indicating an immediate, nonscheduled message
from Langley. Sent over VOA, this sort of signal was second in priority
only to an emergency indicator, and that precedence was used only for
an immediate threat to life. Imagining the worst, Hoyle tuned the
shortwave to 12.3 MHz, where, precisely at 55 minutes 30 seconds
past the hour, a female voice read a stream of five-digit numbers.
Adding his contractor number, 1130, Hoyle transposed the sums

against the master code key, each five-digit number representing a word or phrase rather than a list of characters.

As the message assembled itself, Hoyle sank into a funk. It summoned him to a meeting tomorrow, noon, at a café on the Calle Santa Cruz in La Paz. Thoughts of being paid evaporated, and Hoyle began to wonder how he would come by a ticket home. He drank what was left of the bourbon, decided, rightly, that he needed no supper, and at seventeen minutes past midnight he switched off the light and slept like the damned.

3

ABOVE THE PLAZA San Francisco, the sky was sapphire at its
zenith, an ethereal blue, too pure to be comprehended. In
the shadow of high Catholic architecture, Hoyle sipped his coffee and
looked into the street. The sidewalks were crowded, and beyond them
traffic passed in a steady growl on the Calle Santa Cruz: trucks, cars,
and *minipolos* in an argument of grinding gears and piercing horns.
Trundling between men and women in Western dress were cholas in
voluminous *pollera* skirts, their long black braids tucked into bowler
hats. A woman in a miniskirt passed carrying a green parasol, her heels
clicking on the cobbles. With disconsolate lust, Hoyle watched until
she passed from sight.

A man approached the table and spoke in French. *"Excusez-moi, ma
montre s'est arrêtée. Avez-vous le temps?"*

The man's hair was brown tending to sandy, and he wore round
wire-rimmed spectacles and a tweed jacket.

"I'm sorry, my watch is in the shop." Hoyle answered in English,
completing the bona fides communicated from Langley—embarrassing formalities straight out of a dime novel.

Hoyle took in his contact, greatly surprised at how young he looked.
Hoyle waited a moment to ask, *"Aimez-vous parler ici?"*

"No. We have a car." The man gestured across the street. Behind the wheel of a 1965 Impala sat a man with the dark good looks of a Guaraní Indian.

"Let's go."

Perplexity giving way to irritation, Hoyle tossed a few coins on the table and followed the man down the sidewalk.

"I didn't catch your name."

"Smith," the man said as they crossed the cobbles. "First name's Neil. The Directorate of Operations sent me. I'm going to be taking over the in-country effort."

As they reached the car, the driver popped from behind the wheel and opened the passenger-side door.

"Charlie, boss. I'm the driver," the dark-complected man said. His name was Ovejuyo, a handle unpronounceable by gringos, and for as long as he had worked with the American embassy, everyone had called him Charlie. Dressed in a white shirt, gray jacket, and fedora hat, Charlie looked like a typical Boliviano, a man so inconspicuously dressed as to be invisible.

Smith piled into the passenger seat, and Hoyle fell into the back behind Charlie. Charlie honked and entered traffic, and Smith turned in his seat. "What was your assignment?"

Hoyle's eyes flicked to Charlie.

"He's in," Smith said.

"I was sent down-country to locate Masetti and Atilio."

"Did Langley indicate there would be any follow-on work?"

"No." Hoyle continued: "Did you read my traffic?"

"I've read everything."

"Who hit the convoy in Santa Cruz?" Hoyle asked.

"The latest country brief and intel summaries will be in tomorrow's diplomatic pouch. You can read them yourself," Smith said. After a moment he asked, "How's your Spanish?"

"Bastante bueno."

"What were they paying you, Mr. Hoyle?" Again the young man's tone was disaffected, patronizing.

"A thousand dollars a week," Hoyle answered.

"I have more work. Six months, maybe a year. In-country. I'll have you continue at the same rate. If you're interested."

"You're aware I'm a contractor."

"Yeah. The Company's going to want some distance on some of this."

"Distance" meant deniability. Hoyle assumed Smith had been told about his resignation. Finally, he asked, "What's the job?"

"Paramilitary. Fieldwork."

Hoyle noticed that the collar of Smith's shirt was a size too big. It gave him an even more juvenile appearance. Hoyle thought of all the money he had left, seventy-five dollars U.S., and the words burned in his throat. "I'm interested."

The Impala passed through the cemetery district, down Avenida República, and sharply left onto the Boulevard Jose Maria Asin. There they came upon the first military checkpoint. A dozen Bolivian soldiers sat atop a Sherman tank, blandly watching traffic pass.

The Impala merged into the morning rush; the traffic ran together, slowed, and stopped like too many animals jammed into a pen. As the car turned, something slammed against the windshield. Hoyle suppressed a flinch, thinking as he did so that whatever had struck the glass had not made the noise of a hand grenade. Appearing suddenly on the windshield was a wet rag stuck above the wiper blades. Outside the car, a young beggar started to wipe the glass. The child was dirty, skinny, and maybe ten or twelve years old.

In the backseat, Hoyle reached into his pocket for a few coins. "Let me give him something." Charlie's eyes found Hoyle's in the rearview mirror, but Smith motioned Charlie to drive on.

"Don't give him anything. It only makes them worse."

Charlie snapped out a phrase in Guaraní, firmly but not loudly, and the beggar removed the cloth and skipped away. Hoyle watched the kid dodging between the rows of cars, barefoot and graceful as a toreador.

"How long have you been with the agency, Mr. Smith?"

Smith had introduced himself as Neil, but in this moment Hoyle didn't care to remember.

"Four years," Smith said.

"Right out of college?"

Smith shook his head but did not turn around. He seemed suddenly bored. "I was with the Department of Defense before that," he said.

"One of the McNamara Whiz Kids?"

At this, Smith turned, and the eyes behind the wire-rimmed spectacles glittered. A few seconds passed, and then Smith asked brusquely, "Did Langley promise you some position of authority down here?"

"No."

Charlie gripped the wheel with two hands, pretending to concentrate intently on the traffic stopped in front of him.

"Do you have counterinsurgency experience?" Hoyle asked.

"I was in Cambodia," Smith said. "Three years. I ran the Company's paramilitary operation against the Khmer Rouge. Until last week I worked at MACV Saigon."

MACV was the headquarters of the Military Assistance Command Vietnam. It was responsible for everything from supplying toilet paper for the troops in the field to the conduct of a pair of secret wars in Laos and Cambodia.

"What did you do at MACV?" Hoyle asked.

"Phoenix Program."

In Laos, Hoyle had heard whispers of the project, a combined effort on behalf of CIA, Vietnamese Special Branch, and American Special Forces. Its goal was to kidnap, assassinate, and destroy the Viet Cong infrastructure throughout South Vietnam. It was what the agency called "wet work." Killing. Hoyle had a hard time placing the young man wearing the tweed jacket in a rice paddy, lurking on ambush.

"I read your file," Smith said. "You want to add anything?"

"About what?"

"About what happened in Vientiane."

Vientiane was where Hoyle had come by his latest scar.

"I did what the report said," Hoyle answered. His tone was enough to keep Smith off. But Smith had made his point—he was aware of the charges leveled against Hoyle. He knew they included murder. Hoyle looked directly into the round spectacles, and it was Smith who turned away. Hoyle had made a point of his own. What had happened in Laos was no concern of Smith's.

"Maybe you need someone else," Hoyle said. It was not a bluff. He was suddenly convinced this operation would be a disaster.

"You can take orders?"

"Yeah. I can take orders," Hoyle answered.

Smith took off his glasses, wiped them with a handkerchief, and then slipped them back on. He said, "Then we'll have no problems."

The Impala looped around the Plaza Isabel la Católica, back onto the Avenida Aciento Arce, and turned left into the American embassy. At the gate of the consulate, a squad of dejected Bolivian conscripts piled sandbags in a semicircular heap. Charlie guided the car to the curb, and Smith got out. Hoyle remained in the back.

"Are you coming, Mr. Hoyle?"

"I'm a contractor, Mr. Smith. I try to avoid the flagpole, if you know what I mean."

"I want you in on this." Smith leaned through the window and looked at Charlie. "Pick up his luggage from the safe house at the Plaza España. I want to start for Camiri before dark."

Hoyle opened the door and reluctantly followed Smith.

Charlie called after him, "I'll be waiting out front when your meeting is over, boss."

"Quit calling me boss," Hoyle said.

In the lobby, a secretary looked up from her desk as Smith approached. The woman's hair was auburn and swept up onto her head. She wore blue eye shadow and spectacles that were turned up at the corners, the combined effect giving her a distinctly feline appearance. A stern-faced United States Marine stood at parade rest behind her desk. The woman started to form the words "May I help you" as Smith flashed an ID card.

"This way, sir," the marine said.

They were led up a set of back stairs to a desk, a second marine, and a gray vault door. Smith signed in, Hoyle declined, and they were admitted into a long office lit by fluorescent lights. Typewriters and telex machines chattered, and a pinched-looking CIA officer glared over a filing cabinet as they walked into the office. "What do you need?" he asked.

"Good afternoon," Smith said. "Mr. Hoyle and Mr. Smith to see the acting chief of station?"

The tense-looking man did not move. His eyebrows went up slightly, and Smith again showed his ID.

"He's in a meeting," the man said, going back to his desk. "You're going to have to wait or come back later."

"Okay. We'll wait."

Hoyle watched as Smith found a chair and the officer fed a sheet of onionskin into his typewriter. Hoyle walked over and sat on the corner of his desk. When the man looked up, Hoyle leaned close to his face.

"Listen, dickweed. I'm in-country under nonofficial cover. Every second I sit in this embassy, that cover gets thinner. I suggest you get off your crack and tell your boss we're out here before I jam you under the door frame."

Drawing a collective gasp, the office came to a halt. At that moment a door to the inner office opened, and Cosmo Zeebus came forward, a bluff man with a red face. He recognized Hoyle at once; he was jovial and cheerful. Obviously, he'd missed the outburst.

"Look what we have here . . . Mis-ter Hoyle." Zeebus had a broad Mississippi accent. This, combined with his backslapping manner and potbelly, gave the impression of a deputy sheriff, not an intelligence officer. "Cable traffic said you were down south—I didn't believe it. I thought you were medically retired after that thing in Phu Bia?"

"It was Vientiane." Hoyle shook Zeebus's hand.

"Shot in the face is what I heard." Zeebus scratched his belly and continued, "Good to see you anyway." He nodded at the pinched-faced man, still sitting like a tailor's dummy at his typewriter. "You met Foster? My operations officer?"

"We were just getting acquainted," Hoyle said.

"You down here to help us deal with our bandit problem?"

"I understand there's going to be a briefing. With the ambassador," Hoyle said.

"Briefing? Hell, no one told me." Zeebus huffed. "Come on back, then." He started for the office door then turned, seeming for the first time to have noticed Smith. "You want to bring your case officer in on this?"

"My name's Smith, Mr. Zeebus. I've been placed in charge of the counterguerrilla operation in Santa Cruz."

Zeebus blinked. "What do you mean, in charge?"

Smith handed over an envelope. "Here's my tasking letter, signed by the director—"

"Whose director would that be?"

"The director of the Central Intelligence Agency."

AMBASSADOR HIELMAN'S OFFICE was a mahogany tomb: leather sofas, brocaded draperies, and a desk the size of a small car.

On the green leather blotter in front of him was a photostatic copy of the communiqué given to Major Buran following the ambush. Smith and Hoyle watched while the ambassador lightly traced a pencil under the lines as he read them. Cosmo Zeebus stood by the fireplace and puffed a cigarette.

COMMUNIQUÉ NO 1
TO THE BOLIVIAN PEOPLE Issued March 27, 1967

Revolutionary truth opposes reactionary lies. The military clowns who have seized power, murdered workers, and squandered our resources to U.S. imperialism are now fooling the people with a cruel joke. The hour of truth approaches. Now the people will rise up in arms, responding to the military gangsters with armed struggle.

On March 23, forces of the Fourth Division, based in Abapó and numbering approximately 37 men, under the command of Major Buran, entered guerrilla territory along the Ñancahuazú River. Enemy losses were 17 killed, including a lieutenant, and 14 prisoners, 5 of whom were wounded in the clash. These were given the best medical care by our own doctors. All the prisoners were set free. In making public the details of the first battle of the war, we establish our norm: revolutionary truth. What we do will always be demonstrated by the reliability of our words.

We issue a call to workers, peasants, and intellectuals. We call on those who believe that the time has come to respond to violence with violence, to rescue a country being wholesale to U.S. corporations; and to raise the standard of living for our people, who with each passing day suffer more from unnecessary poverty.

THE NATIONAL LIBERATION ARMY OF BOLIVIA.

Hielman put down the paper. The casualty numbers were correct, and although not publicly admitted by the Bolivian army, they had been confirmed to the ambassador by the minister of defense.

"Mr. Zeebus is of the opinion that this guerrilla organization was of minimal importance," the ambassador said.

"I'm not sure how Mr. Zeebus drew that conclusion, sir." Smith's voice was even.

Zeebus puffed heavily on his cigarette. "What does Langley say about the ambush?"

"They think a new guerrilla organization has formed in Bolivia," Smith answered.

Zeebus exhaled. "New? Not PGA?"

"PGA was Argentine. They're finished."

"What about the communiqué? You agree it was written by the Bolivian Communist Party?" Hielman asked.

"It said the Bolivian people were hungry and oppressed. You don't have to be a Communist to agree with that."

The ambassador's eyes cut to Hoyle. "What is your function in this operation?"

"Mr. Hoyle is a paramilitary operator," Smith answered.

Hielman removed his glasses and placed them on the blotter. "Are you an intelligence officer, Mr. Hoyle?"

"I'm a contractor, Mr. Ambassador." The word "contractor" hung like stink.

"Mr. Hoyle was assigned by the Directorate of Operations, sir. He confirmed the death of Masetti and Atilio in Tarija Province. I've just arranged for him to remain in-country."

"To do what?" Hielman asked.

"I've set up an office in Camiri, close to where the guerrillas are operating. A storefront exporting business. Mr. Hoyle and I will work out of there for now."

Zeebus walked over from the fireplace. He screwed a cigarette butt into the ashtray on Hielman's desk.

"I tell you what—why don't we just cut the Beltway bullshit? They don't want another 'Veetnam' down here, and we're not gonna have one. There's twelve of these guys at most. They're nothing but a Maoist splinter group from the Bolivian Communist Party."

"We may not be dealing with locals," Smith said.

"What do you mean?"

"The National Security Agency has monitored eleven high frequency transmissions out of the Ñancahuazú Valley in the last three weeks," Smith said. "The transmitter is Czech-made. A D47 field radio."

"Who are they talking to?" Hielman asked.

"NSA is still trying to break in to the code groups. The messages were all acknowledged by a twelve-meter station outside of Havana."

Zeebus guffawed. "You telling me these guys are Cubans? Cubans in Bolivia? Bullshit."

Smith chose not to respond. And to Hoyle, sitting quietly, the circumstances of his posting became a bit more sinister: If the guerrillas were Cuban, or Cuban-backed, the situation might very quickly escalate. The agency would need "distance" when things turned bloody. Hoyle was aware at once who in this operation would be expendable.

"Your letter grants you a pretty wide mandate, Mr. Smith. Is it your intention to run a parallel effort?" Hielman asked.

Smith stood. "No, sir. I'm going to run the only effort. I'm going to suspend all other initiatives and contacts immediately."

"Not my contacts," Zeebus said.

"Especially CIA contacts," Smith replied.

The ambassador became red in the face. "I've been a diplomat for thirty years, Mr. Smith. Most of that time in Latin America. You'll find I am not a person who enjoys excitement. You'll have cooperation and support—because I've been ordered to give it to you. I'm going to expect results in return."

Zeebus escorted them from the ambassador's office and down the corridor. His fury eventually found vent. "This is bullshit," he sputtered. "The only reason this thing has stayed out in the boondocks is that we've backed Presidente Barrientos. I'm not gonna let you cowboy in here. We'll just see what Langley says before you go pulling any plugs."

Zeebus tried to brush past, but Smith stopped him. His voice was low. "I *am* what Langley says. Your operation is terminated—period. I find out there's a competing effort, I get surprised by any hidden parts, and I'll personally make sure you get pissed on from a great height."

Zeebus cocked his jaw, and Hoyle watched Smith walk away.

"What does that little shit think he is?"

"In charge," Hoyle answered. "Do yourself a favor, Cosmo. Try not to get pissed on."

4

THE ROAD FROM La Paz was jagged and ghastly, like a scar drawn across a face that might otherwise have been pretty. Long rains had made the hills verdant, almost lush, and it seemed that in each place the land had been made beautiful, the road became suddenly cruel; it was nearly impassible in places where streams tumbled down from cliff sides, or where salt springs leached across the roadbed. Hoyle stretched out as best he could in the front seat of the Land Cruiser, an M16 between his legs and his knees jolting into the underside of the dash each time the vehicle managed to strike a particularly vehement pothole, which was often.

It was a wonder of geological science that the road could be a quagmire in one place and, within the space of a hundred meters, bone-dry and pocked with hard foot-deep craters. The Land Cruiser jerked and pounded across the valley, through several pointless diversions and cuts. Smith sat in the backseat, his rifle across his lap, reading a Bolivian army intelligence estimate, a thick typewritten document as useless as it was voluminous. Behind the wheel, Charlie lit a series of cigarettes, biting down on the filters and grunting "Sorry, boss" after particularly arduous jolts.

As the road climbed from the valley floor, the sky seemed to lower. Cloud bottoms swept the ridges to the right and left, and as they started up the long series of hairpins carved into the mountain, Hoyle could see fingers of mist stir over the top of the road. In one moment, the skyline at the crest would be razor-sharp and lit by sunlight, and in another moment gray and indefinite, as though someone had scrubbed a photograph with a pencil eraser.

Hoyle was the first to spot the wreckage, two burned jeeps looking like charred, rusty bathtubs, and the carcasses of the trucks, all crowded together on the last turn hacked against the steep hillside. The truck bodies were angled across the road, the first still jammed over the guardrail and the second, pointed uphill, with its front wheels knuckled under from a broken axle. One truck had burned completely and the other roughly in half; the cargo bed and the wooden slats on one side were untouched by fire or even smoke. All the vehicles were pocked thoroughly with bullet holes.

Charlie tossed his cigarette from the window, and Smith looked up from his reading as the Land Cruiser slowed.

"Stop here, Charlie," Hoyle said. "We'll walk the rest of the way."

Charlie pulled the vehicle to the inside of one of the hairpins, positioning it in the shadow of the drop-off above, in a place it could not be shot at from the road higher up. Hoyle pushed open the door handle and swung the rifle from between his legs. He allowed the passenger door to swing closed and jacked back the charging handle of his M16. Slipping from the backseat, Smith inserted a magazine and also cycled the charger on his weapon.

Clouds touched the top of the road and swirled over the ridge above them. As the sun slipped in and out, they were dappled with light, shadow, and the gray luminosity that came through the fog.

Hoyle walked up the remaining hairpins, Charlie behind him, followed by Smith, who carried his weapon by the top handle, swinging it like a briefcase. At the base of the last remaining turn, Hoyle stopped and listened. The only noise was the buzzing of flies. Debris littered the roadside, ammunition pouches, spent cartridges, magazines for weapons that had not been fired, souvenirs of the calamity that had befallen the convoy.

Ten feet away was the first body, black and swollen and recently worked over by crows. It was the corpse of a *sargento segundo,* a corporal, his fatigue uniform nearly brown with road dust and soaked through black in places with blood. His bloated hands were clenched tightly into fists that looked like terrible, poisonous mushrooms. At the entrance to the switchback lay a second corpse, that of a *cabo,* a private soldier, shot through the base of the jaw. His body, too, was black with exposure and his head seemed flattened, the skull fractured. His jagged gray mouth was pulled back in a grimace, and his teeth were white in the sun.

At the center of the kill zone, scattered in the road, were seventeen bodies. Hoyle looked around, up the hill to the place he guessed the ambush party had set up, then back at the debris. The wreckage of the vehicles was a uniform ashen color, olive-drab paint showing through only in places that had not burned, the bullet holes already rusting in the mountain damp. "This was a piece of work," he said.

Charlie advanced no farther than the rearmost jeep and averted his eyes from the worst of the murder. Smith looked around with a perfectly impassive expression. Hoyle thought Smith was trying hard to look like he had seen it all. But, in fact, Smith had seen worse.

"The surviving officer says they were engaged with the enemy for forty-five minutes," Smith said, almost like a guide in a museum. "He says that once he realized they were surrounded, he ordered his men to cease fire."

Hoyle knelt and examined tracks in the roadbed, faint and rained over several times but indicative. The wind blew from atop the hill, and a thin cloud rolled down at them. For a moment the scene of the ambush was swallowed in gray mist. The cloud quickly moved past and when Charlie looked up, there was a rainbow around the sun.

"You have an opinion?" Smith asked Hoyle.

"Yeah. Your major is full of shit." Hoyle looked over the turn in the road. He had laid many ambushes of his own, enough to know that this had been a professional and seriously conducted job. "The firefight was over in two minutes," he said. "The guerrillas set up in at least two groups." He jerked his thumb up the road. "Behind us, in the boulder field, and around the outside of the turn." He removed a spent cartridge from the dirt. "It looks like the bad guys were using American weapons."

"You sure?"

Hoyle tossed him the cartridge. "That's thirty-cal. Probably from an M2 carbine."

Smith scanned the hilltop where Guevara and Joaquin had taken cover.

"They set a truck on fire," Hoyle said quietly, "and then they sat and watched the reaction force drive all the way from Abapó." His gaze fell on a pile of stones at the place the road coiled back on itself. There was another one at the exit of the turn, a small cairn, obviously stacked by human hands. "They used those rocks to mark out fields of fire."

Smith followed Hoyle's finger as he pointed out the area swept by the ambush.

Almost talking to himself, Hoyle muttered, "So somebody was good enough to rig a cross fire, but they worried that they were going to miss."

Smith poked at a piece of debris with his boot. "There's a village up the road," he said. "If they moved toward the river, somebody may have seen something."

"Nobody saw anything, Mr. Smith." Hoyle's tone was not arch, merely factual. "Those people aren't going to talk to us. All they want to do is get a pig fat for Christmas."

"We're here to find out what happened, Mr. Hoyle. I don't think the agency will mind if we ask a couple of questions."

Charlie stood sheepishly with his hands in his pockets. Smith started back downhill for the Land Cruiser. Hoyle did not move.

"The road to Vallegrande is a free-fire zone at night," Hoyle called after him. "This whole grid square is bad-guy country."

"I'm aware of that."

The statement hung in the air for an overlong second. "You think it's a good idea to go for a drive around here at night?"

"We'll be back before dark," Smith said tartly.

Charlie watched Hoyle's lips press together. Smith continued toward the Land Cruiser.

"Let's go, Charlie. You're driving," Smith said.

THE LAND CRUISER bumped into Domasco, a cheerless collection of mud-walled and tile-roofed hovels. The dust on the road was like talcum powder. The village, a place that locally was synonymous with bad luck, had missed out on the much-needed rain. As Hoyle climbed from the Land Cruiser, the sun had already slipped behind the ridges to the west, and long shadows projected over the buildings. The town seemed deserted and had an almost stygian gloom about it.

In the doorway of a tumbledown hut, an Indian woman sat at her weaving. She was apparently the only human in the village. Her steel-gray hair was drawn back into long braids joined together with a tuft of black wool. Hoyle's eyes found hers as he stopped in front of the shack. Her face was burned red by decades of sun and wind. On her back the woman carried a sack of banded material, an *ahuayo,* a sort of backpack in which she carried her burden—a small baby, certainly a grandchild. The child slept so still and silent, Hoyle thought at first it might be dead.

"*Hola,*" Smith said. "*¿Dónde está todos?*"

The woman's eyes flicked briefly at Smith and then returned to the loom, her gnarled hands working yarn from a spindle. She seemed as uncomprehending as a tree stump.

Charlie approached and squatted to the right of the woman, careful to kneel with his head slightly lower than hers. "*Mba'éichapa, jar-i,*" he said quietly in Guaraní.

The old woman nodded but did not take her eyes from the loom. Hoyle stood by silently, looking out at the empty village. Smith sank down next to Charlie, taking one knee next to the frame of the loom. Smith's eye fell on a heap of pumpkins on the dirt floor just inside the old woman's house. "Ask her if she went to market this week."

Charlie interpreted, nodding as he did so. The woman answered succinctly, her tongue clicking on her bare pink gums.

"She went."

"The day of the shooting?" Smith asked.

Charlie again put the question into Guaraní. Hoyle could tell he was being deferential, almost reverent, to the old woman.

"She didn't know there was shooting until she came back to the village," Charlie interpreted.

"But she came back up the mountain after the ambush. Did she see the burning trucks?"

The woman answered with one syllable.

"She saw them," Charlie said.

"What about later? Did she see the guerrillas passing? Moving toward the river?"

The woman's voice was like the wind through grass. She continued to tug at the loom, intent on it. Charlie listened, his expression show-ing nothing. "She says it was too dark to see anything when she came back."

Smith stood, looking put out.

Hoyle gently plucked a small lizard from the side of the hut. Its skin was a dull brown, exactly the color of the wall. He held the creature gently, cupping his hand around it. Hoyle said quietly in Spanish, "You know, when I was a kid, I was a champion lizard catcher."

The old woman's hands stopped. Her gaze fell on Hoyle, almost magisterially. He continued, "I don't suppose you could tell me what kind of lizard this is? I see them all over—funny-looking things. They just lie in the sun."

She answered him in Spanish. "They are *brujillos*. They change color to hide." Her Spanish was accented but perfect.

"Where did they go, Señora?" Hoyle asked calmly. "The men who shot at the soldiers?"

"I didn't see."

"What about the men of your village? Where did they go?"

"Hunting. In the mountains."

"All of them?" Hoyle asked.

The woman said nothing. Her hands again picked at the loom.

"Thank you for talking to us, Señora," Hoyle said. "Thank you for your time." He placed the lizard carefully back on the wall, and it scur-ried up and under the eaves.

Smith and Charlie followed Hoyle back to the Land Cruiser.

"Tell me something, Mr. Smith. Was everybody at MACV as gung ho as you?"

Smith's jaw tightened. "She knows which direction they went after the ambush. You know it."

"Her and everybody else," Hoyle shot back. "Why do you think the village was empty? These people are going to have to live here long after we're gone."

"That's not my problem."

"You're making it a problem."

For a moment it looked like the two men might come to blows. Charlie again put his hands in his pockets.

Hoyle said, "By tomorrow morning half of Ñancahuazú will know there were gringos in here asking questions." As he spoke, his voice got lower; it was what he did in anger instead of increasing the volume of his speech.

"I want the bad guys to know we're in here," Smith said. "We can't track the guerrillas unless they move, and we can't predict a move unless we provide a stimulus. That's agency procedure, Mr. Hoyle."

"It's agency procedure to protect our sources. If the Communist Party even thinks she talked to us, that old lady will go before a people's tribunal. If the army thinks she failed to cooperate, they'll cut her tongue out of her head. You might want to remember that the next time you want to stimulate the enemy, Mr. Smith."

Smith watched Hoyle climb into the Land Cruiser.

"Let's get out of here, Charlie," Hoyle growled. "It's getting fucking dark."

5

I T WAS NOT until midafternoon that Che Guevara saw to the departure of Miguel's group, hauling food and supplies up the *escarpa* from Camp 1, which was now to be abandoned. The move had been suggested by Joaquin. Camp 1 was close to the river, which after a week of rain had risen dangerously, eroding the banks and flooding the flat stretch behind the farmhouse. Camp 2, located in the Iñao Mountains twelve kilometers north, would now serve as the column's principal base of operations. It was hoped, also, that radio communications with Havana might be improved, Camp 2 being nearly three hundred meters above the valley of the Ñancahuazú.

Guevara spent most of the rainy morning making sure the encampment was dismantled, the fire pit and clay ovens broken up, and the ashes dispersed. The storage caves located at the camp were sealed and their entrances camouflaged. Five depots contained ammunition, medicine, spare radio equipment, codebooks, and the personal effects of the Cuban comrades. These caches would now comprise the column's strategic reserves.

Early in the afternoon there was thunder, and the rain became constant. Now all that remained of Camp 1 were the rifle pits overlooking the river and a small observation post sited halfway up the trail to Camp 2. The rifle pits were left in place to cover the river crossing, and the observation point had been established so an eye could be kept on the farmhouse in the valley below. It was to this position, and to the duty of sentries, that Guevara assigned two of the Bolivian comrades, Eusebio and Chingolo. They followed the bearing parties from Camp 1 and slogged toward their new posting. As soon as the last of Miguel's men passed through and were away up the mountain, the Bolivians leaned their rifles against a tree. Birds chirped and clicked in the forest around them and Guevara's orders to keep watch were forgotten. Exhausted and pelted by rain, the two Bolivians slung their hammocks among the trees and promptly dropped off to sleep.

Had they chosen to stand guard, the Bolivians could have observed a small farmhouse set down in a scruffy, stump-riddled clearing. From their vantage, the Ñancahuazú Valley ran north and south, one of several basins associated with watercourses in the hilly, wooded *departamento* of Santa Cruz. The Ñancahuazú River had its headwaters south and west, in the adjacent territory of Potosí, and entered the valley after descending steeply from the hills of the Pampa del Tigre. For much of the austral summer, the river was shallow and slow, transected by sandbars and bound on its banks by rocky bluffs. The river, like the people in the valley, appeared tame but remained capable of casual treachery. As the rains began, the Ñancahuazú swelled and then ran implacably; within a week it was uniformly turbulent and would stay that way until the rains stopped, several long months from now.

The farmhouse sat squarely in the center of a 3,700-acre parcel of ranch and forest land purchased six months before by two of Guevara's Cuban lieutenants, Pombo and Tuma. The adobe was roofed with sheets of corrugated calamite, and the comrades had come to call it the Zinc House. Some logging had been carried out for purposes of cover, but the Zinc House was used primarily for storage and as a rendezvous point with urban cadres from La Paz. The land had been purchased with cash, Pombo and Tuma putting out the story that the acquisition had been made for a Peruvian capitalist who planned to build a sawmill.

The property lay almost 250 kilometers south of the provincial seat of Santa Cruz. An additional hundred kilometers south and east was Paraguay, then the Argentine frontier. The terrain was difficult, precipitous, and filled with places of ambush. Guevara knew that to operate in this country with a force of conventional troops would be a nightmare. Hard country always favors the guerrilla.

But the guerrilla cannot operate in a vacuum. It did not bode well that the valley was sparsely populated. Worse, few of its settlers could read or write, and all were politically undeveloped. Several small pueblos were scattered about the hills, most adjoining rivers or seasonal streams. The largest of these settlements, Tatarenda, held no more than a dozen shacks. Local agriculture was slash-and-burn and was not always sufficient to keep its practitioners from hunger. Almost without exception, the peasants of the valley were wary of strangers. Worse, much work and little reward had made them hard and covetous.

Guevara and Moro waited in the remains of Camp 1 for Joaquin to return from across the river. Part of the day had been taken up with physical examinations of the men. After the last of the bearers had trudged away, it was Guevara's turn. He sat on a log, his fatigue shirt balled up and held in his lap. Above him, rain pattered into a poncho strung up between branches.

"Open your mouth?" Moro asked politely.

Guevara tilted back his head as Moro peered down his throat with a penlight and tongue depressor.

"Ahhhhh?" Moro suggested.

Guevara made no sound.

"Make a noise so I can see under your goddamn uvula."

Guevara obliged with a lengthy, unchanging grunt. Moro flicked the tongue depressor into the brush and began palpating the glands in Guevara's neck. He placed a stethoscope on Guevara's back, moved it several times, and frowned. Finally, he pulled out the earpieces. "How many asthma capsules do you take a day?"

Guevara lied badly. "Asthma?"

"Don't bullshit me," Moro said. "What do you take?"

"Theophylline." Then he added, "Three times a day."

"When's the last time you took any medication?"

"A couple of days ago. I'm saving it."

Moro placed his stethoscope back into his rucksack. "You're going to kill yourself. You smoke too much, you eat too little, you're overworked, and there are bats that sleep more than you do."

Guevara stood and pulled on his shirt. "I don't need the lecture. I'm a physician, remember?"

"Big deal. We've got three MDs in the column. We have only one comandante." Moro dug around in his pack and handed Guevara a vial of pills. "Hydrocortisone. Two of these every morning. If you get worse, I'm going to put you on an adrenaline IV." He did not know where he could even find adrenaline, and he had only a dozen hydrocortisone tablets. If Guevara's condition did not improve, Moro would have to send to La Paz for more drugs. A highly uncertain supply route at best.

Guevara's expression became troubled. He was not a man accustomed to asking favors. "Moro, look, I—"

Moro put away his penlight. "My diagnosis stays a secret—if you do what I say. You're off tobacco, period. You start taking your pills and eating full meals, like everybody else. And let someone else carry the goddamn radio once in a while."

"I should have left your ass in Cuba."

"I wish you had." Moro smiled. As Guevara finished buttoning his shirt, Moro said, "It wouldn't hurt you to take a bath once in a while, either."

There was a movement at the fringes of the camp and Joaquin came into the clearing. He had supervised the movement of supplies, getting up at three in the morning to start his task. At forty-one, Joaquin was the oldest man in the expedition, the second in command, and he went out of his way to show the others that he was physically up to the work. His walk today had covered maybe fifteen kilometers, up and down jungle trails and twice across the river.

As Joaquin drew near, Guevara lifted his pistol belt. Joaquin's expression was dour.

"What's the matter?"

"Pombo has just come from the valley. We have visitors at the Zinc House. Comrade Galán has come from La Paz."

Selizar Galán was the general secretary of the Bolivian Communist Party, a man as perfectly contradictory and dilettante as the organization he supervised.

"Wonderful," Guevara said.

Joaquin paused. "Tania brought him." Joaquin watched Guevara closely. His attention seemed to waiver, and he made a slight gesture, something like a shake of the head. Joaquin had expected him to ask about the woman, but he did not.

"There were a dozen bottles of *chicha* at the Zinc House," Guevara said, his voice low, like a man suggesting a doubtful thing.

"There're still there," Joaquin answered.

"Have them brought up to Camp Two." Guevara's eyes brightened, but he seemed to frown as he spoke. "We'll have a party for our guests."

Guevara slung his rifle and climbed up the embankment out of the camp. As he made his way up the mountain, wind stirred through the branches and shook rainwater from the leaves. Soon he was alone on the trail, and as he walked through the forest he was happy to have only himself for company. Guevara's pack and equipment were already at Camp 2, and carrying only his pistol, rifle, and canteen, he made good time. The way led steadily uphill, north, and then abruptly west; the trail had been constructed as much as possible in the cover of the forest.

At the first switchback, he stopped to catch his breath. There was a cold, hollow sensation in his chest, the foretaste of a fit of wheezing. In his pocket, he found the hydrocortisone tablets and rolled one into the palm of his hand. He bit the tablet carefully in half, swallowing one part and placing the other back in the brown plastic tube. The pill was bitter in his mouth, and searing as it slid down his throat, but he made no complaint.

Guevara continued up the mountain and a somber sort of emptiness kept close behind him. He turned to look at the trail winding back down into the valley. Touched by slanting light, the cloud bottoms were lowering and above the ridge the sunset assembled itself in shades of gray. It had been over a decade, almost twelve years, since he'd picked up a rifle and committed his life to the *Idea*. And after all that time, through ten thousand adventures, victory and adulation, frustrations and regret, one thing had not changed: He remained an outsider. The wars he fought, he fought for others. He took up their battles, made their revolution, always and forever in countries other than his own, and now, in this, his fourth month in Bolivia, Guevara was again taking up the struggle.

The trail leveled for a hundred yards and he walked steadily until it rose again, carrying him closer to the gloaming sky. Around him in the forest, birds sang and cackled as they settled to roost. The rain stopped and he walked steadily for an hour more, his shirt and pants drying as he moved. Guevara had few emotions about this war, except that it was unavoidable.

Guevara asked much of himself and often too much of those around him. High expectations came easily to a man who had accomplished nearly everything he attempted. His life meant work, the daily routine of guard rotation, feeding and training the men, reconnoitering the terrain around them, and preparing for the day when combat would open on a broad front. Some might have pitied him over the obligation of this work, the austerity of the reward, but in his heart, Guevara was happy. This life had come to him because he chose it. If he could be young forever, if he could never age beyond this moment, this was the life he would have chosen. His place was in the vanguard, and revolution, *guerra extrema,* was his profession. His rifle, an American-made M2 carbine, was light in his hand. He carried it as naturally as a businessman would carry an umbrella. His rifle was the lever with which he planned to move the world.

Once, for him, the tool had been medicine.

It seemed a million years ago that he had studied to become a physician. The young man who wanted to be a doctor was a stranger to him now. He did not regret leaving medicine; nor did he see that his life had ricocheted through an unending cycle of enthusiasms, disenchantments, and departures. After graduation from medical school, Guevara had sold his few possessions and meandered north, through Chile and Peru, Paraguay, Bolivia, and Brazil. As far north as Miami. He wandered south again, crisscrossing Central America. In Guatemala, in the time just before the CIA's coup d'état in 1954, Guevara became the lover of Hilda Gadea. He thought of her now, a short, curvaceous woman with strong opinions and a quick smile. Hilda was mestiza and an ardent Communist. Guevara remembered Hilda as many things, teacher, nurse, and the architect of his political awakening. It was Hilda who lent him books by Lenin, Trotsky, and Mao. When she became pregnant, Guevara gallantly insisted that they marry. She at first refused, but he would not take no for an answer. Though their marriage would be short and without passion, Guevara had done what he thought was proper. This would be the last act of his life motivated by bourgeois sensibility.

Guevara recalled an aimless time, and then the couple drifted to Mexico. Hilda bore them a daughter whom they named Hilda Beatríz. The little girl, dark-eyed and serious, had never seemed real to Guevara. Nor had his marriage. At a time when most men would settle into the role of father, he knew that his pilgrimage was just beginning. In

Mexico City, he met Fidel Castro, the leader of a ragtag band of Cuban exiles. Even now Guevara felt that their meeting was the most momentous event of his life.

Guevara was nicknamed Che by the Cubans, from an expression that peppered the Argentine patois—a salutation roughly analogous to "Hey, buddy." With no military training and little political development, Guevara knew he was an unlikely combatant. He understood that Castro had admitted him into the ranks because he was a physician. Guevara trained and hardened his body. Nine months after he became a father, he bade Hilda and his daughter goodbye, expecting never to see them again. Of the eighty men to land in Cuba with Fidel Castro, Guevara was one of only ten to survive the first month of combat. A reputation for valor soon attached itself to him. He rose to the rank of comandante, the highest distinction given to guerrilla commanders. Ernesto Guevara was then twenty-seven years old.

It was eight years ago that the dictator Fulgencio Batista had slithered aboard an airplane and ignominiously fled Cuba. The guerrillas had closed on Havana as Batista escaped, and the edifice of dictatorship flew to pieces before them. The joy of the people was indescribable. Guevara entered Havana and rode with Castro in a jeep that was soon filled with flowers. A hundred thousand men and women lined the streets, and their raw joy thrilled Guevara. That afternoon was etched into memory: The revolution had triumphed. No man was more astonished than Che Guevara.

When death would not embrace him, Guevara again wanted life and its pleasures. Despite a frugal streak, he lived fully. He had charisma, great responsibilities, and power. Everywhere he went, there was the fawning, obsequious attention of women. He was not immune to their charms, and no man is untouched by flattery. Guevara fell in love with a beautiful blond revolutionary, Aleida March. Their affair was passionate, and Guevara wrote her poetry. She would become his second wife. The days and months following the victory were even now a blur to him. He was made military governor of La Cabana prison, where a revolutionary tribunal judged Batista's henchmen and officials of the old regime. Daily, Guevara saw to it that enemies of the revolution were brought to account. Firing squads plied their trade day and night. Guevara had killed in war, and it was his duty to sit in judgment of the defeated. For the dead, he had no pangs of regret, not for the slain, and none for the criminals who went before the *pelotóns* in La Cabana. He did not have to be convinced that these criminals had brought justice down upon themselves. *Libertad o muerte. Patria o muerte. Justicia o muerte.* Guevara returned to his quarters each evening with a fine appetite and a clear conscience.

When Hilda joined him from Mexico City, Guevara told her that he had fallen in love with someone else. He remembered a night of tears as Hilda said that whatever had happened during the war was now over and that she still loved him. His heart still beat cold when he remembered saying, "It would have been better if I had been killed." Guevara had a place still in his heart for Hilda, but not love.

Hilda granted him a divorce, and her patience and devotion put into him a nagging sort of remorse. He married Aleida and did his best not to look back on the wreckage in his heart. Aleida would bear him four children, each as different as days of the week. He did his best as he walked now to forget them, Aleida, Hilda, and the children. Love for his family was a thing too precious and fragile to be carried into the field. He could not stand to think of them, not in this place, not in this time, when there was so much to do. And so many enemies to fight.

On the trail, it was full dark. The moon had risen behind him in the valley, and as the clouds opened, the night beyond was a thousand shades of indigo. This was the first time in weeks that stars could be seen, and as the moon labored overhead, it threw a complete shadow before him on the trail. Night through the trees was a sustained whisper, and far below, the sound of the river came onto the ridge, a perfect hiss. Guevara moved on a hundred meters, stopped again, and sank down against a boulder beside the footpath. His chest ached, and he rattled out the half tablet from the pill bottle and swallowed it. He sat and listened to the sound of the distant river, his rifle across his lap.

As the moon shoved between the clouds, Guevara looked down into the valley. The Ñancahuazú was a shining ribbon of silver. The farmhouse was there, a small spark tucked into the apex of a long bend, but when the clouds closed again, the river and valley sank into a void. The blackness descended so suddenly that Guevara sat blinking in perfect wonder. He knew the same shadow had fallen over the Zinc House. And it was there that Comrade Galán now cooled his heels.

The little fucker, Guevara thought. *I should make him wait for a week.*

But with Galán was the woman. Tania. Guevara first reminded himself that he did not love her, then he allowed himself the pleasure of thinking of her. It was six years ago in Berlin when they met. Tania had been for him an unlikely conquest. She had been born in Argentina, Heidi Tamara Vünke, the daughter of a Polish Jew and a German leftist who had fled the Nazis. During the war, Tania's parents became committed Communists and returned to East Germany soon after the end of the conflict. In East Berlin, Tamara worked as an interpreter and was assigned as a protocol officer when Guevara led a trade delegation there in 1960. She remained at his side through a week of mind-numbing exchange discussions, supervising the work of several interpreters and the translation of diplomatic memoranda. Guevara noticed that as she interpreted, she would keep her eyes on his, often not breaking the gaze until long after he was answered. When others spoke, she would again look only at him.

He did not think Tania could be called conventionally beautiful, though she was slim, with dark hair and eyes and an upright, almost military bearing. Her face was slightly long, her jaw pointed daintily, and her cheeks were high. Her nose was aquiline, her lips were thin, and not once in three days did Guevara see her smile. That they had become lovers was more the result of impulse than of infatuation. On his last night in Berlin, Tania arrived at his rooms, late, on the pretext of delivering some documents. As Guevara took them, she stood awkwardly inside the door, and he offered her a glass of wine. She declined politely and said to him, *"Hazme el amor."*

The words electrified him. No woman in his life had ever been so forward. He asked her, "Are you sure?"

She unbuttoned her blouse and said, "I'm very sure."

He pulled her into his arms, and they made love on the floor. In the morning they drove to the airport, and he shook her hand as he boarded the plane. He did not expect to see her again.

A short time later, she was assigned to interpret for the East German Ballet and turned up in Havana. When the dancers left Cuba, Guevara asked her to stay. This was arranged through some friends at the East German embassy, and he found her a job at the Ministry of Education.

Guevara was scrupulously well behaved in public, but he was aware of the rumors. He did his best to ignore them, but Aleida did not. Guevara saw Tania as often as he could, and they spent nights together in a government guest house in San Cristobal. Always she was there for him, always direct, earnest in the way she listened, passionate in her lovemaking, and in time she fell hopelessly in love. There was another night of tears and anguish when he explained to her that he would never leave Aleida or his family. She told him that he had won her heart, and Guevara said, "I did not ask for it."

Guevara did not love Tania, but his trust in her was unconditional. In 1964 he dispatched her to Bolivia as a deep-cover operative. She had been ordered to ingratiate herself with the highest levels of Bolivian society. This she did, with a determined charm and a generous stipend paid by the Cuban intelligence service. As Tania made her arrangements for Guevara's arrival in Bolivia, he would fall precipitously from the Cuban hierarchy.

There were disagreements with Castro, and with his brother, Raúl, some of them theoretical and all of them increasingly personal. Guevara's communism had crystallized, and he became ever more unwavering in his opinions. The break came after he made a particularly incendiary speech in Algeria, referring to the Soviet Union as "an accomplice to imperialism" and tweaking the Russians as "bourgeois Communists" who were unwilling to fight a worldwide revolution. Castro was enraged. Returning from Africa, Guevara was met by Fidel at the airport and whisked to a thirty-six-hour confrontation. Guevara remembered it as an all-night shouting match. Once or twice his own bodyguards had entered the room ashen-faced, as distressed as children listening to their parents fight. Neither Fidel nor Raúl ever publicly spoke of what was said in that long night. Guevara's memories of it even now were tinged with anger, betrayal, and hurt. In one bitter passage of their quarrel, Raúl had reminded Guevara that he was an Argentine, not a Cuban, and that the Cuban revolution could have only one *jefe máximo,* and that leader was Fidel. It was Castro who was in a position to judge what was best for the Cuban people. If Guevara wanted to start the world on fire, Raúl shouted, he could go do it—*on his fucking own.*

The fight ended many hours later, the men hoarse, exhausted, and further apart than they had ever been. The next day, in a confidential letter to Castro, Guevara resigned his posts with the Cuban government. The break between the two men was complete. Fidel accepted his letter, telephoned him at home, and told him to choose a destination.

It was then April 1965. A Cuban military task force was preparing to deploy to Congo, one of several internationalist missions being dispatched to active insurgencies. Guevara now thought it impulsive, and a great mistake, but decided to join and head this contingent. Castro maintained secrecy as Guevara prepared his force. After their fight, rumors swirled that Guevara had been executed, that he had suffered a nervous breakdown, that he had been killed in a plane crash. He no longer spoke on the radio and did not appear on Cuban TV or in the newsreels. Castro remained sphinxlike, answering only that "Comrade Guevara was alive and well and serving the revolution."

Guevara bade his family goodbye and departed for Congo. To cover his departure, the Cuban intelligence service floated rumors that he was in the Dominican Republic, Colombia, even Vietnam.

Traveling incognito via Cairo and Dar es Salaam, Che Guevara stepped from a boat on the Congolese side of Lake Tanganyika in the early evening of April 24, 1965.

Even through the glass of hindsight, he realized how ill advised his expedition had been. The rebels he had gone to aid were illiterate, untrained militarily, and relied as much on tribal magic, *dawa*, as they did on their weapons. They were fighting an equally buffoonish, if vicious, enemy, the armed forces of the Western-backed dictator Joseph Kasa-Vubu. The rebel leaders, among them Maurice Kabila, were accustomed to luxury, prone to high-sounding speeches, and spent their time at conferences in Paris and Cairo. Guevara came to learn, bitterly, that the Congo war was not a revolution, it was a vastly immoral and brutal farce, one of ten thousand tragedies that would befall Africa in the twentieth century.

The entire front collapsed in October. Demoralized and sickened by tropical diseases, the Cubans had no choice but to retreat. Guevara's force scattered back to Cuba, extracted by Soviet aircraft, and he traveled cross-country to the Cuban embassy at Dar es Salaam. There he went to ground. For six weeks he remained hidden in a small room above the embassy guesthouse, dictating his account of the debacle, *Passajes de la Guerra Revolucionaria (Congo)*, to a secretary. He recalled feeling as bad as he'd ever felt; physically, he was exhausted, and his will to live had nearly left him. Then fell a thunderbolt.

While Guevara was in Dar es Salaam, he learned that Castro had broken his silence. Without informing Guevara, Castro had gone on national television and read Guevara's letter of resignation to the astounded people of Cuba. The letter had been written in anger, and for six months Castro had kept it secret. He seemed perfectly somber when he told the Cuban people that Che Guevara had surrendered his posts, his military rank, and even his Cuban citizenship. In a three-hour speech, Fidel heaped praise on Guevara but did not give the reason for the resignation. That he could so calmly sell out Guevara astounded even the crafty Raúl.

At a stroke, Che Guevara had become a man without a country.

For an entire day, he could not believe it—even now Fifo's cunning amazed him. He sat in his small suite of rooms, racked by fever, rereading the cable over and over, cursing himself, then Castro, and finally accepting the fact that he had been cast adrift. His asthma became acute, and the malaria and dysentery that had plagued him during the campaign again took its toll. His health, like his fortune, was in precipitous decline.

Incredibly, Castro sent emissaries to Dar es Salaam, summoning Guevara to Havana. Guevara refused. He arranged instead to fly to Prague with a small cadre of bodyguards. He was taken to a safe house in the Czech countryside and settled in. There he received treatment for his asthma and slowly began to recover his health. And he began to plan.

Guevara had previously dispatched a revolutionary cadre into Argentina, the expedition led by Jorge Masetti. This effort had rapidly come to grief, but Guevara was convinced his own fate would be different. He'd tried to push forward preparations for a second Argentine expedition, but they went nowhere. In March 1966 Castro proposed another destination, a place where the prospects of a properly led insurrection were promising. That place was Bolivia.

Castro was enthusiastic, and Guevara was gradually won over by his arguments. A successful insurgency in Bolivia would allow Guevara to export revolution across the border into Argentina. This, Castro knew, was Guevara's ultimate goal, the liberation of his homeland. Castro was convincing.

Guevara summoned Tania to Prague, and her preparations within Bolivia were reviewed. As spring came over the dull brown countryside, they renewed their affair. Tania still loved him, and in that he took some consolation. He did not love her, and he had told her. She was an intelligent woman. She understood. But it is a literal mind that equates understanding with comprehension, and it was with a broken heart that Tania returned to Bolivia to continue preparations and await word of his arrival.

Guevara was flown to Cuba, arriving at Rancho Boyeros Airport at night. He was whisked to an isolated house outside of Havana. Aleida and the children were brought to him, but their reunion was short-lived. Guevara plunged immediately into plans to leave them again.

Guevara allowed himself scarcely five months to train, equip, and deploy his force. He pronounced the mission ready, assumed a disguise, said goodbye to his family, and headed by a wildly circuitous route to Bolivia. Again, his plans were immense. Guevara dreamed of nothing short of a modern reprise of the liberation wars fought by Simón Bolívar and San Martín in the 1800s. Now, as he readied his Bolivian cadres, Cuban advisers were already serving with guerrilla armies in Venezuela and Colombia. Guevara envisioned these forces pushing south while his own group liberated first Bolivia, then Argentina, Uruguay, and Peru. Nor was this some idle fantasy. He had studied and written extensively on guerrilla warfare. He was fascinated by the work of the Chinese Communist general Lin Biao, who postulated that peasant armies, led by revolutionary cadres, could lay siege to the bastions of capitalism and their degenerate cities. Mao had employed this strategy in China and brought the revolution to one billion people.

As Mao had done in China, Che Guevara would now do in Latin America.

This was the road that had brought him to the Ñancahuazú. A life-long journey had taken him to this short halt, leaning against a boulder on a trail overlooking a forlorn valley in the desperate gut of South America. Guevara looked down at the river and imagined a metaphor for his own life winding through high places and low, meandering around obstacles but rolling on inexorably.

Guevara believed. And his men believed in him.

For a moment he considered that he had once had everything—fame and fine houses, a family. He had no regrets. Fame did not matter to him except as it opened doors for his plans and made things possible. He cared little where he slept. His children were precious to him, but they were not dear enough to put aside his quest. He'd had everything a man could dream for, and now he had the rifle in his hand

and the clothing on his back. Revolution was his true love—revolution as *ideal* and *achievement*. Perhaps he was chasing a mirage. No, it was real. Guevara had seen revolution made true in Cuba, and he told himself that he would make it happen again.

Caesar had crossed the Rubicon, and Guevara's river, the Ñancahuazú, shimmered below, a thin splinter of silver winding around precipitous jungle hillsides. Below in the valley, there was still a single speck of light—it came from the Zinc House, Tania was there—and in the morning she would guide Selizar Galán up this same path to Camp 2.

There was a clicking sound brought up on the wind, the noise of a canteen or a rifle magazine knocking against a belt buckle, and Guevara was instantly alert. He sat perfectly still against the boulder as a shadow moved up the trail below and to his right.

Slowly, from the gloom, Guevara could puzzle out the shape of a man carrying a rifle. At twenty yards, he could tell that the man was tall and of solid build—a soldier, to guess by the steadiness of his pace. The soldier carried a heavy pack, and under this burden, he bent slightly forward at the waist, eyes cast down on the trail before him. As the man found his way around a switchback, Guevara remained still against the boulder; he knew that as long as he did not move, he was part of the shadow, another component of a vast dark night, and the walking man would not see him until it was too late.

It had been an error to rest directly on the trail, a dipshit amateur's mistake, and Guevara cursed himself. He could not shift his rifle off his lap without revealing his position. Several long seconds passed, and the man with the pack climbed steadily. Guevara's hand moved slowly to his hip. Scarcely breathing, he opened the leather flap on his holster, and his fingers closed over the butt of his pistol. He drew the weapon gently and placed his thumb on the hammer. If the soldier was alone, Guevara would kill him. If the soldier was scouting for a larger unit, Guevara would try to slip behind him, leave the trail, and warn the others. As long as the moon stayed behind the clouds, Guevara would have an even chance to escape.

He stared over the man's shoulder, looking behind him and downslope. From the path beyond, there was no other movement and no sound; the man had apparently come up from the valley alone.

This would be enough to seal his doom.

The soldier came on, his eyes still on the trail in front of him, and

Guevara could hear the short chuffing of his breathing. When the man was close enough to touch, Guevara raised his pistol and stood. In that moment, the clouds opened, and a shaft of moonlight struck the trail, lighting Guevara like a specter.

The man's face jerked up, and he staggered back, suddenly and perfectly amazed. Guevara had seemed to materialize out of solid rock.

In the darkness, Guevara could see the soldier's face, his mouth open and eyes white in surprise. With a worried grunt, the man thrust his hand under the strap of his rifle, but there was no time for him to pull it from his shoulder. The soldier heard Guevara thumb-cock the pistol and saw him level it at his face.

"Goddammit," the man said, more in embarrassment than fear.

In the moonlight Guevara smiled, and the man ruefully shook his head.

Guevara placed the pistol back in his holster, and his hand closed over the man's shoulder.

"Come, Joaquin," Guevara said, "we will walk up together."

6

IT SURPRISED NO one that Tania had hurried along with Arturo and Tuma to be the first to arrive at Camp 2. From the barrens above the farmhouse, Marcos watched the three of them climb the ridge, emerging from cloud and disappearing into forest as the trail switched back and they ascended. At the observation post, Marcos nudged Pombo, who lounged against a stump, scraping his nails with the point of a bayonet.

"Here comes the *chiquita*," Marcos said. "You'd better go tell the boss."

Tania arrived at camp red-faced, her hair wet with perspiration, a good forty-five minutes ahead of Galán and his escort.

"Hello, Pombo," she said as she came toward him. She'd known him in Europe and in Cuba, first as a member of Guevara's security detail and then as an agent in Czechoslovakia and La Paz.

"Welcome to the war," Pombo said.

"You look well," Tania said. It was the most hollow of platitudes. Tania was aware, fully, of what Pombo and the others actually thought of her.

"I'll take you to the comandante." Pombo waved his hand, gesturing for her to go first, and she was led through camp to the place above the creek where Guevara had placed his hammock. As they walked, Pombo ran his eyes over her without longing. Tania was dressed in a khaki jacket and shirt, olive-drab slacks, and a pair of sturdy soldiers' boots. She wore sunglasses, the lenses dark and the frames made of faux tortoiseshell; the effect was to make her outfit seem somewhat more chic than utilitarian.

Tania did her best not to appear eager or particularly happy, but her heart was hammering in her chest. "How is he?" she asked.

"Same as ever."

A bit of schoolgirl had crept into her voice, and she regretted the question immediately. As they passed down the leafy trail, she took off her sunglasses and put them in a pocket.

At Guevara's clearing, she caught sight of him lying in his hammock, writing in a notebook. He swung his legs to the ground and tossed the book into the hammock as she approached. Pombo walked her into the clearing and withdrew immediately.

Tania stood smiling, and Guevara came toward her. He hesitated, making sure they were alone, and then they embraced. As she held him, she smelled gunpowder, sweat, and tobacco. She noticed he was thinner than he had been, and that his hands were dirty. To Guevara, his lover seemed older and careworn.

"I'm glad to see you," he said. Tania kissed his neck and cheek; her lips brushed his, but he averted his face. She again kissed his cheek.

She waited for him to say something, to say that he had missed her, that he was glad she'd come safely, she waited for him to tell her she was beautiful, but Guevara said nothing. They embraced for a moment more, Tania holding him tightly, and then he backed away. A look was exchanged, a glance more telling than a thousand words, and Tania felt a needle in her heart. She plainly understood his reserve, and she replied as he had thought she would, with a poignant, almost bewildered submission.

"Are you all right?" Guevara asked.

Tania swallowed and nodded. "Of course," she said flatly. A tree would not have believed her.

Guevara's concern was genuine, but there was much more to Tania's behavior than he could fathom. She was taken with him, and had been since the first moment she saw him, but Tania's real feelings were irrelevant. Perhaps they were indescribable. Perhaps she did not know what she felt; perhaps she had been in this game too long, pretended to be others too long, pretended emotions, and now she did not know who she was or what she felt.

Her throat burned, and she wanted very suddenly to bawl. She could not believe that he could not hear the thoughts swirling around in her head.

"Are you surprised to see me?" she asked.

"No," he said. "When Havana said Galán would come, I expected you to come also."

She said nothing but continued to look at him, her eyes directly on his until he looked away. Guevara gestured to a log positioned next to a campfire, reduced to ashes but left to smolder to annoy the mosquitoes.

"Come on. Step into my office."

Guevara could have no idea that the woman before him was more capable than he imagined, more practiced than he suspected, more dangerous and more deadly than the entire Bolivian army. She sat.

To Guevara, Tania looked frail, almost childlike.

"We have a job to do still."

"I know that," she said.

"You've done important work. I'm very proud of you."

She thought to scold him but suppressed the urge. He could not help, she thought, but to patronize.

"What do you think of him?" Guevara asked.

Tania blinked, then asked, "Do you mean Galán?"

"Yes."

She hesitated, gathering her breath and waiting for an indication that she might speak candidly.

"I talked to him in Havana last year," Guevara said. "I already have an opinion."

This was a test, she realized, so she spoke honestly: "He's a jackass. A liar and an ass—which is rare."

Her words seemed to have a tonic's effect on him. Guevara leaned back and clapped his hands together. "I'm glad there's someone here who can tell me the goddamn truth."

Tania reached into the pocket sewn to the thigh of her trousers and removed a folded envelope. "These are messages from Leche," she said.

Leche, milk, was Castro's code name. Tania knew that fact, and other facts, but she perfectly feigned ignorance. She handed the envelope to Guevara and watched as he opened it and read. She already knew the contents of the messages; they'd been transmitted to her by shortwave, and she had decoded them three nights ago, before she and Galán left La Paz.

She watched Guevara closely as he read. He always tested her, she thought. And she tested him, and perhaps he knew that. Even when they made love, she'd tested him. These proofs had convinced her that he underestimated her, pitied her, even. That perception was exactly what her role in the drama required.

He believed her to be capable but moonstruck. He thought he understood her and, thinking he comprehended her motives, believed what he wished to see.

As Guevara turned the pages, she thought of their nights in Prague and the small safe house. Pombo had told her that not even the Czechs or the Russians knew where Guevara was. She did not tell Pombo that she knew differently. She knew because the Czechs knew, and the Russians knew as well—her case officer had told her that Guevara was in hiding. She knew that he had been living for almost six weeks with a single bodyguard.

When Guevara had contacted Tania in La Paz, summoning her to Czechoslovakia, she had obeyed. She was happy then, happy to be with Guevara and happy to again share his bed. Guevara knew, Tania thought—he knew she had been with other men.

When he sent her away to the training base in Camagüey, she had taken comfort as it was offered. Still, for one glorious month in Prague, a month of rain, Guevara had wanted her, and their affection had been genuine and mutual. She had listened to him talk of his plans, and he had listened to her talk of her childhood and her dreams. She knew Che Guevara as thoroughly as any woman could know a man as self-contained and isolated.

But he did not know her at all. She was quite possibly the only other human being on earth more isolated, more disconnected, and more self-reliant than Guevara. His inability to see her for what she really was was the failing of an honest man. Perhaps it was only the mistake of any man who thinks he knows a woman.

Guevara could see in Tania nothing more than he wanted to see.

Seven thousand miles from the place they had first made love, Tania lowered her head and surrendered to tears. He heard her sob, and he stood and lifted her face. He wiped the tears from her eyes and kissed her.

"Shhhhh, *querida*. Shhhhh," he said.

Guevara could not know that Tania was not crying for herself, but for him.

IN HONOR OF the general secretary's visit a pig was killed and roasted, and Loro arrived from the Zinc House with the *chicha*, late as he usually was for everything, but the comrades were well fed and happy, then happier still as cups of the sour, milky liquor were poured out and a *saludo* was offered to their new endeavor. As the toast was being proposed, the Bolivians were sure to sprinkle a few drops of *chicha* on the ground. This was the traditional portion reserved for the earth goddess, Pachamama. They were just as sure to do this as slyly as possible, so as not to attract the hoots and mockery of the Cubans, for whom religion was a long-running joke. Eusebio and Chingolo exchanged glances as they tipped back their cups. No real Boliviano would think of drinking *chicha* without offering a *cha'lla* to guarantee long life and a rich harvest. Fuck the Cubans, Eusebio thought, what they don't know is probably going to save their asses.

Marcos entered camp and said he could smell roast pig halfway up the mountain. He had been sent ahead to report that Comrade Galán was still on the trail, and was delighted to find that roast pork and *chicha* had been put aside for the men of the escort. The party was expected to arrive not long after full dark. This message he delivered to Guevara, Joaquin, and Tania as they sat by the fire. Guevara nodded, and as Marcos disappeared, Joaquin spat into the coals. "Goddamn. Galán is a slow, lazy fucker."

Tania registered this and said nothing. Guevara stood and stretched. "I just want to get this over with," he said.

It was dark, and the fire had been rekindled by the time Camba stepped into the firelight. With him was a short, shifty-looking man in a waist-length jacket and flannel slacks. Because he was not entirely trusted, Galán had been taken by a deliberately roundabout path to the camp. Guevara noticed that Galán's street shoes were scuffed and down at the counters. The walk from the farmhouse had obviously been an adventure.

Guevara did not rise as the two men advanced into the firelight. Camba spoke. "Comandante, I present Comrade Galán, the general secretary of the Bolivian Party."

Neither man extended a hand. Guevara nodded at the tree trunk facing the fire. "Comrade, I'm glad we have a chance to talk. Have you eaten?"

The pleasantries, if they could be called that, evaporated quickly.

"I'm not hungry." Galán's voice was shrill, almost female in its timbre. "I'd like to speak to you in private, Dr. Guevara."

Guevara nodded, and Camba stepped back into the darkness. Galán peered around the fire. He made out a shadow standing next to Guevara—Joaquin—and then Tania, sitting with her arms folded and her legs crossed.

"Tania is a friend, and Joaquin is my second in command. Whatever you say to me, you may say to them," Guevara said. He also wanted to make sure that others could report on the conversation.

"What are you doing here?" Galán asked.

Guevara ran his hand through his beard. "You were in Havana last month. What did they tell you we would be doing here?"

"No one authorized you to ambush that patrol."

"Authorized?" Joaquin sputtered.

Guevara flicked his eyes, and Joaquin found a seat and was quiet. Galán continued, his words falling quickly against one another.

"Ñancahuazú was to serve as a staging base only, for operations into Argentina."

"The time's not right for an Argentinean operation."

"What makes you think the time's right for Bolivia?" Galán asked hotly. He noticed, rather distastefully, that Tania was jotting down notes of the conversation.

"Well, there are a couple of reasons," Guevara began. "Besides Haiti, this is the poorest nation in the hemisphere. Bolivia has the highest rates of illiteracy, infant mortality, and the lowest life expectancy—"

Galán cut him off. "What about the army?"

"We just kicked their asses. They're clowns."

"You were lucky. Even if you win a hundred times out here, it won't matter. The people, the campesinos, the miners—they aren't ready for revolution. They're not prepared politically or militarily. I said to Fidel—"

Again Joaquin rose to his feet. "Six months ago you told Fidel you'd support our operations. You promised weapons and men. That's why we're here." He stepped close to Galán; Guevara was surprised to see Galán remain seated. The smaller man's eyes glinted in the firelight.

"For an Argentinean operation," Galán said.

"This was never about Argentina," Guevara said, pinning him.

Galán had in fact told many stories. He had told Castro he would support an operation in Bolivia, then told Moscow and the members of his own Party that he would not. He was a facile liar, perhaps a man incapable of telling the truth.

"The Party's reconsidered," Galán said. "The time's not right for armed struggle."

"When will it be right, Comrade?" Joaquin sputtered. "When no babies live? When the North Americans control your streetlights? What's it going to take to get you off your ass?"

Guevara lifted his hand. Joaquin sat once more, shaking his head. Tania looked at Galán in the firelight. He was leaning forward, and his hands were clenched.

"You participated in the last elections, Comrade Galán. The Bolivian Party ran candidates?" Guevara asked.

"We did," Galán answered.

"Did you come here to tell us that you've become a democrat?"

"I'm a realist. You can't make a revolution by bringing in thirty Cuban adventurers."

"Bolivians serve with us," Guevara said.

"They're Maoists, renegades."

"Inti and Coco are Bolivian Party members."

"Not anymore. They've been expelled. I've come to inform you that if you continue this struggle, it must be brought under the control of the Bolivian Party."

"Under your control?" Guevara asked quietly.

"As general secretary of the Bolivian Communist Party."

"You have no military experience."

"And you're not Bolivian. When the people discover the revolution is being led by a foreigner, they will turn their backs and fail to support it. It will fail because it's being led by a band of Cuban mercenaries—not Bolivians. It's our revolution, not yours."

"We're two men sitting around a campfire. In the middle of fucking nowhere. Let's talk like men."

"All right. You fucked up, coming here. The enemy is too strong. The CIA already is in Camiri. Soon the U.S. Army will be here, too. This place, the Ñancahuazú, is a death trap. The country is too hard. It's too sparsely settled. You'll die here."

Joaquin's face reddened with anger. Tania scribbled a few notes and wished furiously that she could jab a pencil up Galán's ass. Only Guevara seemed in control of his emotions.

"You're soft, Galán," he said. "You've gone bourgeois. If this country is hard on us, it's harder on the enemy. Even now the Bolivian army pisses their pants every time they head off-road." Guevara stood and gestured around them. "If I let you play general, everything we've prepared for, everything we've gained, would be blown away in a heartbeat. You're not a revolutionary. You're a party hack."

"I'm the general secretary. I assume control immediately, or the Bolivian Communist Party will not support you. That's my final word."

Guevara dropped his stick into the fire. "Then I'm sorry that your trip has been wasted," he said.

Joaquin stood, and Tania as well. In the yellow flicker, Galán's face was like a weasel's.

"I demand the right to address the men," he said.

"Why?" Guevara asked evenly.

"I have come to offer the Bolivian comrades amnesty if they lay down their arms and return with me to La Paz."

"Whose goddamn side are you on?" Joaquin said.

"My side. And the side of the Bolivian people."

Guevara said calmly, "Joaquin. Muster the men."

In a few moments the men were assembled, twenty-seven, less five on guard and those at the Zinc House. Galán stood before the assembled band of guerrillas. To Tania, he seemed like a little dog yapping before a pantheon.

"Comrades," Galán intoned, "the Party finds those joining this effort to be in error. I offer formal amnesty to any Bolivian comrade who renounces armed struggle, lays down arms, and returns with me to La Paz."

No one moved or spoke. The fires crackled and snapped.

Guevara was sitting on a stump nearby. "You heard him," he said. "It's over for us. We're done. Cubans, Bolivians, anybody who wants to sleep in a real bed can pack up your gear and go home."

"Go home, shit. I just got here," Pombo said.

There was a riffle of assent.

"Comrade Galán is of the opinion that our efforts will be wasted," Guevara went on. "Maybe he's right. Maybe things aren't that bad here in Bolivia. Maybe Barrientos and his gangsters are about to have an epiphany of justice and reason. Maybe the imperialists will pack up and go back to Wall Street—"

"Hey, maybe Pombo will quit picking his nose," Joaquin said.

There was laughter.

"We can always hope for a miracle," Guevara said. His eyes scanned the bright faces before him. "I am a revolutionary. It's the duty of revolutionaries, and the highest calling of man, to make revolution. What we build here will spread to all the nations of Latin America. One, two, a hundred Vietnams can encircle our enemy. This is where it's going to start. Here, in this canyon. Tonight. These fires, from this camp, are going to set the continent on fire."

Tania watched him speak, transfixed, spellbound, as were all who could hear him.

"Anyone who wants to go home and eat from the master's table is free to go. Anyone who wants to kick Barrientos in the ass can stay with me."

Someone shouted, and there were smiles and backslapping.

Galán twitched. "You're making a mistake," he said. "You'll die like heroes. But you'll all die."

"Camba, please escort the good comrade back to the real world," Guevara said. Camba and a dozen men stepped forward.

Galán turned to Guevara. "I wish you luck."

"No, you don't."

Galán could not withstand Guevara's eyes. He turned and followed Camba away into the night. Joaquin watched them go with a disgusted, tired look.

"He's going to screw us," Joaquin said. "The little shit."

"He'll try. I want to have the forward detachment on the trail at sunrise. I want all the paths leading to the camp broken down completely. Have the men bury all their personal effects."

Joaquin moved off to carry out the order. Guevara and Tania stood in the firelight. The night loomed around them, the fire was like a single bright room in a large, dark house.

"What should I do?" Tania asked.

"You're going to be our only link to the city now. We can't risk having you return here. Go with Galán back to La Paz. Use the shortwave and tell Havana what's going on. They'll have orders for you."

"Do you think Galán will inform?"

"I don't know what he'll do." Tania saw that Guevara's expression was stern. "Stay in contact with Havana, but don't bring him back here. For any reason. When we need you, we'll contact you through Leche."

Guevara reached out and cupped her cheek. It was the gesture of a lover, but his fingers were like ice. He held her gaze for a few silent moments. Perhaps words failed him.

She watched Guevara walk away from the firelight. As the night closed over him, Tania felt like she had watched a man stepping off the edge of the world.

7

THE FORTUNES OF the town of Camiri rose and fell with the price of crude oil. Those fortunes had lately been in decline, and it was not difficult for Smith to lease a storefront on the corner of the Avenida Bolívar and the Calle Comercio, near the market. Smith told the landlord that the building would be used by a team of geologists working for the national oil consortium. The cover was serviceable and would explain the comings and goings of several vehicles and the meanderings of sunburned gringos at odd hours of the day and night.

Beyond Camiri's cluster of oil derricks and refineries spread the Chaco, an arid, inhospitable wilderness roamed by jaguar, white-tailed deer, and peccary. Unredeemed by culture, climate, or society, it was mainly proximity to the Ñancahuazú that recommended Camiri as a forward operating base.

Into the second-story rooms of the building Hoyle had placed army cots, and a large closet off the stairs was set aside for the radio. On the ground floor, the rooms adjoining the front door had been made to look like an office, with a desk, typewriter, and telephone. A larger room, reached through a curtain behind the office, held their field desks, files, and weapons. Next to Hoyle's desk there was a thoroughly disreputable-looking sofa and an electric coffeepot that rarely if ever worked. Both had come from a recently raided whorehouse on the Plaza 15 de Abril.

The storefront itself was utterly nondescript. Scotch-taped to the front window was a hand-lettered sign that read TOPÓGRAFOS DE PE-TROLEUM, S.A. Another stuck inside the door glass advised: CERRADO. As much as possible, Hoyle, Smith, and Charlie came and went by the back door. Once a week Hoyle gave a street kid three Bolivianos to wash the front windows clean of the oily grit carried from the road by passing tanker trucks.

Tonight Hoyle and Charlie returned to the office late after a long, dusty drive from a scouting trip to Lagunillas. Hoyle had given Charlie the night off and was amazed and envious when he seemed positively buoyant, skipping off to meet some cousins he said were staying at the Hotel Boyuibe. Hoyle unlocked the back door, dropped his rucksack in front of his desk, and collapsed onto the couch, exhausted. It was most of an hour before he realized that he had not taken off his boots.

Hoyle sat up painfully, his head pounding. He opened the icebox and used a church key hanging from a string to snap the top off a bottle of Postosino beer. He downed a few swallows, the bubbles disagreeable on the back of his throat. Holding the cool bottle against his forehead, he crossed the room.

Stuck into a cardboard tube on his desk were maps, high-quality topographics produced by the Defense Mapping Agency. He gathered several and unrolled them on the large table in the center of the room. These were proper military photomosaics, marked over by one-kilometer-grid squares, aligned perfectly to geopolar north, detailed Mercator projections that had been photographed by American reconnaissance jets and thoughtfully compiled in the cool quiet of graphic studios in Suitland, Maryland. Drawn to 1:25,000 scale, the maps were suitable for planning artillery bombardments, air strikes, and the plotting of grand military campaigns. As far as Hoyle knew, these maps had not yet been supplied to the Bolivian army, which was in any case unlikely to plan, bomb, shell, or campaign anytime soon.

Sipping his beer, Hoyle taped together half a dozen of these pages to cover an area encompassing most of the southern expanse of Santa Cruz. Like the map in Señor Lempira's office, Hoyle's map too had places incognita, huge swaths of terrain not marked by place-names.

On the laminated sheets, mountains, canyons, rivers, and villages were in their places, but almost all were without label: tracts of forest and jungle, hillside, rivers, streams, and stands of forest that were not fixed by language. The hills alone were distinctly identified, each peak bearing a number automatically determined by the radar altimeters of the reconnoitering aircraft. Hill 826, Hill 792, a monotony of numbers.

Hoyle thumbtacked his creation to the wall and stood back to look at it. He could trace out the Ñancahuazú flowing north to the center. Where it met the Rio Grande, the rivers together resembled the letter Y scribbled by a child. Slightly lopsided, the Rio Grande's principal tributaries—the Masacuri, Frias, and Hondo—joined from the upper left. At the center of the Y, the Ñancahuazú jaunted east to become the Rio Grande proper, and that river, much enlarged, departed in a slow turn to the north. The watershed occupied perhaps fifty thousand square kilometers and was bound to the east by the Camiri–Santa Cruz Highway and, slightly beyond, the Yacuiba Railway. The highway and railroad were the sole north-south communication in the entire eastern part of the country. For three hundred kilometers north and south and almost two hundred kilometers east and west, the area was wilderness. Not a single road crossed the valley, and not one bridge spanned the Ñancahuazú, Masacuri, or Frias. Somewhere in a thousand-square-mile expanse of territory, a guerrilla band had established a base, perhaps several bases. To fix their location, Hoyle had to now become a guerrilla. He had operated in the bush and knew its requirements. In the field, good guy and bad guy had the same needs and wants. Somewhere out in the Ñancahuazú, his opposite number lived and breathed and slept. He had placed down caches, stored ammunition, food, and medical supplies. At least one of his permanent positions held a radio. He cooked rice, ate what game he could shoot; he took shits, washed his clothes, and cleaned his weapons. Maybe he read letters from home and he sent out reports and estimates to someone, somewhere.

Hoyle opened another beer and grunted. *Okay, fucker. You didn't just throw a dart at the map. You planned this. Where are you?*

He first plotted the location of the double ambush. After walking the terrain, he had noticed two things. The scene of the first ambush was far from perfect; aside from boulders and scrub, there was little cover. If the site was chosen, it had been chosen badly. The follow-on ambush, the firefight with the reaction force, had been conducted flawlessly. That suggested to him that the ambush of the first truck was a chance encounter. The second engagement, the ambush of Major Buran, had been deliberate. The guerrilla commander had elected to stay and wait, and sprang a second attack with ruthless aplomb.

Hoyle knew that no competent guerrilla would have lured the enemy into battle if the location were close to his base. Hoyle took a grease pencil and drew a broad circle around the ambush site. Its radius was what he considered a brisk two days' march, approximately fifty kilometers. It was unlikely that the guerrillas' main base would be inside this circle.

Assuming the base area was not close to the initial contact, it would still have the same general requirements: water and food, as well as cover and concealment. This meant, specifically, that the guerrillas' main camp must be near a river and would likely be hidden in a mountainous, wooded area. There might be one camp, but it was more likely that there were several close together. The requirements of logistical support meant that at least one of the guerrillas' camps had to be located within half a day's march of a road head. Without this, a supply line to the city, no guerrilla unit in the field could long sustain itself.

In the north, the lower edges of the Rio Grande Valley below Samaipata offered both haven and road access. In the east, the Capinirini Mountains between the Santa Cruz Highway and Lake Pirirenda met the necessities of concealment, water, and communications. In the west, the canyons and rolling countryside around La Higuera were not especially good but would suffice. And in the south, the headwaters of the Ñancahuazú above Lagunillas were also a venue. There were several other, less plausible locations, all falling within the approximate rectangle marked out by the leading possibilities.

His headwork had reduced the guerrillas' probable base locations from a range of several thousand square miles to an area of several hundred. The entire Bolivian army did not have sufficient forces to cordon and sweep even this reduced area. Nor did they have the expertise to reconnoiter it, in force or clandestinely. The enemy was hidden and kept safe by Bolivia's formidable terrain and the incompetence of its armed forces.

Lost in thought, Hoyle had not noticed that it was raining until the door blew open in a sodden gust. Outside, water poured off the roof in a torrent. Smith kicked the door closed and shook the rain off his poncho.

"Goddamn this place," he said. He tossed the poncho over a chair back, pulled a folder from under his shirt, and put it on his desk.

Hoyle watched him wipe the raindrops from his glasses. Smith's eyes appeared red and small until he threaded the earpieces back over his ears and blinked at the map.

"You want a beer?" Hoyle asked.

"I want bourbon," Smith said. He walked to his desk, officiously unlocked the center drawer, and pulled out two glasses and a bottle of Jim Beam. A somewhat uneasy détente had evolved between them; it was founded more on the necessities of compartmentalized operation rather than friendship. Smith and Hoyle still got along better when they were apart. Still, Smith was happy for the company tonight; he had driven alone all day from Sucre.

Hoyle watched him pour two tumblers half full of whiskey. "What was up in Sucre?" he asked.

"I checked with the National Police. Since the state of emergency, they've been making foreigners register. You have to get a Vaitmento Abriganda if you're going to spend the night in town. I checked out a couple of Peruvians who went through a week before the ambush. Dirtbags. I think they were cocaine dealers."

"That convoy wasn't ambushed by druggies," Hoyle said. "They had their shit together. They engaged a superior force in broad daylight, kicked its ass, and vanished like a virgin on a troopship."

"You sound like you admire them, Mr. Hoyle."

"I'm trying not to."

Smith sat at his desk and swung his feet onto the blotter.

"At the ambush, they marked out fields of fire with piles of rocks," Hoyle said. "We used to do the same thing with the Montagnards. That convoy ambush was on-the-job training."

"Bolivians and Cubans?"

"People. People who knew what they were doing and people who did not."

Smith made a face. "If it's locals, somebody's filled their heads with a lot of Marxist bullshit. They get them spun up, and they grab some guns." He sipped whiskey and shook his head. "Every time they take a potshot at a soldier, the army burns a village. That's not a revolution—it's bad math."

"It's only a revolution if you win," Hoyle said.

The rain beat down for a few moments. Smith reached for the bottle and said to Hoyle, "Would you—"

In that instant there was a flash of reddish light. Hoyle was turned to face the map on the wall, so he sensed it with his right eye first. He knew what it was immediately; there was a *crack-bang* and then a gust of hot, acrid wind as the shock wave of a massive explosion sucked the air out of his lungs. Some piece of debris struck him behind the knees, and his feet were swept out from under him. The explosion roiled through the building, part cloud and part fire, smashing windows and splintering doors.

For Smith, turned with his back to the front office, the first impression of the detonation was a deep, thudding concussion perceived as much with his chest as with his ears. As the explosion ripped into the room, Smith tumbled forward, instinctively covering his face as a hurricane of shattered glass flew past him. In the resulting chaos, desks were overturned and the typewriter from the front office punched through the back door. The overhead lights were blown out, but incredibly, both desk lamps survived and remained illuminated, pointing up through the swirling smoke.

Hoyle's ears were screaming, but he didn't think he'd been pierced anywhere. He came to his hands and knees, drew his pistol, and half crawled, half dived behind an overturned file cabinet. "Kill the lights!" he shouted. "Kill the lights!"

Smith kicked out the closest desk lamp and swung his fist down on the other, smashing it like a kid exterminating a particularly annoying insect. Hoyle peered over his cover toward the front window. The street side of the building was torn open. From the Calle Comercio, Hoyle could hear dogs barking and then people yelling.

Smith was standing, pushing his glasses back up on his nose. He said in a clear, calm voice, "Car bomb."

Both men reeled through the debris to the front of the building and out into the street. To the right and left of the offices, shopwindows were shattered, and at the corner of the marketplace, the awnings and stalls of the coca-leaf vendors were in tatters.

As Hoyle looked back at the front of the office, he realized the charge had been placed in a car across the street, an expedient and deadly means of attack. Car parts and shrapnel had peppered the front of buildings for a hundred meters up and down the street. Hoyle grasped how narrowly they had escaped. As adrenaline ebbed, he clenched his teeth and felt an odd tremor in his legs.

Smith's eyes adjusted to the darkness, and he surveyed the damage. White paint had been daubed on a wall nearby. It said: VIVA LAS GUERRILLAS. YANQUI GO HOME. A hammer and sickle was painted under it.

"We're going to need people. More agents," Smith said. There was an edge in his voice. He was taking this personally.

"That's a bad idea," Hoyle said. "We're not going to beat this by pouring in bodies."

"What is it that you're not getting here? We just got car-bombed.

Hoyle flicked his head at the graffiti in the firelight. "Look at the hammer and sickle. It's upside down." He threaded his pistol back into its shoulder holster. "There's been no Communist bombings before this."

"Then who put the bomb down?" Smith spat back.

"Landowners, Barrientos, the army, take your pick. They make it look worse than it is. We panic and escalate."

From out of the rain came the noise of police cars and fire trucks.

Hoyle touched Smith on the shoulder. "Let's beat it."

They headed quickly down the alley and toward the back of the office. As the rain beat down, Hoyle realized for the first time that he was barefoot. Although he felt no pain, his right heel was putting down a series of crimson puddles as he walked to the Land Cruiser parked behind the back door. Very suddenly, his foot started to hurt.

"I'm going back to La Paz, ask some questions," Smith mumbled. "I can spread some dollars around . . ." He seemed almost to be talking to himself.

Hoyle slipped behind the wheel of the Land Cruiser. Smith climbed into the truck with him. The rain still fell heavily, drumming on the roof until its sound was extinguished by the starting of the engine.

"We don't want informants," Hoyle said. "We need people on payroll. Native speakers—people who can move between La Paz and Ñancahuazú with a very small footprint."

"Where are you going to get people like that?" Smith asked.

"Miami," Hoyle said.

8

T HEY WOULD BE organized for movement like this: A vanguard column, led by Marcos, seconded by Pacho; Begnino would serve as the point element's machine gunner. All Cuban officers. In this first column would be placed the most reliable of the Bolivians: Aniceto, Coco, Dario, Julio, Loro (though Guevara considered Loro somewhat more amusing than reliable). The center group, commanded by Guevara, would be mostly Cuban. Pombo and Tuma would serve as bodyguards and aides-de-camp, Urbano, Rolando, Ricardo, and Alejandro as cadres. Moro would accompany the center group as combatant/ physician and could be trusted to keep Guevara's asthma medicines. The following Bolivians were assigned to the center column: Inti, Serapio, Chapaco, Léon, and Willy. The rear column would be commanded by Joaquin and seconded by Rubio. Braulio and Miguel would oversee nine Bolivian comrades: Apolinar, Pedro, Benjamin, Victor, Walter, Chingolo, Eusebio, Paco, and Pepe. El Negro, a Bolivian medical student, would serve as the rear guard's physician.

In the three columns were thirty-five combatants; slightly over half—nineteen—were Bolivianos. In each group was a solid nucleus of Cuban fighters, all experienced, and Guevara knew he could trust Joaquin and Miguel to act logically. On point, Marcos could be counted on to find trouble before it found them, and Joaquin, solid, dependable Joaquin, would be ready to support or retreat as the situation dictated. Guevara had made his dispositions well.

On Monday the last of the food had been brought up from Camp 1 and divided as marching provisions among the men. Each column leader admonished the comrades that this was not a holiday ration but was intended for use on the march. Guevara personally laid down the penalty for breaking open the rations: two days without sleep and three days without food. Though an effort was made to evenly allocate the loads, the most onerous cargoes fell to the rear guard. Three mules and a mare were also assigned to the trailing column, the animals carrying crated ammunition, a small cache of plastic explosives, and the largest of the cooking pots.

As the column leaders inspected the troops, Guevara took up his books and maps and walked back to his clearing. As he sat in his hammock, a dull sort of apprehension came over him. The feeling was hard to understand—plain in its effect but incomprehensible in it origins. He was satisfied with the preparations, and the men seemed happy. Why was he low? Some of the reason was physical. His asthma had circled him the last several days. He hadn't needed to take the small, bitter pills Moro had given him—he'd managed by force of will to stave off a full-blown attack—but he felt the tightness in his chest and knew that worry was a ready trigger.

Still hanging over all was the issue of Galán and the position of the Bolivian Party. Fucking Galán. Monkey-faced shit-eater. It would happen in due course that Galán would turn the Bolivian Party against them, *actively* against them, and there was danger in that. This peril was most acute early on. The Party would be split along the lines of conflict: Those embracing the armed struggle would be with them, and the prevaricators, the deviationists, the *Galáns* would be swept aside and blown away. The faint of heart were at least identified at the outset. The drawing-room revolutionaries would fall by the wayside; stalwart comrades would see that the time for revolution was upon them. Even now the first of the volunteers from the Communist Youth Organization had broken with Galán and would be arriving at the camps in the next month. More Bolivians for the Bolivians.

There was still the issue of what to do with the Bolivian comrades Guevara had now. Some of them held promise, but others were already

showing signs of becoming shit connoisseurs. There had been instances of tension between Cubans and Bolivians, nothing serious, but
noted. It was natural that there would be some teething pains; the Bolivian comrades were being brought under revolutionary discipline,
and for now that meant answering to Cuban officers. When there were
successes in the field, there would be more volunteers. The force
would expand, and Bolivians would eventually be appointed to positions of responsibility.

But first Guevara must make good with what he had. Cubans and
Bolivians had to be forged together into a cohesive *guerrillo,* and to do
that Guevara planned a monthlong training march, a reconnaissance in
force, down the Ñancahuazú and up the Rio Grande, perhaps west to
the Masacuri.

In truth, Guevara had no destination. The objective of the march
was to reconnoiter the theater of operations and condition the men.
There was, of course, the possibility of contact with the enemy, but
that was not the object. Not yet. This was to be a training march.

From the main camp, Guevara heard an argument involving the
loading of the mules, Joaquin holding firm that ammunition crates be
loaded last, so they might be unloaded quickly in case of need, and
someone, Marcos perhaps, insisting that because they were heavy, they
should be loaded first, close to the pack frame. Guevara ignored the
words and the problem. The men needed this march—first as a trial
and then as an accomplishment. There were maneuvers to be practiced, envelopment and ambush, attack and retreat, procedures for
splitting up and then joining together. All of these evolutions needed
to be practiced and practiced until even the most inept Bolivian could
lead the columns. That would take time. Until then the hard country
favored them, held them secure in its vastness. Kept them safe.

Guevara took the journal and pen from his pack and wrote:

> *The last day at camp. A bearing party cleaned out camp number one
> and the sentries were brought back. Antonio, Ñato, Camba, and Ar-
> turo will be left behind to guard the farmhouse and receive Moises and
> the volunteers when they arrive in the coming weeks.*

Guevara lifted his pen, staring down at the spidery handwriting
tilted across the date book at his knee.

He wrote a last sentence: *I spoke to the troops, giving them final instructions about the march.*

In fact, he had told the men only that they were heading north and that the trip would last at least two weeks. In the absence of facts, rumor wafted through the columns, the Cubans knowing to expect one of Guevara's *pruebas duras,* another hard test, and the Bolivians carelessly expecting to be back in camp after a fortnight's walk in the woods.

Everything is right, Guevara told himself, not proudly but to reassure himself. He put his journal back in his pack and snapped the cap on his pen. It's time to get these people off their asses. It's time to begin.

9

MR. VALDÉZ DECIDED to follow Miami station's advice and bought a ticket to La Paz via New York. It would have been less expensive to travel direct to Panama, but he thought it prudent to follow the suggested route. Hoyle had mentioned in his cable that the job was "getting interesting," which might mean anything—difficulties, extra pay, or the enchantments of the fairer sex. None of these possibilities troubled Valdéz, who had a pretty good idea what the work might entail, and when Hoyle asked him to forward "two sets of tools" via diplomatic pouch, Valdéz had required no further explanation. Four Samsonite suitcases had been air-expressed from Miami to the American embassy in Santo Domingo, then sent on to Bolivia by diplomatic courier. Valdéz could pick up his equipment at the embassy in La Paz at his leisure.

Once into La Paz, Valdéz disposed of his suitcase—it was a prop filled with secondhand clothing—and meandered through the city. He enjoyed an early lunch of *sopa de mani*, creamy peanut soup, and *sajta de pollo*, half a chicken cooked with garlic, cumin, salt, parsley, yellow peppers, and onion. After the overwhelming lunch, Valdéz purchased a razor, toothbrush, and tooth powder. Leaving the pharmacy, he twice took public transportation and twice doubled back on his own route, completing a standard CIA surveillance detection protocol called a "two-island tour." Satisfied that he had not been followed,

Valdéz arrived at the American embassy at precisely 2:17 P.M. and was met in the lobby by a staff sergeant of the marine security detachment. Valdéz was led up two flights of stairs through the armored door and into the communications station, then into a steel-walled room where his luggage waited for him. The marine apologized as Valdéz unlocked the yellow nylon diplomatic mailbags that contained his suitcases. The bags had been deposited between the embassy's code machines.

"I'm sorry, sir," the marine droned, "I can't leave you alone in the crypto vault."

Valdéz smiled. "That's quite all right." And in fact, Valdéz rather liked the Marine Corps. He would be the first to admit that he was a man of firm convictions, and that he enjoyed the certainty of absolutes. The Marine Corps dealt in moral certainties; for marines, things were either right or wrong, good or evil, and Valdéz appreciated that. He especially appreciated this simple and enduring philosophy because so often in his work things were anything but absolute.

Valdéz opened the first of the diplomatic pouches and removed a cheap plastic-sided suitcase printed with a black plaid pattern. He threw the locks and opened the case. Inside were street clothes and a Dopp kit. Within an empty can of shaving cream was concealed a Mexican passport bearing the name Jorge Castillo Morales. Affixed to the document was Valdéz's photograph, stamped with a Bolivian visa bearing today's date. The visa listed his profession as petrochemical engineer. Tucked into the passport was a Jalisco driver's license and business cards.

These small lies bundled together were Morales's "legend," the tissue of fabrication that was to be Valdéz's new identity. The phone numbers on the business cards were each appropriately backstopped, meaning there was an office in Jalisco and the telephone would be answered with the name of Jorge Morales's nominal employer, Pemex Development S.A. If anyone bothered to call, the friendly people on the other end of the line would verify that Jorge was a longtime employee, a graduate of Oklahoma State University, and presently in Bolivia to consult on a petroleum natural gas injection project at Camiri.

Like Hoyle, Valdéz was a CIA contract operator entering Bolivia under nonofficial cover, meaning that his presence in the country would not be sanctioned by the American government. This sort of cover, somewhat dramatically, was called "illegal," although use of that word was reserved mostly for Communists who entered target countries under similar arrangements. His camouflage was more often called "civil cover," or simply "nock," the phonetic of "NOC," or nonofficial cover.

Valdéz knew that if he were to be arrested in Bolivia, the Mexican passport would allow the embassy, State Department, and CIA to deny they knew him. In some countries, for NOCs, the game ended at the end of a piece of piano wire. In Bolivia that bit of ugliness was unlikely—Bolivia was a staunch U.S. ally, if not an outright vassal. The country was a Partner for Peace, a greedy recipient of increasing amounts of American aid, money, and military assistance.

When Hoyle contacted Miami for additional operators, it had been decided that the augmentation would go forward in the most discreet manner possible. For this reason, Valdéz had traveled under alias.

In a second, larger suitcase were Valdéz's weapons, held in place by cut blocks of Styrofoam. The sergeant watched intently as Valdéz removed and assembled a Colt model 609 Commando assault rifle. The weapon was intended for U.S. Special Forces fighting in Vietnam, and it was from there that Valdéz had come.

"Seen one of those before," the sergeant said. And he had, only once, at night, when a patrol of Rangers had passed by the sergeant's squad on a hot landing zone. Valdéz's weapon would eventually be called the CAR-15—it was the apex of American assault-rifle design, a shortened, faster-shooting M16. As the sergeant gaped at the rifle, Valdéz glanced at the decorations on his uniform blouse. They included a Vietnam service ribbon and a Purple Heart.

"Where'd you get hit?" Valdéz asked.

"Shot through the ass," the sergeant said. "Both cheeks."

"I meant where in-country."

"Quang Tri. In I Corps."

Valdéz murmured an acknowledgment. His rifle assembled, he clicked on the safety and set about putting together his pistol, a 9mm Beretta.

"You been over, sir?"

"I have had the privilege," Valdéz answered.

When Valdéz looked up, the marine was staring. There was a distant, troubled look on the sergeant's face.

The marine said quietly: "Privilege? To be over there? You gotta be kidding me."

Valdéz looked down and was quite surprised to find the pistol assembled in his hand. He had put the weapon together without realizing it—an exercise conducted utterly by rote. He tried to say something, but his mind was blank. Suddenly embarrassed, he closed up the last of his suitcases, and the sergeant made a mental note: *This motherfucker is out of his goddamn mind.*

MR. SANTAVANES FOUND it difficult to sleep. Once or twice lightning flashed through the drawn blinds and a whimper of thunder crept into his room, an oppressively furnished corner suite in a small, neat hotel on the Calle Loayza. Beside him, the girl snored slightly, breathing in and out, and Santavanes stared at the ceiling, which seemed an especially long way off when you were drunk. There was still the metallic taste of Singani in his mouth.

When it starts to get light, I will wake her, Santavanes thought. But that could be a long time from now, longer than he could easily determine, because before he had the girl sent up to his room, Santavanes had hidden his wristwatch. Not all whores steal, he knew, and looking at the girl, he found it hard to think that this one would, but Santavanes did not believe in testing the goodness of others. That is why before the porter brought the girl along with a bottle of Singani, limes, and ice, Santavanes put away his watch. And now, lying drunk and sated in his bed, he did not know exactly where his watch was. I'll find it in the morning, he thought.

Santavanes pulled the blanket up. He was still cold in his bones from the long truck journey from Peru. For most of the trip, he'd crouched in the back of a *camión* with about forty campesinos, pushed together and jostled as the truck lurched south, past the eastern shore of Lake Titicaca, then across the frontier into Bolivia. With the other passengers, Santavanes had simply stared back blank-faced when the Bolivian customs officer lifted up the tarp and shined his flashlight into the truck. The driver paid the customs officer a few hundred Bolivianos and Santavanes and the others were in, the driver hardly inconvenienced by the five-minute delay and the officers at the Desaguadero border post satisfied with a spongy wad of currency.

The *camión* continued south during the cold night, and at a truck stop in Huraini, Santavanes went to the counter of the small café and asked the owner for his valise. It was waiting, having been brought to the truck stop two days earlier, and Santavanes asked for the use of a room to change. This, too, was ready for him.

In the half an hour or so it took the driver to fuel the truck and re- fill the radiator, Santavanes disposed of his campesino outfit, a battered felt hat, dark pants, jacket, and sandals. Santavanes then removed from his valise a clean shirt, slacks, a brown wool suit jacket, socks, and a pair of brogans. In the shoes was tucked five hundred American dollars. When Santavanes returned to the truck, he simply handed the driver a five-dollar bill and climbed into the cab with his suitcase. For the rest of the two-hundred-kilometer drive into La Paz, they did not speak, the driver quite certain that his passenger was a smuggler and Santa- vanes content to cultivate that impression.

For the next several hours, Santavanes had watched the scenery, which was reasonably beautiful as they passed beneath the snow- covered dome of Illimani and then into La Paz.

In bed the girl stirred next to him, and Santavanes could see the out- line of her shoulders in the small light that made it past the window blinds. He thought of waking her and making love again, but he knew this would involve some negotiation, perhaps even an ultimatum. That task was beyond his present level of enthusiasm, and at last he was con- tent to fall asleep with his arms around her.

In the morning the porter brought coffee and Salteñas, and the girl ate and washed herself in the sink, and when breakfast was finished, the porter again tapped on the door and took the plates and the girl away.

Santavanes checked out of the hotel and was picked up by a white Land Cruiser. Behind the wheel was a sturdy-looking Guaraní Indian who introduced himself as Charlie. Also in the vehicle was a tall, mus- cular-looking Latin man who introduced himself as Eduardo Valdéz. Santavanes shook his hand, and as he did, he introduced himself as Felix. Names might change, and often did, during the course of an as- signment, but they would begin with Eduardo and Felix. Unless oper- ational factors made disclosure necessary, it was not essential or even desirable to know much more.

As they drove away from the hotel, Santavanes asked in English, "So, where are we going?"

Charlie answered in English. "We have a safe house in Vallegrande. You're going to base out of there."

"What happened to Camiri?" Santavanes asked.

"Bombed," Valdéz answered, as though commenting on the weather.

"Everything go okay on the border crossing?"

"Fine, no problems."

Valdéz guessed his new colleague was Cubano, like himself, but he did not make his observation a point of discussion. Santavanes was indeed a countryman, a Guantanemero, and a veteran of a dozen CIA assignments. For most of Santavanes's deployments, he had been infiltrated as an illegal, in many of them he had operated solo, and all of his situations had been what the community called "direct action"—killing.

Mr. Valdéz and Mr. Santavanes were peers.

Valdéz gestured at the suitcases piled into the cargo compartment. "I brought you a standard load-out."

"What did you get me?"

"An FN rifle. They told me you liked the range."

The weapon was familiar to Santavanes, an implement as basic and necessary as a hammer to a carpenter.

"How about a pistol?"

"A .45 Browning. Four magazines."

"That's fine," Santavanes said.

Charlie drove on for a while, the truck shifting gears and starting the long climb out of La Paz. In the front seat, Santavanes absently touched his wrist and thought, *Goddamm it, I forgot my watch.*

10

THE SUN SLIPPED out of the sky, and dusk lowered over the city like a cupped hand. In a dinner jacket and cummerbund, Hoyle made his way across the Plaza Murillo, approaching the monument and scattering a flock of listless pigeons. On either side of the square, floodlights pushed sharp beams against the president's house and the congress building, each glowing a citrus shade of yellow.

As Hoyle continued into the square, the buildings on either side seemed somehow to recede. This was not merely a trick of the light. Although the plaza itself was level, the street fronting the congress, Ayacucho Bolívar, dropped slightly as it exited to the north. The result was that the right side of the congress building seemed to be sinking. A similar wrinkle of topography vexed the presidential palace, and as Hoyle came closer, it, too, gave the impression of a wounded ship.

Shouldered against a doughty Spanish cathedral, the house of Bolivia's president had about it an expectant, almost fretful air. Assaulted many times, pocked by bullets, and repaired contritely, the president's house was known throughout Bolivia as Palacio Quemado, the burnt palace. Twenty years before, almost to this very night, Bolivia's most unfortunate head of state, Gualberto Villarroel, had been seized by a mob, thrown from a balcony, then hanged in the square. A martyr to extemporaneous democracy.

In spite of this grim anniversary—perhaps because of it—the palace would tonight be the scene of a grand cotillion. As the beau monde of La Paz converged on the Plaza Murillo, the army flattered them with a daunting show of force. Watched over by a squad of paratroopers, arriving guests passed first through a barricade of sawhorses and barbed wire. As Hoyle joined the crowd, he noticed that the paratroopers concentrated their attention on the people in line, not on the plaza or adjoining streets. If an attack should come, the paras would be as surprised as everyone else.

In the portico, Hoyle passed a pair of Bolivian ceremonial guards, red-coated infantrymen exactly like a matched set of tin soldiers. A liveried servant presented a silver tray upon which Hoyle laid his engraved invitation; a second butler smiled back, gesturing Hoyle toward the sound of conversation and the jingle of crystal. The party and the courtyard then opened around him.

The quadrangle was overlooked by galleries, and a fountain bubbled in its center. The balconies were turned out in luminaria and a profusion of Bolivian flags. In a corner, a fifteen-piece orchestra crooned Glenn Miller's "Moonlight Serenade." The crowd was a thoroughgoing cross-section of Bolivian plutocracy: politicians, generals, oil merchants, the owners of tin mines and smelters, the scions of landed families, newly wealthy coca barons, grand dames, concubines, journalists, and the merely beautiful. The courtyard swirled with ladies in evening gowns. The dresses were decidedly European, since the rich in this country, like the women of the diplomatic corps, could afford clothes from Paris.

Hoyle plucked a glass from a passing tray, settled into a corner, and took in the crowd. It had been almost six years since his previous posting in La Paz, and he was not recognized. This allowed him to study every face, and even for a man of his profession, Hoyle was thought to have a keen eye for faces. He had the unique talent of drawing into himself and blending seamlessly with a background; this skill enabled him to see and not be seen, to watch and not be noticed. As dancers sailed past, conversations drifted to him. Hoyle affected a disinterested smile but attended as much as his ear could sort out. He noted in particular the conduct of the great ladies as lesser mortals passed them. A quick cut of their eyes or a whispered comment told more than an inch of dossier.

Hoyle took it all in, as he had been trained to do, adding faces to

names, names to innuendo, and all of it condensed and stowed away
with an idea toward furthering his goals in Bolivia. This was the only
reason he had come. He was here on an open-ended mission, part
reconnaissance, part recruitment survey. Hoyle knew that any of the
embassies of a dozen other nations—Britain, Germany, France, Spain,
Italy—had intelligence officers here to do the same thing. Only absent
were the Soviets. Following the Cuban missile crisis, the government
of Bolivia had acceded to a U.S. suggestion that they break off rela-
tions with Cuba. The Bolivians went one better and kicked out the
Russians as well. Across town, the Soviet embassy was shuttered, and
their espionage activities had been farmed out to the less urbane but
equally ruthless Bulgarians.

Hoyle drank a second champagne without the slightest sensation of
irony. There were a million places in the world where the rich danced
while the poor starved. Hoyle had been around the world, and it had
beaten sense into him. He knew that injustice was a phenomenon as irresistible and inescapable as gravity. The privileged always danced and
drank champagne. They did so in Saigon, in Johannesburg, in Havana;
it could not be different here.

Hoyle was not cruel, but he was not an empathetic man. He looked
at the crowd with narrowed eyes and thought, *It's coming for you.* It
did not matter that Hoyle was here to stop that day of reckoning, or at
least to forestall it. In that mission, he took no joy beyond a certain
dark pride in his work. His was an assignment, not a personal aspira-
tion. There remained the very real possibility that Bolivia would succumb to revolution. If it came, the people around him would be swept
away, perhaps even liquidated as a class. Hoyle did not pity them. In
plain truth, he hardly cared for them at all.

Hoyle was attached to no nation except the United States, and that
attachment, though deep, was more intellectual than conventionally
patriotic. His profession involved the surgical application of violence to
produce a political result. If his assignment had been to sow revolution
rather than suppress it, Hoyle would now happily be in the hills building bombs and plotting assassinations. He did not bestow a sense of
right or wrong on the jobs he did. He was a professional, and his conscience allowed him to stand in the courtyard of a palace, in the presence of people he despised, sipping champagne and smiling like a man
who wished them well.

The band played another song from the 1940s, "I'm Gettin' Senti-mental Over You" by Tommy Dorsey. The combination of the music and couture put forward an awkwardly nostalgic air. Sprinkled in the crowd were Bolivian officers in peaked caps, Sam Browne belts, and jodhpurs. The uniforms were jarringly familiar. For decades, the Boli-vian army had been advised by the Germans on matters of both tactics and fashion.

"Ever feel like you stepped into the wrong war?"

Hoyle turned, the English at first puzzling him. It was a bigger sur-prise to see Cosmo Zeebus standing in a trendy evening jacket. Before Hoyle could think of a pithy comment, Zeebus stopped a waiter and plucked a glass from his tray. "I thought you avoided flagpoles."

"American flagpoles."

Zeebus drank down his wine in one gulp. "Where's your asshole buddy?"

Hoyle assumed this referred to Smith, but he took a moment to an-swer. "He might show up."

"Too bad about Camiri," Zeebus said, referring without sympathy to the bombing of their base.

"We've moved. We're set up in Muyupampa." This was a lie, tech-nically disinformation, but Zeebus was not written into Hoyle's work, and if he didn't know the location of the new base, it could not be leaked.

A moment passed, Zeebus breathing steadily, as large men do. "You know where he used to work? That Smith fucker?" he asked.

"He told me."

"Yeah, well, the MACV bullshit was cover. He worked in the Par-rot's Beak. Cambodian border. Had a troop of tribesmen and a SEAL team with him. They used to go out at night and cut the heads off gooks."

"Did someone show you the heads, Cosmo?"

"Look, I'm telling you as a friend."

"Smith is going to cut off my head?"

"Laugh now, amigo. The guy is a menace." It occurred to Hoyle that Zeebus was a bit drunk. "They got him out of Washington," he went on. "They sent him down here before there could be a congres-sional inquiry."

Hoyle exchanged his glass with a passing waiter. Again he found it impossible to imagine Smith in combat, let alone directing atrocities. Smith looked like an English professor.

"I'm glad you told me, Cosmo. This guy could wreck my career."

"You don't have a career, pal. I'm just clueing you in. They're going to watch what he does down here. You better watch yourself, too."

A spatter of applause spread and redoubled across the courtyard. Bedecked in the uniform of a major general, President René Barrientos Ortuño made his entrance. Behind him streamed his retinue, generals, staff officers, and a pod of their bejeweled and heavily perfumed wives. As he waded into the crowd, Barrientos conducted himself regally, acknowledging the applause with papal satisfaction.

"He looks taller on television," Hoyle said. The applause now was unanimous. Zeebus put down his glass and joined in tepidly.

The crowd opened, and Hoyle caught sight of a woman standing to the left and behind the president. She was of medium height and had dark hair. Even across the courtyard, Hoyle could see that her eyes were a pale, unearthly shade of green.

"Who's that?" Hoyle asked.

"Narrow it down for me, buddy."

"The woman," Hoyle said.

Zeebus squinted indifferently. Among the followers of the president, Maria Agular was the only woman dressed in a business suit, a skirt and jacket, not evening clothes. Her hair was loose about her shoulders, not piled in a bouffant, and it shone like onyx. Zeebus stared for a moment. "Beats the hell out of me."

Maria was listening closely to a polished-looking gentleman of about forty. The man had quick, penetrating eyes and was dressed in a Savile Row suit.

"Who's she talking to?"

"Alameda, minister of information. He and Barrientos came into the embassy today. Alameda whipped out the graphs and pie charts. They asked the ambassador for a fifteen-thousand-foot runway, six Phantom jets, and one hundred tons of napalm."

Hoyle ignored Zeebus. "Is that his wife?"

Zeebus shook his head. "Uh-uh. Alameda likes sweet things. And money. Mostly money. The Company's had him on payroll since sixty-five."

Hoyle began to shift his gaze. He'd made the calculation that if he looked any longer, he would be noticed. It is an odd fact that a person watched closely will unconsciously turn and look right back at the on-looker. And this is what happened: Maria turned, and her eyes fell di-rectly on Hoyle.

He did not turn away, and in every second that he looked at her, he had the distinct impression that he was making a mistake. He would think later that when he first looked at her, he'd felt the exact sensation he had when he parachuted from an airplane. It was not exhilaration, it was not fear or even the glum impression of concentration. Hoyle looked at the woman and thought, *I have just done something stupid.*

Zeebus's voice was close, and Hoyle could feel his hot-sweet breath against his ear. "Shit," Zeebus said. "See you later."

Hoyle turned to see Smith crossing toward them. Zeebus spun on his heel, pushed into the crowd, and was gone. Hoyle felt for an instant like a man alone on a thinly frozen lake.

"Thought you'd be here," Smith said. He looked after the depart-ing fat man. "I guess he's still a little sore."

"Yeah, he is," Hoyle answered.

Smith looked at a passing waiter but did not summon him. "How's the wine?"

"Not very good." Hoyle looked over his shoulder. President Barrien-tos was now speaking with Alameda. Hoyle no longer saw the woman.

Smith was the first to notice a tall, unpleasant-looking colonel ap-proaching from the presidential retinue. He wore pince-nez spectacles and the pompous uniform of a Bolivian staff officer. Behind him trailed Lieutenant Castañeda. Heels clicking on flagstone, the two officers walked across the courtyard, dancers and partygoers opening before them. Hoyle first saw Castañeda, his companion from Señor Lempira's office, then the taller officer.

"Who's the scarecrow?" Smith asked.

"Colonel Arquero. Director of intelligence." Hoyle continued softly, "He was a major during my first tour. He assigned a national po-lice officer to help me find the bodies in Tarija."

Smith watched Arquero and Castañeda come on. Arquero was well over six feet and seemed almost cadaverous, a man who rarely ventured out in daylight. His promotion to colonel had come for providing in-dispensable, if unspeakable, services to the coup plotters who had brought Barrientos to power.

"He doesn't look like a leg breaker," Smith said.

"That's not his worst habit," Hoyle answered, quickly emptying his glass. *"Ce que le colonel aime vraiment sont les petis fils."*

Two steps ahead of Arquero, Lieutenant Castañeda stopped and put his heels together in the grating manner of a Prussian officer. "Mr. Hoyle," he said. "It is a pleasure to see you." He crisply did a half left and gestured to Arquero. "May I present—"

"Mr. Hoyle." The colonel offered three fingers and stood with the corners of his mouth pulled back.

Hoyle took what part of Arquero's hand that he could and shook it warily. "A pleasure to see you again, Colonel," he said, his expression perfectly concealing an incalculable reservoir of contempt.

Castañeda stood by, somewhat deflated, introductions being one of his reasons for living. To Castañeda, Hoyle said, "The colonel and I are well acquainted." Hoyle moved his head without taking his eyes off Arquero—exactly what he would have done had he been in a room with a viper.

"Colonel, may I present my colleague Mr. Smith?"

This time Arquero did not offer his hand, but tilted his head back slightly, examining Smith through the bottoms of his pince-nez.

"Good evening, Mr. Smith." The colonel's tone was entirely bland, an effect accentuated by the baritone of his voice and the slow timbre of his speech.

"*Mucho gusto,* Colonel," Smith said.

Hoyle noticed two perfect red depressions where the glasses clamped the colonel's nose.

"Mr. Hoyle, I was relieved to hear you were not injured in the Camiri bombing. I understand you lost some windows?"

Hoyle suspected that Arquero had ordered the bombing. He contented himself by saying simply: "We were lucky the bomb was placed a safe distance from our building."

"Yes. That was fortunate. Wasn't it?"

Defeated in his introductions, Castañeda now did his best to be affable. "Mr. Smith," he chirped, "I understand you were out to survey the site of the ambush in Muyupampa?"

"Major Buran was kind enough to explain the engagement to us."

"Major Buran has been reassigned." Arquero sniffed. "I think you'll find the next time Bolivian forces meet the enemy, things will be different."

"The army has not made an announcement about the ambush," Smith said. "May I make a suggestion?"

"Your Voice of America reported the story fully," Arquero said.

"But the army said nothing," Smith answered. "Tell the truth," he went on. "Give accurate casualty figures. Say exactly what happened."

"I think you may have misapprehended the gravity of our defeat."

Smith did not share Hoyle's affinity for Latin obfuscation. Truth be told, Smith was somewhat of a blunt man, a true Rhode Islander, and he came at the subject directly. "It'll happen again before the situation turns around. Guerrilla propaganda expects the government to lie. What they don't know how to handle are facts."

Hoyle did not expect this vein of conversation to become constructive or even particularly pleasant, and he was soon proved correct.

Arquero tipped his head back again and looked at Smith. "You make an interesting point, Mr. Smith. But I think we are going to need weapons, as well as advice, if we are to mount a successful counter-guerrilla operation, one on a broader scale, like your own in Vietnam."

His thesis declared, Arquero was now happy to annoy elsewhere. "Well, I'll not trouble you with business any longer. Enjoy your evening. If I may be of assistance, gentlemen, please do not hesitate to call on me personally."

Arquero bowed and departed. Castañeda again struck together his heels, then scurried along after his boss.

"Where did you think you were going with that one?" Hoyle asked.

"Not very far." Smith had his hands in his pockets. He looked at the ground for a moment, then seemed to remember something. "What time do your friends get in from Miami?" he asked.

"They're in. Charlie's driving them to Vallegrande."

"They can establish the safe house and comm link. I want you to stick around with me in La Paz for a couple more days," Smith said.

"You want them to set up the station by themselves?"

"You said they were good."

Hoyle nodded. "They're good."

"Then they can set it up. Call me in the morning." Smith walked away.

Across the courtyard, Hoyle watched Alameda gesture sharply at Maria Agular. As he looked on, Maria turned and made her way toward the portico. Hoyle watched the expressions of the grand dames as she walked by. Not one looked at her kindly.

Maria moved gracefully, her head held slightly back and her jaw fixed resolutely. As she passed, Hoyle noticed that her eyes were wet.

11

THE CUBANS PREFERRED things to happen quickly. When they made arrangements, there were urgent meetings, and occasionally, operational matters were even discussed on the telephone, a glaring breach of security that Tania had been careful to avoid. Sometimes, dealing with the Cubans, things developed so rapidly, and often so chaotically, it was almost impossible to keep track of who had done what.

It was important that Tania keep a correct record of what happened; she managed this by maintaining a daily log of her assignments—who in Guevara's organization had tasked her, what she had been assigned to do, and when the job was completed. In a separate set of files, she kept the names of comrades with whom she had been put in contact, their code names, and whatever biographical details she was able to learn about them. Tania updated these dossiers at the end of each month.

After the files were updated, she photographed the pages using a thumb-sized microdot camera. The film was processed in her sink, and she used an X-Acto blade to make innocuous cuts on the edges of postcards into which the microdots could be hidden. These cards were sent to various addresses in Europe, all of them mail drops for Soviet embassies. A month, sometimes six weeks later, Tania would receive a letter from a friend in Paraguay; an underlined signature indicated that the latest batch of microdots had been received.

All of her work was done by post, which was time-consuming, but in the ponderous course of the mails, there was safety. Tania's reporting was steady, secure, and unremitting. It was also extremely secret. Only a handful of senior officers at Moscow Center knew of Tania's dispatches or the manner in which she sent them. She was, in KGB parlance, a "deep placement," and her reporting on Guevara had made more than one career blossom in Moscow. Tania's efforts had been extremely gratifying for Aleksandr Mikhailovich Sakhovosky, the supervisor of the First Chief Directorate, the KGB's division responsible for all foreign operations and intelligence-gathering activities.

In what had been considered a fairly routine "honey trap" operation, the East German Ministry for State Security, the Stasi, had placed Tania in Guevara's entourage during his 1960 visit to Berlin. Guevara was then the Cuban minister of industry. The Stasi ordered Tania to attempt the seduction of Guevara, and routinely informed Moscow when she had succeeded. It was Sakhovosky who first prevailed on the East Germans to turn over control of Tania to the KGB.

Two months later, Tania was made available as an interpreter for the East German national ballet and departed with the company on a tour of Cuba. Her duties were sufficiently carefree to allow her time to renew a relationship with the handsome minister of industry. When the ballet left to continue dancing, Guevara himself arranged for Tania to stay on in Havana. Her reports had flowed to the center ever since.

Tania's connection to Guevara was much fretted over within the KGB. Next to Castro, Che Guevara was perhaps the most important personality of the Cuban revolution. Tania was seen from the outset as a long-term asset, and her KGB controllers ran her with great care. As she became infatuated with Guevara, her handlers were careful not to allow her to develop a sense of disloyalty. They could not allow her emotions to interfere with her reporting. Her assignment was too important.

She was kept in line by a fine balance of flattery and an appeal to the spirit of socialist sacrifice. Her work within Cuba was highly classified and communicated to Moscow using the ambassador's personal codes. As her relationship with Guevara continued, Tania was debriefed in an increasingly deferential manner. She was asked what Guevara thought, how she assessed his opinions, and what she felt he might do. She was constantly reminded that her work was important and served the broader goals of international socialism.

Guevara had no idea of her double life; nor would he until it was too late.

By 1964 Tania's love for Guevara was so apparent that she had become something of an embarrassment. Although many in Havana had *amores secretos,* the revolution was not without a puritanical streak. Castro quietly advised Guevara to lower Tania's profile. This he did by sending her two hundred miles away, to the Interior Ministry's covert operations course in Camegüey. The curriculum was basic, the simple tradecraft skills required of an intelligence officer, and it was bitterly ironic to Tania that the Cubans had no idea *she* had been spying on *them* for over three years. When she was informed that Guevara had personally chosen her to go into Latin America on a deep-cover operation, something in her snapped. She did not see this assignment as a sign of her lover's confidence; she saw it as a dismissal.

Dejected, Tania asked her KGB handlers to allow her to return to East Germany. From this she was gently dissuaded. Again her controllers urged her to continue her association with Guevara, however distant or peripheral. Their leverage now was strictly internationalist, and her service was humbly for the betterment of socialism. She agreed resignedly. It was growing obvious even to Tania that her romantic devotion to Guevara was a one-way thing.

Tania attended the Cuban operations course, and a slow sort of carelessness overtook her. She was a failed romantic and reacted in a predictably irrational manner. She initiated an affair with one of her instructors, a tall, wiry black man who had previously served as the head of the Asia and African section of Cuban intelligence. Tania was his lover eagerly, if unemotionally, until she left for La Paz.

Rusticated to Bolivia, the KGB expected little else from Tania. And then, late in 1965, Guevara summoned her to Prague. At the center, there was much self-congratulation—their window on Guevara had reopened.

For Tania, the matter was still one of the heart. Her love for Guevara had only been cast in amber by her year alone in La Paz, and as she traveled first to Havana and then on to Czechoslovakia, she wanted nothing more in the world than to have Che Guevara as her own.

Her hope was to prove a desperate and dangerous thing.

In Prague, Guevara again took her into his bed, but not fully into his heart. He had just returned from the catastrophe in Africa, his health was broken, and his political fortunes in Cuba were nil. She found him a man much diminished from the august hero of the revolution. The wounds and the calamities he had survived only made him more beloved, and in that spring she cherished him with a will and a purpose. That Tania could hold him in the night, that she could be assigned with his dreams and trusted to carry out his most confidential missions but not possess his heart—this nearly destroyed her.

She did her best not to show her anguish, and he was insensitive enough or abstracted enough not to notice. At the end of their month together, he calmly summoned her to sit at the small table in the kitchen of the safe house and gave her a list of things he wanted accomplished in La Paz. He sat there pedantically and made her memorize them.

That night he made love to her, and afterward she sobbed like a child.

On a long, numb journey back to Bolivia, Tania sometimes felt simple heartache, sometimes self-loathing, and sometimes a murderous rage. It was, she told herself, her own fault, all of it. When she returned to La Paz, she vowed to end her work and signaled her controllers at the center for an emergency meeting.

A woman twice Tania's age arrived a week later, posing as an aunt. This was perhaps the center's most cynical tactic to date. The woman moved in with Tania for a month, listened to her, cooked for her, and bought her clothes. Tania had accomplished much as an agent, and was extremely sophisticated operationally, but she was human. Moscow knew, even if Guevara had forgotten, that Tania was twenty-eight years old, alone, and vulnerable.

The woman sent by the center was a specialist—an experienced intelligence officer with a Ph.D. in clinical psychology. She praised Tania's efforts in La Paz, flattering her on the social connections she had made and praising her for all she had done to lay the groundwork for Guevara's expedition. The woman commiserated, cajoled, and convinced Tania to stay in place one more year, until a successor could be groomed, vetted, and sent to Bolivia to take her place.

Then Tania could go back to Germany. Then it would be over.

Tania stayed, and her new friend departed, directly for the Soviet embassy in Mexico City. There it was reported frankly that Tania was burned out and unfit for further service. The center made the decision to leave her in place. In the cold calculus of spycraft, it was determined that Moscow could gain by doing nothing. The work Tania had done in La Paz was on behalf of Cuba, not the Soviet Union. Moscow was not yet certain where Guevara would go. If he did come to Bolivia, Tania would be there to monitor him; if he did not, Tania would remain in La Paz as a useful, if unreliable, agent in place.

And if she self-destructed, it would not be the KGB that suffered.

For a while Tania willed herself on. Guevara's advance team came and went, and then, finally, she was asked to guide Selizar Galán to the Ñancahuazú camp.

The day she saw Guevara again was like a dream.

Even now she marveled that it had happened, and wondered also at the odd, cold moment of their reunion. When she saw him, a sudden wave of pity had broken over her. He stood as she walked toward him, handsome, unfaltering, radiating confidence and strength. He could not know, as Tania did, that all his plans were exposed and that great powers were arrayed against him. When Tania felt his arms around her, the conflicting emotions within her nearly made her swoon.

When she returned to La Paz from Guevara's camp, the strain of her betrayal, the anxiety of a secret life, of the lies within lies, the loneliness, all became overwhelming. Tania cried in the night, she cried when she was alone, she cried when she was walking down the street.

But still she reported. When she'd returned from the camp, she communicated to Moscow that Havana had charged her to go to Buenos Aires and contact a friend of Guevara's. On the evening she sent her last report, she took a dozen Seconal, drank half a bottle of cognac, and sprawled nude on her bed. It was a shock to her when she woke two days later. Piss and shit were dried on the sheets around her, and flies crawled across her face. These were the first things to tell her that she was still alive.

She walked to the bath, cleaned herself, and sobbed. She had failed even to kill herself. She squatted in the small living room of her flat and stared at the floor. There was no one she could even tell.

Two days after her suicide attempt, Tania received a postcard, a glossy beach scene from Rio, signed by a person named Robert. Although the card bore Argentine postage, *par avion,* Tania was certain it had been placed directly in her mailbox. When she saw the card among her other letters, it was as though she'd been touched by an electric current. The postcard was a prearranged signal, hand-delivered by Tania's Soviet controllers. The beach scene indicated an emergency matter. Had the card been sent from Belgium or someplace colder, it would have indicated a matter of less importance. Tania tossed aside the other mail and staggered into her bedroom.

At her desk, she read the card. In the short paragraph scribbled on the back, the words "beach," "dancing," and "sunburn" were used in innocuous sentences. A curious reader could guess nothing more than Robert was enjoying a seaside holiday.

In a shoe box under Tania's bed was a sheaf of water-soluble paper, and typed on it was a code key. Tania needed only to look up the nouns written on the card and compare them against a column of about a hundred words grouped alphabetically. She was still stupid from the drugs, and this routine task took her the better part of half an hour. The message at last revealed itself: "Beach" denoted a meeting place, in this case a park bench on the Plaza 14 de Septiembre, two or three kilometers away from her apartment. The word "dance" meant that a meeting should take place today, and "sunburn" indicated that her contact would be there at four-thirty P.M.

It was now a bit past two o'clock. This was just sufficient time for Tania to dress, leave the apartment, and take a meandering, indirect route to the plaza.

She arrived precisely on time and took a seat on the appointed bench. Ten minutes passed—a sufficient interval, she knew, for her contact to observe the plaza and its approaches and make sure that Tania had not been followed. She watched a man and woman circle the square twice. With some relief, she figured out that they were pick-pockets, cruising. After the couple left, a tall, heavyset man walked to the bench and smiled at her.

"Excuse me," he said in accented Spanish. "Could this have fallen from your purse?"

In his hand was a duplicate of Robert's postcard.

"I've never been to Rio," Tania said, and he sat down. He was a careworn man in his mid- to late forties. His shoulders were broad, and his belly was heavy. As he put away the postcard, Tania noticed that his hands were small, almost feminine.

"I am Robert."

Tania only nodded.

"Were you followed?" he asked. This man operated excruciatingly by the book. She shook her head.

"You know the secondary meeting place?"

Tania now noticed that the man had a Slavic accent. She answered curtly that she knew her procedures.

"You'll forgive me for standing on ceremony," he said. The man was definitely Russian and of middling rank. She guessed, correctly, that he was a KGB colonel. His real name was Iosif Seergevich Diminov, and he'd traveled to Bolivia in the guise of a Bulgarian diplomat. None of that mattered to Tania; whoever this man was, he was merely a messenger from the intelligence agency she served, and while they were together, in direct contact, she was in some jeopardy.

"*Sollen wir Deutsches sprechen?*" he asked.

"I prefer to speak Spanish."

"Just so." He smiled at her with a mixture of admiration and mundane sexual appetite. "I first want to tell you that the center is very happy with your work." Diminov seemed to pause, waiting for her to acknowledge this praise, but she was silent.

"We have read your reports on Guevara and are very pleased. The work is thorough and of great benefit."

"You didn't contact me to tell me I am doing a good job."

"No."

A group of children passed, and he was quiet. When they were gone, he said, "We have some questions about Guevara beyond the facts stated in your report."

"Yes?"

"When you saw him, did he seem well?"

"He was thinner."

"But healthy?"

"I think so."

Diminov looked out on the square. It was infuriating how casual he was attempting to be. After an interminable pause, he asked, "The man you are to meet in Buenos Aires, Guevara's friend, is he known to you?"

"Not personally."

"We want to make sure that he reaches Guevara safely." As an afterthought, Diminov added, "And that you are safe."

All at once Tania was anxious. She knew that none of this could have been the purpose for an urgent meeting. She had been brought here, out into the Plaza 14 de Septiembre, in broad daylight, and now she wondered why. A dull paranoia clutched at her. Perhaps they were going to shoot her.

"How did you find the camps? Were they well ordered?" Diminov asked.

"All of this is in my report."

"Does Guevara sleep apart from the others or close by?"

"Close by."

"Did he make love to you?"

Tania had not anticipated the question and heard herself answering almost before she could respond to it emotionally. "No. He did not."

"Why not?"

At this Tania paused, measuring her words. "He does not love me."

"Is it possible he will rekindle this relationship?"

"I don't think so," Tania said.

"You had close contact with Guevara at the camp?"

"Yes."

"How frequently?"

"Constantly."

"Do you think on a future meeting you would have an opportunity to place a drug into his food?"

"Drug" meant poison, and Tania felt a physical pang. She reflected rapidly on the act of murdering Guevara with a vial of cyanide. The thought seemed without beginning or end, and without duration— she turned over the act in her mind like a rational person might briefly consider jumping off a bridge. Murder him? She had never thought to do that, never, even when her heart was shattered, not once until this second.

Diminov looked at Tania, but her face revealed nothing. She sat trying to push down thoughts she did not want to understand. She was ashamed that there was some small place in the broken part of her that wanted Guevara dead.

"Did you hear the question?"

The words seemed to be tumbling from someone else's mouth as she answered. "In camp the food is prepared communally. Guevara makes a point of eating after the others have been served. It could not be done without . . . drugging all the men."

Diminov grunted. "You would not object to the assignment?"

"Is my loyalty being tested, Comrade?"

Diminov smiled insincerely. "Of course not. You have extraordinary access to an important person. It is important to know what options we possess."

Tania could hear the wind blowing through the trees and the traffic circling the edge of the plaza, a thousand small sounds building into a roar in her head.

She said at last, "I can be counted on."

12

WITHIN THE MINISTRY of the Interior, Hoyle followed Smith down an impossibly long corridor, a cloister actually, the warm wind following them through the archways. Distracted, Hoyle hardly remembered entering the building from the street, and then they were inside a big, sprawling compound, all columns and arcades and courtyards. This place might once have been a nunnery. They turned right and then left, and Hoyle had to marvel that Smith seemed to know where they were headed. They came at last to an impressively carved door and pushed it open. Behind the door was a large room, a reception area, and beyond the offices of His Excellency Enrique Ruíz de Estrada Alameda, minister of information, and deputy minister of the interior.

Three secretarial desks faced the reception area. Oddly, the place was lit by fluorescent lights held in boxes suspended from a gracefully arched ceiling. Smith approached the closest secretary, a severe-looking woman, obviously the head gatekeeper. Hoyle turned slightly to his left and was taken aback to see the woman from the party at the presidential palace. The woman with the sea-green eyes.

Hoyle smiled as she turned from a filing cabinet and walked to a desk at his right. She nodded at him as she sat, but in her expression was no trace of recognition.

"*Hola.*"

"*Salud,*" Hoyle said.

Maria did remember him but perfectly gave the opposite impression. She fed a form and carbon paper into her typewriter, turning away as she did so, and Hoyle sighted a nameplate on her desk: Maria Agular. As Maria worked, Hoyle slightly averted his gaze, but his eyes stayed on her. He noticed her graceful, long neck and the way her black hair curled over her shoulders. Her eyes were so striking that he had almost failed to notice the simple perfection of her features. She was wearing a gray wool skirt and a shimmering silver top, and he could see the shape of her small, upturned breasts under her blouse. He made a deliberate effort to look someplace else and felt an odd twitching in his throat.

Smith finally prevailed upon the gatekeeper to use her intercom, and Hoyle cast his eyes about the office. Prominently placed were photographs of Minister Alameda with various luminaries. There was the de rigueur shot of the minister smiling with General Barrientos, but he was posed with other, better-known people as well: the United Nations secretary general, U Thant, Raquel Welch, and Fidel Castro.

The door to the inner office opened, and Alameda stepped out, impeccably turned out in a dark suit and a Harvard crimson tie. He crossed immediately to Smith, holding out his hand and smiling broadly as he came on. "Mr. Smith. I am delighted that I have a few moments between appointments."

As they shook hands, Hoyle had a second to wonder how it was the minister had known which of the two gringos was Smith.

"I know you're busy, Excellency, this will only take a moment. I was hoping we could discuss coordinating a press strategy for the areas affected by the bandits . . ."

Alameda's eyes flicked to Smith's briefcase, and he smiled again. "I do have a moment," he said.

Smith and Alameda disappeared into the inner office. Hoyle drifted closer to Maria's desk.

"Please don't let me interrupt," he said as she looked up at him. He did his best to charmingly continue the interruption. "When it's something that's only going to take a moment, I usually get to wait in the lobby." This made Maria smile. He nodded to a photograph on the wall. "Is that—?"

"John Wayne." Behind her, Alameda and a man with a big neck smiled from a posh restaurant booth. "When the people are famous, I usually wait in the lobby, too," Maria said.

They both smiled. Hoyle wondered if people walked by her blinking in amazement. Her eyes were preternaturally green, the color of a mid-Atlantic swell, a wave that could kill a ship.

"Can I get you something? Coffee?"

"Nothing, thank you." Hoyle looked around. "This is quite an office." The space was grand, carved stone columns supported a ceiling comprised of several vaulted sections.

"It's a little imperial," Maria said. At that moment the gatekeeper stood behind her desk and crossed to some distant filing cabinets.

"You don't sound Bolivian," Hoyle said. "I'm sorry . . . your accent . . . I'm kind of an amateur language sleuth."

"Nicaraguan."

"Nicaraguan? Really? I've never been."

"I was hired as a translator—at first, in the Ministry of Health. I am a nurse, actually. I speak French and German. Someone found out, and then I wound up here."

They shared language as a calling, an attribute Hoyle self-consciously attributed to a need to please.

Smith appeared from the inner office. "Mr. Hoyle?"

Hoyle looked over Maria's shoulder. Smith and Alameda were shaking hands by the door. Hoyle noticed that Smith was now without his briefcase.

Hoyle smiled at Maria. "I'd better go," he said. "Nice talking to you."

"A pleasure, sir."

In the time it took Smith and the minister to walk to the door, Hoyle had scanned Maria's desk, as well as the desk of the gatekeeper. His glance seemed so casual, they could have no idea that he had committed to memory the numbers on the dials of their telephones, and had scanned the papers on their blotters.

"You must be Mr. Hoyle?" Alameda said, smiling through impeccable teeth.

"*Mucho gusto*, Excellency."

Alameda was about Hoyle's age and slightly smaller; he had a disconcerting habit of standing too close as he spoke. "Colonel Arquero speaks of you very highly."

"I'm flattered, Minister," Hoyle said. The remark was a bit of a jab. Alameda knew Arquero well enough to despise him. Still smiling, Hoyle marked Alameda down as someone to remain wary of.

Alameda's fingers came down on the corner of Maria's desk. "Maria, I'll need the lists for the UPI pool. In my office."

"Yes, Minister."

Smith opened the formidable door and stepped out of the office. Stealing a glimpse at Maria, Hoyle followed and pulled the door closed behind them.

They walked down the cloister some distance, allowing two uniformed police officers to pass before they spoke.

"Problems?" Hoyle asked. Inside the briefcase had been ten thousand dollars in crisp twenties, as well as a Cartier wristwatch.

"He liked the watch. From now on, we type it, and he preaches it like the gospel." The gratuity accepted by the minister would allow Smith and Hoyle to control, or at least influence, the news from the battle area. Other payments would follow—the minister was a machine that burned money—but Smith would decide when the truth would be told and when the truth would be in short supply. There was an old saw in the CIA: "If it's typed, it's true." What people were told would always be more important than what actually happened. In Bolivia, perception would now become reality.

"What's with the picture of him and Castro?" Hoyle asked.

Smith shrugged. "His options are open."

They walked on through the cloister, shadows streaming at them in slabs of light and dark.

"Anything interesting on the desks?"

Hoyle shook his head. But there had been something on Maria's desk. Jumbled together on her blotter were a list of journalists seeking expedited visas, a memo regarding mail deliveries, and an envelope with Maria's home address: 312 Calle Cochabamba, No. 2. Hoyle meant to see Maria Agular again, and he intended to do it without Smith knowing.

They walked on, Hoyle again feeling his awkwardness and the disconcerted, agitated way he felt when he looked into her eyes. He did not mention this; nor did he reveal to Smith that Maria Agular from Nicaragua had lied to him about her accent.

Hoyle had recognized her inflection at once, and it was not the rapid-fire patois of Managua.

Maria's voice was richly, and distinctively, that of an upper-class Cuban.

13

THEN IT WAS evening; pale blue with the first, bravest stars beginning to shine above the peak of Illimani, and La Paz finding its own lights, the modest neon of shops and cafés of the Prado and the yellow-orange of kerosene lamps blinking down from shanties on the hillsides. Maria Agular walked without hurry toward her meeting, scarcely even sauntering, she moved so slowly. She found reason to pause in front of a shopwindow on the Avenida Ismael Montes; the reflection was a genuine surprise because her expression was so grim.

The night deepened, and so did her mood, from distracted to disappointed and, finally, to something like glum surrender. Maria crossed the street at the Calle Potosí, a taxi slowing to toot its horn at her. She did not turn her head but kept on toward the lights of the Hotel Presidente. She *wanted* to be late, because she was certain *he* would be, lateness being the prerogative of great men, the privilege of any person who holds himself above another. The offhandedness with which he would greet her was even now an ache she felt. As she walked the last half block down the Calle Genaro Sanjinés, a pair of soldiers watched from across the street. They looked like boys, wide-eyed at the goings-on of the city, innocents except for the weapons in their hands, short, fatal-looking contraptions with magazines curved under them like the horns of beasts. She glanced at the two soldiers but willed herself not to see them, because seeing them would make her think. It would make her think of things that were no more and things that would never be again.

It never became familiar to her, La Paz. She had no affection for the place and never would—the high, cool mountain air, the incomparably sapphire skies—sometimes she felt she was on another planet. It was so far from her home, the home in her heart, a tropical place of verdant, steep-sided mountains, of music and laughter and of the sea. And that was what she missed most, the sea—it was the only thing left for her to long for. Almost everything else in her life had been taken, and she had mourned for it so desperately that now she was numb. Her family was gone, wiped away like the film on a dirty window, gone and made an example of, her family name whispered from house to house, and all manner of things blamed on them, as many things as possible, because they were dead and now others had to live in the shadow of death and the knock on the door. Every person in her hometown of Playa Baracoa knew that any one of them could be denounced as a counterrevolutionary, lose their job, their possessions, and their home, or, worse, simply vanish into the night. Perhaps that was better—to disappear into the night. Better to go gently than be shot down, as was Maria's father, Colonel Ignacio Augusto Cienfuegos. They killed him, *los rebeldes,* then his corpse was dragged behind a jeep and left on the beach for gulls to pick at. A day later, they came for Consuela, *Madre,* and her brother, too, and when they were gone, the house was divided into flats and given over to cane cutters. Maria's home in Cuba was gone. Everything was gone except her memories of things that were no more, and she held on in La Paz like a discarded object, a tropical thing that had been drawn up by a hurricane swirling through the atmosphere and dropped in a high mountain place where the air was so pure and thin that it sometimes tasted to her like metal.

As she approached the revolving brass door, she blamed herself, for want of courage, for want of judgment, for everything, but now, more than anything, she blamed herself because she was *on time,* and at the indulgence of someone for whom she was a whim. But she put a smile on her face, her beautiful angel's face, and the doorman held the door for her and tipped his hat. She crossed the lobby and promised herself that she would ask about the passport. She would insist, *insist.* And as she entered the grand lounge with its candlelit tables, she was so astonished to see Enrique Alameda—the great man himself—waiting that she forgot for a moment even where she was.

"Beautiful Maria," Alameda said, and he stood. His fingers touched her elbow, and he lightly kissed her cheek.

There were only a dozen other people in the bar, half of them North Americans, and Maria felt a small flush of shame. She felt eyes upon her, as she always did; eyes that put her in context with him, Enrique Alameda, Excellency, *ministerio de información,* and her, *esa mujer,* that woman. It was a demeaning thing for her to see the sideways glances, to know what they thought—that she was the plaything of a powerful man, not much beyond flesh and paint and perfume.

Alameda smiled and gestured into the leather booth. Maria smiled back, her face a perfect mask, and sat. He took her wrap off her shoulders, and he was not the only person in the bar to notice the whiteness of her skin.

Two drinks appeared magically, Scotch for him and a glass of champagne for Maria. Predictable magic, these drinks would have appeared on any table in town.

"You are lovely," he said. In response, she only looked at him through the candlelight; she knew it was not necessary to acknowledge so empty a blandishment. Alameda quickly went into an apology, just as meaningless, but he kept his eyes on hers as he spoke.

"I'm so glad that I'm able to see you," he said. "After the misunderstanding at the reception." He had invited Maria to the reception, then asked her not to wear evening clothes, and when she'd shown up, he'd calmly asked her to leave because she was underdressed. The hurt in this was lost on him. He apologized now only because she had made a trip all the way to the Plaza Murillo. Maria did not pay attention to the apology itself, or the heartfelt, regrettable circumstances that supported it. She took a sip from her glass and heard him saying: "I'm glad we have some time together now."

She swallowed champagne.

"Please don't be cross with me," he said.

"We don't have to talk of it," Maria answered. "I am not angry." Alameda had no idea that this meant exactly the opposite. He was happy to move on to other things, and inside a small part of her heart, she was happy that she would not have to unravel his thin excuses. She was angry at herself still because he had made her cry that night.

"Enrique," she said, slightly louder than needed to carry across the small table. At this Alameda stopped speaking. He owned her, really, had dominion over her, but she had some small hold on him, a slight bit of purchase, and she used it now, again saying his name. "Enrique?"

"Yes?"

"I don't wish to annoy you."

"What makes you think you do?"

"You are busy, and to nag you is to annoy you."

"Nag me about what?" he asked, sipping his drink. The ice rattled against the short, fat glass.

"My passport," Maria said. She made her face empty, blank, and beautiful, as she did not want this to become a contended issue.

"I have it," Alameda said. "It'll all be taken care of."

Maria's Bolivian passport had expired, and Alameda had collected it from her, promising a new one. That was two weeks ago, and Maria had no papers, nothing to show at the roadblocks except her card from the ministry, and although that had worked until now, there might come a night when it would not.

Maria considered her words. She could not directly ask for her passport back—it was not hers, technically. The picture on it was hers, but the name Maria Celestine Agular, that was not her name. The passport had been issued fraudulently, a genuine document with an alias typed on it. Maria was her Christian name, but the rest of the neatly filled spaces were fiction. Her birthday, the supposed place of birth, all lies save the address of the flat on the Calle Cochabamba that Alameda paid for out of ministry funds.

It was on the basis of this Bolivian passport that Maria had been able to travel from Mexico and work in Bolivia. After she had fled Cuba, there was an ugly incident with the Mexican immigration authorities—her Cuban papers were a hastily purchased forgery, barely good enough to allow her to purchase an airplane ticket, and when she arrived in Mexico, her documents were taken and she was made to register with the police. She had no money to ensure that she was granted asylum, and was three days from being deported back to Cuba when she met Alameda at a party at the French embassy. He took care of everything. Soon the police stopped harassing her, soon she had a residence permit and an apartment, and soon she was his lover. He promised her work in Bolivia and a place to stay. All of these things became debts that bound her to him. There were many: continuing protection and clothing and a bigger apartment, her job at the ministry and money to spend and food and jewelry—these things made her safe and kept, but now he had her passport, and that made her vulnerable again. Everything he had given her rested on the nationality, the false identity, the uncomplicated disguise that the passport sustained.

"I only ask about it," she said evenly, "because of the state of emergency."

"You have your card from the ministry." He smiled.

"Of course."

"It will do for the roadblocks." He took a sip of his drink. "If you should ever have trouble, all you need is to call me. Even at home." Now the power was his. Alameda knew women well enough to know a proud one. Maria would be eaten by rats before she would call him at home.

"Are you planning a trip?" he asked, toying with her.

"Where would I go?"

"I'd be very sad if you left me," he said, pouting. It made Alameda feel powerful to do this—yank her about. Maria was his plaything, but she was, after all, his *favorite* plaything. "You really shouldn't worry, Maria."

"I ask for a reason. The state of emergency troubles me."

"You can't be afraid of the bandits?" Alameda scoffed. It was irrelevant that he had just asked the American ambassador for a hundred metric tons of napalm to battle the "antisocial elements" who now roamed the Ñancahuazú.

"I have already lost my home once," Maria said. "And I very nearly lost my life." She waited a moment, choosing her words carefully. "If you had not helped me, I wouldn't be here. I am grateful. I'm still grateful."

"I am your friend," Alameda said.

"You are more than my friend."

Alameda looked at her in the candlelight. She was a mistress, and he'd had several; he would have several more; but there was not a single man in the world of flesh and blood who would not be swayed by Maria now, moved by her, enraptured by her.

Alameda leaned back in the leather booth. "You'll have your passport back," he said. "Perhaps we'll get you a diplomatic one. Would you like that?"

He was pompous, and she wanted to toss a drink at him, but she maintained a remarkable poise.

"Just valid papers to show at the roadblocks," she said.

He smiled.

"And really, if there is a problem . . ."

"A revolution?" Alameda sniffed as though one might be hiding under the table.

"Yes. A revolution." Maria looked at him and did not vary her gaze. "I don't want to be left here."

"I would not leave you, *querida*," Alameda said. "I would never do that. You couldn't think that I would do that?"

She smiled at him, but she had seen all of it happen before; she knew what happened when the toys were left behind, and she did not trust him any more than she loved him.

"No," she lied smoothly, and she reached across the table. "I know you would not leave me."

14

T HEY CAME AROUND the base of the hill, still in the shadow of
the trees, to a place where the trail turned uphill, away from the
river, and a small track branched off, running parallel to the stream.
Guevara crossed to this path and worked gradually through a thicker
copse of trees. The column behind him moved quietly, no one speaking; the only sounds were the scuffing of boots against the places
bedrock revealed itself under the dirt. The smaller trail continued beneath the hill, in stages swinging north, and above the treetops, the
sun revealed itself to the left, twenty or so degrees below zenith. In
the places the sun broke through the canopy, Guevara could make out
the boot prints of the vanguard. Then he came upon Pombo, who was
kneeling behind a tree with his carbine cradled in his arms.

Pombo held up his palm, signaling halt, and Guevara crouched next
to him. Beyond a low-hanging branch, he saw the cornfield—the first
trace of human presence they had seen in a week of marching.

Guevara listened, as Pombo did. There was the sound of the wind
through the corn, and from somewhere came the rattle of a crow. At the
far end of the field, on a slight rise, was a small house made of mudbrick
and palm frond. Its front door faced west, affording a view of the river,
and the corn between the tree line and the house prevented Guevara
from seeing directly into the clearing around the house. There was no
chimney, just an open space in the roof where the smoke could come

out. Guevara could not hear voices or the sound of an ax, but the smoke said for certain that the house was occupied. The corn was chest-high in the places the insects had not attacked it, and the orderly rows told a story of hard labor. The cornfield was not large enough to be worked by more than a single family, but there was a possibility that other houses were nearby, so Guevara sent Miguel and Coco around to the right.

He kept his voice low and said to Pombo, "Tell Joaquin to take the rear guard to the river. Tell them to cover the approach."

Pombo nodded and moved off. Loro watched eagerly, but there was nothing to do until the scouts came back. Guevara sat back against a tree. Their cover was good, and the wind was blowing toward them, so he took out his pipe and sucked on it. After ten minutes, the scouts returned, walking unhurriedly, and Guevara stood as they approached.

"Just one house," Miguel said. "Some kids playing in the yard, and a couple of pigs."

"No one else?"

"We didn't see anyone."

It was unlikely that parents would run off and leave their children, so it was almost certain the column had not been detected. One or both of the parents were sure to be about, perhaps working in another field or inside the shack. Guevara ordered the first column forward and sent back word for the others to follow, bringing up the mules and the packhorse.

Skirting the cornfield, they approached the house, which looked even more decrepit and sorry as they drew closer. There were a dozen chickens scratching the dirt in front of the house, and a quartet of skinny pigs was penned into a wallow between the woodpile and the cornfield. As the column came near, Guevara saw a little boy and a girl under a tree beside the pigsty. The little boy ran for the house, and the girl stood and watched them come on. Her dark hair was bobbed short, and she wore a white cotton dress with yellow flowers printed on it. Her feet were bare, and her face was dirty. She did not move as the boy ran away, feet slapping.

Guevara swung his carbine behind him and smiled at the little girl. "Hello," he said.

The child seemed rooted in place, like a sapling. She looked up, and Guevara noticed that there was a honey-colored sore on the corner of her mouth.

"My mama is hurt," the little girl said.

"How did your mommy get hurt?"

The little girl stood on her tiptoes. "She's going to have a baby. Papa went for a doctor."

THE DELIVERY WAS straightforward, though the woman bled considerably, there being some difficulty in passing the placenta after the child was breeched. Guevara detailed Moro to handle the birth; Che was no obstetrician, and although he could by no means be called prim, he preferred a bit more mystery regarding women. The infant, a girl, was healthy, though underweight, and the mother did as well as she could to feed her daughter with a flat, wrinkled tit.

While the woman gave birth, Guevara treated the remaining children, two boys, aged six and ten, and two girls, aged five and three. Their afflictions were all symptoms of rural poverty: impetigo, ringworm, and an obvious case of conjunctivitis. The youngest shyly pulled up her sleeve to reveal a scarlet-colored boil. This was discovered to be furuncular myiasis, and the child then bravely endured the removal of a living boro fly larva from the oval-shaped cyst on her forearm. Guevara afterward inoculated each of the children, their smiles by then dissolving into tears, three injections each and the surgical excision of a live maggot being more than most children will bear. This was made right by Pombo giving them each half a stick of chewing gum—the only candy of any sort to be had in the entire column. The tears were soon dry, and the children ran and played. Joaquin, whom they called *El Oso,* became their favorite.

Just before sundown, the sentries relayed that a man with a rifle was approaching. It was determined that he was the farmer, leading a broken-down mule. Willy and Rubio were sent to meet him on the trail and escort him to the farmhouse. The farmer was exhausted, and the mule was sullen; they both had jogged as far as Tatarenda, looking for the doctor, who was drunk and had anyway driven his car to the whorehouse at Abapó.

The farmer was named Honradez Rulon, and he was dressed in a pair of creaseless brown pants, a white shirt, and a torn wool sweater. On his head was a battered brown fedora, the brim pulled down. With one hand, Honradez led his mule, and in the other, he carried an old Mauser rifle. The rifle's bolt was back, and the receiver was open; Willy had made Honradez jack the bolt and put the bullets in his pockets when they met on the trail. Honradez had heard rumors that there were armed men in the forest, and he had thought they must be smugglers. It only slowly dawned on him that the men who surrounded his farm were *insurrectos,* not smugglers, and he was astounded.

As he entered the clearing, his children ran toward him, jabbering happily, and as Honradez tied the mule to the woodpile, there was nothing else for him to do except grin the way people do when there is a possibility that they might inadvertently give offense and be killed.

"Congratulations," Guevara said. "Your wife had a little girl."

At this Honradez broke into a childlike laugh, so honest and heartfelt that it spread instantly to every one of the comrades who heard it.

"A girl!"

Honradez had prayed hard all the way from the river that the Virgin of Urkupiña would spare his wife and that he *please God* would return home and not find his children gathered around a dead woman. Tears streaming down his face, Honradez handed Guevara the rusty gun and rushed into the house.

Later, they roasted a pig and made *humitas* of moist corn dough flavored with onions and chilies and rolled up in corn husks. Moro carved great hunks of pork with his scalpel, and they each used a piece of banana leaf as plates. Honradez sat with Guevara, Inti, and Moro as they ate. During the meal, Inti was introduced as the guerrilla column's leader, a ruse Guevara would repeat each time they met peasants. Honradez pretended enraptured attention as Inti held forth on the reasons the guerrillas had come and the need to take up arms against La Paz. Guevara listened as Inti spoke, and he watched Honradez closely. To Inti's points Honradez would only nod and say, *"Es verdad,"* and in the end the farmer proved as noncommittal and inscrutable as any peasant in history.

As Inti talked, Honradez became certain that this thin Boliviano was not really the man in charge; Honradez's nose for authority proving as acute and unfailing as a dog's. He also detected the Cubans' accents, which, implausibly, Honradez thought were North American. After midnight, mostly to change the subject from politics, Honradez offered Inti, Marcos, and Guevara each one of the bottles of beer he had been saving for carnival. The beer was poured out into tin cups and downed with *saludos* all around.

"I'm in your debt," Honradez said. "I don't know how I can begin to thank you."

Joaquin patted his stomach. "Listen, man, you're even with me."

"There is something you could do for us." Guevara opened his map case and spread the paper on the dirt at their feet. Honradez's face betrayed no expression, but he thought, *So this is the one in charge, the one with the papers.*

It had grown dark, and Guevara angled the map sheet at the fire to light it. "Which trail did you take to Tatarenda?"

"I'm sorry," Honradez said. "I can't read, Señor."

"This is like a picture. From the air." Guevara's finger touched the map, to the left of where the Ñancahuazú flowed into the Rio Grande, a place roughly in the center of the map. "We're here," he said. His fingernail touched a dotted pencil line on the map where he had marked down the trail. "This is the path by the river. This is the one on the ridge."

Honradez looked puzzled, the expression accentuated by the light of the fire and an earnest attempt to look harmless.

"You headed east to Tatarenda," Guevara said patiently.

East was something Honradez understood. The map was a swirl of colored splotches and made no sense.

"I took the river trail," Honradez said. "They told me the doctor had gone to Abapó, so I came back."

"Did you see soldiers?"

"With beards? Like you?"

"Army soldiers," Guevara said.

"I didn't see any soldiers. Anywhere. Only trucks of the oil company when I got to the Camiri road."

Inside the house, the baby cried, and Honradez stood. He said, "Excuse me, kind gentlemen," then bowed out of the firelight and into the house.

"We've made a friend," Joaquin said.

"It's been six weeks since we ambushed the convoy. You think it's possible that the army hasn't put out one patrol, even on the highway?"

"Why would he lie to us?" Moro asked.

Guevara popped a last bit of *humita* into his mouth and chewed as he spoke. "That rifle he was carrying—it's army surplus. The government gives them out to the peasant militias."

"You think he's militia?"

Guevara tossed his banana leaf into the fire. Whether or not the farmer was a member of the home guard was moot. The army would soon know the column had passed the river.

"What do we do?"

"We thank him for dinner," Guevara said.

The column leaders readied their groups for movement, this taking a bit longer than expected, as Eusebio and Chingolo had already put their hammocks up and removed their boots. The animals were again loaded and backpacks swung up onto shoulders. Honradez came out of the house holding a kerosene lantern as the men were assembling into lines.

"I hoped you would stay. It's safe here. I was going to milk the cow in the morning," Honradez said.

Inti was already leading the vanguard back around the cornfield, so Guevara answered: "You've been kind, sir, but we'd better move on. We don't want to bring any attention onto your family."

"Where are you going? I can show you the way," Honradez said.

"We know the way, friend." Guevara's gaze was piercing. Honradez could not hold it.

"Thank you for the food," Guevara said. "Good night."

At the tree line, Guevara paused with Joaquin, watching the men walk past and into the jungle, humpbacked shapes against a thin sliver of moonlight.

"The moon's almost down," Guevara said. "When it's full dark, have the men exchange packs and weapons, then circle back past the farmhouse. Have everyone pass through at least twice."

Joaquin smiled. Doubling the column would make the force seem twice as large.

"If this *pendejo* is going to sing," Guevara said, "he might as well sing a tune we like."

15

CARRYING HIS M16, Hoyle moved toward the sound of the river. The path was loomed over by an endless arch of trees, so the light that fell on the ground was yellow and green. As it neared the Rio Grande, the trail became broad and sandy, and there were signs that it had been used to drive cattle to market. In most places, the track paralleled the river above the valley floor, staying predictably just inside the tree line. It was exactly the type of trail to be avoided in Southeast Asia: a jungle altar upon which lazy soldiers were sacrificed.

To the left and right along the path, Bolivian conscripts sprawled in various states of repose. Some squatted on their packs; a few sat directly on the trail as they chatted, their rifles leaning against trees or in the dirt at their feet. The patrol had halted for the fifth time in as many hours, and had progressed, Hoyle guessed, no farther then ten kilometers from the road head at Tatarenda. They'd started from the trucks before dawn, and Charlie was frankly delighted to be left behind with the vehicles. Hoyle remembered him saying *adios* with a limp and fatalistic shrug when they moved off into the forest.

As he passed up the column, Hoyle did his best to appear pleasant and kept his corrections to a minimum. Here and there he asked an NCO to stand and keep watch, pointing in a direction away from the trail. Occasionally, he'd ask a *cabo* how he was doing—he'd fix a rifle strap for one, close a pack flap for another—and by the time he'd reached the head of the column, Hoyle was convinced that he had just walked through a convention of military retards. For almost all of the Bolivian soldiers, this was the first time they had been issued live ammunition, and their sergeants had been busy all morning reminding the men not to be fucking idiots and shoot themselves.

Fretting for the Bolivian republic, Hoyle continued down the trail, negotiating a steep stretch just before the river. Inside the tree line, above the place where a dozen large boulders loomed over the watercourse, Hoyle and Valdéz exchanged silent glances. Their impressions were the same, and their moods similarly depressed. The morning's walk had been a farce—they had individually and collectively overestimated the Bolivian army, and now there was nothing to do but complete the planned march and hope there would not be trouble. To the right, Smith crouched at a boulder, shooting a compass bearing down the river and marking their position should support become necessary. A Bolivian radio operator stood next to him, smoking a cigarette and looking up into the sky. *The sky!*

"Jesus Christ," Valdéz said, disgusted.

He wore a pair of khaki pants with cargo pockets and expensive Austrian hiking boots. Over an Izod shirt, he wore a flak jacket and web gear, canteens, magazines, grenades, and first-aid pouches all arranged just so. On his face was a pair of swept-back Ray-Ban sunglasses that gave him a slightly debonair aspect, though Hoyle knew him to be a thorough-going killer. The Colt model 609 rifle in his hand was oiled immaculately.

They were at a place along the Rio Grande where the valley opened and the Ñancahuazú joined from the south. A ford called Vado del Yeso was somewhere to the west. Or it was supposed to be. The maps had proved less than perfect, but that was to be expected—a map was always someone else's best guess, and navigation, Hoyle knew, was the art of eventually getting home. The scouts had said that Vado del Yeso was the only safe place to cross the river for twenty kilometers. It looked like the river could be forded directly in front of them, but again, that was only because the water was low; Hoyle noted several large tree trunks jammed into boulders well up from the water. This quiet river had run in deadly spate and had done so recently. Half an hour ago, Santavanes had taken two Bolivian troopers and gone to look for a place to cross.

"Who did he take?" Hoyle asked Valdéz.

"Two sergeants. One of them used to be French Foreign Legion. The other guy's a paratrooper."

Hoyle had no idea how the Bolivians would work out, but he knew Santavanes well. Santavanes worked best on his own, and it could not be said that he suffered fools gladly. He might wind up shooting his Bolivian charges, but he would not allow them to tumble into folly.

"Do me a favor," Hoyle said to Valdéz.

"Sure."

"Go back to the rear of the column, get some pickets out on the flanks, and tell the first sergeant to get ready to move the column forward."

"All right."

"Better get back there before they all fall asleep."

Valdéz scrambled back up the steep part of the trail and disappeared into the tree line. Hoyle stood and watched the bank across the river and the ridges in the places the woods thinned out. Now and again a muffled order came drifting from the trail behind him, the rattle of a piece of equipment or a shouted curse, but mostly, there was just the white noise of the river and the tittering, almost crackling calls of birds in the forest.

Smith came back over from the boulders, and the Bolivian radioman came with him. Hoyle noticed that the radio operator wore round wire-rimmed glasses almost exactly like Smith's.

"How long has Santavanes been gone?" Hoyle asked.

"I'm not worried about him," Smith said. "The sergeants seem okay. The Legionnaire especially."

"You sure he's Legion?"

"His French was good," Smith said.

Hoyle stared at the river and shook his head. Five years in the French Foreign Legion would have granted the sergeant a clean passport and French citizenship. If you'd served in the Legion, why the hell would you come back here?

Hoyle continued to watch the riverbank above the small rapids, and then he saw Santavanes appear from the brush on the opposite shore. Santavanes was dressed in a plain olive uniform, the same one worn by the Bolivian *cabos*. Holding his rifle over his head, he waded the river right in front of Hoyle and Smith, then walked, dripping, up the boulders toward them. So much for the search for a crossing place.

"There's a cornfield around the bend," Santavanes said. Smith wiped his glasses as Santavanes stamped the water out of his boots.

"The farmer says he's a corporal in the home guard. He says he's seen the guerrillas."

"When?" Smith asked.

"He wants money," Santavanes said.

THE RIVER CROSSING went without major incident. The Bolivian troops were herded back together and marched, for they were incapable of patrolling, down a sketchy set of paths toward the cornfield and the small mudbrick house of the farmer. As they drew closer, Smith dispatched Valdéz to the right and Santavanes to the left, sending with them ten Bolivian soldiers each. This was intended as a blocking force. Hoyle and Smith led the remaining troops directly toward the house, the Bolivian lieutenant insisting that he be allowed to let his men fix bayonets, form a line, and walk dramatically through the cornfield.

As they approached the farmhouse, a little girl peeked at them from behind the pigsty. She was not afraid, and Hoyle walked over to her and knelt down. *"Hola, princesa,"* he said.

The princess was not amused. Hoyle slung his rifle behind his back and waved his fingers in front of the little girl's face. He then did the simple magic trick of making two centavos appear behind her ear. He handed the little girl the coins, and she laughed delightedly. Hoyle noticed a rectangular patch of surgical gauze taped to her forearm.

"What happened here?" he asked.

"The men with beards," she said, "they gave me medicine."

"Medicine?" Hoyle asked. "Can I see?"

The little girl allowed him to lift the gauze, and he saw a smooth incision—definitely the mark of a scalpel—and a crusted-over punctum.

The little girl turned and showed off a perfectly circular scab on her shoulder. "Angels kissed me," she said.

"What's that?" Smith asked.

"She's been vaccinated for smallpox," Hoyle said.

They were both silent, the evidence of the little girl's inoculation and the surgical scar on her forearm were as unlikely as Truth and Justice.

The chickens scattered across the dirt front yard, and Honradez Rulon stepped out of the house. Hoyle stood as the farmer walked toward them.

"I understand that you have seen the *insurrectos*," Smith said.

"I told the other man I would like to be paid."

"We're willing to pay you," Smith said. "It depends on what you know." Smith pulled open the Velcro on his flak jacket and removed a soft wad of Bolivian currency. Honradez's eyes fell on it. Hoyle shooed away the little girl as Smith counted out a hundred Bolivianos in slightly wet cash.

"The guerrillas gave your children medicine," Hoyle said. "Why are you willing to inform on them?"

"My family is hungry, Señor," the farmer said, "and the Communists hate Jesus and the Blessed Virgin."

"When did you see them?" Smith asked.

"Three days ago."

"How many men?" Hoyle asked.

"Eighty-three," Honradez said. "I counted them as they passed the house."

Smith spoke for a while with the farmer, listening to the story repeatedly and nurturing what rapport he could with so avaricious a creature. The soldiers not deployed to the blocking forces had started a fire and cooked lunch. Hoyle rejoined them under a tree by the woodpile.

"Trail's old, but it looks like the guerrillas did a couple of circles around the house," Hoyle said.

"What's the count?" Smith asked. He looked over at Honradez, who was sitting next to the Bolivian officer.

Hoyle said, "Forty, maybe less. They doubled back past the house, so Greenjeans was seeing double."

Smith considered the map for a moment and said, "We have a couple hours of daylight. I want to keep pushing west—maybe we can cross their trail on the other side of Vado del Yeso."

Santavanes and Valdéz remained quiet out of respect for Smith, but none of them thought that taking the Bolivians any deeper was a good idea. Hoyle looked out at the soldiers sitting resentfully around the farmhouse. Since they'd crossed the river, the Bolivian troops had become increasingly grim, and it was certain that an order to continue west would not be welcomed.

"I'm not sure they'll go," Hoyle said.

"They'll do what we tell them," Smith answered.

Somewhere a thrush clattered out a long, worrying call.

Hoyle spoke quietly. "Look, if you order that lieutenant any deeper, you're going to put him in a box. If he refuses you, his authority goes to zero. If he says yes and his men won't go, we have a mutiny."

Smith's combat experience was considerable, but his experience with balky troops was nil. He was in no mood to mollycoddle the Bolivians. He looked at Valdéz. "Do you think they'll fight?"

"A few. I think the rest will run."

"Let me take a couple of volunteers and recon toward the river," Hoyle said. "If it's clear, I'll signal for you to come forward."

"I'll give you one hour, Hoyle, and then I'm ordering the company west."

ABOVE VADO DEL YESO, the Masacuri River was a little more than a hundred meters wide. A pair of sandbars cut across it diagonally, and there was a sallow-colored stretch of sand, almost a beach, on the east bank just before the river turned. Below the farmhouse, the river ran in fast waters and occasionally even in rapids, but around the ford, it was tame, the tea-colored water between the sandbars moving slowly.

Hoyle was not surprised when the Legion sergeant again volunteered to scout. His name was Gustavo Merán, and he was by far the best soldier in the company. They spoke briefly as they set out from the cornfield, and Hoyle learned that he had indeed served with the French, seeing combat in Algeria and service in Chad before he returned home to Bolivia. Merán organized the men for movement, a dozen *obligados* he had selected from the first platoon, and when they reentered the forest, Merán walked point two places in front of Hoyle. Smith's radio operator, the one with the round glasses, had also been volunteered and now slouched along next to Hoyle like a kid being sent to the principal's office.

Above the crossing place, the river turned sharply west, and Merán halted the patrol. Together, Hoyle and the sergeant went ahead to scout the bend and check the sandbars. They had gone only a few dozen yards before Hoyle noticed a broken tree limb along the bank. It was snapped off neatly.

Hoyle knelt next to the cracked branch and found a boot print in a shallow eddy. Merán nodded silently as Hoyle put his hand to the surface of the pool and waved water over the track. Two inches below the surface, the boot print vanished in a small reddish-brown cloud of mud. The track was probably less than five minutes old. Without a word, Merán signaled behind him for the men to take cover.

Hoyle strained to hear above the sounds of the river. It seemed that the calling of the birds had died away; there were only the clicks and hum of insects and the smooth rush of water across the rocks. Hoyle moved forward, his rifle held chest-high, and he slipped the strap from around his neck and let it hang down. He quietly sank to a crouch. The wind stirred through the tops of the trees, and sunlight dappled his arms. There were low sounds intermingled with the ticks and chirps, a distant grunting, maybe the hooting of a monkey, and then it came distinctly: the sound of men. There was laughter and then a clacking noise, metal against rock. Merán heard it all and cut his eyes to Hoyle.

Hoyle kept his rifle vertical and pressed his body against a tree. Merán started to come forward, but Hoyle signaled him to stop with a slight shake of the head. Through a shimmer of leaves, Hoyle could just see the apex of the bend. Not quite a hundred meters away, a dozen men were clustered on a sandbar, washing in the river. Their weapons and packs were heaped together in a pile on the near side of the stream. Guerrillas. Nearly all the men had beards, and their hair was long. Hoyle looked again down the riverbank and scanned the tree limbs overhead. Incredibly, the bathers seemed not to have posted a sentry.

Hoyle was aware of the slow, hard beating of his heart. There was the question of how to open the engagement. If he had reliable troops—shit, if he had taken Valdéz and Santavanes—he only would have to pull the trigger, and they would have moved to support him. Merán could be counted on to do the same, but that made only two rifles against ten. Of the Bolivian squad behind, Hoyle thought nothing. It was his experience that reluctant troops would flatten at the sound of unexpected gunfire—they would hide, and then they would scatter.

Hoyle was turning these factors over in his mind when a twig snapped behind him.

Then several things happened very quickly.

Hoyle turned at the noise of the branch, as did Merán. They were both experienced soldiers and swung their weapons along with their heads, Hoyle's thumb rocking down the safety on the M16 and smoothly, automatically, swinging the butt stock into the hollow of his shoulder. He saw them, two dark-haired, bearded men in faded green fatigues. Both carried a pole on their shoulders, and hung on it between them was a wild javelina, freshly killed. Both the bearded men had their rifles slung uselessly over their shoulders and were astonished to have stumbled on the Bolivian soldiers.

Half a second passed, a span of time unfolded by adrenaline into a month, a season, an instant that would be seared into the mind of every man who survived. For a frozen moment, the two groups of men blinked at each other.

Then one of the Bolivian soldiers shouted and fumbled for his rifle. The closer of the two guerrillas shoved the pole off his shoulder, smoothly drew his pistol, and shot the soldier in the face. As the trooper tumbled back, Hoyle and Merán opened fire. Hoyle's first bullet struck the pole just behind the pig's feet and snapped it in an explosion of bark. His second shot struck the pistol from the guerrilla's hand, and as time spun out, Hoyle had an instant to reflect that he'd aimed for the man's head and missed. Both of the guerrillas dropped their burden and ran as quickly as they could away from the river. Hoyle fired two shots after them and Merán a dozen, but the forest swallowed the guerrillas as quickly as they had appeared, and in the blink of an eye, they were gone.

Not one of the Bolivian soldiers had yet raised a weapon. Time continued to expand, and Hoyle was aware that the crashing noise of his rifle had deafened him; what he heard were muffled noises, like sounds made underwater.

There was a pause, and several seconds filled with shouting. Hoyle spun around and saw that the men on the sandbar were scrambling for their weapons. One of the guerrillas, a tall, broad-shouldered man, had already aimed and fired. Two bullets snapped past Hoyle and smashed into a tree behind him. Then there was much firing from the sandbar, all of the guerrillas shooting steadily, and Hoyle instinctively slid down low against the tree trunk and returned fire. Bullets ripped past him and banged about the branches. Cut away by tracers, twigs and leaves rained down from the canopy, turning over and over as they fluttered to the forest floor. Behind Hoyle, Merán continued to shoot, the close and sharp report of his rifle like a slap on the back of Hoyle's neck.

Hoyle's mind raced with clear, rapid thought. Rates of fire, avenues of retreat, places of cover. The firefight seemed to be unfolding like a film run too slowly. Hoyle was aware of the oddly muted sounds, the steady hammering of single shots and the trembling bursts of automatic fire, but they were sorted by his mind into a distant place. Beside him, Merán continued to fight, a fearless man, but the Bolivian conscripts had flattened down onto the riverbank, and as Hoyle reloaded, two soldiers stood and ran. Both were cut down. One fell into the water, and the other let out a holler and crumpled onto a shallow pool, then crawled quickly back up into the trees, his voice broken and squeaking, *"Ai, ai, ai, ai."*

Hoyle calculated that there were fewer than a dozen guerrilla fighters on the sandbar, and the two who had run away were now someplace behind him. That meant more than twenty enemy were unaccounted for, and Hoyle was certain they would rush to the sound of gunfire. When the entire guerrilla band joined, Hoyle knew that he and Merán would be hopelessly outnumbered. Already they were being outfought.

The guerrillas on the sandbar spread out, and soon a converging fire came through the trees. This barrage missed Hoyle and Merán only because the bend in the river made the guerrillas misjudge the range and concentrate their fire slightly short. Behind Hoyle, Bolivian soldiers threw down their weapons and equipment and ran as fast as they could downriver, away from the fight. More leaves were falling around them, a blizzard of green cut through with the deadly light of tracers bouncing among the tree trunks, red and green, slow and fast, a perplexing and fatal sight. The guerrillas' fire turned at the moving bodies, and in the seconds it took Hoyle to reload his weapon, he saw three more Bolivian soldiers tumble, shot in the back as they tried to escape.

Hoyle turned to Merán, three feet away and firing steadily. Hoyle signaled to him, pointing back the way they'd come, and Merán nodded. The sergeant did not fall back, though he understood they would soon retreat. He kept up a slow, steady fire.

Something brushed Hoyle's calf and he looked down. At his feet was the radio operator. He had thrown away his rifle and was curled into a ball against the roots of the tree. How long he had been there, Hoyle could not know. He bent forward and lifted the young soldier by his pack straps. The radio operator's glasses had fogged thickly, and his cheeks were slick with tears. Hoyle noticed that the radio had been shot through twice, once through the casing and once through the control panel. The radio was as useless as the man who carried it.

"Are you hit?" Hoyle asked.

The radio operator blinked behind the steamy lenses. He was too terrified to speak.

There was an outcry from the sandbar, and the guerrillas were joined by another group, maybe fifteen or twenty men. It was remarkable and improbable, but the fire diminished. Hoyle rolled a glance around the tree trunk. On the sandbar, the second group of guerrillas had begun firing upslope and into the woods behind them. They had mistaken the Bolivians' naked flight as a flanking maneuver. Thinking they might be surrounded, the guerrillas now sprayed the trees upriver and away from Hoyle and Merán. Hoyle knew this mistake would soon be corrected; if there was to be any chance of escape, they had to move immediately.

GUEVARA HEARD TWO sharp reports, gunshots close together. The sounds came from the riverbed below him and somewhere to the east. As a second weapon spat out a dozen quick shots, he realized there had been contact with the enemy, and he threw off his pack and tumbled downhill toward the water. The vegetation was heavy, and for several long moments, as he clawed his way downslope, Guevara could see neither the river nor his own men. He could only guess that they were being shot at from somewhere near where the river turned, but his was an ear tuned to battle, and his hunch would prove correct. As he scrambled through the brush, he heard Joaquin bellowing orders. The men sent to draw water ran quickly for their weapons, and almost at once the firing became general. Guevara could not yet see who was shooting at the sandbar, but he again heard the high, piercing crack of weapons downstream, and the *tick tick tick* of bullets flying through the tree branches around him.

Guevara toppled down the riverbank and out onto the sandbar. He ran crouching to the place Joaquin was directing fire and dropped into cover beside him. The noise of the guerrillas' weapons, almost twenty all together, was an ear-shattering roar. Half the men were shooting downriver, and the others were firing into a patch of hardwood up behind them. Guevara realized quickly that the noise of rifles was mostly that of outgoing fire, and he banged Joaquin on the shoulder. He signaled for the men to cease fire, shaking his head and pulling his finger across his throat. Gradually, the order was passed by hand gestures and by the shouted command *pare fuego*. The guerrillas' weapons sputtered and fell silent. As the echoes rolled off against the hillside, Guevara was able to hear the sound of short bursts from downriver. There was no gunfire behind them. Guevara realized, and Joaquin did, too, that only a single weapon was firing at the sandbar.

"Fuck," Joaquin yelled, "I thought they were in back of us."

It was obvious now that there were no Bolivian soldiers anywhere on the hill. Still, a steady stream of bullets plinked at them from the river bend, punctuated by short bursts of automatic fire aimed low and walked into the shallows.

Guevara peered over the top of the fallen log behind which they'd taken cover. He did this for only a second, since the bullets fired at them were very accurately aimed. A hundred meters away, Guevara could see the riverbank and the corpses of half a dozen Bolivian soldiers scattered about. He could see no movement, nor could he detect the place from which the gunfire came. A second after he ducked back, a bullet smashed into the log a few feet away from his face, tearing out a chunk of termite-infested wood and slinging it off nearly straight up into the tree canopy above him.

"How many?" Guevara said to Joaquin.

"Two squads . . . I don't know. Half of them ran away downriver."

"Army or militia?" Guevara asked.

"Green uniforms," Joaquin answered. "Army."

Rolando spoke. "I thought they were trying to flank us."

"There's only one rifle there now," Guevara said. On cue, five shots passed close overhead, a testament to the marksmanship of this lone rifleman.

"Just one? Where are the others?" Joaquin asked.

"Have we driven them off?" Rolando's face was bright, and his eyes shone. Adrenaline and the intoxication of combat had enraptured him.

"They're falling back," Guevara said. One brave or foolish soul was covering the retreat. It was likely that the Bolivians had run away, but Guevara could not be certain that the enemy had not feigned retreat in order to draw the guerrillas into the open and strike them with enfiladed fire. That was what Guevara would have done.

"Have Marcos take the forward detachment and advance on this side of the river," Guevara said, and as these words left his mouth, Rolando did an impetuous and fatal thing. He jumped up from behind the log, placed his weapon on his hip, and ran forward, spraying bullets at the bend in the river. Guevara reached up and tried to stop him, and his hand caught Rolando's belt, but he jerked forward. Unbidden, two or three of the others stood and broke cover like Rolando, shooting and moving toward the bend in the river and yelling as they scrambled forward.

They were charging without orders, five or six of them, Bolivians and Cubans together; the veterans knew better, and they knew the comandante better. It was not yet time to break cover, and definitely not time to crash through the jungle toward a hidden shooter. Guevara and Joaquin remained behind the fallen log; both knew that to stand and join the stampede would be folly and maybe death. All that could be done was to fire in support of Rolando's improvisation, attempt to lay down a suppressive fire as the charge went forward, and this Guevara did, firing and yelling himself hoarse, shouting for Rolando and the others to find cover and break off the attack.

HOYLE SHOVED THE radio operator toward Sergeant Merán. Hoyle changed magazines, put the bolt forward on his weapon, and said, "Get him out of here."

Merán's eyes fell on the radio; he saw that the casing was shot through, and he knew that it meant help would not be soon coming.

"Find Smith and bring him here. Tell him we found the main body—forty guerrillas."

"Come with us," Merán shouted, but in that instant the firing from the sandbar slowed and then stopped.

Hoyle pulled the useless radio from the Bolivian soldier's back and dropped it into the leaf clutter. "They're regrouping," he said. "Run." Merán pulled the young man forward by his shirtfront. "Come on, you dumb bastard," he said. And they ran.

Hoyle peered around the tree again, and for a few more seconds, there was no firing. He could hear Merán and the radio operator crashing through the brush behind him. There was no shouting from the sandbar, no noise at all, birds and insects shocked into silence by the ferocious noise of the firefight, and Hoyle strained his ringing ears for any sound at all. Then it came, one voice, and then another, a sound like *haaaaaaa*, through the bush, and there was the racket of several weapons shooting intermittently.

Hoyle lifted the rifle to his cheek and sighted across it. Through the trees, he saw half a dozen guerrillas in a staggered row running toward him. Hoyle's mind was almost a perfect blank as he aimed and fired at the closest guerrilla. The M16 bucked twice, the barrel hardly moving, and Hoyle watched the man tumble forward. It happened slowly enough that Hoyle could see that both his shots had struck the guerrilla in the right thigh, maybe six inches above the knee. The M16 fired a small bullet, barely larger than .22-caliber, but the round was designed to cause maximum damage to a human body, and as these bullets found their mark the guerrilla wheeled about and Hoyle could hear two distinct thumps, the sound of the steel-jacketed slugs ripping flesh and breaking bone. Not over a dozen yards in front of Hoyle, the man went down, and the other guerrillas charging with him soon flattened behind cover.

Hoyle ran quickly to another tree. From the sandbar, he heard an order being repeated again and again, relayed man to man and he was surprised, embarrassed even, that in this moment his Spanish failed him. Hoyle's brain buzzed, and his throat was dry as dirt. As he crouched, panting, against a tree trunk, it astounded him that he had no idea what the guerrillas were saying to one another.

GUEVARA WATCHED AS the men ran forward, he cursed and called for them to take cover, and then he saw Rolando stagger and lurch forward. Before Rolando's body struck the ground, his pants were soaked through with blood. In an instant gore pumped through the perforations, spraying like water from a hose, and Guevara was certain an artery had been severed. Without thought or plan, Guevara leaped over the log and ran toward the wounded man.

Sprawled in an open place beneath a large hardwood, Rolando lay on his back. His rifle was at this side, and both his hands were pressed down hard on the wound. As Guevara knelt over him, Rolando smiled. Guevara recognized the expression—he had seen it before—it was the most absurd and inexplicable thing in the world: a young comrade, curiously and frankly delighted to have been wounded. But as Guevara laid hold of Rolando, blood gushed between his fists, the wound spraying blood two feet into the air, ejecting it in spurts timed to the rhythm of Rolando's fast-beating heart. The bleeding would not stop, and in a few moments Rolando's expression became one of shock. Until this he'd felt no pain, not even a twinge from his obviously broken leg, but as the blood spewed into the air, his eyes became wide with fear. He gripped his pants leg and squeezed his fingers into the mangled flesh, but still the blood came, jetting over him, ruby in the air and black and sticky as it pumped against the bark of the tree.

"Shit, shit, shit," Rolando said.

The satisfaction at being wounded evaporated into mortal dread. Guevara ripped off his belt and quickly made a tourniquet. Guevara hitched on the belt, and Rolando screamed in agony, the artery and pulverized muscles shoved against raw, broken bone. Guevara began to drag the wounded man back toward cover.

NOW THEY WERE all moving, coming at him, and for the first time since the contact opened, Hoyle felt that he was in danger. Merán was gone, away through the jungle behind him, and Hoyle was conclusively aware that he was alone and facing a superior and well-led enemy.

Hoyle again took aim. A hundred yards away, two dozen guerrillas were visible; they were being marshaled into a line and were coming on, shooting. Close to his right, he saw one man lift a wounded guerrilla under the armpits and drag him backward. Hoyle positioned the chest of the rescuer under his front sight and narrowed his eye. His index finger drew slack out of the trigger, but Hoyle did not fire.

To shoot would be simple murder.

Across the space of the clearing, Guevara's eyes found Hoyle; rather, Guevara ascertained a man with a black rifle, an enemy taking aim. There was an incalculable instant, one half a millisecond of connection, one veteran recognizing another, and insensibly and without reflection or mercy, Hoyle moved the muzzle of his rifle up and to the left. In the swirling calculus of combat, Hoyle recognized that the wounded man and his savior were not an immediate threat, the advancing men were, and his thumb pressed the safety switch from fire all the way back to auto. He aimed waist-high at the advancing guerrillas and fired half the magazine in short, sharp bursts. He had spared Guevara and Rolando, but to the others, he intended maximum harm. He aimed and fired again; bullets crashed through the trees, and Hoyle felt a brief twinge of satisfaction when he heard a human yelp from somewhere in the brush.

It was time to disappear. Hoyle pulled a smoke grenade from his flak jacket, yanked the pin, and tossed it upwind. Hissing, the grenade bounced onto the riverbank; purple smoke gushed between him and the guerrillas. Screened by the cloud, Hoyle turned and ran.

He could hear the weapons of the guerrillas firing steadily, and again everything seemed to slow. The small patches of sunlight that made it through the forest seemed impossibly bright, and the noise of the river seemed like a roar in his ears. Hoyle felt as though he were trying to run through concrete: He willed himself onward, but his legs would not do his bidding. His heart pounded in his throat, and he could feel the concussion of the weapons being fired at him—sharp, tearing explosions that rattled his guts. Hoyle jumped over the bodies of the Bolivian soldiers in the shallows next to the riverbank, and when the first bullet hit the sand in front of him, he knew that he would soon be shot down.

His senses started to flee him; the light on the forest floor dimmed, the sounds of the river froze in his ears, and he thought, calmly, that he had not expected to die this morning.

It was a mistake to cross the river, he thought. All of this was a colossal fuckup.

Two bullets struck Hoyle nearly simultaneously, the first cutting away the heel of his right boot, abruptly and violently spinning him through the air and sweeping his feet from under him. Something passed his ear with the sound of a bullwhip. As he fell, a bullet struck him in the front of his flak jacket, punching the breath from his lungs in a short, excruciating grunt, and Hoyle was knocked senseless. Oblivion closed over him like the lid of a box.

WHEN THE LAST man fell onto the riverbank, Joaquin ordered a cease-fire. The veterans quickly reloaded, anticipating Joaquin's next command, and Moro turned back to the place Guevara had dragged Rolando. He knelt as Guevara struggled to further tighten the tourniquet. Moro knew, as Guevara did, that the femoral artery had been severed. Guevara called for stretcher bearers, and Rolando was wrapped into a poncho and carried back up the trail.

"I'm sorry, Comandante," Rolando said. "Shit, I'm sorry."

"Go with him," Guevara said to Moro.

"The surgical kits are all the way back with the horse," Moro said.

"Go quickly. Do what you can," Guevara said. Moro hustled off after the stretcher, following the black trail of blood. Guevara moved toward the bend in the river. Joaquin had already taken charge, deploying squads on the flanks and ordering Urbano and Alejandro to gather weapons and search the bodies. These actions were carried out with sufficient haste, as all knew more soldiers would be drawn to the sound of the fight.

Guevara scanned the riverbank; half a dozen Bolivian army dead, and seven more corpses would be found in the brush, making for a total of thirteen killed.

"Willy and Chapaco were hunting," Joaquin said. "They stumbled into a patrol. Willy was shot through the hand."

"Who else is wounded?"

Joaquin shook his head; there had been no other casualties. Thirteen Bolivian soldiers were dead, and an unknown number were scattered and hiding in the forest.

Guevara walked through the small clearing where Rolando had fallen, then toward the stretch of beach where the river turned. Fingers of violet-colored smoke still floated through the trees. He found the casing of the smoke grenade, burned out and smoldering in a wet spot on the trail.

On the sand by the river, Guevara came upon the pieces of Hoyle's rifle, black plastic and aluminum, and then the weapon itself, a remarkably skeletal and fragile-looking thing. Guevara lifted it from the sand. Even half-smashed, the rifle's distinctive front sight and carrying handle were obvious. Joaquin looked at it and recognized the weapon at once. The M16 rifle was emblematic, an icon of the United States. "That weapon," Joaquin said. "It's North American."

Sprawled a dozen yards from Joaquin, Hoyle heard these words spoken plainly. They came to him through a dark veil of hurt.

His eyes flickered open, but he saw nothing—sand pressed against his face, and he could feel the grit between his teeth. A gash had opened on his forehead. He felt numb in his legs. At first he thought this a symptom of paralysis, and it took him a good several seconds to realize that he was lying across one of the shallow sandbars, immersed up to his waist in water.

Hoyle remained perfectly still and could hear the voices of the other guerrillas counting bodies and calling to one another from down the riverbank. Hoyle was not sure that he could move; there was an overpowering pain in his chest, and as he heard the crunching of stones, he realized someone was approaching. He had no chance of escape, so he closed his eyes, hoping to play dead.

Guevara tossed away the broken rifle and looked over at the place where Hoyle lay. Guevara could not see the man's face but recognized that his clothing was different from that of the Bolivian *cabos,* and over his flak jacket he wore a pistol in a shoulder holster. It was the pistol that first attracted Guevara's attention, pistols being a universal mark of military status. Guevara clicked his lips, and Joaquin looked over. Joaquin, too, saw the pistol and knew at once what it meant.

As Guevara walked closer, he recognized this person as the same man who'd spared his life as he struggled to drag Rolando to cover.

Joaquin aimed his rifle at the back of Hoyle's skull. He said quietly, "I think this one is a gringo."

Hoyle held his breath, waiting for a bullet. And then the forest exploded.

From both sides of the river, rifles fired and machine guns prattled. The air was filled with bullets; a perfect and dreadfully executed cross fire swept the ground and the sandbars. Guevara knew at once that the Bolivian army had returned and that they had been flanked. Guevara's forward column was still gathering weapons; he realized his troops were spread thin and the enemy was concentrated. The only choice was to disengage and run.

Guevara yelled to the others, *"Fall back! Fall back!"*

A hundred bullets came through the trees at them, then hundreds more. Guevara fired and Joaquin did as well, and the comrades scrambled back up and into the brush, away from the river and the deadly triangle of fire.

Hoyle pressed himself into the sand, daring not to even flinch as the torrent of lead swarmed above him. He could hear yelling and then cheering as Bolivian soldiers started to splash across the river.

It was a testimony to Guevara's leadership and the pathetic shooting of the Bolivian army that all of his men would escape the counterattack. The guerrillas quickly disappeared into the brush, breaking contact, leaving the Bolivian troopers to spray bullets at specters glimmering across the forest floor.

Smith and Merán waded up onto the sandbar. Hoyle felt a hand close over the shoulder of his flak vest and roll him over. It was Smith, and the expression on his face was stern.

Smith was shocked to see that Hoyle was covered with blood.

Hoyle had survived, which both amazed and pained him. He had expected to be shot or captured; he had not even conceived that the Bolivians would return, and now that he was delivered from harm, he felt oddly miserable. He'd led the two squads into contact, and they had been mauled. It did not matter that Hoyle had covered Merán's retreat, nor did it matter that the Bolivians who'd fallen had fled without firing a shot. It mattered only that others had been killed and he had lived. As fear released its grip, what descended on Hoyle was something like shame.

He tried to speak, but his mouth was full of sand. Blood from the wound to his scalp covered half his face. Santavanes stood over Hoyle, looking down coldly.

"Is he alive?" Santavanes asked. The tone of his voice was so blasé as to be laughable.

Hoyle finally managed to sputter, "Are you?"

Smith ran his fingers through Hoyle's hair, looking for a punctured skull. He didn't find a hole.

"Help me up."

"Stay put," Smith said. Smith pulled open Hoyle's flak jacket, the Velcro making a ripping sound. Hoyle stifled a groan. The pain in his chest was excruciating; ribs were broken, and each breath was a stabbing agony.

Smith scanned Hoyle's shirt: Incredibly, he was not punctured. A single bullet, smashed and mangled, dropped from a vertical gash inside Hoyle's body armor. The slug fell to the sand. It looked like a flat, ugly mollusk.

"Damn."

Hoyle's fingers touched the front of his chest. There was already a nasty black-and-red blister rising on the skin below his sternum.

"Jesus," Santavanes said. "You are one lucky son of a bitch."

16

A N HOUR PAST midnight, Guevara sat, watching the ash on the end of his cigar, deliberately trying to make his mind a blank. A single thought kept working its way into his head, and he tried repeatedly to defeat it. *One man is nothing.* He weighed this idea, dismissing it but not rejecting it, and it came to him again and again, a chorus, a dirge. When his cigar was done, he tossed the chewed end into the fire and stood. He walked over to the place where they had laid Rolando and knelt down. Rolando's eyes were closed, and a poncho was pulled up around his shoulders. He appeared to be merely sleeping, but his face was pale, and made paler by the weak sputter of the fire, now only embers. It had taken Rolando only twenty minutes to die: twenty minutes from the time the bullets smashed his leg, and in truth, he was dead the instant he stood and ran forward because there was no remedy within seven hundred miles that could have saved him. As the column withdrew, he'd been carried uphill toward the place the pack animals had been picketed. Moro had worked desperately to staunch the bleeding, but he was a physician, not a surgeon, and by the time the femoral artery had been dredged up from the shattered leg and clamped off, most of the life within the young man had drained away and slopped off the rubber poncho.

He had been twenty-three years old.

From out of the darkness came the sound of the pick breaking up the rocky earth and the chuffing of a shovel. A proper grave was being dug, a meter deep, anyway, and Rolando would soon be buried as befitted a man who'd given his life for what he believed. There would be no graveside eulogies. Guevara had spoken to the men when the column had stopped and the guards had been posted. He'd reminded them that the first to fall in combat was Cuban. He told them that sacrifice would unify them, Bolivians and Cubans together, and unity was the only way their army would grow. What lay before them was more toil and more sacrifice, but all of them knew that.

What Guevara did not tell them was that he had searched the length and breadth of his heart and found it impossible to feel grief. He was not uncaring, but death had taken from him so many comrades, so many friends, that he had accepted its demands as a matter of doing business. These words, he knew, the others would find incomprehensible, even heartless, and he kept them to himself.

Guevara had long expected the first loss, but it had come somewhat sooner than he anticipated. That was possibly good. The comrades had been blooded. Now it was important that the men be kept hard at it, and after he'd concluded his remarks, he had them distribute and cook three days' rations. He told the column leaders that they would be moving soon after moonrise. Guevara planned to march fifty kilometers, up the Masacuri River and then east into the San Marco Mountains. He planned to outdistance and outmarch any army unit sent to pursue them. The mules and horse were again loaded, and all the men had eaten and drawn water. Now all that remained was for the grave to be finished and for Guevara, somehow, to smother the thought that had embroidered itself onto his consciousness: *Rolando was nothing.*

There was a voice at his elbow.

"It's time, Comandante," Joaquin said.

Guevara took the beret from his head and placed it in Rolando's dead hands. Tuma and Willy pulled the poncho over his face and snapped the buttons all around. Carefully, they lifted the corpse and carried it to the grave. Guevara stood and slipped his rifle sling over his shoulder.

As the rations were being prepared, Joaquin had set up the radio and listened to the government's news broadcast out of Santa Cruz. In a conversational tone, he reported what he had heard. "The army claims to have killed nineteen guerrillas."

"They always win on the radio," Guevara answered. "What did they report for casualties?"

"Thirteen dead, seven wounded."

It was curious that the government had revealed a true statement of its own losses. Joaquin continued: "Voice of America is reporting the army has sealed the roads into Santa Cruz."

"If they want the roads, they can have the roads."

Guevara looked up into the sky. It was gray where the clouds were and blue and silver around the moon. "The moon's high. We'll move until daylight, then rest the men. We should be able to find some cattle to eat north of the Masacuri."

The word was passed, and the columns moved out. Guevara stood and watched the men go by, nodding occasionally to the shadowed figures as they passed up the trail and into the darkened woods.

Pombo walked out of the gloom, and Guevara heard his voice.

"Where is the boss?"

"Here."

Pombo stepped over to Guevara. "Did you find my pack?" Guevara asked.

"We searched the ambush site, Comandante. It's gone. They took everything. I'm sorry."

Guevara cursed himself. The pack had contained a clean pair of trousers and a uniform shirt as well as extra magazines for his pistol and rifle. More important were his books and some papers. The loss was not irreplaceable; his operational diary and maps were carried on the old mare. But Guevara was certain he'd sent Pombo to the exact place he'd dropped his rucksack. It was likely that the army had recovered it.

"Did you eat?" Guevara asked.

"Yes," Pombo said. "I've had plenty."

Pombo joined the column and stepped off into shadow. Guevara walked with Joaquin awhile in silence. The platoon hiked past Tuma and Willy, placing the last stones on Rolando's grave.

They continued for a while, neither speaking, and then Joaquin said quietly, "I fucked up. If I had put guards farther upstream—"

"What would be different?" Guevara asked. "Someone else would be dead. Maybe you. Maybe the hunting party. Maybe me."

Joaquin shook his head. He was not as unbreakable as Guevara.

"A commander prepares the field of battle, but he doesn't roll the dice."

"I placed the men on the sandbar—in the open."

"And they beat back and defeated the enemy," Guevara said. "You did your job, friend. Your men did well. Go on, join your unit."

Joaquin entered the column behind Tuma, and Guevara stood off the trail watching the pack animals shuffle past. Dark on dark, the men walked past him like ghosts.

We are nothing.

Guevara glanced up again at the moon. He held his hand up and looked hard at it. He was shaking, but no one could see. No one but him.

17

"YOU GOT LUCKY they were only shooting thirty-caliber. Fat bullets. Cracked ribs are better than being dead." Charlie said this slowly as he wrapped a long bandage around Hoyle's chest. Santavanes stood by, helping to hold Hoyle's left arm above his head and watching him sweat and grunt.

"Does it hurt?"

"Like Chinese opera," Hoyle said.

Curiously, only Charlie laughed.

Hoyle sat at a long table in the casita at Vallegrande. The house sat on an isolated tract of woodland to the north and west of town. Lighting was provided by kerosene lamps, and a ten-horsepower generator noisily made electricity for the radio and safety lights in a photographic darkroom Smith had set up in the back part of the house. It was a low building, stucco with a tile roof, unremarkable inside and out. It was here that Valdéz and Santavanes had established the comm station, and Smith had decided that it would become their base of operations after the bombing in Camiri.

Charlie finished binding Hoyle's ribs and turned him toward the lamp to examine the gash on his forehead. "You have a head like an anvil," Charlie said.

Blood was still caked behind Hoyle's ears, though the wound to his scalp had been stitched in the field. Charlie fiddled with the cut for a few moments, pouring iodine on it, and Hoyle finally shooed him away.

"How do you feel?" Smith asked.

"Like shit," Hoyle said, and he stood and tried to stretch. The pain thwarted him, and Santavanes guided him back to the chair.

"Jesus," Hoyle muttered. There was still the possibility that he had suffered internal injuries, though after hiking back to the road, he had been pronounced healthy by a Bolivian army doctor. That meant nothing. Twice during the long, clanking truck ride to Vallegrande, Hoyle had pissed blood. In the morning a Bolivian army helicopter would take him to La Paz, where he was to be examined by a surgeon from the American embassy. Hoyle knew, as Smith did, that it would be a couple of weeks before his broken ribs would heal. Until then he was useless in the field.

Hoyle was more self-critical than critically wounded, though his chest felt like someone had run him through with a dull shovel. His indignity was not eased by the fantastic tale of bravery told by Sergeant Merán, or the offer made by the young lieutenant to write Hoyle up for a Bolivian Legion of the Condor. Hoyle told Smith plainly what had happened—that they had blundered into the guerrillas and that the Bolivians had melted away at the first shot. Of the fifteen Bolivian soldiers who had accompanied Hoyle upriver, Sergeant Merán was the only person not killed or wounded. Death, once again, had taken Hoyle into its mouth and vomited him out.

The swirl of adrenaline still gripped him, and as he remembered the firefight for the hundredth time, it seemed he had been transported outside his body. When the images from those terrible minutes flashed to mind, Hoyle saw himself as though he had watched the fight from above the trees. He saw himself lift the radio operator from the ground; he saw Merán pull the young soldier away; and he very plainly saw his own figure, a tall man carrying a black rifle, running through the brush, shoulders hunched as the bullets and tracers ripped bark off the trees around him. These memories came back so vividly that for several seconds he was unaware of Charlie standing in front of him, holding a glass of bourbon and a codeine tablet. At last Charlie said, "Boss?"

Hoyle swallowed the tablet with a shot of whiskey. The bourbon warmed away the tang of blood in his mouth.

He sat quietly, trying to extinguish the memory of the fight. It could not be said that Hoyle had been unafraid as the bullets flew. Fear snatched at him as it did any person. But fear, especially fear in combat, was something Hoyle had long ago learned how to deconstruct. A quiet sort of fatalism was his armor; even in the moment he was struck down, when the first bullet ripped off the heel of his boot and the second slammed into his flak jacket, Hoyle did not fear. The rest of it was a darkening blur.

Contact was never as bad as what came after—the empty space behind his heart, the sweat and the sustained effort to keep dreams at bay. All of this Hoyle would try to compartmentalize. This was not done consciously, but as a matter of routine. He had a place prepared for the remembrances of battle, a place without nostalgia, deep and out of the way. This was the mechanism by which he kept the violent moments from having power over him. From the memory of the firefight, he would strip all emotion, boil it down into the essence of tactical fact, a perfectly aloof nugget of history. Hoyle could not know that this method of denial would not work forever—he knew only that it had worked so far.

As the memory of the actual fight was dismantled, other things surfaced in his mind. It was more difficult for him to forget the confusing, terrifying seconds when he had regained consciousness on the sandbar. Unable to move, hardly able to breathe, he'd heard the guerrillas coming closer, counting the dead and numbering him among the corpses. This was what gnawed him, that confused moment and then the long, dreadful seconds when the shadow fell across him, when he knew the guerrillas were standing over him and all he could do was play dead and wait for the explosion of a point-blank shot behind his ear.

Hoyle was gradually aware that Valdéz and Santavanes were looking at him. They were not staring, just looking thoughtfully, for both had been in Hoyle's place. Santavanes knew Hoyle from Vietnam, and Valdéz had worked with him in Laos. They shared history as well as the profession of violence. Like Hoyle, they'd both had to dig graves in their minds.

Hoyle looked past the lantern's steady light out the front door. The dusk was a deep shade of blue. In the forest around the house, crickets sang steadily, and somewhere a monkey hooted. Even after the whiskey and the pill, something ached in Hoyle's guts, burned him like a spark thrown off of a hot fire. It was a plain, uncomplicated emotion, but like a spark, it could expand, open out, and blossom into something complex and soul-destroying. What smoldered within him was a thing more virulent and lethal than fear: It was shame.

Hoyle had lived, and men in his charge had died. He could not rationalize their deaths. The Bolivian soldiers were cowardly, and when they ran away, they were shot down. They had run and died, and Hoyle had played dead and lived. He was no better than the Bolivian corpses and he held up his glass, and Charlie came again with the bottle, pouring it nearly full.

It would be Smith's job to write a report of the firefight, detailing the accidental contact with the main body of the guerrilla force and listing the army's casualties. After the guerrillas fled, a search was made of the riverbanks. Hoyle had thought it likely that at least two guerrillas were hit, but no bodies were found. In the brush above the river, the army found a rucksack and cartridge belt, the only items, besides footprints and spent cartridges, left by the guerrillas on the field.

Now the rucksack sat on the table in the main room of the casita. Santavanes snapped open a switchblade knife, cut open the straps, and dumped the contents on the table. Smith spread them out with his hands, and Santavanes sliced his way into each pocket of the backpack, looking for concealments.

Valdéz was an extremely well-organized man, and he meticulously laid the contents of the pack out on the table. There was a pair of olive-green trousers and a uniform blouse, a pocketknife, spoon, tin cup, plastic bowl, and box of waterproof matches. A poncho and a blue plastic waterproof tarp. Some rope, a hatchet, and a folding shovel. A lensatic compass—U.S. Army issue—two magazines for an automatic pistol, and two magazines for an M2 carbine. There were colored pencils, red, green, and black, a ballpoint pen, and a spiral-bound student's notebook. The notebook's pages were blank. These were the tools, trinkets, and treasure of a common soldier.

Bound up with rubber bands, a green plastic sheet was wrapped around three books. Santavanes popped open the elastic and handed the books to Hoyle. The topmost was a dog-eared copy of *Man and His Symbols* by Carl Jung, in French. A psychology text was an odd thing to carry into combat. As Hoyle ran his thumb down the back cover, the fly sheet peeled away. Under it, pasted against the end board of the book, was a Paraguayan passport. Hoyle removed the document and opened its front cover. The picture was of a balding, middle-aged man in horn-rimmed glasses. The name on the document was Ramito Belendiz Ramerize; his occupation was listed as trade representative for the Organization of American States. There were several visas stamped into the pages, European and South American travels, but Hoyle dismissed the document as stolen and set it aside.

He reached into the pile and lifted a small memoranda book bound in fake green leather. He thumbed through it; printed on page after page were columns of three-digit numbers. "Looks like communication codes."

Folded in half, and half again, a piece of notebook paper was stuck in the leaves of the little book. A spidery hand had drafted a brief message, acknowledging receipt of something called "Manila transmission 156." The note was half encoded, three-digit numbers positioned above half the words, a fairly routine use of a communication system called a one-time pad. But under the text and its cipher was a scrawled three-letter signature: *Che*. The letters were in cursive, all lowercase and slanted up and to the right. They were underlined by a single stroke.

Santavanes looked over Hoyle's shoulder at the signature. His voice was hoarse, and it seemed as though his words were never meant to be said aloud. They had simply escaped his mouth.

"Che?" he said. "Che Guevara?"

"Bullshit," Valdéz spat. "That asshole is dead."

Hoyle looked at the signature. Perhaps it was half a signature, perhaps someone's initials.

Valdéz crowded in and looked at the paper himself. "No" was all he said.

Hoyle handed the paper and the memoranda book across the table to Smith, who took them both by the corners and held them in the lantern light to peer at them intently. His round spectacles became pools of light.

"Mr. Santavanes, we'll need photographs of all of this stuff. Make a transcript of the documents. Cable them urgent to Langley."

"You can't do that," Valdéz said. "They'll go apeshit—"

"They can make their own assessment," Hoyle said.

"No one's seen Che Guevara in public in three years—don't you think there's a reason?" Valdéz waved his hand over the little green book, like a magician trying to make it disappear.

Smith was silent. Hoyle poured himself another whiskey—just half. His ribs no longer ached, and the codeine was making him feel magnanimous.

"Do you know where he is, Mr. Valdéz?" Hoyle asked.

"He's not here. He got killed in the Congo. And if he didn't die there, Castro killed his ass when he tried to come back to Cuba," Valdéz said.

In fact, no one Western intelligence service knew where Guevara was, or even for certain that he had been in Congo. Despite the various and strongly held opinions of its operatives and analysts, the CIA didn't know. Hoyle was Guevara agnostic; he knew only that whoever commanded the guerrilla column was a master practitioner.

As the silence lengthened, Valdéz sputtered: "You send that up there, and the Directorate of Operations is going to go hermatile."

"The directorate thinks it's possible there are already Cubans in here," Smith said.

"Santavanes and me are the only Cubans in here," Valdéz scoffed. He was taking this personally.

Hoyle casually set aside the booklet and the paper. "Three years ago, Guevara gave a speech at the United Nations." He leaned back slowly in the chair, and his face was lit by the lantern. "The Cuban delegation stayed at the Algonquin Hotel. We did a black-bag job and got Guevara's fingerprints off a glass in the bathroom."

"How do you know that?" Valdéz asked, like a kid quizzing his father about Santa Claus.

"I was on the entry team," Hoyle said.

Santavanes smiled at Hoyle. *"Mi hombre,"* he said slyly.

"Bag that stuff and courier it to Langley," Smith said. "Have it dusted for prints and run against the files." He used the back of his fingernail to push the items across the table to Santavanes. "If this stuff is Guevara's, it'll have prints."

While Santavanes gathered up the books and papers, Charlie looked at the small possessions on the table. He noticed that the rifle magazines were .30-caliber—the same sort of bullet that had smashed Hoyle's ribs. Charlie kept this observation to himself.

There was another book in the waterproof packaging, a worn-out hardback that had done much traveling. A russet-colored stain sauntered across the cover of André Malraux's *La Condition Humaine*. Hoyle lifted the book, and a photograph slid from the pages.

Tucked into the front was a black-and-white picture of a plump blond woman and three small children. All were smiling, happy. The woman and the children were sitting behind a table heaped with birthday presents and, oddly, a dozen unopened bottles of Coca-Cola. The photograph had been cut with scissors. A man's face, the head and shoulders of the father, had been clipped from the picture.

Hoyle studied the photograph and ran his finger over the cut.

"What kind of guy cuts himself out of his own pictures?" Santavanes asked.

"Somebody who thinks he's already dead," Charlie said.

18

A SENSE OF extraordinary peace came to Maria as the rain shivered against the grand windows of the office. She had pushed apart the heavy floor-length curtains and lifted the sashes, throwing open the place as far as was possible to the wind outside. This was hardly ever done; His Excellency insisted that the windows be closed and the curtains drawn at all times, and it was not often that Maria was left alone in the office and free to do as she wished. Minister Alameda was at a conference in Santiago—he would be traveling for the next ten days—and Maria's officemate, the dour and contrary Señora Truillo, had departed on her annual holiday to Sucre.

Light and shadow came alternately through the great windows, and Maria could hear the rain splash down off the roof tiles and pour into the courtyard. The mail was opened, the telegrams sorted, and the phones seldom rang. There most likely would be nothing else to do for the entire day. Maria had dared even to quietly play the radio. On the Voice of America, a man sang about San Francisco, a glorious name for a city, a place where people put flowers in their hair. The music was a special luxury. Señora Truillo (no one called her Delores) did not allow the radio to be played in the office; at least, not merely for the purposes of listening to music. The radio atop the file cabinets was there to monitor news broadcasts, more particularly to listen to news reports issued by the minister, and it was properly switched off when not used for business. As the music played, Señora Truillo's empty chair seemed to assume a sort of vacant scowl.

It was not merely the absence of Señora Truillo that brightened the morning. His Excellency put out quite a bow wave himself. Maria was amazed at the difference his absence made. This morning there seemed to be something gentler, less momentous, and far less anxious about the entire place. There were, of course, the things between Maria and the minister—intimacies more than those of employer and secretary. But Alameda did his best not to show obvious attention to Maria, and though this sort of affair was not uncommon, Alameda's attitude toward it was not typically Bolivian. During the hours they worked together, the issue was not denied or even specifically hidden—it was ignored. In his workplace demeanor, the minister was almost North American. For eight hours every day, Alameda pretended, as Maria did, that there was nothing romantic between them. When they were together—alone together or around the city in the presence of others—Alameda was fawning, or remote, or amorous, as it suited him. He was a man, flesh and blood like any other. Alameda's foibles were those common to public men: He was vain, narcissistic about his person, and haughty about his position in government. But he was also taken with her—"smitten" might be the word—although he would never admit this, nor would he ever say to Maria that he loved her. And Maria knew that Alameda loved himself too much to ever really love anyone else.

Maria had come to terms with loneliness. She had few friends in La Paz. There was Señora Truillo, who was a polite though always disapproving acquaintance; they were not confidantes. Beyond a handful of contacts from work, Maria rarely spoke to other women. The wives of the other ministers avoided Maria as though she carried an electric charge. She had met one or two other mistresses but found absolutely nothing in common with them. Most were Bolivians, a few Brazilians. Many were in situations exactly like Maria's—they had apartments and stipends. Maria was friendly to them, but it went nowhere. By the mistresses Maria was resented for her education, by the wives of the other grandees Maria was resented for her beauty and for being what she was: a paramour.

Maria was a thoughtful woman, and in the face of nearly universal approbation, she'd taken refuge in the world of ideas. Books had eased her loneliness in La Paz. She read widely, in Spanish mostly, but also in French and English. That she was bright was undoubtedly one of the things that had attracted Alameda to her. She was well read and pretty and was not falsely demure. She'd come to know what was expected of her; Alameda liked conversation, and she understood what he liked in bed. Maria knew that she provided a service. In exchange, she was given a job, an apartment, and a few luxuries. Almost immediately, she'd found most social avenues were closed to her. There were occasions, rare circumstances, when other of the great men came together with their mistresses. These events were so furtive as to be untoward—celebrations in private dining rooms, or parties in another of the mistresses' apartments (the drivers would park a block away). These gatherings had about them an air of conspiracy and vice; Maria disliked them immensely. Alameda sensed her discomfort and spared her these occasions as often as possible. In this way, Maria's small, not wholly unpleasant world had constricted in the three years she'd been in La Paz.

The morning's gloom improved in a series of sun showers, and then, at last, noontime came with a high, timid sunshine. It was about then that Maria turned around in her seat and was shocked to see a man standing in front of her desk. She had not heard the door open; nor had she seen movement out of the corner of her eye. It was inconceivable that a person could enter the office and cross the space toward her desk so silently. Though she was startled, she recognized the man's face, and her alarm melted into a genuine smile.

"I didn't mean to frighten you," Hoyle said.

Maria recognized the tall North American who'd waited while his friend delivered a briefcase. She remembered the jokes about famous people, but she did not remember the man as quite so handsome. He was wearing a tweed jacket and a tie. There was a bandage high on his forehead, and his expression was disarmingly bashful.

"I don't know if you remember me," he said. "My name is Hoyle."

"I remember," Maria said.

A second passed, both of them, grown people, inwardly made into schoolchildren. Hoyle's eyes were on hers just an instant too long. He felt a pang in his chest, and the pain in his ribs redoubled it.

"I hope it's all right I dropped by," he heard himself saying. "There were a couple of things I needed to check with you."

Maria stood behind her desk and did not exactly know why. She noticed for the first time that Hoyle towered over her, a big, solidly built man.

"The minister is not in," she said.

"Actually, it was you I wanted to talk to."

"Me? Please, sit down." She gestured to a chair in front of her desk. "What is it that I can help you with?"

Hoyle sat on a couch next to a coffee table. The furniture was Scandinavian, sleek and ridiculous beneath the vaulted roof of the minister's palatial offices. As Hoyle settled into the cushions, he winced. The pain in his ribs was still sharp.

"Are you all right?"

"I'm fine," Hoyle said. He touched the bandage on his forehead. "I had an accident." He lied, as he always did, flawlessly. An embassy doctor had examined him that morning and announced that he had a bruised kidney in addition to a pair of broken ribs. Maria was looking at him with an expression of concern that required a bit more information. Hoyle said, "I bumped my head on the steering wheel."

Maria shook her head. "They drive like crazy people here."

Hoyle placed his hands in his lap. Maria noticed that he was carrying a small clutch of purple flowers.

"Hadn't you better put your flowers in some water?"

"They're for you."

"For me? Thank you." Hoyle handed them to her. "They're beautiful."

The flowers were purple and yellow inside, paper flowers sold by the cholas in the marketplace.

Hoyle smiled. "A bribe."

"Oh, I've become an important person," Maria said. She stood and placed the flowers on her desk. "Would you like some coffee?"

"Yes, thank you," Hoyle said. He did not often drink coffee but wanted any excuse for the meeting to go on. Maria walked to the coffee urn next to Señora Truillo's desk and prepared two cups.

"I'm sorry, there's no sugar. Señora Truillo locks it in her desk." Maria's expression was an encyclopedia about Señora Truillo.

"Doesn't she worry about ants?"

Maria smiled. "The ants worry about her."

She handed him a cup and saucer. Hoyle returned to the seat on the couch. He'd noticed that Señora Truillo's desk was adorned with pictures of her family. He did not know this was another of her means to register disapproval at Maria's affair.

"Do you have children?" Hoyle asked.

"Me? No. Señora Truillo is very fond of her family." A moment passed. "You're not married?"

"I was. I married my high school sweetheart. It turned out not to have been such a good idea. My job kept me gone a lot. I don't think I really blame her now. It's hard to be alone." Hoyle shrugged. "That was a long time ago. How about you?"

Maria shook her head. "I've been moving around. Nicaragua and then here."

Hoyle did not react to the lie. Maria continued, "I was in Miami once. As a little girl. My father took me for a visit."

"That's a funny town," Hoyle said.

"I don't remember much. I remember there were palm trees and people put cement birds in their front yards."

"Flamingos."

"That was it. Flamingos."

Hoyle finally got to the point. Almost to the point. "What I needed to talk to you about was a procedural thing."

Maria sat across from him, her knees primly together.

Hoyle told himself inwardly not to look at her legs and went on, "I needed some information—hypothetical, really—I needed to find out how a group of people could get into the country."

"Visas?"

"Yes. What I needed to ask you about was the procedure for visa applications. Visas into Bolivia."

Maria's eyes stayed on him, testing. "What did you want to know?"

"I wondered how a group of people might make sure their visas were granted—so they could travel together. If a group of, say, journalists were trying to get their papers all at the same time."

"We don't normally handle those requests here."

They both knew she was lying. Maria knew it acutely, and Hoyle less compellingly.

He made his voice a perfect blank. "You don't?"

"It was done in the past. Before I came to work in the ministry. All visas are handled by the Immigration Police now."

Hoyle knew that Alameda sold visas and passports. Charlie had confirmed this on their first day back in La Paz. "Oh. That's too bad," he said. "Because now I don't have an excuse for hanging around." He stood. "I won't take up any more of your time. Thank you for the coffee."

Hoyle walked toward the door, and Maria followed. The fluorescent lights buzzed overhead.

"Thank you for the flowers," she said.

"Sure." Hoyle stopped at the door.

"Do you know what kind they are?" Maria asked.

"We have some that look just like them where I was raised—in Colorado. They grow in the mountains. They're called columbines. They grow right in the snow."

"Brave little flowers," Maria said.

Hoyle felt oddly as if the world were spinning under his feet. He noticed that her skin seemed to glow, and her eyes made him think of tigers crouching in green forests. This impression took him away for a second, and when he came back, he remembered awkwardly that he had used his excuse and now he was utterly at a loss.

"Would you like to have lunch?"

"I really shouldn't," she said. "There's no one else in the office this week."

"They'll never know," he said hopefully.

"Sorry."

"Dinner?"

"I really shouldn't."

"Don't you ever eat?" Hoyle asked. He had no idea that his smile was crooked in an irresistible way. It was now Maria's turn to feel the world turning. "Coffee, something. In the future sometime?"

Maria was disarmed and answered, "Sometime, perhaps, Mr. Hoyle."

"Paul."

"All right. Paul."

Hoyle heard the massive door click behind him. He walked down the cloister, and the last few clouds rolled away from the sun, and then the wind started to blow like it was never going to stop.

.   .   .

THE POLICEMAN AT the corner was large and fat, and his gray uniform jacket was pulled tight across his belly, the buttons under enormous strain. His face was full, and below his nose was a small, square mustache flecked through with gray. As Maria passed him, he shook his head and pointed across the street.

"Where are you going?" he asked.

"Home," she said. "Calle Cochabamba."

Others tried to pass on the sidewalk, and the policeman held out his arms, pointing again back down the block. He raised his voice but did not shout, addressing the pedestrians on the corner: "They are going to close the Plaza Murillo."

"Why?" someone asked.

"Because of the protesters," he answered, and looked again at Maria. "Don't get caught in the crowd, *chica,*" he said. "Army troops are coming. Everyone move back, please. Move back."

A few people turned around, while others stood perplexed and dumb. Two young men came across the street carrying a placard emblazoned with a hammer and sickle. The policeman set after them, waddling across the street and blowing his whistle. The men shouted back at him, calling him a fascist, and quickly ran around the corner, the policeman breathlessly following. For a moment the crowd on the sidewalk milled together, the sight of the policeman chasing the protesters more comical than sinister, and most people chose to ignore the entire thing.

Maria continued down the street, prepared to turn back, but by the time she had reached Avenida Colón, she neither saw nor heard anything out of the ordinary, so she continued on her usual route home.

Hoyle had counted on this as well, that Maria would stay on her normal path. He sat parked in the Land Cruiser at the corner of Mercado and Socabaya, scanning the crowd as it passed. Neither Hoyle nor Maria had counted on a protest march. No one could have foreseen it. What had begun as a rumor in the morning was compounded by a second rumor of the deployment of military police to the congress—this drew students and, during the early afternoon, crowds of the curious. More people swarmed toward the congress building and the Plaza Murillo, and the crowds became dense. Engine idling, Hoyle waited for Maria, his meticulously planned chance encounter made increasingly unlikely by the volume of people in the street and the real possibility of a riot.

He waited, and at half past five, he was convinced he had missed her.

Within a few blocks, Maria became aware that the crowd had grown both larger and more discordant. She noticed also that it was overwhelmingly male, and younger than the office workers and professionals who normally filled the streets in the late afternoon. She attempted to turn back, but the crowd pushed her forward, and she took refuge in the door of a shop. The mood of the passing groups changed by the minute, jubilant then agitated, determined and silent, then shouting slogans and singing. Maria waited for a break in the throng, then scurried down a block, an instinct for refuge propelling her toward her apartment.

Around the corner, she was quite surprised to see a tank at the intersection. Atop it a dozen soldiers stood unemotionally, weapons on their hips, bayonets pointed into the air. The crowd moved respectfully past the high olive sides of the tank. Now and again someone in the crowd would shout "Viva Bolivia" as though it were a magic charm against being shot down by one's own army.

Maria stopped on the corner across from the tank. The sight of it and the size of it were amazing to her. She did not wish to get any closer to the square or to the large number of soldiers jumping down from the sides of a dozen trucks parked in front of the Hotel Austria. A confrontation seemed inevitable, and Maria was aware that bullets fired into crowds created random tragedy. She recrossed the street, increasingly worried, and saw a white Land Cruiser stopped at the curb. The driver leaned across the front seat and opened the passenger door.

"I think you better get in," Hoyle said.

In the crowd, someone threw a paving stone at the tank. It bounced off the armored side with a dull clang. There were a few more shouts of "Viva Bolivia," and as the tank's engine coughed over, the crowd surged away from it, like a wave drawing away from a beach.

"Get in," Hoyle said again, and this time Maria did not hesitate but climbed in and snapped the door shut after her.

"Thank you," Maria said. "I'm lucky you came by."

That he had waited for her, Maria could not know; it was Hoyle who had been lucky to pick her out from the crowd.

"Are you always this gallant?"

"It's all a question of timing," Hoyle said. He spun over the steering wheel and turned around in the street. He leaned on the horn, and the crowd parted in front of him. A clutch of students drifted past. They were carrying a blackboard taken from a classroom. On it was chalked ABAJO PULPO YANQUI, Down with the Yankee Octopus, and the slogan struck Hoyle as oddly poetic.

"Anti-invertebrates," Hoyle said, and Maria laughed brightly.

"You don't take this personally."

"Why should I? I'm not an octopus," he said, and she laughed again.

The tension was broken, and within a matter of blocks, the crowds had abated. By the time they turned up the Mariscal de Santa Cruz, traffic was returned to its normal state of chaos. It seemed incredible to Maria that three blocks away, the city went about its business, willfully ignorant to the human storm gathering at Plaza Murillo.

"Where can I drop you?" Hoyle asked.

"I live on the other side of the plaza. I'm not sure we can get there."

"We can go around."

"Optimism is a charming American trait," Maria said.

"Well, I'm doing my best to be charming."

They drove for a while, and Hoyle said, "I know you don't eat. Do you drink?"

"May I call you Paul?"

"That's still my name," he said, smiling.

"I'm not sure you understand my situation, Paul."

"I think I do," Hoyle said, and he looked at her squarely. Her beauty so unsettled him that he said again: "I think I do."

Maria looked out the window and watched the city pass. "I hope that doesn't make you judge me."

"Of course not."

They surveyed the space between them, a place measured in moral and sexual dimensions; they both knew where this could go, Maria aware of only some of the danger this liaison could pose to her. She did not know Hoyle in any more than the most superficial way. The fact that she was attracted to him did not make her any more judicious.

"I don't mean to pressure you," Hoyle said.

"You're not. It's just been a while since someone asked me to have a drink."

"I think we could find someplace quiet," Hoyle said. Quiet meant anonymous, someplace Maria would not be known. "That is, if you'd like . . ."

Maria considered the invitation. During her silence, a dozen things passed through Hoyle's mind, a host of issues beyond the normal circumstances of a man asking a woman out for a drink, factors beyond the complications of flirtation with the mistress of a powerful man. Like Maria, Hoyle had secrets to protect.

"What do you do at the embassy?" Maria asked.

"I don't work at the embassy," Hoyle said. "I'm a contractor."

"What sort of work do you do?"

"I work for a petroleum survey company." A steady enough cover, eminently plausible and much less interesting than the truth.

"And your friend Mr. Smith?"

"He's a cultural attaché."

Even Maria knew that this bland title usually denoted a spy. Again she became guarded. Spies and the friends of spies. It was a small, wild voice in her heart that said, *Go ahead, no one will know.* No one will ever know. Her life was now all given over to the demands of someone else, and for the first time in almost three years, she was alone, her time completely her own. The voice said, *This man is attractive, he is an American, and he might be of some help to you.*

"I'd love to have a drink," she said.

19

HOYLE HAD NOT slept well, drink and excitement and the pain from his ribs keeping him awake most of the night. But he knew what had kept him awake mostly was the woman. Hoyle felt sometimes that his heart was like a burned-down house, but he had been struck by her, affected the first moment he saw her, and the second, and the third. And now he sat crossing and uncrossing his legs at the small café table, remembering the moment late last night when he went to bed at the safe house on the Plaza España and caught the faintest smell of Maria's perfume on his skin. The most fleeting trace, for when he dropped her off, she had held him briefly and touched her lips to his cheek, and then she said to him that she would see him tomorrow, and they might go away together for the weekend. She had said she would like this more than anything, and now he waited in the café where Maria had said she would meet him, and he was as nervous as a man in an overturning boat. Hoyle could not know if she would really come, and he could scarcely tell if last night was real, the drinks and laughter, and now he sat trying to separate the time he had spent with her and the time that he had dreamed of her, this strangely beguiling woman.

He had been kept from sleep by the line between what he should do and what he should not. Going away with Maria, slipping off with her to the place he knew outside the city, spending the night with her—

this was a thing he should not do. If she was to be a lover, and only a lover, that would be enough. But if Maria was to be an informant (the cold, brutal word in the trade was "asset"), if she was to be a source, then he should not go away with her. He must not sleep with her. He must not be attracted, charmed, or ensnared. He must not grow beguiled.

Hoyle ordered a Paceña as cold as could be had. He needed time to wind down his thoughts. He stared out into the street. It was ten minutes to two, ten minutes until the time she had said she would meet him, and Hoyle mulled over the standards of his profession; chief among the rules was not to sleep with the help. Sex was often the handmaiden of espionage, frequently the "handle" by which intelligence assets were levered, but case officers—controllers—were not supposed to take lovers from among the ranks of their spies. Hoyle had the examples of many, many failures to guide him to this immutable law. His friend Pyle had been murdered in Saigon, and it had been over a woman. Pyle, gung ho, dumbass Pyle, chivvied and tossed off the Dakow Bridge and into a river of shit.

Hoyle's attention drifted to a table behind him. A pair of elderly men had taken to arguing over their coffee in perfect High German. They were obviously, and proudly, ex-Nazis, but Hoyle chose not to turn in his seat. He listened absently for a moment, and his mind slowly drifted back to Maria.

Hoyle had thought of nothing, exactly nothing, when he'd said, "Let's go away tomorrow—let's get out of La Paz." He'd said it as though he were a normal man who did normal things for a living. He'd said it as though Maria were a normal woman and not the possession of a minister of government.

Hoyle could not know what went on behind the cascade of dark hair and the bright, perceiving eyes. There might be danger, hazard beyond the sudden reckless moment when he'd put his arms around her and her lips had pressed against his neck and she'd whispered to him, "I'd like to see you again."

Maria might be very much more than a willing sexual partner.

And she might be nothing more.

At three minutes past two, Maria appeared around the corner of Mariscal de Santa Cruz and Avenida Camacho. She was dressed in a short aqua-colored dress and jacket; over her shoulder she carried a dark satchel, larger than a purse, and under her right arm, she clutched a small handbag. Hoyle stood and walked toward the curb, and she came on without seeing him. As she came closer, she seemed first to notice the Land Cruiser, and then her eyes fell on Hoyle. He knew that the crowd made her uneasy, and was careful not to smile so brightly. He met her at the curb and opened the door of the Land Cruiser.

"Shall we go?" he asked.

Maria glanced across the tables of La Confitería, hearing the German men still arguing, and she nodded. She stepped nimbly into the passenger seat, and Hoyle closed the door. Behind the tinted windows, Maria seemed immediately to relax; in her mind, this departure had been something of a jailbreak, and as Hoyle pulled into the stream of traffic and then sharply left onto Mercado, she let herself smile and exhale. She was free.

"How are you?"

"I am all right."

Hoyle looked over at her. To his surprise, she came close and kissed his cheek. "Hello," she said in English.

"Hi."

She said, "I'm nervous. A little nervous."

He said, "I am, too."

The city was a wonderful thing to leave behind, and they drove through the last of the roadblocks as they turned onto the *autopista* and toward the hulking mass of Huayana Pitosí, lit brilliantly by the slanting sun. Four miles up into the sky, the summit was a rolled knuckle; a white, sputtering veil of snow was torn by the wind and whirled off to the north and east. Soon the city grew thin behind them, and the highway turned toward Lake Titicaca. They talked the entire way, from exactly the place they had stopped last night, before their small kiss. Maria and Hoyle talked about themselves, and after the first lies they had told each other, everything they said was true.

She told him about boarding school in Germany and how she had hated it. About her roommate, Nusheen, an Iranian, a Baha'i, whose father was a general in the shah's army. She told him about nursing school in France. She told him it was her mother, also Maria, who had made her choose nursing as a profession. "Nurses never go hungry," her mother had told her.

Hoyle paid attention, as he had the night before, and he was entertained, engrossed, even, but he compared the things she said, sifted through them, the small facts taken together, looking for inconsistencies and contradictions. There were none. The story of Maria's life fit together and made sense. Hoyle knew it was a difficult, almost impossible thing to counterfeit. But he listened also to the things Maria did not say. She did not once mention Nicaragua. She did not once say what her father did to pay for boarding school at a German convent and nursing school in Lyon.

"I'm boring you," Maria said.

"I don't think you could do that."

"You look distracted."

"You distract me," Hoyle answered. He meant it.

"Generally, I ignore flattery," Maria said. "But I could get used to it."

They had driven for nearly an hour before she even thought to ask where they were going.

"To a place I know, the Hotel Casino de la Selva." He added, "On the Lago de Huyñaymarka. We'll be there before five o'clock."

That was far enough away, Maria thought, three hours from the city and at the southern end of the lake. Far enough away for her to be herself and no one else. She asked him to tell her about Colorado.

"I lived in Colorado Springs when I was a little boy. We moved to Chicago when my father died. I was ten."

"You miss your father."

"I guess. I didn't know him well. He didn't get along well with my mother. I don't think she really got along with anyone." Hoyle drove for a moment and then said, "Mother drank."

Maria was silent, listening.

"Anyway, I was sent to military school. And to summer camps during vacations. After I graduated from high school, I went to Colorado College. That first Christmas I went back to Chicago. Mother had remarried, a man named Mansullen. He'd been a tennis pro at the Winnetka country club." Hoyle smiled. "We didn't get along too well, either. I haven't been back to Chicago since."

"What was your mother's name?" Maria asked.

Hoyle had not said it, and he stared at Maria blankly. For an instant he could not remember, and it was as though he were an imposter, a thing masquerading as human, a creature that had been hatched from some cuckoo's egg. Hoyle narrowed his eyes, remembering his mother's tall elegance—even drunk, she was regal—and a hundred other things came to his mind, the smell of her perfume, the clink of her jewelry, the gloves she wore to luncheon. Hoyle's mind threatened to collapse into a howling blank, and then he said finally, "Viveca."

All of this was more than Hoyle had ever told one person. It was more than he ought to have said, and it was more candid, more true, than he should have revealed. Why didn't he care? Why hadn't he told Maria one of the dozen covers he had memorized? Why had he told her anything at all?

"Now I've bored you," Hoyle said.

"Of course not."

Maria had listened carefully.

The long, dusty road from Pucarani jogged west, and just as unexpectedly, the rutted track became an asphalt road and rounded the base of a hill. Hoyle turned his eyes to the road and said quietly, "We're almost there."

THE HOTEL CASINO de la Selva perched on a thumb of land jutting into Lago de Huyñaymarka, a vast C-shaped embayment at the extreme southern end of Lake Titicaca. The hotel pointed exactly northwest toward the Estrecho de Tiquina, the narrow gap separating Huyñaymarka from Lake Titicaca proper.

The road switched back and climbed the rolling scrub-covered hills. Clinging to an almost precipitous slope, the hotel came into sight, the main building and dozen yellow bungalows scattered along terraced walks and these surrounded by several stands of pine. The trees were peculiar because the hills beyond were mostly bare, and their dusky green color was extraordinary. The hotel had been built by an eccentric British gentleman, Lowry, once a consul and now a quiet and dignified alcoholic. The place never really caught on, perhaps because of its name; there was no casino, nor was there a forest, just the few pines, scrub, juniper, and cactus. But these were the only things that might disappoint. The Hotel Casino de la Selva commanded what might well be the most beautiful view in the world.

Immediately below the terraces were the Islas de Huyñaymarka, Kalahuta, Incas, Suriqui, and Pariti. To the north, visible beyond the narrow Tiquina Straits, were the Island of the Sun and the Island of the

Moon. The Inca called these Manco Capac and Mama Ocllo, husband and wife, brother and sister, and Titicaca itself was the cradle of the entire universe. That was not hard to believe. In the dusk, the entire place seemed perched on the pinnacle of the world, and the islands jewels in the crown of the setting sun.

Hoyle parked just away from the portico under a stand of pine, and Maria watched the sun edge into the silver vastness beyond the islands. In the three years she had been in Bolivia, Maria had never left the city. She never could have imagined a place like this existed just hours from the crowded, dusty place called La Paz. Maria thought, *Enrique would not come here,* and then she thought, rather sadly, that perhaps he had always come here.

"I'll check us in," Hoyle said.

Maria took her eyes from the sunset and smiled at him.

"Would you like to come in with me? It's okay." "Okay" meant that this was a place without judgment, and it was. Lowry cohabitated here famously with an Argentinean opera singer while his wife lived wrathfully in London. The clientele was almost entirely European; more specifically, the guests were almost always members of the diplomatic community. The couples who stayed at the hotel were not always spouses.

"I'll wait here," Maria said. "I hope you don't mind."

"I don't mind," Hoyle said.

She found his hand and said, "Thank you for bringing me here." Her eyes stayed on his, and he bent forward. Her lips touched his lightly, then again, more firmly, and her heart seemed to be beating like a drum in a parade.

THE WALK TO the bungalow was an eternity, and then purgatory on top of that. Maria paced the terrace for the few minutes it took the bellman to set the luggage into the bedrooms, fluff open the curtains, and mumble, *"Gracias, Señor,"* for the dollars Hoyle pressed into his hand. As the latch clicked behind him, Maria stood rooted by the open doors to the terrace, a cold wind already rising from the lake and the bright red sky of sundown. Hoyle took a step toward her, and he meant to say that there was a bottle in his suitcase, he meant to offer her a drink, her choice of bedrooms, he meant to say anything, but instead the words choked off in his throat and they moved toward each other and his arms went around her waist. Her perfume befuddled him, made him dizzy, and then he felt her lips open on his, he tasted her tongue, and his breathing almost stopped.

Three days ago he had been struck down by bullets, and now he was here. Hoyle could not have been more surprised if he had been dragged into heaven by angels with trumpets.

Maria tilted her head back and turned around in his arms. Hoyle embraced her, his chest against her back and his lips against the back of her neck. He kissed her ears and her cheeks, holding her from behind.

Maria said aloud, not whispering, "This is the most perfect place I have ever been."

She could feel his arms moving around her waist, and again he kissed her neck. As she turned her head, his lips found hers. He slipped his tongue into her mouth and tasted her kiss, hot and pleasant, and Maria dropped her jacket off her shoulders.

He ran his hands down her sides, down to her narrow little waist, and onto her lovely back. She pressed herself up against him, and they fumbled with each other's clothing. Zippers and buttons, then straps and elastics and the heady smell of flesh, and Hoyle felt the heat of her naked breasts against his skin. He touched them first with his finger-tips. Touched them where the skin was white and most tender. And then lightly, lightly, his fingertips passed over her nipples, gently over each one. He again kissed her neck, and his tongue ran across her mouth. She felt his hands close over her breasts, cupping them, gently squeezing. And then his hands went down, down her chest, down across her stomach. One hand stopped on her hip, and one hand slid slowly, slowly, onto the mound between her legs.

They tumbled then into one of the beds, a sighing, grunting tangle of limbs. He ran his hands through her dark hair, and kisses were with-out number. She rolled on top of him; he felt her beautiful thighs opening, and she guided him into her. She gasped and he heard her say his name, once, twice, and he pushed into her. Hoyle pressed against her with his entire weight. A warmth started to spread from her ab-domen, and tingling, hot jolts expanded across her body. She clutched her nails into his back and shivered. Maria felt like a million feathers had avalanched over them. Hoyle again kissed her neck, and this time he tasted sweat. He rejoiced in the taste of her. It gave him a primal, wild joy to hear her cry out. And as she climaxed, he pressed her down on the bed and held her tightly.

Now he was beyond anything but desire for her, and he felt her legs shift and the soft caress of thigh around his waist. They had both abandoned reason, thought, tossed away everything but the want of pleasure. She whispered almost in a hiss, "Take me. Take me. Take me." The words amazed him, electrified him. With this she conquered, lured him to that place where his soul touched hers, and it was chaos and lightning, and he heard her again calling out, and his skin was on fire, and then ten thousand colors of light exploded in his head, and for a split second he was stunned, as baffled as though he had been pulled into a whirlpool. His breath escaped in a long groan, and Maria held on for both of their lives, clutching him, pulling him back from the yawning brink of emptiness.

HOYLE WOKE AS dawn rolled down from the hilltop behind the bungalow, and the lake below was like a sheet of unpolished garnet. His eyes opened, but he remained perfectly still in the bed, as was his habit. He listened to the sound of Maria breathing steadily next to him, and he was surprised when she reached out her hand and touched him. She was awake as well.

"I'm here," he said.

He turned to face her. Maria had pulled her hair back with a rubber band, and with her face half buried in the pillow, she looked like a child. Hoyle's head rested against his arm, and he pushed a strand of hair away from her face.

"Good morning," she said.

"Did that really happen?"

"It did."

"How are you?"

She looked at him, and he held her hand. "I suppose I should be used to all this sneaking around."

"We didn't sneak," Hoyle offered.

"Of course we did," she said.

"Are you okay?"

"I'm fine. I want to stay here. I want La Paz to drop off the end of the world."

"I'll make sure that happens."

Maria smiled and they kissed. The light from the terrace spilled on them, and for the first time, she noticed the scar under Hoyle's jaw. The former nurse realized that the wound had probably been life-threatening. "What happened here?" she asked, touching under his chin.

"I was shot."

Maria did not seem surprised. "Were you in the war?"

"What war?"

"Vietnam."

"I was in Vietnam," Hoyle said. Vietnam and other places, but Vietnam was not a lie.

"Were you a contractor also in Vietnam?"

"I did the same kind of work."

"Who shot you?"

"A man who killed my friend. His name was Fowler."

"He was not Vietnamese."

"He was an enemy."

A moment passed, and Maria did not see in Hoyle's eyes the burden of any sin.

"Is Hoyle your real name?"

"Yes," he answered. "What is your real name?"

Maria pressed her lips together. They each had secrets, and since they'd made love, they had secrets together. She said evenly, "Maria is my given name. My family name is Cienfuegos."

Hoyle held her steadily in his gaze. He had already bared his soul to her, his life, if not what he did for a living, and he knew that Maria had suspected he was a spy from almost the first moment she'd laid eyes on him.

"You are Cuban," Hoyle said.

"I am."

"Did Alameda help you leave Cuba?"

"No. He helps me to stay here. I left Cuba on my own. Enrique gave me papers and work." Her eyes seemed tired, weary of the world. "He gives me a place to live, clothing, and money. I guess what we have is a pretty standard arrangement."

"Don't be cruel to yourself."

"You really don't judge me, do you?"

"No. I don't judge you. I try not to judge anyone."

"Very Christian."

"I'm not a Christian," Hoyle said. "At least not much of one. I try not to judge people because I have never done it well."

Maria got up to bathe, and Hoyle sent out for a breakfast of coffee, Salteñas, and fruit. They were brought to the bungalow by a young man in a crisp white jacket. There were also Sunday newspapers, *The New York Times* and the *Times* of London, both exactly one week old, folded and ironed to look as though they were as new as the day. This bit of anachronism was considered part of the hotel's charm, as Lowry always arranged to have British, American, French, and German newspapers shipped by air and driven to the lake. Even a week late, his guests appreciated news of home.

Wrapped in a robe, Maria padded to where Hoyle sat in front of the terrace doors. It was still too cold to sit on the balcony.

Maria looked out over the lake. The drive back to La Paz stood in the room with them, as real as any human interloper. It was that part of Sunday morning when the illusion collapses and the week looms ahead.

"What are we going to do now, Paul Hoyle?" she asked. "Now that we have this thing together?"

"I want to continue to see you."

"And make love to me?"

"Yes. Can you trust me?"

"I don't trust easily," she said.

"You shouldn't."

"I don't trust, and you don't judge," she said. "Do you think we can go on like that?"

Hoyle looked again at her. She was the most beautiful and mercurial woman he had ever seen in his life. He had almost forgotten that he should not be here.

"There's no point in going on if we can't trust each other," Hoyle said.

"Then we will trust each other," Maria said.

20

ON THE AERO chart, the place was called LV-36. It was an airfield mostly because the map said it was—a forlorn piece of real estate gouged out of the trees in hopes that an airplane might come. Hills stood close around it, some dappled by cloud, some washed out by the hazy sky and lolling away, one after another, each less distinct than the next. There was no tower, not even a wind sock, and the field was decidedly higher on its northern end. This made the place seem off-axis, as though it were a facet cut from a lopsided rock, a bewitched surface where nothing could be plumb, straight, or level.

It was not yet noon, and already the heat was punishing. Standing with Valdéz and Santavanes, Smith was exhausted and jangled from a twelve-hour drive from Tatarenda, north all the way to Santa Cruz and then east over a hundred miles of bad road to Vallegrande and the airfield. The drive had given him hours to think of the cable he'd sent to Langley, the details of the fight at the river, an account of Hoyle's injury, and the particulars of the ambush. His message had been a masterpiece, for although it had acknowledged that the Bolivians had been soundly defeated, it distracted with the details of the counterattack and tantalized with the list of items recovered from the rucksack. Between every line, a jackass could read that the guerrillas controlled the countryside. This fact was easily ignored.

Defeat for the Bolivian army was routine; the contents of the rucksack were an astonishment. Smith's cable had fallen like a bombshell in the hallways at Langley. Code breakers set to work on ciphers, hand-writing experts peered though magnifying glasses, fingerprint technicians sweated over smudges, information analysts and middle managers were all put into a dither. The entire American intelligence apparatus was jolted by the possibility that the insurgency in Bolivia might be led by Che Guevara, a man the Company officially considered dead. When Langley cabled back, Smith half expected to be ordered home. But he was not. Instead of being recalled, he had his mandate vastly expanded.

Smith was being sent an airplane, and its contents were fierce.

The Directorate of Operations had assigned a new code name to the Bolivian venture. This itself was a mark of front-burner status and keen interest. Smith's operation would henceforth be called Bush Mechanic, and the mission was now specifically to terminate the insurgents. The previous tasking had been to frustrate the insurgency, the rhetorical difference translating into a full measure of force, murder, and mayhem to be applied individually and collectively against the guerrillas.

With these expanded responsibilities, two operational entities were being assigned to Smith. These units were code-named Famous, this prefix indicating that they were U.S. Army Special Forces operating under CIA control. The first outfit was to be called Famous Lawyer and the second, to follow in three weeks, Famous Traveler.

Lawyer was a hunter-killer group, a thirteen-man Special Forces A Team armed to the teeth. All were experienced operators seasoned in Vietnam, and until this assignment, they'd been serving as instructors at the School of the Americas in Panama. Famous Lawyer was a black outfit, meaning it did not officially exist, and neither the ambassador nor the military attaché would be informed of their presence.

The follow-on group, Traveler, *did* exist and would be deliberately inserted with much hoopla. The job of Famous Traveler would be to train a Bolivian Ranger battalion; their activities would take place in the public domain, with press and photo opportunities. They would also provide a perfect diversion.

While training took place in the wide open, Famous Lawyer would surreptitiously find and fix the enemy, locating the guerrilla forces and base camps so the Bolivian army could at least try to take the field. The hunters were the lethal doppelgänger of the teaching team—American intervention in covert and deadly earnest.

About half an hour after noon, a C-130 cargo plane materialized from the heat. The huge aircraft droned through the sky, struggling to make itself visible, and then touched earth in a ruddy cloud of dust. As the propellers reversed pitch, the plane came toward them, lurching over the uneven places like some great clumsy animal that had broken free from a pen. The plane was bare metal, painted with a pair of small blue stripes down the length of the fuselage. There was a decal on the tail that advertised SOUTHERN AIRWAYS, but it might well have said anything. The paint job was what the industry called "low viz"; not camouflaged, just nonmilitary and forgettable. The paperwork indicated that the aircraft was a charter out of Panama, and its livery meant nothing. Even its tail number, N-8675J, was fake. The plane turned around at the end of the runway; its pilot was a dirt-strip maestro, shutting down the starboard engines so that not a wisp of dust blew in the direction of the waiting men.

The tail of the aircraft inched open, vehicle ramps were thrown over, and two jeeps and a truck were driven out of the plane as the engines idled. Smith and the others walked forward; a tall man with fair hair and a drooping mustache swung his legs from behind the steering wheel of the first jeep. He wore khaki trousers and a green polo shirt. His men were dressed in similar getups—chinos or blue jeans and short-sleeved shirts. None wore uniforms, though some carried rifles and others wore pistols in shoulder holsters. They were a hard-looking bunch.

Smith walked to the jeep and shook the tall man's hand. "Welcome to Bolivia," he said.

"I'm Holland," the tall man answered. "We're your lawyers." Valdéz noticed that the jeeps were filled with Russian-made weapons and the truck was loaded with ammunition.

"Man, you brought some stuff," Valdéz said.

"Enough to get started." Holland wore a .45 automatic in a leather holster under his left arm. Smith noted that he was tanned. All of his men were; the lawyers had spent much time in the open.

"Who's the head spook?" Holland asked.

"I'm running the in-country effort," Smith said, then he nodded to Santavanes and Valdéz. "These are my associates."

Holland put out his hand. "Name's Rollo."

"Javier," Valdéz said.

"Santavanes."

"Didn't catch your first name?" Holland said.

"Señor Santavanes."

Holland took Santavanes's measure. It wasn't likely that they would ever get along, but they understood each other at once.

"We didn't get much notice from Panama that you were coming," Smith said.

"Neither did we," Holland answered.

Behind them, the aircraft's engines roared, and they were all silent while the noise broke over them. Holland looked down the length of the runway as the C-130 took off. Trailing a plume of red dust, the huge aircraft climbed gracelessly into the sky. In a moment it was swallowed by cloud and lost from sight, and a few seconds later, even the sound of its engines had faded. The aircraft had been on the ground under five minutes.

"Where do you want us to set up?" Holland asked.

BY NIGHTFALL THE casita at the end of the runway had been augmented with sandbags and concertina wire. The Lawyers erected three large tents behind the house, one in which to sleep, one where they would cook and eat, and a third as an operations shop. They'd also placed three complicated-looking antennae on the roof of the adobe, a high-frequency wire, a short UHF antenna, and a odd-looking contraption, a set of aluminum tubes resembling a caduceus that would enable them to ricochet messages off orbiting satellites. To Valdéz, it was all very interesting, but for Santavanes, the tents, sandbags, and comm gear gradually bred a smoldering sort of annoyance. He did not like Green Berets much. Santavanes considered them a blunt instrument, while he considered himself to be a scalpel.

After dinner, Smith, Valdéz, Santavanes, and Holland sat in the main room of the adobe. Smith lit a lantern and poured some bourbon. Holland studied Hoyle's map, which had been salvaged from the bombed offices in Camiri. Santavanes ate the last of his dinner, beans and rice, and watched Holland pace in front of the map.

"Who put this together?" Holland asked.

"Hoyle," Smith answered. "He got his ribs broken in the ambush. He's back in La Paz for a couple of weeks."

Holland studied the terrain. On the map, the likeliest places for

guerrilla bases had been circled with grease pencil. Holland's understanding of topography was as keen as Hoyle's. In the Ñancahuazú
Valley and the adjoining countryside, there were tens of thousands of
places to hide but only so much water. Holland knew, as Hoyle did,
that water was as necessary to the guerrillas as ammunition.

It was likely that they would move and operate close to the watercourses. The places the rivers met, the junctions of valleys, were likely
locations for base camps, storage caches, and communications stations.
The networks of rivers and tributaries suggested a probable set of paths
and intersections; places that were safe and places to be avoided. These
facts of geography reduced the searchable areas considerably.

"How long will it take Traveler to train a counterguerrilla unit?"
Smith asked.

"That depends—on how screwed up the Bolivians are and how
good you want them to be."

"They have to be good."

"Six months," Holland said.

August, Smith thought. It will be August before the Bolivians have
any reliable units.

"You might get some faster tactical results if I put some of my people forward," Holland said. "To advise the Bolivian field commanders."

Santavanes snorted. "You go out with the Bolos, and you'll get
waxed."

"You think so." Holland's eyes were directly on Santavanes. His
statement ended flatly, not like a question. Like a statement.

"I'll tell you something, Major. Paul Hoyle is one of the best field
operators I ever met. He's got more jungle time than you could ever
dream about. He went out there and got hit by two bullets. It's a fucking miracle he's alive. I don't know how good you think you are, but
the people we are up against—they are goddamn good. As good as
Charlie. As good as the Khmer Rouge. Good. This isn't going to be
over in a weekend."

Holland said nothing; he turned and again looked at the map.

Smith was not a conciliatory person, but his words lessened the tension. "I want to limit your contact with the Bolivian army. Your people
will operate solo. I want to start with recons and long-range patrols.

First I want you to find the bad guys and tell me where they're moving. Then I'll make a decision on how to kill them."

"Your call," Holland said. "If you want this thing over fast, put some of my people into the field to lead the Bolivians."

"Not yet," Smith said.

Holland drank down the rest of his bourbon.

"When can you get started?" Smith asked.

"I'd like to get an overflight of the area," Holland said. "I want my team leaders to see the valley from head to foot."

"We can arrange that."

"I can start putting teams out by the end of the week."

"Good."

The meeting was over.

"Thanks for the whiskey," Holland said, and he walked back to his tents.

When he was gone, Santavanes tossed his tin plate into the bucket in the kitchen. "I think his beret's too tight."

Smith swung his feet up on a table and leaned back in his chair.

Scrubbing his plate in the lukewarm water, Santavanes continued to lay it on, cynical and facetious. "But I gotta admit, we've got a great location here. Five-thousand-foot runway—we can bring in a squadron of gunships. A hundred more advisers. We can really escalate."

"There isn't going to be any escalation," Smith said.

"It's already escalating, Mr. Smith. We got two teams of Green Berets we didn't ask for."

"They'll be kept on a leash," Smith said. He hoped that would be true.

Santavanes wiped his plate with a dishrag and waxed nostalgic. "You know, I was in Congo when it went to shit. In Brazzaville. Very dramatic. The CIA station chief and I got pulled off a roof by a Belgian helicopter. Tracers flying all over the place—it looked like New Year's Eve."

"And your point is?"

"That was six months after they sent in the Green Berets."

Smith gave Santavanes a withering look.

"Hey, it's just a story," Santavanes said. "It could never happen here."

21

TANIA WOKE ON the bed in her apartment. One of her shoes was on, one was off. Her suitcases were piled in the corner of the bedroom, and her coat was pulled over her. When she fell into bed, she had been too exhausted even to pull down the covers.

Beyond the windows, night sounds from the Calle Campero lifted her slowly out of her dark, calamitous sleep. She opened her eyes but did not move. The lights burned brightly in her bedroom; she recognized a few of her possessions and the noises from the street, but it took her a few minutes to realize where she was.

She had been traveling, and now she was home.

No. Not home. She was back in La Paz.

It was now two A.M. Tania sat up and swung her legs under her. She took off her dress, then her stockings. In her underwear, she picked up the Venezuelan passport and padded through the dark apartment out into the kitchen. She opened the window above the sink and ripped pages from the passport. She used a cigarette lighter to burn these one by one, turning on the faucet to put out the flames when each of the pages had burned, and then she stirred the ashes with her fingers so they would pass easily down the drain with the running water.

The Venezuelan passport was an expert forgery. It bore Tania's photograph but was issued in the name of Maragethe Isabel Bastos, a stenographer from Caracas. Tania had used the papers to travel from

La Paz to Buenos Aires. The passport had served her on her mission, and now it must be destroyed. Tania burned the page with her photograph, and last she burned the cover of the passport, this taking a while longer. After she had run tap water on these ashes, she scooped them up with her hand, wrapped them in tissue, and flushed them down the commode.

Tania had used the passport to carry out the errand assigned by Guevara—meeting with the Argentinean Communist Carlos Sandoval. While in Buenos Aires, Tania had arranged travel for Sandoval and a French leftist, Rene D'Esperey. They would arrive in La Paz in ten days. After they entered Bolivia, Tania would guide them to Guevara's base in the Ñancahuazú.

While in Buenos Aires, Tania had done the work Havana requested of her. She had impressed Sandoval and D'Esperey as a dedicated and accomplished agent. After their meetings, after their travel was arranged and she had gathered messages to be communicated to Guevara, Tania dutifully reported to her KGB controllers.

This had been done with great care and secrecy, for not only did Tania have to evade the Argentine *gendermaeria,* she also had to make sure she was not under countersurveillance by Sandoval or D'Esperey. In a posh hotel in Buenos Aires, Tania again met the fat man she knew as Robert. Tania was ushered into a luxurious, sprawling suite where she was quite surprised once more to meet her "auntie," the Soviet agent who'd visited La Paz after her breakdown.

Tea was delivered on a silver tray, and Tania was thoroughly debriefed on her meetings with Sandoval and D'Esperey. She did not know the reasons why Guevara wanted these men to be taken into Bolivia, and neither Sandoval nor D'Esperey had offered much information. Robert gave Tania written orders to cooperate with Guevara and to safely guide Sandoval and D'Esperey to the base camp.

The aunt told Tania that her work continued to be of the greatest importance to Moscow. As a token of the esteem in which she was held, Tania had been promoted to the rank of major in the KGB. This recognition came complete with a copy of a personnel file stating that Tania held a regular commission with a date of rank effective from January 1, 1967. The paperwork was legitimate; Tania had indeed been inducted into the Komitet Gosudarstvennoy Bezopasnosti as a regular officer. The aunt was particularly pleased to show Tania a medal in a folding leatherette case, the Order of the Red Star, a Soviet decoration for distinguished intelligence service. Tania saw instantly through the charade but pretended happiness and pride. She knew exactly what they were attempting to do. The medal and the dossier were stratagems, psychological ploys to keep Tania on the team.

She wondered just how stupid Robert and the aunt thought she must be.

Tania made notes about operational procedures and was given a second series of postcards to mail and an accommodation address in Mexico City, and Robert promised they would not directly contact Tania unless it was a dire emergency. He continued to make promises, and Tania quit listening but came back to reality when Robert handed over a cash bonus and operational funds totaling twenty-five thousand U.S. dollars. The money was something she could use. It was something real.

At the end of their meeting, the auntie gave Tania a vial of yellow triangular pills. These, she said, were from a doctor friend in Mexico. They would help Tania sleep. Tania accepted the drugs and put them in her purse.

Tania returned to La Paz and passed through customs using the Venezuelan passport. She then took a taxi to a pharmacist's shop near her apartment. Fearing the auntie had given her some kind of slow-acting poison, Tania took the pills to the chemist. She told the man behind the counter that she had lost the label from the pill bottle; she wondered if he could tell her what sort of medicine it was. The man went into the back of the shop, consulted a few thick books, and returned to tell her that the pills were lithium carbonate. Tania asked what the drug was for. With some embarrassment, the chemist told her that the pills were for manic depression. Tania thanked him and went directly from the shop to her apartment. The pills, like the ashes of her passport, were flushed down the commode.

Tania put two kettles on to boil and drew a bath. She allowed the tub to fill, then added the contents of the kettles, for she liked the water punishing hot. She stepped out of her panties, slipped her bra from her shoulders, then stepped into the tub. The water at first burned her feet and ankles, the sensation a delicious wave of scorching, then numbness. She lowered herself into the water, felt the same wave of stinging, then heat, then a prickly numbness as the nearly scalding water inched up her thighs to her groin and then carried over her tummy and hips. Last lowered into the hot liquid was her back, the water again nearly blistering her, the sensation of hot wires touching up her spine, then over her shoulders, then her breasts and nipples as she submerged.

Tania pointed her toes toward the base of the tub, her body totally covered by hot water except for the circle of her face. Her skin reddened as her thighs, shoulders, and breasts sank just an inch below the surface, and as she submerged her ears, she could no longer hear the small sounds from the street outside the window. The silence was complete; she was isolated in a world of nearly burning water. All she had was the pain it caused her, and that was all she needed. This place of silence and torment she had made for herself, and had often made for herself, since she was a little girl in Germany, this had been her private ritual and place of refuge.

Tania closed her eyes. She had only to wait a few moments, and the dream would come. It was always the same dream. The sensation of the hot water seemed to go away, and Tania was transported to a brook overarched by boughs of hemlock. Cattails rustled at the edge of the deep, tea-colored stream. She was drifting, being carried slowly by the water. Gentle but unimaginably strong, the current moved her along the bank. White flower petals rained from the trees above.

The same dream. Always the same dream.

Perhaps it was a thousand years ago. Tania was a woman of noble birth. Various calamities befell her family—murder, insanity, circumstances that were not elaborated on—and Tania went off to gather flowers in the forest. On the bank of a stream, she fell; in the dream, Tania could not swim and did not try. A flowing gown buoyed her up for a while, only a while, before the stream turned to a deeper place. The woods loomed over the water, and weeds and tangle brush clutched at her dress; slowly, inescapably, the stream pulled her down, first her hips, then her legs tangled in skirts, her long hair spreading like an aura around her. She was drawn underwater, her hands languidly clutching at air, her head tipped back, her mouth half open. Slowly, with exquisite finality, she drowned.

It was there, on the banks of the stream, that her beloved prince would find her. In her dream, Tania imagined the grief and shock of the man who would chance upon her body, her spirit borne away and the corpse white and waxlike yet still enchantingly beautiful. No man could look upon that body without being extinguished by sorrow and grief.

She would finally be loved.

The simple tragedy was that she would be loved too late, and her prince would mourn her unto the point of madness. This was always Tania's dream. A beauty not reckoned by the world would at last be embraced—taken whole and made beyond value only by death.

TANIA WOKE HOURS later. Morning light was spilling through the bathroom window, and the sounds from the street had grown angry. The quiet of the wee hours had been devoured by the calamitous grinding of the morning's rush. The water in the tub had grown cold. Tania's skin was cold. But she continued to lie in the tub, not moving and doing her best not to sob. She had hoped that she would not wake from the dream. She had hoped that the water in the bath would do what the water in her dream could not—end this suffering.

Slowly, with dawdling bending of elbows and knees, like an old, old woman, Tania lifted herself from the tub. Dripping, nude, she walked through the hall and into the living room. She caught a glimpse of herself in the mirror. Her wide hips, her breasts hanging lower than she had remembered, her hair dark, wet, and matted in ringlets against her skin.

I am a fright, she thought. I am a horror.

It was then that she caught sight of an envelope that had been slipped under the apartment door. A white envelope on the carpet a few inches from the frame. In blue ink, a flowing hand had written: TANIA.

She stood, naked, and felt her heart begin to pound. The handwriting, she knew, was Robert's.

The Russians wanted more from her. Greater efforts, more elaborate betrayals. Supreme sacrifices.

Tania's mind seemed to be opening, and all the world poured in, like the ocean flowing into a stricken ship. The weight of it all was overwhelming, and for the first time since she had begun her double life, she thought of running away. But where could she go? Where could she run from Robert and Auntie? Where could she go that they would not find her?

Tania's knees buckled, and she hit the floor.

Nude, wet, and shivering, she held her face in her hands and began to sob.

PART
II

By Necessary
Means

22

A HUNDRED STEPS ON, then another hundred, and what had appeared from the valley to be the ridgeline was only a false summit. Behind Guevara, the sun was slipping from the sky, and for a long minute he stared upslope, panting. His hands trembled as he wiped the sweat from his eyes. Almost exactly twelve hours ago, his asthma had returned, and throughout an arduous day's march, he'd felt the coils of it winding about his throat. This day had been hell on two legs. As the column moved out of the valley, he found himself farther and farther behind; first with the center group, then the rear guard, and finally, as the men marched to the ridgeline where they would spend the night, Guevara found himself alone on the trail. He was the last man to make the ridge.

Below him, a steep hillside plunged west, and under the bluffs spread the gathering dark. Guevara had continued to press the training march north, following first the Ñancahuazú and then the Masacuri. Two weeks had stretched into three, then four. The passage since they left the banks of the Masacuri had been a nightmare; the terrain was a torment, and the maps were a joke. These mountains, the San Marcos by name, had proved an implacable foe.

At least a dozen times since the ambush on the river, the column had to retrace their steps when cliffs barred the way. Yesterday there had been no water, and the men suffered from thirst. The day before, it had rained for eighteen straight hours. Today, as they parched beneath a merciless sun, mud sucked the boots from their feet. Even on the steepest hillsides, the earth oozed up to their ankles. Guevara had never seen such mud.

From his vantage on the ridge, he considered the low, undulating set of mountains. Beyond this final obstacle lay his immediate goal: the Rosita River. In the reddish light, the mountains very much resembled waves on the ocean, lined up one after another. He was not given to pessimism, but the distance to the plain staggered him. If they continued to move at the same pace, it would be five days before they hit the plain and the Rosita. Then and only then would he turn back for base.

A smudge of blue smoke wafted from the ridgeline above, indicating that the fires had been started for dinner. He knew that the eyes of his men were upon him. He did not want to be seen as a straggler. Using his rifle as a staff, Guevara pulled himself up and trundled on. Sagging beneath the weight of his pack, he lurched past the clearing where the mules and the red mare had been picketed. He said not a word to anyone but wobbled to the edge of the camp and dropped his rucksack. Joaquin could see that the comandante was exhausted and did his best to busy the men as Guevara set up his hammock. Joaquin organized the gathering of wood and water and the posting of sentries—the simple tasks that would grant them hot food and security for a night's rest.

Wheezing, Guevara went through the motions of preparing his sleeping place and then walked to the edge of the tree line. His heart still pounded, but it was better now that he was off the trail. His throat rattled as he drew breath. He popped a hydrocortisone tablet into his mouth and crushed it between his teeth. The bitter powder slid down his throat, and he imagined that the medicine would scald his asthma. Like biting his tongue, it was a tactic he'd employed since childhood. He somehow believed that the disease itself would be discomforted by the sour medicine. In a few moments he did breathe easier, but he still felt the high, sharp ache in the back of his chest and a hammering in his throat that mimicked his heartbeat.

Guevara sat on his hammock, his body pounded with fatigue. From the camp, he could hear the coming and going of the men, and slightly downslope, the mules shuffling about. He concentrated, trying to gain control of his breathing. He took out his journal and wrote: *A bad day for me. I was exhausted and made it through on willpower alone.*

His pen stopped, and he thought. He had entered the camp like some sort of shuffling hobo. It would not do that he sat alone while the others worked and prepared the meal. He was in command, and bad day or not, he must still be seen to lead. Carrying his notebook, he went toward the sound of voices. It was full dark now, and he felt a bit recovered. He straightened his back as he walked toward the fire. The clearing smelled of sweat and lard and gun grease; the last of the cornmeal was being boiled together with jerky made from a wild hog.

As Guevara drew near, Pombo smiled and said, "Hey, Comandante, that trail was a whore."

Joaquin made a joke to the effect that Pombo would know a whore if he walked on one, and the others laughed. Guevara smiled, and the tension and worry of the men was broken. It was enough that they knew the boss had suffered and triumphed. Few thought it their place to even whisper of Guevara's illness, certainly not Moro, his physician, and no one other than Pombo dared to address the comandante directly.

Guevara felt well enough to order the radio set up, and at 2030 hours, he monitored a coded broadcast from Havana. As dinner was served out, he deciphered the message in his notebook. The unworking of the puzzle occupied him completely, and his food went ignored. The others ate like hyenas. The fact that the comandante seldom ate was also noticed and communicated by meaningful glances. As Guevara worked on the cipher, letters assembled themselves into words and words into phrases, and the message spread out across the pages of his journal. Havana advised that Tania had returned from Buenos Aires. Sandoval and D'Esperey were to travel next week from Argentina and could be expected to arrive at the main camp over the coming weeks. Havana said also that the Bolivian Communist Party had declared itself against the armed struggle and would do nothing further to support the guerrillas in the field.

Guevara did not share the contents of the message with Joaquin or with anyone. He closed his journal and then picked at his dinner, two small *humitas* wrapped in soggy corn husks. When the food no longer amused him, Guevara asked to speak with Joaquin privately.

When they were alone, the big man asked, "How are you, Comandante?"

"I'll be better tomorrow."

"I can send a runner back to the caves," Joaquin said, "if you need more medicine."

"I'll be all right."

Joaquin said nothing, but he did not think Guevara was well. He knew that the comandante was capable of running himself into the ground.

"I figure it's five days to the Rosita," Guevara said.

"Four, if I can get these assholes to move," Joaquin answered. A few of the Bolivians had been lagging on the march. Worse, there had been grumbling.

"I wasn't up front very much today. How did they do?"

"The comrades are tired. There's some frustration that the maps are so bad."

Guevara considered this and then said, "We'll get to the Rosita, then turn back for base camp."

Joaquin computed the time they had already been on the trail, twenty-three days, and the time to the river, another five. Even if they returned by the most direct route, Joaquin figured it would be twenty more days, at least, before the column returned to the relative comforts of the main camp.

"Can I speak to you frankly, Che?"

"Always, friend."

"Why don't we turn for base now? We've already had contact with the enemy. We're pushing the men hard. We're at least three weeks from base."

"I want the men to be pushed," Guevara said. "I need to stress the column in order to have it meld together." He paused and took a wheezing breath. Guevara measured Joaquin's expression in the firelight. "Anyway, it wouldn't make sense to turn south, not until we get across these fucking mountains."

"The Rosita," Joaquin said.

"The Rosita and then back to base."

"There's one other thing," Joaquin said.

"Go on." Guevara yawned. He felt like he might fall asleep on his feet.

"It's Marcos," Joaquin said. "He's been getting after the Bolivians in the forward detachment."

"The stragglers?"

"Yeah, there's a couple of shit-eaters. But it's going a bit far. He's constantly riding their asses—"

Guevara cut Joaquin off. "I'll keep an eye on it."

Joaquin felt like some sort of stool pigeon, but as second in command, he had to report on the conduct of the men, especially when their conduct was detrimental. "Did you eat?"

"Some."

"Eat more," Joaquin said. "Tomorrow is going to be a bitch."

Joaquin walked back toward the fire, and Guevara stood alone. The night around him droned with the sound of insects. He found his way to his hammock and removed his boots. Almost against his will, he ducked under the mosquito net and let himself fall into his hammock. He fought off sleep the way a child might—by trying to outthink it.

Four or five days between them and the Rosita. Another kick in the balls. There was no question of reversing his decision; it was final. But Guevara now examined the factors that had led him to it. Rules of iron. He was aware that the morale of his men was being tested, but that was the purpose of the march. It *was* a test. Combat was a test.

A few did not need to be tested—Joaquin, Pombo, Moro, Begnino, men who had been with him for years. They were his stalwarts. It was not for them that he did this. It was for the others. For the Bolivians. They must learn that a mountain range would be crossed. They must learn that these privations were an introduction to what they would experience in the future.

Guevara's eyelids fluttered closed, and he concentrated on his breathing. Three weeks and he would be back at base. They would reach the Rosita exactly as he said. They must learn war, he thought. They must learn that it would be war always until victory. Rules of iron would make iron men.

Guevara tried to make his mind a blank. He knew that to sleep, he must clear his mind, though he knew that this was rarely accomplished. He shifted the focus of his senses to the dark night around him; he concentrated on the insect songs and the gentle noise of the wind flowing downslope. He did what he could to separate mind from body, but the pain in his chest gnawed him. The hydrocortisone was wearing off.

Questions without answers swirled in Guevara's head. Voices called to him, voices without language, shouts and cries, reverberating like echoes. The voices were answered by a rattle of ideas, plans, small steps, and great leaps, revolution, and the fires of a hundred Vietnams smoldering in Uncle Sam's long striped trousers. All that was left for him to remember were the burden of his pack and the sweat that stung his eyes. Perhaps he would be better tomorrow.

Then sleep found Che Guevara and dropped him like a sniper's bullet.

23

TWO DAYS HAD passed as though they were a dream. It was the evenings, the incredible, delicious evenings, that made time evaporate. Hoyle and Maria had spent every night together since they'd returned from the lake. This surprised them both. But they found that not only did they delight in making love, they enjoyed each other's company, even though they often spent long periods in silence.

Minster Alameda was still abroad—he would be until Sunday—and they intended to spend each of the coming nights together until he returned. Beyond that, they had no plans, and Hoyle himself hadn't the vaguest idea what they would do once Alameda returned to La Paz. Neither Hoyle nor Maria thought it prudent to stay over at her flat, and Hoyle was too professional to use the safe house at Plaza España for their assignations. They spent their evenings at the Hotel Cochabamba, a decent though somewhat gloomy place off the Calle Sagamaga. Hoyle had arranged, discreetly, for them to have adjoining rooms.

Each morning they left the hotel, and Hoyle drove Maria to within a block of her apartment; she was careful to leave for work in time to be at her desk promptly. Maria shared with Hoyle an uncanny ability to dissemble, and when Señora Truillo returned from her holiday in Sucre, she found everything in the office in its place (even the curtains were drawn correctly) and had no reason to despise Maria any more than usual. Maria was buoyant, almost beaming, and the cantankerous señora put this down to His Excellency's coming return. Had she known that Maria was carrying on another affair, she might have been driven to distraction. Maria was happier than she had been in years, as was Hoyle, and for them both, it was a delight made sweeter because it was secret.

Yet during these days, Hoyle was nagged by regret—not anguish over his affair but guilt that he was not in the jungle. His ribs still were knitting painfully, and there was no question that he had to recover before he could return to the Ñancahuazú. Since childhood, Hoyle had felt a desperate need to be useful, and this want had been made keen by the defeat at the river. Although he had analyzed the engagement in detail, and he knew that no one, technically, was to blame, there was something in him that felt responsible. Culpable. This was a failing that could be atoned for, even undone, by being of use.

If Hoyle could not yet return to the mountains, then he would work in the city. On his first afternoon back from Titicaca, Hoyle summoned Charlie from Vallegrande. Hoyle knew the guerrillas had to be supported by an urban network, and he wanted Charlie to help him find it.

Charlie met Hoyle at the Plaza España and filled him in on Famous Lawyer and Famous Traveler. The deployment of a hunter-killer group did not surprise Hoyle; he knew that Washington was turning up the volume. The arrival of the Lawyers showed how deadly serious the game had become. About the contents of the rucksack, there was no word. That would be the next shoe to drop.

Charlie said also that since the Lawyers had joined in Vallegrande, Santavanes had taken to sulking. It was not a surprise the next day when Santavanes arrived in La Paz. He said he'd rather be away from the casita for a while, and anyway, Smith was getting on his nerves.

Hoyle had Santavanes go to the embassy and draw funds; this money was given to Charlie. He was to spread a couple thousand dollars around to Communist Party members and see what could be learned about the guerrillas' urban network. Santavanes expected little from this effort and suggested they kidnap a few relatives instead. After some consideration, Hoyle declined. Kidnapping relatives was always effective in the short run, but it quickly spiraled out of control; for the time being, he thought it best to see what Charlie came up with.

At the end of each day, Hoyle met Maria at the hotel. They ate and drank and made love. They talked and made love again. In the morning, Hoyle drove her to her apartment and then went to Plaza España to work. In this manner, four days passed. Then Charlie telephoned and said he had urgent news.

CHARLIE ARRIVED AT the Plaza España carrying a brown envelope and three bottles of Pepsi, the drinks being his traditional beverage of celebration; besides being inscrutable, Charlie was also a teetotaler. He left the envelope on the table and went through his ritual of opening the bottles and pouring out three glasses without ice. Hoyle waited patiently for him to do this because he liked Charlie, and Santavanes was silent because he was thirsty and it was too early in the day for beer.

Charlie lifted his glass and smiled a Cheshire smile. "I made a big score," he said, nearly capturing the idiom.

Hoyle watched as Charlie used a pocketknife to open the envelope. Half a dozen eight-by-ten photographs spilled out on the table. Charlie angled the desk light at them. "These men joined the guerrillas. Some of them must have been on the riverbank."

Hoyle looked down at a series of blowups of the national ID cards of several dark-complected men. Unblinking, unreadable faces stared up from the blotter. These were Guevara's Bolivian combatants. There were other pieces of paper, mimeographed copies of Bolivian National Police subject cards.

"Eleven Bolivians total," Charlie said. "They were members of Oscar Zamora's pro-Chinese splinter group in Oruro."

Hoyle was certain the ambush had been staged by more than a dozen men, probably as many as forty. These might be some of the fighters who had hit them at the river, though they were not all of them.

"How reliable is your source?" Hoyle asked.

Charlie looked at him over his glass. "I paid cash. The general secretary of the Bolivian Party sold these names to the National Police six days ago. I have a cousin—"

"In the police?"

Charlie smiled crookedly. The question answered itself.

"Why would the Bolivian Communist Party burn their own guys?" Santavanes asked.

"They've been expelled." Charlie's dark eyes held Hoyle's steadily. "There's a power struggle in the Bolivian Party. The pro-Moscow fac-

tion wants to go mainstream. They elected members to Parliament."
Charlie's finger tapped a photograph on the table. "These men want a
war right now. They broke with the Central Committee and headed
into the mountains."

"Okay," Santavanes said. "So let's say these are the guys. *Some* of the
guys. Where did the others come from?"

"That's what Langley is going to tell us," Hoyle said.

"You think there's a Cuban team in here?" Charlie asked.

"Yeah," Hoyle said, "I do."

"If there are Cubans in the field, there are Cubans in the city," Santavanes said.

Hoyle looked at Charlie. "Do you have any objection to running
back on your source?"

Charlie's eyes flicked to Santavanes. "I don't want people dead."

"Not dead," Hoyle said, "followed. I want to see who they know.
Who they're dealing with."

Charlie nodded. "We can do that."

Hoyle swept the photos back into the envelope. "Then we start tomorrow," he said.

Neither Charlie nor Santavanes knew that Hoyle's evening was already planned.

HOYLE CAME INTO the hotel room, and Maria turned in surprise as he
entered.

"I didn't mean to startle you."

They kissed, and Hoyle then noticed that a tray had been set on the
table. There were olives and slices of cold ham and Bolivian cheese.
Pukacapas were wrapped in paper fresh from the market, there were
also oranges and red apples and a bottle of wine.

"I thought you might be hungry."

He was, and they ate and washed the food down with a bottle of
Veuve Clicquot and then a very unimpressive bottle of claret. Beyond
the balcony, the sun slouched down in the sky, and a cathedral's bell
tolled for vespers. Although it would have been pleasant to sit outside,
neither thought to do so. They talked and became mildly intoxicated,
first Maria, then Hoyle, who went next door to his room and called
down for another bottle of champagne. When it came, Maria insisted

on prying off the cork, saying she loved the noise and the smell of the wine when it was first opened.

"My father used to open champagne bottles with a sword," she said.

"A daring man."

"He was," she said. "He hardly ever missed."

"Much neater than trying to open a bottle with a revolver."

"Now you're making fun of me."

"No," he said. Again he kissed her. The cork came off with a pop, and Maria refilled their glasses; they were the straight-up tumblers she had taken from the bathroom.

"What did your father do?" Hoyle asked.

Maria was tipsy enough to speak her thoughts directly as they came to her. "The sins of my father?"

"We are all sinners."

"You should have been a priest, Paul Hoyle."

"I don't think so," he said, and kissed her again. This time he could taste the wine on her lips. "What did he do?"

"He was a colonel."

"An officer in the Cuban army?"

"He worked for General Batista." At the dictator's name, Maria hesitated, but again the wine loosened her tongue. "He was a police colonel."

She said nothing else, and Hoyle asked nothing. He knew very well what sorts of things happened to police colonels after revolutions. Hoyle knew also that Maria's parents were dead, and he was fairly certain they had not died of old age.

He changed the subject as blithely as he could. "I think you would like to go out tonight," he said.

"I don't think so."

"Dancing?"

"We can't be seen dancing together."

"You must have seen me dance before."

"Never."

"I dance like a bear in a cheap Russian circus. It's astounding."

This made Maria smile. She embraced him, and they sat back on the sofa, her head resting on his shoulder.

"I want to stay here tonight, with you," she said.

"You don't want to dance?"

"I don't want to share you."

A few moments passed, and Hoyle drank wine from the bathroom glass. He watched Maria delicately sip at hers. The champagne had begun to go flat.

"What will we do after Sunday?"

It was the awful moment when parting was mentioned, and Hoyle's jaw stiffened to meet it.

"I don't know," he said.

"Do you want to see me?"

"Very much."

A quiet between them lengthened and became deeper. The night crept through from the balcony, and the room darkened around them. They sat together, holding each other, content in silence. Both felt they had something precious and fragile to conceal and keep safe.

This evening was the point at which physical attraction passed into some greater thing. And it was the moment when Hoyle's feelings would place them most in peril. Hoyle and Maria were like shipwreck victims set adrift on a vast, indifferent sea. They could hope to survive this thing, and indeed they might, but from now on small mistakes, even plain bad luck, could overturn them and cast them into the deep.

24

BEYOND THE OPEN doors of the casita, rain fell on the dirt runway in a constant snarl. It streamed from the roof tiles and off the tents behind the casita and threatened to overwhelm the neat drainage ditches dug by the Green Berets. The rain was biblical, epic, and sitting next to the chattering Teletype, Smith could not help but think that a rain like this could sink the world. It amazed him that radio signals could pass through air filled with so much falling water, yet the Teletype nattered on, and Smith sipped coffee and watched as the message was revealed inch by inch from the KY-17 cable printer.

SECRET

CENTRAL INTELLIGENCE AGENCY
Intelligence Information Cable

COUNTRY: CUBA/BOLIVIA   PRIORITY: ROUTINE
DISTR: IAWD

Subject

1. INTELLIGENCE ESTIMATE. ERNESTO /CHE/ GUEVARA IN BOLIVIA.

2. GUEVARA LEADS BOLIVIAN COMMUNIST INSURGENT GROUP NUMBERING AT LEAST 50 EFFECTIVES.

The printer's bell chimed three times, rather like a nickel slot machine spilling out a stingy jackpot. The machine clanked on, details, specifics, and bureaucratese, but the truth had been set free by the subject line. The fact of Guevara's presence filled the room as though he had walked through the door and stood dripping.

The Teletype chimed again, and a second message rolled from the printer. Smith tore the message from the machine, careful to make the edge as straight as possible against the row of metal teeth built into the machine, like those of a tiny aluminum shark. He held the paper, already becoming damp, its edges curling against themselves. The message was succinct and assigned to Che Guevara a new CIA handle, a cryptoglyph. This was to be used from now on in place of the target's name; Ernesto "Che" Guevara was now SL/APOSTLE. The first letters, Sierra Lima, denoted his Argentinean birth, and the code name was obviously the hobbyhorse of some wit back at Langley.

Guevara was now tagged, and Smith was on the clock.

On the tiled roof, a crow skittered and jumped about, driven from the sky by the pouring rain. Smith could hear the scratch of its claws against the tiles, a grating, annoying sound quite separate from the clicking of the code machine and the buzz of the downpour. This was one of the occasions when senses and circumstances assembled in a mind and created a mark on memory; for the rest of his life, Smith would remember this instant whenever he heard the rattle of a crow or the sound of rain beating against the roof. Sounds that would otherwise be meaningless or even pleasant would now be associated with the instant he had learned the name of his enemy.

The rain continued to fall in a protracted hiss, and it occurred to Smith to take for himself the code name PILATE, since he had been tasked to kill an apostle.

IN THE CIRCLE of light from a kerosene lamp, Smith bent over a small field desk. A rack of radios and code machines formed a barrier between him and the door, and in the yellow pool of light, Smith worked slowly at his codebooks, encrypting a cable to Langley. He was careful to get the details and the phrases just right; he was looking out not only for his operation but for his career. Above, on the wall, one of the Lawyers had put up a calendar—airbrushed, leggy girls posing with parts for hot-rod cars. Neither much interested Smith, though he did look up and check the date as he scribbled. There was much to say, but for the sake of brevity and ease of coding, he kept his text to a minimum.

It was important to get down on paper what the mission had become, for Smith had been tasked in small bits, and gradually, his job had expanded. He acknowledged the last message, concurring with Langley's assessment that Guevara was leading the guerrillas and then stating plainly that Guevara and the Cubans were now his target. Smith reiterated to Langley that the objective of Bush Mechanic was the termination of the insurgents, and he was careful to use the plural. Smith had seen operations "blow back" in the halls of Langley when things went badly, and he had seen them do likewise when they went too well. Smith could not know what excesses might be committed by the Bolivian army, or what parts of his own operations might eventually leak. This message was an insurance policy. Its confirmation would be his receipt—his proof of payment. Smith was many things, but he was no fool.

He stated that Famous Lawyer had already conducted an aerial survey of the Ñancahuazú and had identified the likely locations for guerrilla base camps. Starting next week, these areas would be systematically searched. Recon teams would be inserted at key trail junctures and river crossings. Smith said that his plan was to first track and pinpoint the enemy. The guerrilla column would then be engaged and annihilated piece by piece. Smith had enough experience in jungle warfare to know what a Green Beret A Team could do. He did not doubt for one instant that Holland and his men would destroy the insurgents. Finally, Smith added that an encampment had been readied for the arrival of Famous Traveler, and that the training of the Bolivian army would remain separate from his efforts. Ambassador Hielman had been reluctantly forced to play ball.

Smith completed his encode; rows and columns of numbers swam before his eyes. He wrote the header of the cable: TS/SCI, TOP SECRET SPECIAL COMPARTMENTED INFORMATION, and its priority, ROUTINE.

Death, Smith thought, death is routine. This mundane bit of traffic would make certain that Langley understood what it had asked for— the death of Che Guevara.

Smith removed his glasses and rubbed his eyes. He walked behind the casita to the radio tent and gave the code groups to one of Holland's men to transmit. The sergeant's finger pressed on a radio key, clicks that translated to dits and das, an electric pulse that would bridge the distance of ten thousand miles—6574, 3544, 3122, 7162—numbers blasted into the ether, numbers that added up to zero. Zero for Guevara and more zeros, cold zeros, for his men.

25

COSMO ZEEBUS SHOVELED up the last of his flan, then pushed away the plate with his thumb. He had quite possibly eaten the largest dessert ever served in La Paz.

"By God," he said, "I've lost my appetite."

Zeebus had eaten all of two desserts, custard and gelato, not to mention a platter of *papas rellenos* and a full plate of *silpancho*, a Bolivian beefsteak smothered with tomato concassé and topped with a fried egg. It was a meal that would have choked a timber wolf.

"You can say a lot of shitty things about this place," Zeebus said, "but you gotta love the food."

Hoyle sipped a beer and averted his eyes. Zeebus was a gastronomic spectacle, a trencherman of the first order, and the owner of the place, a chola named Magda, loved to watch him eat. Zeebus had single-handedly added her restaurant, Los Escudos, to the diplomatic corps's culinary map. As the plates were cleared away, Hoyle's eyes were met by a pair of Swiss consuls at an adjoining table. They had watched Zeebus set about his lunch with an air of disgust and awe. Magda hurried along the busboys and smiled a gold-plated smile. Zeebus was like money in the bank.

Zeebus dropped a cube of sugar into his coffee. "What?" he asked.

Hoyle had watched Zeebus eat a hundred meals in maybe sixty different places around the world, and each time the sight shocked him.

"You're amazing," Hoyle said.

"Son, what's amazing is how little you eat," Zeebus said. "I never see you eat."

That was true enough for this meal, a lunch spanning the period of the Bolivian siesta, between noon and two. It had taken Zeebus roughly this long to demolish his midday repast. Since early morning, Hoyle, Charlie, and Santavanes had been surveilling Selizar Galán, the general secretary of the Bolivian Communist Party. A loose but unbroken tail was kept on Galán as he carried out a morning perambulation, a trip to the market, a bus ride to a midcity café, and then a relaxing browse through a bookstore. Galán's morning errands were erratic precisely to detect if someone was following. Twice the general secretary had doubled back on his own route, and twice he had rounded corners and waited, and each time his tails had eluded detection. Hoyle and Santavanes were impressed throughout the morning by Charlie's diligence and his knowledge of the city and the target. Charlie was a natural-born operative.

Galán had met no one, dropped nothing off, nor picked anything up. He had retired to his apartment about noon, and while Charlie and Santavanes waited him out, Hoyle had elected to join Zeebus for lunch. The hunt would be resumed at two, when it was thought that Galán would reemerge. Until then Hoyle and Zeebus broke bread and buried the hatchet. Rather, it was Zeebus who broke the bread, and the way to this man's heart was truly through his stomach.

"How are your ribs?" Zeebus asked, not convincingly.

"Better."

"You get shot more than anybody I know."

That was true. Though Hoyle tried not to think of it.

"Son, Ambassador Hielman wishes you were dead. He doesn't like being told what to do. Even if it does come from on high."

"We all dance for somebody, Cosmo," Hoyle said.

"Yeah, well, I'm gonna dance right out of here. Thanks to you and the boy wonder."

"Smith?"

"Son of a bitch. Yeah. Him. They officially made me chief of station since this thing heated up."

"Then you owe him a thank-you note."

"I'm chief of station of Turd City, pal. This place is nowhere."

"It's my second tour in nowhere," Hoyle said.

"Yeah, well, we can't all be as screwed up as you." Zeebus looked at his napkin but did not use it to wipe his mouth. "One thing good came out of this."

"Good for who?" Hoyle asked.

"Good for me," Zeebus said. "As COS, I was able to sign my own request for transfer. I put in for somewhere there's some action."

"Maybe there'll be some action here."

"Shit. All you're gonna do is try to get the Bolivians out from under their own beds. And besides, if there is any action around here, you aren't gonna share."

"I'm not the guy running this."

"Save it. I know. I just want out of fucking beaner world. And I got it yesterday. A cable with my transfer—"

"Saigon?"

"Shit, why would I want to go there? I'm talking Berlin. U.S.A. versus the Commie Menace. The real show. Ninety days and I'm G-O-N-E. You and four eyes can fight the Frito Bandito without Cosmo." Zeebus laughed at himself.

"Congratulations."

Berlin *was* the big time. An island of the West surrounded by barbed wire—a place the game was played for real. Hoyle had no chance of ever being assigned there—not unless he was rehabilitated, and that was unlikely given the discontent Smith was sowing. It was also not the sort of place they sent contractors. Not as long as there was dirty work to do elsewhere.

"I don't know why I'm telling you this."

"You don't think I care?" Hoyle's tone was wry.

"No, ya dope. I'm gonna give you a little inside info. Back channel." Zeebus leaned a little closer. Hoyle noticed a fleck of egg yolk on his chin.

"About?"

"The people you pissed off."

Hoyle's face was a pleasant blank.

"Yeah, you. After your little powwow, Hielman's knickers were in a knot. It doesn't make it any better that there isn't anything he can do about it. State Department is telling him to buck up and do as he's told. It's MacDonald, the military attaché, who's gonna fry your ass."

"How so?"

"Hoyle, sometimes you *are* a dope. Where's Hielman gonna go? He's an ambassador already. He's at the end of the rainbow. Ambassador to Bolivia—last stop. But MacDonald—he's a colonel. And he wants to be a general. He's not going to get to be a general writing press releases for a group of Green Beanies training up a mess of Bolivians. Especially when he's figured out that you and Smith have something going up in Vallegrande."

"What does he know?" Now Hoyle's tone was serious.

"Relax, son. He doesn't 'know' anything—except that you got at least two Cuban contractors in here. He's heard the rumors that there's Communist mercenaries up-country. He's heard that you and Smith got the green light to take them out."

Hoyle's voice was even. "If there's been any leaks, Cosmo . . ."

"Son, cool down. If MacDonald knows about you, it's because you got a reputation. Hell, *I* don't even know what you got going up there. I'm just telling you. This thing isn't over for MacDonald. He wants a piece of the action. He ain't gonna sit by and watch the medals get passed out and him get passed over."

Hoyle looked at his watch. It was ten minutes to two. "I have to run."

"Who are you tailing?"

Hoyle said nothing but put a wad of Bolivianos down on the table.

Zeebus continued to fish. "Two o'clock. All the Bolos get up from siesta."

Hoyle liked Zeebus, even if he was a pain in the ass. "Thank me for lunch, Cosmo," he said.

"Thank me for the information," Cosmo said.

They walked for the door.

At the door, Zeebus stopped and kissed Magda's hand. He turned on the charm, his Spanish thick with a Mississippi drawl: *"Esa comida era fantástica. ¡Algo de su mejor alimento! Gracias, Señora."*

Before Zeebus could introduce him, Hoyle slipped out the door and disappeared into the crowd.

26

A BLOCK AND a half down, on the left side of the street, Selizar Galán exited his apartment and strolled east down Avenida America.

"It's about goddamn time," Hoyle muttered. He was sitting behind the wheel of a 1965 Impala staked out half a block down from the corner of Avenida America and Calle Viacha.

Santavanes stirred in the seat next to him, pretending never to have slept in his life. "*¿Qué paso?*"

"There he goes."

Santavanes opened the car door and started after Galán, keeping the distance of half a block between them. The street was not crowded, but there were pedestrians about, the city beginning to stir after the midday's lull. Galán stopped at a yellow street cart tended by a young chola in a bowler hat. He fished some coins out of his pocket and bought a Salteña. At the cart, he ate it slowly, turned twice, facing Hoyle, but did not see him or Santavanes among the cars and people streaming down the sidewalks. Whatever Galán had been doing in his house for the last three hours, it had not involved eating. As Galán ate, Santavanes stopped at a news kiosk and purchased a packet of cigarettes. He stood by the stall, smoking casually, until Galán had finished his lunch.

Galán wiped his mouth with his handkerchief and continued down the street, again heading east. Santavanes followed, staying a block down, placing his left hand in his jacket pocket, a signal for Hoyle to keep back. Hoyle and Santavanes had worked together so often, in jungle and city, that they had a dozen such signals. A change of pockets to the right hand would mean to close up; a conspicuous checking of the wristwatch would mean that the tail was made—surveillance was blown—and the following units should pass on adjoining blocks and then regroup.

Hoyle checked his rearview mirror. Charlie puttered up on a motorbike and stopped next to the driver's-side window. Down the block, a tall, heavyset man in a blue suit approached Galán; this was a surprise. The rules, and common sense, dictated that Galán would run a second surveillance detection route before he conducted any business. Made smug by his morning's walk, Galán obviously considered himself to be free of observation. Santavanes was likewise caught unaware but smoothly turned into a ladies' dress shop and waited. Hoyle squinted down the block.

"Who's the gringo?" Charlie asked. He instantly regretted the remark, but Hoyle took no offense. He lifted a 35mm camera and used its long lens to zoom in on the man's face. There was a brief moment's disbelief, but Hoyle recognized the man at once.

"He's not gringo," Hoyle said, "he's Russian." The fat man was an opponent from Europe. "His name's Diminov; he's a light colonel in the KGB."

Hoyle was amazed to see the Russian half a world away from their last encounter. He usually operated under diplomatic cover, but the Soviet embassy was closed in La Paz. The Bolivians had knuckled under to Uncle Sam, expelling both the Cubans and Russians after the missile crisis in 1962. That meant that Diminov had inserted under "illegal" cover. Like Santavanes and Valdéz—and Hoyle, for that matter—Diminov was not shielded by diplomatic immunity. The Russian was fair game.

Hoyle lowered the camera and watched the two men speak. Diminov was carrying a newspaper folded in half, perhaps the most obvious prop in the world of espionage.

"Right out in the street." Charlie shook his head. This was not how the game was played.

"Tradecraft isn't Diminov's long ball," Hoyle said. "He's more of a brass-knuckles kind of guy. I played against him in Vienna. He's lazy. Likes to work in parks."

A third person joined them, a Bolivian dressed in a cardigan sweater and navy slacks.

"Who's the lightweight?" Hoyle asked.

"Galliego. He's a leader of the Communist Youth Organization."

"You sure?"

"Trust me," Charlie said.

Galán had balls. He was holding a Party conclave right out in the street. Direct contact between the Bolivian Communist Party and a Russian intelligence officer in broad goddamn daylight. It was either idiotic or brilliant.

"Who do you have on the other side of the market?"

"My cousin. Don't worry."

Galán, Diminov, and Galliego started to stroll toward the Mercado Lanza, a warren of stalls and vendors. Charlie revved his motorbike.

"If they split up, stay with the new guy," Hoyle said.

Charlie threaded his Honda into the stream of traffic. Hoyle opened the car door and jogged across the street. Down the block, Santavanes emerged from the dress shop with his hand in his right pocket—the signal to close the distance. Hoyle hustled down the sidewalk and caught up to Santavanes at the edge of the market.

The market opened on three sides around them. There were hundreds of people, vendors and shoppers, tables laid out with bread and produce, stalls with shelves sagging under bright boxes and bottles and cauldrons filled with *chicha* and *somo frío*.

"I still have them," Santavanes said as Hoyle trotted up, "fifty yards down by the blankets."

Hoyle saw them through the crowd. He watched as Galliego handed an envelope to Diminov. The Russian stuffed the envelope into the newspaper and walked in the other direction. Galán turned back and headed directly at them.

"They've made a pass," Santavanes said. "Who do you want?"

"I'll stay with the Russian. You stay with Galán."

Diminov walked casually through the crowded stalls, leaving the market at Avenida Figueroa. Hoyle sprinted across the street, nearly getting hit by a taxi as he cut across the corner to stay within sight. The Russian moved leisurely, unaware that frantic movements were being made in his wake. He sauntered two blocks down, then another. Ahead loomed the Plaza 14 de Septiembre, a likely place for Diminov to work. Hoyle had a good view of the subject and covering traffic around him. He seemed to be in a decent position to keep Diminov under observation. And then on the corner of Calle Illampu, he ran into Charlie.

"Where's the guy in the sweater?" Hoyle said.

"I lost him."

How the hell? "I thought you had a cousin on the other side of the market."

"He lost him, too."

"Get on the other side of the plaza," Hoyle said. Chastised, Charlie gunned the motorbike and took off.

Hoyle jostled through the crowd. He finally regained sight of Diminov half a block down, standing in the doorway of a shop. As Diminov turned from the doorway, a striking dark-haired young woman appeared from the crowd.

Tania saw the man she knew as Robert fully a block away as she approached northwest up the Calle Max Paredes. He was precisely on time, as was she. The Russian was in exactly the right location, the doorway of a stationery shop called El Correo. As Tania moved toward him, she saw that he displayed the safety signal, a newspaper carried in his right hand, indicating that it was safe for her to approach. Tania carried a red clutch purse under her arm, her signal telling him that she had not been followed.

As she came closer, her heart began to race. It had been pounding since her last cover stop, a purchase at the gift shop of the Hotel Milton. Unlike Galán, Tania had kept her tradecraft sound. Her surveillance detection route had taken her across the city all morning. She had not been followed, but she could have no idea that Diminov had been. She was on edge, even paranoid, and she grew more tense as she approached Robert.

As Tania came near, Diminov stepped from the doorway. He seemed to look through her as though she were a stranger in the crowd, but as he stepped past, he flipped her the folded newspaper with an underhanded motion. They passed, not acknowledging each other, the newspaper now snapped into Tania's left hand. Without looking back, Diminov headed back to his hotel, and Tania crossed the street. They had completed a brush pass. Hoyle had seen it all. As had Santavanes, who'd brought up the car and now was double-parked a block from the plaza.

"We've got another player," Hoyle said.

What had been a cakewalk in the morning had turned into a complex nightmare. Now Diminov was going one way and the dark-haired woman the other. Galán was somewhere back in the market, and Charlie had slipped from sight.

"We're out of tails," Santavanes said. It was an admission of defeat and a grudging tribute for the crafty Galán. They had been lulled by his sloppiness all morning and then overwhelmed. Galán's ruse had worked perfectly. Frustrated, Hoyle watched as Tania moved away down the sidewalk.

There was suddenly the chirp of car tires, and that sound lengthened into a long skid. Tania was aware that a vehicle had swerved quickly, and a second later, it jerked up over the curb in front of her and onto the sidewalk, blocking her path. Tania thought at first, as everyone did, that it was a traffic accident.

The car doors were thrown open, and two men jumped out. Tania heard them shouting but could not make out the words; still she thought it only a mishap until she registered the glint of a chrome-plated pistol. She saw clearly that it was a snub-nosed revolver, not an automatic, and she felt the muzzle of the weapon jam into her ribs. The closer of the two men grabbed the front of Tania's blouse and swung her toward the hood of the car. Tania was taken utterly by surprise, and she collided with the roof of the car and then the hood before she could shield herself with her hands. Her face was cut as she was whipped past the antenna. She heard the words "Policía Nacional," and she knew the game was up.

Her ankles were kicked apart, and she was spread-eagled across the hood. As the arrest occurred, Tania had an odd sense that it had all happened before. It had not, but the event—compromise and detainment—had been in the back of her mind as long as she had undertaken clandestine work. A thousand times it had unfolded in her nightmares, a thing of dread and wonder, and now, as it happened to her, Tania felt oddly set apart from it. Like the people on the street, she could only observe with horror and dread. As she was searched, she lifted her head briefly to look down the block after Robert. It was instinct, a gesture she could not help, and one that a proper counterintelligence operative would have looked for as confirmation that a meeting had taken place. The Bolivian officers were more brutal than astute, and Tania's head was shoved back down against the fender. Her head was jerked back and her arm twisted behind her. The newspaper dropped into the gutter as she was shoved headlong into the backseat of the car. One of the men jumped on top of her and slammed the door. The dark sedan accelerated back onto the street with tires smoking. The entire arrest had taken under fifteen seconds.

Hoyle swam through a tide of dumbstruck pedestrians and made it to the sidewalk. He found the newspaper, folded and lying in the gutter. As he bent to pick it up, a spit-shined boot came down, nearly pinning his hand.

Hoyle looked up in shock. Colonel Arquero stood above him.

Hoyle lifted the newspaper. Two machine-gun-toting National Police officers moved to the curb. Santavanes trotted up, his hand in his coat.

"*Fácil, muchachos,*" Santavanes said. "*Somos amigos.*"

The muzzles of the guns flicked off Hoyle and on to Santavanes. The triggers tightened. Arquero's face remained oddly pleasant, although Santavanes and the two uniformed policemen were quite capable of shooting one another.

"I'm a bit surprised to see you here," Arquero said to Hoyle.

With a certain amount of embarrassment, Hoyle looked at Santavanes; not only had they lost everyone they were tailing, they had blundered into Arquero's web. The National Police obviously had the plaza under constant surveillance. Hoyle had not picked up on this, nor had Charlie.

Arquero cleared his throat. "May I have the newspaper, please?"

Perhaps Arquero knew of the envelope stuffed inside the paper; perhaps he did not.

"This?" Hoyle tapped the rolled-up paper against his hand.

"Give it to me, please," Arquero hissed.

The machine pistols remained pointed. Hoyle handed over the paper. Arquero put it under his arm and walked away.

Smiling broadly, Hoyle climbed into the Impala.

"How'd that little bastard put the swerve on us?" Santavanes asked.

Hoyle did not answer.

Santavanes looked over. "What are you grinning about?"
Hoyle reached into his lapel and pulled out the envelope. "This," he said. By some sleight of hand, he had removed the envelope from the newspaper, right under Arquero's nose. Right under the muzzles of a pair of machine guns. An audacious and elegant move.

"Very nice," Santavanes said. "Did Mama give you a magic set for Christmas?"

AT THE SAFE house at Plaza España, the envelope was steamed open. Inside was an Austrian passport bearing the name Michel Nemick. The passport was filled out and appeared genuine—all that was missing was a photograph. This document Hoyle laid aside. Of more immediate interest was an innocuous letter from "Beatríz" to Tania—fifteen harmless lines about looking forward to seeing her after vacation. The envelope and letter were examined under ultraviolet light; this revealed no secret writing or invisible inks. Inch by inch, the paper was scanned with a binocular microscope. Particular attention was paid to the periods and the meticulously dotted "i"s, "j"s, and the accents over letters written in flowing longhand.

In the thirteenth line, Santavanes found a microdot placed over the "i" in the word *vacación*. As Hoyle watched, the microdot was laid on a clear slide, floated in mineral oil, and placed on a projector. The wall flashed white as the slide was clicked into the light stream; projected on the wall were three typewritten pages. The first page contained two columns of names, with noms de guerre in capital letters. It was a list of all forty-one of Che Guevara's combatants, real names and code names, and a list of twelve Communist Youth volunteers who had made the trip to the Zinc House and now waited Guevara's return in the Ñancahuazú Valley. The second page was a letter from the general secretary of the Bolivian Communist Party saying that they would no longer support combatant operations. The third page instructed Tania to deliver the two personnel (D'Esperey and Sandoval) to the guerrillas' base and then return to La Paz. Tania was then to use the enclosed Austrian passport to leave Bolivia.

It took until just after midnight to examine the letter, and Hoyle told Santavanes to draft a message summarizing its contents to Smith. Hoyle excused himself, saying he had a previous engagement, and

Santavanes set about typing and encoding the contents of the microdot for transmission to Vallegrande. It had been a fruitful day's work.

CURFEW HAD BEEN lifted, but there were few people or vehicles on the street. Hoyle drove back to the Hotel Cochabamba and found Maria waiting in their rooms. Her small overnight bag was zipped closed and placed by the door.

"I'm sorry I'm late," Hoyle said. An evening they'd planned to spend together was gone. "Work," he said, "and I could not get away."

They embraced. "I have to get back to my apartment. I'm going to have to leave in a few minutes," she said.

"Well, then we have a few minutes. There's still some champagne."

"No, save it," she said. "For next time."

A military truck passed below on the street.

"When will I see you again?"

"I don't know. Can you call me?" Maria asked.

"I've rented a post office box near the ministry. I can leave messages for you there."

"So much intrigue."

"I'm sorry."

She kissed him. "I'm not," she said. "I'm not sorry."

He still had questions to ask, questions about Alameda, questions about visas and passports issued by the minister's office, and questions about a hundred things, but this was not the time to ask.

"I'm afraid that this might become too much for you . . ." he said, his voice trailing off.

"It might. But I want to continue."

"So do I."

"May I speak honestly to you, Paul Hoyle?"

"Of course."

"I am afraid that it will end badly, this thing between us."

"Don't say that, please."

"No, I am a grown person, and I see that this is becoming complicated. It is complicated because of what you do for a living, and because of the way that I live. It is complicated because we must sneak about like mice. I am used to it, I am a mistress—"

"Maria, please—"

"No, listen to me. I am someone else's mistress, and that makes me several other things, a liar and sneak, and I am used to it. I look in a mirror, and I see what I am. And for that reason alone, I know that one day you will grow tired of this and of me."

Hoyle held her and stopped her talking by kissing her. "Please, don't say any more," he said.

"You can't pretend it isn't true."

"I won't listen to you put yourself down."

Hoyle held her and was astonished again by the warm, complex spice of her smell. "Are you sorry this happened?" he asked.

"No."

"Then let's go on," he said, "let's go on carefully."

"I want to go on with you, Paul Hoyle. I want it more than anything, and that frightens me. It frightens me also that my time is not my own. My time belongs to Alameda. It bothers me that I must steal what time I can to give to you."

It all revolved around time, the lives of mistress and spies. Both Hoyle and Maria performed sleights of hand, both stole time, hoarded it, trafficked in it, both used it as a cloak, pretending to be one place when they were actually another. Hoyle did it professionally, and Maria did it to live. Both played cards from a crooked deck. Hoyle knew that Maria was right. He knew from a life of professional intrigue that time always ran out. He had lived this, and Maria was discerning enough to see that ahead of them was the very real possibility of disaster.

"I won't hurt you," he whispered.

"Then you must take me to my apartment, for I am a proper lady, and it will not do to have my neighbors set to gossiping." Maria had intended this as a joke, but it fell a bit awkward, close as it was to the truth.

He helped her on with her coat.

"Will you save the champagne for me?"

"I'll even find a sword to open it."

Gallantry took precedence over operational security, and Hoyle drove Maria back to the apartment on Cochabamba. He promised to leave a note for her the following afternoon. As they approached her building, there was no one on the street and no lights on, and Hoyle impetuously kissed her on the stairs. He would remember this kiss for the rest of his life, fraught as it was with the danger of being observed and the escalating sentiment between them. Hoyle held her hand as she pulled away, and after she had gone in the front door, Hoyle drove to an all-night café and ate an entire *silpancho*, he was so ravenous.

27

DARKNESS AND NEARLY SILENCE.

Tania was naked, thrown into a room without light or air. Tall enough for her to stand, perhaps ten feet long by eight feet wide, but in total, all-consuming darkness, so it was not possible to know exactly. She had been blindfolded when they shoved her inside, and when the door closed, the cell was as dark as a crypt. It may well have been a tomb, for feeling her way around in the darkness, Tania found that there were two corpses tossed on the floor. She could not tell if they were male or female, only that they were human and decaying.

She crouched in the corner and listened to water drip from the walls. She had been stripped, beaten, and assaulted, though not raped. Not yet. Tania had not anticipated being arrested, but after her capture, almost everything had gone as she expected.

Tania had been trained in the methods of interrogation, as well as in techniques likely to be used against her, and the Bolivian National Police were playing from a predictable if brutal script. She had been roughed up, beaten, had her clothing pulled off. Blindfolded, Tania had been marched through a corridor and exposed to the hooting and verbal assaults of male prisoners. She had expected the questions shouted at her, punctuated by blows and threats of rape and murder and acid and electric shocks. Through it all, she had played innocent but listened carefully to what her interrogators asked and what they did not ask.

Outside the cell, a door clanged, and there was shouting. In the darkness, a rat skittered close by her. Tania's body was scratched and bruised; her lip was cut where one of the policemen had slapped her. They would soon search her apartment, and they would find her photographic darkroom. Her codes and the microdot viewer were concealed in a false-bottomed suitcase, and they would eventually find these as well. Worse was to come, much worse, and Tania knew that the anticipation was part of the process. The next round of questioning would be fiercer still. They would leave her in the cell until their questions were in order. They would let her cook, as the saying went. It was part of the process, part of the rendering.

Perhaps Robert had not been arrested. Perhaps he was working right now to have her released. Perhaps the comrades would raise money to bribe the guards.

Tania must not give in to fear, but just as determinedly, she did her best not to hope. She put her hands around the back of her neck. Her wrists were bruised from the handcuffs, and she could hear the blood pounding through her veins.

Above everything else, she must not hope. Hope was the only thing that could break her.

28

I N THE SMALL hours before dawn, Hoyle rolled over and listened
to the sound of wind through the hotel window. For what remained of the night, he slept badly, and when he did at last succumb,
he dreamed that he had lost something important—he did not know if
it was an object or a person, but something had been entrusted to his
care, and through negligence or bad luck, he'd misplaced it. He woke
feeling guilty.

There was the smell of Maria still on the pillowcases, and this made
him feel even more guilt.

Hoyle dozed again, he did not know for how long, and as he fell
into sleep, a thousand images of the day flashed under his eyelids. A
hypnogogic parade. He saw again scenes of the street, the lunch taken
with Cosmo Zeebus, the trail of Galán through the warren of the *mercado*, and, hauntingly, the passport hidden within the newspaper, the
passport that had a name but not a face. He saw again the sudden, concise violence of the woman's arrest. He saw her dark hair thrown back
as a policeman clasped a hand across her mouth. He saw the newspaper drop into the gutter and her blouse fold open. These things occupied Hoyle's mind, and then, as quickly, they discolored and bled away.

There was an indefinite period of warm, comfortable darkness, and
then Hoyle had something that was very close to a nightmare. He
dreamed that he was again a cadet at his military school: It was a fall

day, gray, as everything was gray in his dream. The uniforms, the food, the books, the blankets, all shades of gray. Hoyle was again a cadet, but he was grown—an adult, sentenced somehow eternally to prep school. The uniform did not fit him, the shoulders too narrow and the pants too tight. His cadet collar cut into his neck. His brother cadets were as they had been in Hoyle's student days: adolescents, young men, carbuncular and awkward. Hoyle was the age of his professors, almost the age of the warhorse sergeants and officers who had taught him military science. Yet he marched with the other cadets to Latin class, to government, taught by the formidable Colonel Wease, to algebra and *Beowulf* and dissected frogs. Semesters passed in this dream. He was trapped in a wrinkle of time, a grown man unable to escape from a world of petty rules, dress parades, spit and polish, and rifles without firing pins. Hoyle came away slowly from this dream; it did not so much end as unravel, a purgatory interminable and inane.

Hoyle woke to the real world with something like relief, but his consolation changed at once to alarm.

A man was standing at the end of his bed.

It was Diminov, the KGB officer he'd seen in the market.

Hoyle blinked and at once threw off the bedclothes; he made a rush at Diminov, but there were two other men in the room. Hoyle struck the closest one and knocked him across a table. A truncheon came down on the back of Hoyle's neck, and his breath escaped in a guttural shout. The blow staggered him, and his knees buckled. Hoyle went out for a second, the wits and wind knocked from him, and the two men lifted him half conscious and tossed him bodily onto the couch.

Hoyle sat in a heap, his T-shirt bunched up where fists had grappled him, and with a high-pitched ringing in his ears.

Diminov sat down casually in a chair next to the bed. "My old friend Mr. Hoyle," he said. "How I miss Europe. Latin America is filthy. And things are so much more . . . hands-on than they were in Vienna."

Hoyle's eyes darted, looking for an angle. The man standing behind Diminov unholstered a pistol and thumb-cocked it.

"Please sit and listen, Mr. Hoyle," Diminov said. "It would be a pity to have Sergev shoot you in the head."

Hoyle leaned back into the couch. His jaw worked against a bit of chipped molar. It was like sand in his teeth.

"Although we remain enemies, ideological enemies, I find that our interests coincide to a remarkable degree." Diminov's voice was high-pitched. To Hoyle, it seemed annoyingly feline.

"The National Police arrested a colleague of mine yesterday," Diminov continued. "Her name is Tania Vünke. She is an operative for Cuban intelligence. A very enterprising young woman. You see, she also works for KGB. We are her principal employer. I believe you at CIA call that a 'false flag' operation, don't you? Just so."

"Why tell me? You want me to put you in for secret agent of the month?"

"It should be obvious. I want you to have her released."

"Get bent."

"Mr. Hoyle, I didn't come here to ask for a favor. I came here to make a proposition. If you have Fräulein Vünke released, I will give you the location of the guerrilla leader."

"Che Guevara."

"You impress me, Mr. Hoyle. You really do."

"Why would you want to help us screw up a perfectly good revolution?"

"That's where our interests coincide. My government does not see the benefit of a Bolivian revolution. Not right now."

"You're willing to sell out Guevara?"

"You seem surprised," Diminov purred.

"He's a Communist—"

"He is an anachronism. A romantic. A throwback to the time of revolution for the sake of itself. My country finds his radical positions inappropriate to the realpolitik of the modern world."

"You support Cuba," Hoyle said.

"We support Castro. Do you really think Castro wants Guevara alive?"

"Why would he want him dead?"

Diminov reached into the bowl on the coffee table and helped himself to a clementine. He peeled it with his thumb as he spoke. "Our countries very nearly went to war. Nuclear war. The issue was over spheres of influence." He broke the peeled fruit into three sections. "The first world, you in the West. The second world, the socialist and progressive nations." He placed the smallest section on the table. "And the third world—Africa, Southeast Asia, all countries that are postcolonial, developing nations. Holes of shit you call them. Places like Bolivia.

"The United States and the USSR have come to an agreement. An arrangement regarding influence in these three worlds. There will be border issues, but what's been proposed will allow both our countries to exist outside the shadow of nuclear confrontation."

"What's this have to do with burning Che Guevara?"

"Stability between these worlds. Cuba and its revolution were at the root of our disagreements, Mr. Hoyle. Castro and especially Guevara are enthusiasts for world conflagration. They want revolutions to sweep the third world. But their outlook is not strictly Marxist-Leninist. It is Maoist. A small point for you, perhaps, as a capitalist exploiter, but an important point for the faithful. The USSR does not feel that the political and economic conditions are right for a worldwide revolution. Not now. Not while a hot war is raging in Vietnam. The Soviet Union does not want a South American revolution. And not a Cuban-sponsored revolution, in any case."

Diminov pushed a section of clementine into his mouth and chewed on it. It was the second-world section.

"I'm listening," Hoyle said.

"Tania Vünke was placed into Guevara's entourage seven years ago. She has been our access to him. If not for her, we would not have even known where Guevara was. It is now time to extract her. That's why I've taken the liberty of visiting you. I want you to exfiltrate Fräulein Vünke from Bolivia back to Austria. Under a Western passport. A clean document. From Vienna, we will transport her back to a fraternal socialist country."

"Have a great trip."

Diminov ate another section of fruit. "I'm an enemy here, Mr. Hoyle. There is a limit to what I can do. Bolivia is not, for me, a permissive environment. As much as it pains me to ask, I need your assistance."

"What's the big deal about this woman?"

"My organization does have a certain reputation for matters dealing with personnel. But we do not wish to forfeit Tania Vünke."

"Why not?"

"Have you not heard of professional courtesy?" Diminov spat a seed into his hand. "Besides, there is certain information she possesses that would prove embarrassing to my country, beyond the fact that we have engaged in espionage against our ersatz Cuban allies. Even if I did manage to bribe her release from prison, she is now a marked person.

Fräulein Vünke has no diplomatic status. If she attempted to leave, she would immediately come under the scrutiny of the immigration police."

"We have your Austrian passport."

"I suspected that. The document is of the highest quality. As are its visas. It needs only a photograph."

"So you need a body."

"As do you. That is why I propose a trade." Diminov exhaled though his nose. "Arquero is your stooge, is he not? Pay him money and have Fräulein Vünke released."

"What's in it for me?"

"Che Guevara, as you say, on a platter."

"What makes you think we don't already know where he is?"

"Because he's alive. You know some of the places he has been. And you suspect some of the places he may go in the future. But you have not located him. If you had, it would be a simple thing to drop napalm on him."

"You want this woman released, I get more than a circle drawn on a map."

"What else do you need, Mr. Hoyle?"

"I want his radio frequencies and his communication plan with Havana."

Diminov put down the fruit. "How do you expect me—"

"I'm not done. We know there's going to be a rendezvous. Two more men are being sent to the guerrillas. I get this fräulein of yours released, and she guides them in direct to the main camp."

Hoyle stood. Sergev kept the pistol aimed. "That's preposterous."

"That's the deal. Take it or leave it."

"She is released—alive—and we will continue our discussion." Diminov wiped his hands on the tablecloth. "Since it is I who have found you, if you wish contact, place an ad in the classified section of *La Paz Tiempo*. Perhaps asking Saint Jude to help you find lost love." The religious allusion made Diminov smile. "I will contact you here at this hotel. You seem to like this place." Diminov nodded, and Sergev and the man with the truncheon walked out.

"You burn me, and I'll make sure she disappears."

"Don't do anything rash, Mr. Hoyle," Diminov said. "We don't have to be enemies on this one." The fat man pulled the door closed behind him.

29

LIGHT SLANTED THROUGH the windows in Colonel Arquero's grand office. The clock ticked slowly, and Lieutenant Castañeda stood by the door, as immobile and unthinking as a piece of furniture. Hoyle and Smith watched the colonel frown over the folder placed before him. He examined each of the three photographic prints, holding them close to his shiny pince-nez spectacles, then checking each photograph against a typed transcript of the microdot. This he did with deliberate and self-conscious care, and the clock ticked through diligence to insolence and finally to absurdity. It was a blessing when Arquero's small hands pushed the photos and papers back into the folder and he squinted up from the blotter.

"This is obviously a ruse," he said. "A provocation. Do you expect me to believe that Che Guevara is in Bolivia?"

"We believe it," Hoyle said.

Unfolding in Arquero's office was a battle of words, wills, and manners. Hoyle, who had more experience in Latin nuance, put himself forward in the struggle. "We're sure that a Cuban team is in the Ñancahuazú."

"Maybe you are playing a game within a game, Mr. Hoyle. You say there was a microdot on the letter. And you say this is what it contained."

Smith had long ago lost what little patience he'd brought to La Paz. "Where's the woman you arrested?"

"You need not be concerned about her." The colonel lit a cigarette; the extinguished match was a perfect metaphor for Tania's hold on life.

"Is she alive?"

"She is a Communist agent, Mr. Hoyle. Do you really expect me to release her because the KGB asked you?"

"She's the only direct link we have with the guerrillas," Smith said. He stood and paced; the colonel seemed to take a smug, quiet delight in Smith's agitation.

"Besides," Arquero went on, "what makes you think she would cooperate?"

"She doesn't have to cooperate," Hoyle said. "We give her the letter back—opened—obviously, you would have examined it."

Arquero smirked. "And obviously, we would be too stupid to have found the microdot."

"We replace the microdot, Colonel," Hoyle said. "You release her. Tell her it was a mistake, tell her you were after Galán."

Hoyle's patience amazed Smith.

"And the passport? Do we ignore that as well?"

"It doesn't matter," Hoyle said. "Tell her anything, just make her think she's free of surveillance. After the arrest, she'll try to contact her controller. They'll transfer the two new guys direct to the guerrillas. We'll transmit a message to Guevara, pretending to be Havana. We'll tell him there's going to be a supply drop. Food, clothing, ammunition. When Guevara shows up at the drop site, we'll hit him."

"Then what do you need the woman for?"

"Guevara won't just fall for a radio message. She'll confirm the drop site to him. Personally."

"Oh," Arquero said. "This is based on trust." The clock ticked. Smoke swirled from the end of Arquero's cigarette. "Your plan doesn't seem very well thought out, Mr. Hoyle."

"How does keeping her in prison serve any purpose?"

"She is a Communist agent. And if I am to believe you, a Cuban operative working simultaneously for the Soviets. We have searched her apartment thoroughly and found codebooks and photographic equipment; her radio set is now being examined by our technical section. In short, she is a spy. We would be within our rights to shoot her."

"She can deliver Guevara to us."

"You presume, rather hopefully, that she will see the justness of our cause and the mistake of her ways. I have no doubt she is a hard case. Nor do I doubt that she will flee the country at the first opportunity."

"How can she run from the Ñancahuazú Valley? It's surrounded by the entire Bolivian army."

"The guerrillas operate at will within the Ñancahuazú. You're asking me to throw a rabbit into the briar patch." Arquero delighted himself with this bit of Yankee wisdom. It felt wonderful to club Hoyle with his own language.

"Colonel," Hoyle said evenly, "this woman is the quickest way, and the only way, we can eliminate the guerrillas."

"Assume for a moment that I share your sense of urgency, Mr. Hoyle. Let's also assume that this woman will deliver Guevara into a trap. Do you think our forces are ready to take on the guerrillas in a head-on engagement?"

"We have to find them first."

"Then who will fight them? The Presidential Guard?"

"The forces at our disposal—"

"Oh," Arquero said with high derision, "the forces at *your* disposal."

At this, even Hoyle grew disgusted. The clock continued to click away, each fleeing second an ally of the colonel.

"I have been instructed to inform you that our ambassador in Washington has formally requested that three hundred more military advisers be dispatched to Bolivia."

"You don't need more Green Berets, Arquero. You need to get people into the field," Smith said.

"We need arms. And American troops, Mr. Smith, not cheerleading."

Arquero stood by way of bringing the meeting to an end.

"Let's go, Mr. Hoyle," Smith said.

Hoyle reached for the folder. Arquero's hand got there first. "I will keep the letter to examine. With your permission, of course." Arquero smiled like a lizard.

Hoyle lifted the passport from the blotter. "Then we'll keep the passport," he said. He added, slightly less gracefully, "With your permission, Colonel."

"As you wish. Good afternoon, gentlemen."

30

THE RAINS HAD ended, and steam rose from the earth like puffs of smoke. Boro flies were everywhere in swarms, and this was but a nuisance on top of a week of torment. The column had not yet gained the Rosita River, and this fact alone disappointed and annoyed Guevara. He was too much a leader to show his men, and he did his best to appear at all times upbeat and positive. His asthma, at least, had declined, and this was a lucky thing, for he was out of medication, and should his illness return, he could expect nothing but unmitigated suffocation.

The terrain continued to be an enemy. The mountains came on in succession, though their altitude had lessened. The underbrush more than made up for it, as did cliffs and bluffs that stuck up from the dirt in places like the bones of gigantic, buried monsters. After five days on the trail, Guevara labored under his pack, determined to make the river; and now there was little choice but to do so. The maps had proved so unreliable that they could scarcely be trusted to aid navigation. The only sure way back to base was to reach the Rosita, descend it to the Rio Grande, and then join the Ñancahuazú and follow it south. Even this route was sketchy, since the column frequently came on streams where there should be none, and dry gorges that the maps claimed were rivers in full glory.

There was also the issue with Marcos, who continued a quarrelsome attitude with the Bolivians. This reached a head when the forward detachment wandered onto yet another false trail. The error resulted in an entire morning lost to a laborious backtrack. At noon Marcos radioed the main column and asked Guevara for help clearing a new trail. He was sent Braulio, Tuma, and Pacho. Three hours later, Pacho returned from the forward detachment in a lather of rage, demanding to speak with Guevara and stating that conditions up front were unendurable. He said he'd left his post after an altercation with Marcos. It began about a question of map reading and very quickly escalated from insults to assault.

His voice cracking with anger, Pacho said that Marcos had become a bully on the trail, capriciously ordering the comrades about, and after they'd gotten lost, he had threatened the men with a machete. When Pacho got involved on behalf of the Bolivians, Marcos had struck him with the handle, giving him a shove and tearing his shirt.

Guevara called Inti and Dario, the most senior Bolivian comrades, and they confirmed that the low morale in the forward detachment was a result of Marco's arrogance. Inti added, however, that Marcos had been provoked by Pacho's disrespect. He said also that four of the Bolivian comrades—Chingolo, Eusebio, Paco, and Pepe—were slackers, disheartened and lazy. This was especially disappointing to Guevara. The Bolivian comrades were all volunteers, so he had expected more, especially since the struggle was being fought for them.

Guevara spoke that evening with Joaquin, reliable, steadfast Joaquin, and the decision was made to replace Marcos as commander of the forward detachment. Guevara made this choice not out of deference to the Bolivians, though it was important that they be respected; he dismissed Marcos because in adversity he'd found him short-tempered and wanting in judgment. Joaquin suggested that Marcos be replaced after they had returned to base camp, so that his relief would not provide a distraction. In his suggestion was also the small hope that Marcos might redeem himself during the journey back to base.

Joaquin estimated that they were still one or two days' hard travel from the Rosita, and it would take at least six or seven more days to descend the Ñancahuazú and regain the base. Guevara concurred. If Joaquin had any faults at all, they were his optimism and that he overestimated the stamina of the men around him. There were few combatants anywhere who were as worthy as the big man, or as tough.

Guevara slept badly that night, as he did most nights. Dinner had hardly satisfied—a few hearts of palm stewed together with a rancid hunk of jerky. The palm hearts and chewy, reeking meat did nothing to settle his stomach. As unpleasant as their dinner had been, it was better than nothing. Guevara knew also that the men had only three days' rations left, a few cans of meat and condensed milk and twenty pounds of rice and beans. After that, unless game rendered itself plentiful, they would have to eat the pack animals. The specter of hunger wafted outside of the light of each campfire; this, too, added to the anxiety of the men. As Guevara closed his eyes, he reminded himself that there was food in plenty at base camp. But first they would make the Rosita; then and only then would they turn for base.

The morning came as gray as a smudge, and the sky above was mottled with high, colorless clouds. The sugar ration Guevara intended to distribute turned up missing, and as a result, breakfast was only a mug of tea. The mood was sullen all around, and the brooding, slow-motion preparations for movement compelled Guevara to gather together all the comrades and give them a talk.

"This isn't the way I wanted to start the day." Around him, the wind stirred through the trees. "It's been an unpleasant surprise for me to find that comrades already tested on the field of battle—men I hand-picked for this mission—are the first to become a problem."

His eyes passed deliberately over Pacho and Marcos. They were seated at opposite ends of the group like bookends, arms and legs crossed, heads cocked, and eyes narrowed.

"The march we are on has a purpose. It is intended to prepare the Bolivian comrades for the trials and difficulties of guerrilla life. We are out here to come to grips with hunger and thirst, constant marches, and the separation from our families. We do this so that we might become stronger. We do this so we will meld together as a combat *guerrillo*—a unit that operates cohesively, instinctively, and without friction.

"We have been on the trail many days now. We have twice encountered the enemy, and twice we have inflicted on him defeat." Guevara paused again, scanning the faces, meeting the eyes of almost every man in the column.

"But the events of the last several days tell me that we have not yet achieved the goal of this march. We do not yet function as a unit. We are far from operating together as a team.

"Some of us have physical limitations. I am aware of that. I have them myself. Some of us are out of condition. Some of us are simply not used to life in the forest. This worries me less. Physical shortcomings can always be overcome by a willing mind and a combative spirit.

"This morning the sugar ration was found missing. I will use the word 'stolen,' for I am certain it was not misplaced or dropped along the trail. I will point out to you all the great truth that theft is incompatible with socialism, and it is incompatible with the principles followed by this guerrilla unit. Anyone caught committing the crime of theft—the crime of stealing food from the mouths of his brothers—will be punished.

"What bothers me is that it is not the Bolivians who are having problems, but Cubanos—comrades I think of as veterans, men who have smelled powder on the battlefield. Men who have fought the enemy on two continents. I could point out to you many instances of carelessness and lack of discipline on the part of Cubans and Bolivians alike. This tells me that we are not yet complete revolutionaries. We are still individuals. This should provide a lesson for the future: Men who once gave blood and sweat and their hearts for a cause have become used to lives of ease. Marcos has commanded large units, and Pacho is a comrade who has been in combat. It seems now that they have become bureaucrats, used to life in an office—working apart and above others—accustomed to having everything come back to them already worked out. A relatively easy life has made them forget the rigors and sacrifices of the guerrilla life in the field."

Guevara did not shy from naming names or citing specific instances or attitudes. His criticisms were always direct, not intended to alleviate a problem as much as to excise it. This was almost his unconscious style—to reduce the offending individuals, to throw a brilliant light on their failings, and in so doing, to lower them in the eyes of their compatriots. He now went for the jugular.

"I don't want to think that the reason for Marcos and Pacho's constant problems is that they do not have the courage to say they want to quit. I don't want to think that they have had enough. I do not want to think they have lost their revolutionary zeal."

The men held their breath. Even Joaquin was surprised by the cold fury in Guevara's words.

"The next time Pacho leaves a post, he will be dishonorably expelled from the column. Comrade Marcos is now formally placed on probation. He must change his manner of addressing comrades—his insulting manner undermines his authority and is a detriment to good order. We have enemies enough around us. I will not tolerate enemies within.

"When we return to base, we will be joined by new comrades, men who are untested and who will not have the benefits of this march and the trials on which we have embarked. When these new members join us, it is vital that they feel the positive influence of the group. Some of you men are examples. Most of you are not."

Even the insects in the jungle seemed to have fallen quiet.

"If any of you, Bolivian or Cuban, feels weak or discouraged, don't resort to deceit and laziness. If you want out, if you've had enough, speak to me, and we'll discharge you peacefully from the group.

"Does anyone wish to say anything?"

Silence.

"Then this meeting is closed. Vanguard detachment, resume the trail; center and rear guard, prepare to move. We will travel in a forced march, night and day if necessary, until we reach the river. That is all."

IT WAS SWEAT, toil, and misery, ten hours' worth, and exactly what Guevara felt the command required. An hour before sundown, a runner came back through the column to report that the vanguard had come to a muddy brown river, not as big as the Masacuri but larger than the Ñancahuazú. Guevara had Joaquin double up the formation, and when all the comrades had assembled on the riverbank, scouting parties were sent upstream and up the bluffs facing the river. The day's march had been exhausting, at least twelve kilometers long, and for much of the way the forward detachment had to chop a trail.

But the river would prove a far harsher disciplinarian than Che Guevara.

The column was directed north, up the Rosita, and within a kilometer, the banks again closed in. The river was running high, and rough brown water shoved through a number of steep gorges. Benjamin, a Bolivian assigned to the forward detachment, lost the ascending trail and staggered out onto one of the narrow fingers of rock above the river. It was possible to traverse a ledge and make it to higher ground, and two men before him safely passed up onto a gentler patch of riverbank. Benjamin had chopped trail with his machete most of the day and was reeling with exhaustion. Lumbering under the weight of his pack and rifle, he stepped out onto the outcrop, lost his footing, and plunged into the river.

He did not know how to swim.

Benjamin splashed into the water and then managed to get his face above the rushing stream. His rifle was ripped from his hands, but his pack straps held fast. For a few moments, he was floated along, and then the air in his pack burbled out the top and the contents filled with water. The current through the gorge ran him downstream and into a deep, churning pool.

Guevara tossed away his rifle and kicked off his boots. He dove into the river, and the water shocked him, it was so cold. He swam toward Benjamin, but as he did so, the young man shouted and went under. Guevara dove after him, but the current dragged him past the crook in the river. Guevara ran up the bank again and dove into the whirlpool, as did Begnino, but in ten minutes there was no sign of the boy, not even a scrap of his clothing or a single piece of gear from his pack. He had been swallowed by the river without a trace.

The column stood on the banks and on the rock ledges, transfixed. Guevara kept staring at the river, expecting Benjamin to wade out of it, expecting him to surface and say everything was all right. Minutes passed, then a quarter of an hour. The river had taken the young man and would not give him back.

Guevara stood dripping on the ledge, and Joaquin handed him back his rifle. Guevara panted and wiped the water off his face and again looked at the gushing ribbon of brown and the yellowish rapids. How could it be? How could the river have so quickly eaten a man?

"How many of you can swim?" Joaquin asked loudly.

Only about a dozen hands went up. Thirteen men out of nearly forty.

"Fuck me to death," Joaquin muttered. What else could go wrong with this outfit?

There was nothing else to do, nothing but continue to march. Guevara pulled on his boots.

"Forward detachment," Joaquin said, "move out."

"Keep back from the banks," Guevara called after them. "I don't want to lose another rifle."

This day had been abysmal. Nearly twelve hours without break on the trail, and the one moment that might have been savored was marred forever by a ridiculous and senseless death.

This day was a stick, a shitty stick, but now Guevara held out a carrot. After the evening's halt, he ordered the rear detachment to begin preparing a feast, rice and beans for all, condensed milk for their tea, and the meat of a urinia that Begnino managed to kill with a hatchet. These small luxuries were the last of the reserve rations; hereafter, the column would be dependent on the hunters for their food. Hearts of palm had proved plentiful, and now that they were heading south, it might be possible to purchase corn or livestock from one of the small farms strung out along the river.

The smell of food cooking elevated morale, and even the men gathering firewood went about their heavy labors with smiles and a few jokes. By full dark, rations were served out, and there was enough for all to eat twice. Food was saved for the scouts, who returned by midnight to say they had traveled almost three hours downriver and had not found Benjamin's corpse. This was a disappointment, but given the state of the river, not a surprise, and as the scouts ate and the men hung their hammocks, Guevara announced that in the morning, the column would turn south for base. There was no cheering—the death on the river had stilled them all—but the quiet satisfaction of the men was evident. They had reached the river and completed a task that most men would have abandoned. This, too, was what Guevara wanted. He spent no words praising them; the food in their bellies and a night's rest were commendation enough.

Long after the others had fallen asleep, Guevara swung in his hammock and wrote these words by flashlight:

Everything is proceeding more or less satisfactorily. With one fatal exception. Benjamin was physically weak but was determined to make himself into a combatant. He was not up to this test. His physical strength did not match his will.

Although there's been no word from main camp, or news from the outside concerning Sandoval and D'Esperey, they are due to arrive to complete the group. They should be in La Paz by now and will be guided to the main camp in a few days. I do not know what arrangements have been made to transport them from La Paz. Tania will handle it. The Bo-

livian Party's stance continues to be treacherous. Luckily, I expected nothing of them.

The days of short rations have imparted a slackening of enthusiasm. There have been problems in the forward detachment. Joaquin and Pombo have consistently performed well. Among the other Cubans, Marcos is a constant headache. I am a bit concerned that discipline may also have slackened back at main camp. Just a hunch. The others, generally, are doing well.

The next stage will be one of combat and decision.

31

THE CABIN OF the helicopter smelled of nylon and kerosene; it was too new to have taken on the more familiar smells of a combat aircraft, namely blood and piss and gun grease. Hoyle sat in the door gunner's seat, letting the wind flutter his trousers and balloon out his jacket. He watched the dusty towns and dirt roads flash below until the countryside became more hilly as they continued south and then southwest from Vallegrande.

Sprawled about the cabin were Charlie, Smith, and Santavanes; none seemed much interested in the countryside passing below. Santavanes read a book by Mikhail Sholokhov, and Smith sat with his rifle between his knees, staring without pause at the clouds drifting slightly below them. Seated behind the pilots was Major Holland, who held a map in his fist. Hoyle noticed that as they flew, the officer kept his thumb on the spot over which they were traveling, advancing it slowly as new landmarks came into view. This was a precaution Hoyle had also employed with third-world pilots. But on this glorious blue morning, Hoyle kept his map in his pocket and trusted the Bolivians to deliver them and the brand-new UH-1 Huey safely to their destination.

The day was astonishingly clear, and as the helicopter gained altitude, the ground seemed like a sheet of crumpled paper, hills and mountains depicted by penciled shades and the tracks of rivers all marked like squiggly lines. As the Ñancahuazú River came into sight,

Hoyle plugged in a set of headphones and listened to the Bolivian radio frequencies. The pilot announced his approach to the command element of the Fourth Battalion—the same luckless outfit that had been ambushed on the Camiri Highway. There was a considerable amount of radio traffic; beyond the Latin propensity for explanation, the air crackled with orders and counterorders, movements toward and away from the objective, and oddly, a continually repeated request for a pneumatic jackhammer.

Holland put his map in the front pocket of his jacket as the helicopter descended and turned north into a broad, shallow valley. The countryside was well watered and looked as though it would support cattle, but there were none. A single-track dirt road threaded along the valley floor, running north and south, and the pilot followed this at three hundred feet, heading toward an oxbow in the river where the Fourth Division had established a command post. Just north of the landing zone, the river cut across the valley floor from one side of the mountains to the foot of another range. There, tucked into a bend, was a small adobe ranch house with a corrugated zinc roof.

The helicopter landed in a brown, swirling cloud and a dozen Bolivian soldiers slouched away as Hoyle and Smith dropped from one set of doors and Santavanes and Holland the other. The helicopter remained on the landing zone, its engines whining and the huge blades turning almost slowly enough to see.

Valdéz trotted up from the farmhouse. "We hit paydirt." He jerked his thumb back at the house; it was surrounded by soldiers digging holes.

"What's going on?" Smith asked.

"Two days ago the local constabulary got a line on this house," Valdéz said. "They thought it might have been a cocaine lab. When they came to search, they found guns."

Valdéz led the men toward the house. There were no fewer than a company of Bolivian soldiers swarming around. Stacks of weapons were leaned against the house, as were about a dozen suitcases. All had been unearthed from pits scattered around the property.

"The chief of police came down last night, probably to get a payoff. Nobody was home, and he got pissed. He called the army."

"It don't pay to piss off the sheriff," Holland said. He spat a wad of tobacco.

A hundred yards from the house, two Bolivian soldiers were tying up a pair of prisoners, a man of about forty and a sixteen-year-old boy. Both looked as though they'd been beaten savagely.

"Who are they?" Hoyle asked.

"Terrorists," the corporal said. "We found them walking on the trail to Yaquí."

In the first place, there was no trail to Yaquí, it was a goat path; in the second place, Yaquí was twenty miles away, a long day and night's walk. The men in the dirt looked frightened and bewildered.

"Déjeme ver sus manos," Smith said to them.

Wrists tied together, the prisoners held out their palms. Their hands were calloused and their fingernails broken and dirty.

"They were armed," the corporal puffed. He held up an old Mauser rifle. Its leaf sight was broken, and the leather sling had been replaced by a piece of rope.

"These guys aren't guerrillas," Hoyle said. "They're farmers."

Charlie spoke to the two men in Guaraní. "They said they were hunting," he translated. "They crossed the field about three miles to the south when the military arrested them. They want to go home."

Hoyle believed Charlie, and he'd seen enough guerrillas in his life to suspect that the man and the boy were just what they said. Hunters.

A captain strode up then, his boots polished immaculately. "What is going on here?" he demanded.

"These men are not combatants," Hoyle said.

"Who are you?" the captain asked. He looked at Santavanes and at Smith, and he began to get an idea.

"Somos consejeros militares," Smith said. *"Del ministerio de la defensa."* Smith's Spanish was perfect, and his light hair seemed to make the young officer nervous.

"These people are being taken to Lagunillas for interrogation," he said.

"We don't think that's necessary."

"Those are my orders." The captain gestured, and a truck backed up. Soldiers tossed the boy bodily into the cargo bed.

"Let the boy go, at least," Hoyle said.

"They will be interrogated first," the captain snapped, and walked back toward the house.

Smith said to Charlie, "Go with them."

"All right."

"Charlie," Hoyle said, "when you get to town, make sure an officer signs for the prisoners."

Charlie said something in Guaraní to the man, who seemed relieved. Charlie pulled himself into the truck with the prisoners, a guard climbed up after them, and they drove away.

Valdéz returned from inside the house. He dumped the contents of a canvas bag at Smith's feet. "This came from under the fireplace."

In the sack were three M3A1 machine pistols wrapped in ocher-colored waxed paper. With the guns there were thirty-round magazines and cleaning kits. Santavanes picked up one of the weapons and examined it. "These are American," he said. "The serial numbers have been ground off."

"How did these guys get a cache of American guns?"

"They look like *Company* guns," Santavanes said. Communist insurgents didn't normally go to the trouble to conceal the provenance of their weapons. But the CIA did. Nor were they the only American weapons found—there were a dozen M1 carbines and as many Garand rifles; hand grenades; mortar rounds; and small-arms ammunition, all of it stamped U.S.

"What else did they bury?"

"Food, radios, ammunition, shit, you name it. They're still digging stuff up."

Smith looked at one of the machine pistols. It was daubed in cosmoline—packing grease. The weapons were not just unfired, they were new.

"Major Holland, do you have night-vision equipment?"

"We've got starlight scopes."

"Mr. Valdéz has a radio. Get on it, and get a team of your people in here. If anyone's moving around this river at night, I want to know about it."

"My guys?"

"Parachute them in here if you have to. I want night-vision-capable observation points inserted on the ridges east and west. I want them in by tomorrow night and kept in place until I tell you otherwise."

Holland nodded and walked off. Hoyle looked up at the ridgeline across the river. He was certain the enemy's main encampment was near.

"This is just a road head," Hoyle said. "If there's a base camp, it's going to be up there in the sticks." He scanned the mountains around the valley and pointed at the roughest stretch of terrain he could see. "It's going to be overlooking the river and the house, or they'll have observation posts. Probably there to the east."

"I'm aware of that." Smith walked purposefully for the house, and Hoyle followed.

"Look, I don't want to sound like Mr. Safety here, but are you sure you want to put Green Berets in? If they get contact, you're going to have U.S. troops in a shooting war."

"It was a war long before we got here, Mr. Hoyle."

THE ROAD TO Lagunillas gave sunstroke and chilblains in turn. The truck bounced about on a long mountain road that brought both sunlight and remarkably cool air. Swept over by wind and diesel exhaust, Charlie shivered with his back against the cab, and the soldier guarding the prisoners slept on one of the benches with his rifle wrapped in his arms and the stock tucked between his knees. It seemed hard to believe that a human being could sleep in such a position, in a truck that banged and rumbled about so, but the soldier was out for most of the long drive, sun and shade, heat and miserably foggy cold.

The prisoners had been untied and warned that if they tried to run, they would be shot. This was deterrent enough, and they sat close together for warmth and reassurance. The boy was quiet, but the man was eager to talk. Charlie learned that his name was Estlano and his son's name was Rodolfo. They were from the countryside outside of Yaquí and raised pigs and corn. Estlano made a point of saying that he had not seen the guerrillas, but it was known through the valley that they were about. He asked what he and Rodolfo might be charged with and was concerned that the army not confiscate his rifle because without it, he could not hunt. They spoke mostly in Guaraní, occasionally in Spanish, but Charlie could do little more than try to reassure them. If they knew nothing, he said, they would probably be let go.

"Are you an officer, Excellency?"

"I am an interpreter," Charlie said. "Please don't call me Excellency."

"I hope you will tell them that we are innocent."

"I'm sure they will just ask you questions, and then you will be free to go."

"Do you have a family?" Estlano asked.

"No," Charlie said.

"Then I am sorry for you."

The sky lowered and became uniformly gray. There was a change in the feel of the wind; it grew hard, and the air took on a worrying, almost prickly smell. As it grew much colder, it seemed almost certain that it would rain, and when the truck passed over a hilltop, they drove through a dark, dewy cloud and the sun was lost. On the other side, as the truck shifted gears and lurched through a long downgrade, the sun returned and the clouds cracked open in small brilliant patches of sunlight, and the greens around them became almost painfully sharp. That was when a jeep carrying two officers passed them and waved the driver to pull over to the side of the road.

The truck stopped at a place where a stream came steeply down a hillside and was directed into a wide culvert under the road. The driver turned off the engine, and there was the strong rushing sound of water over rocks. Charlie nudged the guard awake.

"¿Estamos allí todavía?" The guard yawned.

"No, we have been stopped," Charlie answered. "You'd better get up."

He looked over the top of the cab, but all he could see was the face of one of the two officers; they spoke with the driver, and some papers were handed back and forth, and then the two officers walked to the rear of the truck and pulled open the tailgate. One officer was a major, and the other was a captain. The captain wore his garrison cap, but the major did not.

"Get them off the truck," the major said.

Charlie noticed that the major limped badly and was missing a finger on his left hand. The soldier prodded Estlano and the boy out of the truck, and they jumped down onto the road. The soldier came to attention and saluted awkwardly. Charlie stood in the truck but did not jump down.

"These are the prisoners?"

"Yes, sir."

The major with the mutilated hand pointed up at Charlie. "Who is this man?"

"I work for the American embassy," Charlie said.

"He is the gringo's ass worm," the captain said. Charlie noticed a slight slurring of his words. He jumped down from the truck, and as he did so, he caught the distinct odor of *chicha*. The officers had been drinking.

The major drew a pistol from the shiny holster on his belt.

"The prisoners are going to Lagunillas for questioning," Charlie said.

The major acknowledged nothing and, in a smooth, concise movement, placed the muzzle of his weapon against the boy's face and pulled the trigger. The sharp bang of the weapon stunned Charlie. The boy's legs buckled under him, and he collapsed straight down on the road, folding up where he'd stood. Blood gushed from a hole above his right eye, an astonishing amount of blood, and the road grew black in a widening pool.

Charlie moved toward the major and tried to deflect the pistol. "What are you doing?"

"Get back, you fucking *indio*," the major spat. He pushed Charlie against the truck. "Get back or I'll shoot you, too."

Estlano choked and knelt in the dirt next to his son. The captain pulled him up by the arm and wheeled him around, shoving him against the truck. Charlie could see plainly now that the officers were drunk. Their eyes were wild.

"Why are you doing this?" Estlano sobbed. "We are only farmers."

"You are insurgents. Bandits."

"No. No. You are wrong—"

The major with the mutilated hand stood with the soldier and watched the captain jerk Estlano about.

"This man is in my custody," Charlie said.

The major hit Charlie in the face with the butt of his pistol. "Fuck you and your custody."

The captain slammed Estlano against the fender. "Tell me, *pendejo*, why you betrayed your country. The foreigners, I can understand, the Cubanos—they are Communists, mercenaries."

"I am not Cuban, Excellency, I am Bolivian."

"You are a Communist. A homegrown enemy. You betray the country that has nurtured you, protected you."

"Please, don't kill me . . . please . . . I have done nothing."

"How can decent people, loyal citizens, expect to have liberty and peace while traitors like you are allowed to live?" The captain was livid. His eyes were wide, and there was saliva collecting in the corners of his mouth.

"Oh, Jesus, oh, Mary, Mother of God, please help me . . ."

Estlano dropped to his knees. The captain aimed the pistol, and the report of the gun was a sharp, hard bang. Blood spattered on the front of Charlie's shirt with a whiff of gunpowder and brains. The shot echoed and rolled over the hillside. The officers walked back to their jeep, the major limping and the captain rolling as he walked like a sailor turned ashore. A welt had opened under Charlie's eye, and blood dripped onto his shirt, mingling with the blood of Estlano.

Charlie stood trembling in shock and rage. Absurdity was added to brutality when the soldier called after the officers: "Your Excellencies? Should I shoot the other one?"

The major put on his cap and looked back at Charlie. "No. Don't shoot him, take him to Lagunillas."

The jeep drove off, and somewhere a pair of crows called out from above the road. Then it began to rain.

32

THE FOURTH INFANTRY Division had companies billeted all over Lagunillas, and there were a number of detachments assigned to roadblocks. Santavanes had spent an hour on the radio, trying to locate the prisoners and Charlie. All of his inquiries were met adamantly with the statement that the military district had no one in custody, and it was not until Hoyle suggested that Santavanes ask if the battalion was keeping any *guests* that they were told Charlie was being questioned at a military police detachment outside of the city.

The road led to the fringes of the town and to the ruin of a church, or rather, a half-constructed cathedral that looked as though it had long ago been abandoned and forgotten. A warren of shanties had sprung up on the hillside around the site, a sort of parasitical annex made from parts of the uncompleted church. It gave the neighborhood a Neverland quality, as though the ants had somehow made off with the picnic. Some of the shacks had windows made of leaded glass; others had walls of cardboard but roofs of red tile, or doors cut together from wood taken out of pews and confessionals. Mud was splashed waist-high on the walls, and metallic blue flies took off and landed in a yellow trickle of sewage that ran down the middle of the street. The furtive nature of the buildings added a sense of heresy to what was already a heartbreaking little slum.

Hoyle pulled the Land Cruiser up to a place that might once have been intended to be a cloister. Charlie was seated on a pile of flagstone stacked under a set of half-completed arches. Hoyle could see that Charlie's eye was appallingly blackened and that there was blood on his shirt. His legs were crossed, as a prisoner might do to reduce the anxiety of his captors. There were two military policemen standing by the door to the church. One went inside, and the other marched away as Hoyle and Santavanes walked toward Charlie. None of the soldiers appeared the least concerned about their guest.

Hoyle came close, and Charlie did not stand up. His eyes met Hoyle's and said everything. The blood said everything. Hoyle did not need to ask what had happened.

"Get the first-aid kit," Hoyle said to Santavanes.

"Where are the prisoners, Charlie?"

"Out back," Charlie said. He shook his head. "I tried to stop it."

Santavanes returned from the truck, knelt down, and tended to Charlie's eye. His face was bruised the color of wine, and the cut below his eye could have probably taken a few stitches. Clotted with blood, it had started to ooze over, and it was too late to stitch it.

"Who hit you?"

"*Putos,*" Charlie said quietly. It was the first time anyone had heard him curse.

Hoyle walked into the church. Under the half-constructed apse, radios hissed and orderlies sat back in chairs, as unmoving as if they were made of stone. A few military policemen sat against the naves, their white helmets balanced on the muzzles of their rifles.

"Who's in charge here?"

No one answered. Hoyle finally walked up to a corporal slouched indolently next to a radio. "Where are your officers?"

"They are eating dinner."

"Where are the prisoners who were brought from the valley?"

No one answered, and the men seated against the walls averted their eyes. Hoyle felt for a moment like a schoolteacher asking about a forgotten assignment.

"Where are the bodies?"

One of the military policemen said, "We put them behind the building."

Hoyle walked through the church with the roof opened to the sky. Blocks had been cut and laid along what was once to be the transept, but now weeds and a few struggling saplings stuck up from between the stones. Where the shadow of the building gave way to sunlight, Hoyle could see the bodies wrapped in green waterproof tarps and bound about with rope. They had been tossed into tall grass. A pair of bare feet stuck from one lump and a smaller pair from the other, man and boy, father and son, swept into war on a whim and killed for half a reason.

For a moment Hoyle just stood. His mind was blurred.

He did not feel anything for these people. He did not know them and did not even know about them except to believe that they had nothing at all to do with the business in the Ñancahuazú. There was no reason for Hoyle to be affected, but he was. He had seen bodies before, untold hundreds, and even counting the ones killed for good reason, he had seen enough to be unmoved. But these two struck him with pathos, perhaps because he'd tried to vouchsafe for them, perhaps because he had not expected Charlie to be beaten and these people murdered, or perhaps because Hoyle was beginning to have had enough. Flies buzzed and crawled around the toes of the dead men. Thirty miles from the place they had been captured, and maybe fifty miles from their home, their bodies would probably never be claimed. It was certain the army would not admit to their murder. Guests of the Bolivian army often went missing.

Somewhere across the road, Hoyle heard the sound of children laughing and calling to one another. There was some daylight left, and after the officers had finished their meal, one of the corporals would be told to dig a hole, and two of the privates would do so, and then the bodies would be dumped in and covered over, and it would be as though the man and boy had never lived. Hoyle turned and made his way back through the church, and as he passed them, the orderlies and the military policemen all came to their feet. Not out of respect, or condolence, or any other reason except self-preservation.

The look on Hoyle's face was stone-cold murder.

THE OFFICERS' CLUB of the Fourth Division was a former plantation house, stucco and red-tiled with wide verandas that looked across Lagunillas and its hillsides. It was set away from the main highway, and around it were gardens and terraces, tended not quite immaculately but kept up enough to be verdant. There were two tennis courts and

several smaller outbuildings that had once been offices for the works
and quarters for the managers and administrators. For all its desperately coveted luxury, the place had about it a feeling of crash and bank-
ruptcy, for the sugar no longer grew and the mill that stood beside it
was a vast, rusted derelict, grown up through the middle with trees and
frequented only by bats and crows.

Hoyle drove up the long gravel drive past private soldiers who'd
been set to raking and slow-moving sergeants who oversaw them. He
parked, and as he walked up the steps into the mansion, he could not
help but marvel at a view that commanded every direction. The long
day was not yet over, and slivers of clouds rode the valley beyond. A bit
north, the mountains of the Ñancahuazú were first low and green and
then higher and blue and the sky above them bluer still now that
evening lurked in the east. Back over Lagunillas, the sun was surrendering peacefully in a few patches of red.

There was a sentry posted on the terrace, but he did not even make
eye contact with Hoyle. The fact that he was gringo was apparently
reason enough for Hoyle to be there, so the sentry clicked his heels
and opened the door. The foyer was stark though elegant, with a
sweeping staircase and terra-cotta floors. Laughter echoed off marble
and crystal as Hoyle walked into the first floor, where white-jacketed
stewards walked in hush, switching on electric lights and fussing over
immense silver candlesticks.

At a long bar near the veranda, Hoyle found the source of the laughter: Colonel Arquero and about a dozen officers, perfect in crisp linen
and field gray, looking like they'd never done a day of dirt-soldiering in
their entire life. As Hoyle entered, the laughter stopped instantly, and
every eye in the place was on him. Hoyle wore rumpled khaki trousers,
work boots, and a furrowed jacket, the same outfit he'd worn into the
field that morning. If it was disrespect he meant to communicate with
his clothing, he succeeded at once. The officers at the bar individually
and collectively took offense that anyone would join them so slovenly
dressed.

Hovering in the air was also the question of an invitation, and Hoyle
unquestionably lacked one. Nevertheless, he sauntered up and found a
seat. "Bourbon, please," he said.

Nobody spoke. Not a word of greeting or a word of derision,
though that note held strongly in the air.

"This is nice," Hoyle said, looking around. "Very posh. Who wants to go crashing around the bush when you can spend time in a place like this?"

The bartender's eyes were wide, and he seemed paralyzed. It was only after Arquero nodded that the man found a bottle and poured Hoyle a neat shot and placed it on the bar. The silence extended as Hoyle lifted the glass and downed it in several long swallows. He set the empty glass back down on the bar and sought out the barman's gaze.

"Un otro," Hoyle said, pursing his lips and giving back insolence for silence.

The barman poured again, in the absence of any negative guidance.

"That's the taste I've been missing." Hoyle managed to smile, though no one else did, not even the usually facetious Colonel Arquero.

One of the officers, a major, leaned toward Hoyle; the man seemed prepared to say something, but Colonel Arquero made a slight gesture, and the officer retreated to his bar stool. Hoyle noticed the limp and that the man's left hand was shattered. A finger was missing, but the deformity seemed more like a birth defect than a combat wound. From Charlie's description, Hoyle was certain this man was one of the murderers.

"To what do we owe the pleasure, Mr. Hoyle?" Colonel Arquero asked.

"Nothing special. I was out all day, Colonel, and I got thirsty."

Hoyle gave back the long, blank gazes. Beyond the veranda, a chorus of insects began to sing, as loud as the noise of a thousand alarm clocks.

Hoyle sipped at his drink. "You know, when I was in Laos," he said, "I knew a man who really loved whiskey. He was a military adviser. He had a C-130 parachute in a bulldozer—a Caterpillar D9, a big one—right into the jungle. Crashed through the trees, triple canopy; this was just outside Mu Gia. Somehow it landed upright. This guy, he got together a bunch of villagers and used machetes—he hacked his way through the jungle. It took two whole days, but they got to the bulldozer and started it up. And he scraped the top off this hill, cut it right out and made a helicopter landing zone. An epic piece of civil engineering, and he did it all so he could have cases of Jim Beam flown in."

The silence was excruciating. Colonel Arquero shifted on his stool. "What you did in Asia is of no interest to us here."

"Well, see, I think it could be," Hoyle said. "Once we had that landing zone, we started flying in a doctor once a week. And then we built a clinic. And the Kha tribesmen, they'd bring their children. Their sick, you know, to get treated. And pretty soon we had volunteers. We pulled together a militia—they elected their own officers and organized companies to fight the Pathet Lao."

The major with the crippled hand pushed his drink away and leaned close. His voice was a rasp. "If you were so successful, Mr. CIA Man, why don't you just go back there?"

"I didn't catch your name, sir."

"Placido," the man said, sharply, abruptly, like a challenge to a duel.

Hoyle looked the major full in the face. "Funny thing is, *Major,* I volunteered to come here."

"And do what, Mr. Hoyle?" Colonel Arquero asked. "Give us the benefit of your funny stories? We need arms, we need ammunition and aircraft. We were promised these things before you came. And now— nothing. You have consistently opposed the arming of our military. Why?"

"I think you need to use what you have, Colonel."

"How would you know what we need?" Placido hissed. "I have just served in Abapó. I saw what was done to a company of my men."

"And what happened today, Major? What happened to the two people who were captured at Yaquí?"

"They were traitors," Placido said, "vermin. If Bolivia is to survive, it needs hard measures. And you need countries like mine to resist communism. To keep it away from you—out of Latin America—out of Mexico. Off your doorstep, so you can have your hamburgers and television."

Placido jammed a finger into Hoyle's chest. "We fight because you haven't got the guts to." He shook his finger in Hoyle's face. "How dare you come in here with your Yankee courage—"

Hoyle's hand moved from the bar rail so quickly that it was a blur. His open hand struck the major in the throat just below the chin, and his thumb hooked into the muscle above the man's Adam's apple. This blow was struck full force, without thought or self-control, and the power of it lifted Major Placido from his feet. As the major was thrust back, Hoyle levered his elbow and smashed the officer down onto the bar. Placido's hand went quickly to his holster, and he managed to extract his pistol, a blue-steel Walther PPK. Hoyle punched the heel of his palm under the major's nose and just as quickly slapped the weapon from his hand. The gun went skittering across the bar and crashed into a rack of glasses behind the barman. The instant of violence was so profound and astonishing that a second or two seemed to pass before the sound of breaking glass could be perceived. Hoyle had struck Placido very nearly a killing blow, and now his arm looped under the man's chin and he held the major's head in the vice formed by forearm and bicep. Eyes bulging, Placido choked off a muffled gasp. No one dared come to the major's aid, and Hoyle's hold was so obviously deadly that a jerk would be enough to break the man's neck.

Hoyle's face was against Placido's ear, and his voice was hoarse, choked with a slow-burning and thoughtful rage. "I didn't come down here to watch you assholes play Nazi. Every time one of your stormtroopers shoots a prisoner or burns a cornfield, you make the enemy that much stronger."

Hoyle's chokehold tightened, and something like the mewing of a cat came from the major's throat.

"Outside that door, children are eating *rats*. They don't have clean water to drink. They can't read. And you can't understand why there's a war on. You don't like gringos—tough shit. We'll pull out, the CIA, the Green Berets, everybody. In three days, assholes like you will be hanging from the streetlights."

Hoyle shoved Placido back against the others. He fell to the floor, legs sprawling, and a bar stool fell on top of him. Hoyle's jacket was open. The officers could plainly see a .45-caliber Colt automatic hanging in his shoulder holster. Hoyle turned to Arquero. "What about you, Colonel? You want to kill some traitors, too? Or is that little pistol of yours just for show?"

Arquero seethed. "Leave, Mr. Hoyle."

"I think I will," Hoyle said. "Thanks for the drink."

As he walked through the mansion, cooks, mess boys, and sentries peeked through doorways and around corners, horror-struck. Not one of them said a word, or thought to do so, and as Hoyle started the Land Cruiser and drove away, he was quite surprised that no one took the opportunity to shoot him in the back.

. . .

A LANTERN BURNED on the table in Hoyle's room at the casita. The parts of his pistol were laid out on a blanket-covered table before him, as were oil and rags and a bore brush. Smith had burst in, throwing the curtain back and thrusting his face into the lamplight, as angry as any man would ever see him.

"Jesus, goddammit! Do you have any idea what kind of cable traffic is flying around? Everybody from Ambassador Hielman to President Jesus goddamn Barrientos." The edges of his glasses were collecting condensation. His voice had risen an octave, and it now bore the strong imprint of his New England upbringing, broad "A"s and swallowed "R"s, all rapid-fire and high-pitched, like the snarling of a terrier.

"What's the problem?"

"You know goddamn well. I'm talking about that cripple you grabbed by the tonsils."

Hoyle made a show of assembling his pistol. "He was annoying me."

Smith's hand came down on the unassembled pieces. He leaned his face into the circle of lantern light. "That cripple's old man just happens to be the Bolivian ambassador to the UN. You got the entire southern half of the planet going apeshit right now. What the hell were you doing in Lagunillas?"

"Looking for Charlie."

"What were you doing at the officers' club?"

"That asshole shot the prisoners."

"So?"

"He murdered them."

"Shooting prisoners around here is a national fucking pastime! What the fuck were you thinking?"

Hoyle stood and walked from the casita. As he passed through the front room, Valdéz and Major Holland tried their best to look deaf and invisible. Smith followed Hoyle out of the house, jabbering at him; the argument had taken on the character of a domestic dispute.

"We don't need this shit, Hoyle. We don't need you going hostile on Bolivian officers." Smith's voice was getting louder.

A head poked out of one of the tents behind the house. Hoyle and Smith were making a scene, and the Green Berets loved it.

Hoyle said, "I punched him out. Big deal. You think it really matters if one more asshole gets punched out in this shitty country?"

"It matters if *you* do it."

"I'm not going to sit by and watch peasants get shot."

"Yes, you are," Smith said. "This is just a job. Bolivia is just another third-world shithole. Sometimes we prop them up, and sometimes we take them down. Don't go righteous on me."

"Maybe it's time somebody did."

Smith pulled Hoyle's sleeve and turned his face into the light from the doorway. "What were you doing at the Ministry of Information last week?"

"Who told you I was there?"

"It doesn't matter who told me. What were you doing?"

Hoyle had no idea how much Smith knew, if he knew about Maria, or if he knew about the lake.

"What were you doing there?"

"Asking a few questions. I didn't think the agency would mind."

"If it's intelligence-related, I need to know about it," Smith said. "If it's personal, emotional, or physical, you're goddamn right I mind."

"What are you, Mr. Tradecraft now?"

"What were you doing at the ministry?"

"The woman, Maria, she said she was Nicaraguan. Her accent is Cuban. I looked on her desk while you were in with the minister; she was working on visa requests. I saw the lists on her desk, but she lied about it. Alameda is selling passports. He probably did the paper for the Cuban team that's operating in Ñancahuazú."

"You don't *know* that. You *think* that. You don't have any proof."

"The girl has proof."

"Maybe she does, maybe she doesn't. What are you gonna do? Screw it out of her?"

Hoyle began to feel anger. Smith's next words would push him into fury. "Don't go fucking this up over a piece of ass."

Hoyle grabbed Smith by the collar and slammed him into the wall of the house. His physical power astonished Smith—he had been pulled off his feet and whirled through the air. Hoyle bounced him off the wall, and Smith reached into his holster and jammed the muzzle of a snub-nosed .38 into Hoyle's throat. Hoyle froze instantly at the flash of the gun in the moonlight.

Smith's voice was like death. "Let go of me."

Hoyle held on, fists full of shirt. His voice was devoid of even a wisp of fear. "You little fuck. You don't have the balls to shoot me."

Smith's thumb snapped back the hammer. The chrome gun was steady in his fist and now jammed tight against Hoyle's jugular.

"I'll splatter your ass right here. Now listen." Hoyle's fist gripped harder on Smith's collar. Smith yelled again: "LISTEN!"

Panting in rage, Hoyle shoved Smith away.

Smith still kept the pistol trained on Hoyle's face. "The rifles we found at the farmhouse were part of a CIA shipment sent to the Bolivian National Police. Your friend Zeebus initiated the transfer back in October. It was supposed to be part of a routine assistance package. Colonel Arquero took delivery of the guns in Mexico City."

"What are you saying?"

"The guns we found at the guerrillas' farmhouse came from the CIA."

"Who told you this?"

"CIA Station Mexico City. Confirmed. In writing."

"Why would Arquero sell weapons to a Cuban expeditionary force?" Hoyle asked.

"You're going to find out."

Hoyle was bowled over. He'd expected corruption but not such perfect duplicity.

Smith lowered the pistol. "We've got new orders from Langley. Guevara goes down. They don't care how it gets done. We do whatever it takes to get Bolivians into the field."

"Is this Langley talking, or are you just bucking for a corner office?"

"Both," Smith said. "Langley wants this thing pinched off before it becomes a full-blown civil war. If the Bolivians won't stomp the Cubans, we will."

Hoyle's breathing became labored. The night around him seemed suddenly suffocating and hot as an open oven. How could this be? How could Arquero have tricked the CIA into shipping weapons? And why did no one notice when he just turned around and sold them on the open market?

"How do I get Arquero to talk?"

"I don't care," Smith said. "Do what you have to."

"Then no protocol. No more ass kissing."

"Do what you have to. Just make it deniable on our end."

Smith went back into the casita, and the sound of insects, billions of insects, swelled around Hoyle and filled the night as high up as the stars.

Hoyle's hands were trembling. Perhaps it was the revelation of Arquero's treachery, perhaps it was anger, perhaps it was fear that this operation was spiraling wildly out of control. Hoyle was aware suddenly that people were staring. Half a dozen Green Berets had assembled by their tents. They'd enjoyed the show but probably would have preferred it if the argument had ended in a serious ass kicking. Hoyle stooped with embarrassment as they returned to their tents. Closer behind him, Charlie was waiting by the Land Cruiser.

He, too, had seen everything. The night around them was alive with the buzzing of insects and the hoots of monkeys. Ten thousand sounds had been substituted for the colors of the day.

Hoyle shook his head, self-conscious, still angry, still breathing like a man who'd climbed a ladder to a fifth-story window. "I'm sorry you had to see that, Charlie."

Charlie smiled. It was a rare and agreeable thing when he did.

"Do you think he would've shot me?" Hoyle asked.

"I don't know," Charlie answered. "You think he would have missed?"

33

WORD OF HOYLE'S altercation with Major Placido had spread through the army faster than a list of promotions. Bolivian opinion of the incident was mixed. Brass, like blood, is thicker than water. Predictably, the murder of the two prisoners was not a topic of discussion. Prisoners, almost by definition, were guilty, and Placido had been within his rights to do with them as he chose. A few found it hard to believe that the execution of prisoners could be the real reason for Hoyle's outburst.

By the end of the week, all talk of the incident had faded. Placido's thrashing was largely eclipsed by the discovery of the guerrillas' equipment at the Zinc House. The newspapers, too, had learned of the operation in the Ñancahuazú, and Smith had flown to La Paz to ensure that Minister Alameda's office handled the news without hysteria. That some of the weapons were American-made was known to the press, and through Alameda, Smith put out word that the arms were Korean War surplus. Kept secret was Arquero's duplicity and the fact that a CIA arms shipment had been diverted to aid Communist insurgents.

Also secret was Hoyle's scheme to force Colonel Arquero to release Tania from prison. He planned this through a combination of physical coercion and blackmail. Hoyle's arrangements were not yet complete, and though he'd wanted very much to accompany Smith and see Maria, Hoyle had not pressed to go to La Paz. Not yet.

"At a safe house, awaiting transfer," Diminov said. "Come, Tania."
Hoyle held Tania back. "I want Guevara's codes and frequencies."
The request stunned her. But causing more consternation and fear
was Diminov's bland reply: "I have them."

Tania watched, dumbfounded, as Diminov reached into his coat,
pulled out a white envelope, and held it out. Tania's mouth opened;
words strangled in her throat. Tania felt as though she were being
pulled down a rabbit hole into a mortal and false-hearted wonderland.
The revelation exploded in her head: Robert, the Soviets—they were
selling Guevara out. The question Robert had put to her in the plaza,
when he'd asked if Tania thought it possible to drug Guevara, this
question uncoiled in her mind in a grand, staggering burst of darkness
and grief. Tania comprehended suddenly and horribly what the
arrangement was: Guevara was to be betrayed to the Americans. She
herself was to betray Che and receive her own freedom. Tania was to
be made into Judas. She staggered backward and felt Hoyle's hand
steadying her arm.

"Where are her travel documents?" Diminov asked.

"She gets the passport after she makes the rendezvous," Hoyle answered.

"That wasn't the arrangement."

Behind Diminov, Santavanes stepped from the shadow of the
gallery. He carried an FN rifle.

"It is now," Smith said. "This is the deal. After she guides in the two
new players, she makes sure Guevara goes to the junction of the Ñancahuazú and Iripiti rivers."

"And then what?" Diminov's tone was arch, but Hoyle and Smith
knew he held no cards.

Smith felt not the slightest twinge of sympathy. In an equation that
must always add up to zero, Tania, like Guevara, was a negative number, an enemy, and simply that.

"After the guerrilla column has been liquidated, a Special Forces
team will extract her." Smith's voice was bland, as though he were describing a trip to the store.

Tania rolled her head from side to side. The word "no" fell from her
lips like a pebble dropped down a well. She saw Robert standing by a
wall filled with dead, but the light seemed to swallow them and smear
out his shape, as it had done to her jailers just hours before.

None of this could be real. The world had fallen off its axis and capsized into insanity.

She heard Diminov say, "She's in no condition to be placed back in the field."

Smith was pitiless. "She guides the messengers, and we get the codes, or I shove her in the trunk and drive back to the Palace of Justice. Your call."

A thin wind blew over them.

"What is going on?" Tania finally sputtered. "How can this be?"

Diminov put up his hand. "You will have your orders," he said.

"Orders to do what?" Tania asked.

Diminov ignored the question as if it had been spoken by a child. He handed Sergev the envelope. Sergev stepped forward and stuck it against the glass of one of the small crypts. He backed off warily.

Smith moved forward, tore open the envelope, and read. Several sheets of foolscap listed recognition and response signals, radio frequencies, and the map locations of half a dozen of the guerrillas' storage caves.

Smith nodded, and Hoyle let go of Tania's arm. She walked several lurching steps toward Diminov. As Tania reached the fat man, her knees gave way, and she collapsed into his arms. Hoyle fought off a twinge of conscience. He had helped engineer her release, but he knew that she had not been delivered from harm. She had been placed in mortal danger; worse for her, she was to betray a man she loved.

Above them, the sky put down light that made the afternoon painfully stark; the colors were so fervent and the shadows so black that it seemed like the choice between life and death, good and evil. A gust of melancholy swept over Hoyle. It was not sympathy. He felt suddenly done in, fed up with the Game. The quicker all was lost, the quicker he could leave this place and become something other than a trafficker in the broken and the dead.

Smith and Hoyle turned and walked back for the car, leaving Tania and Diminov in a wilderness of graves.

36

J UST AFTER NINE P.M., Hoyle glided through the lobby of the
Hotel Cochabamba to the desk of the concierge, who handed
him a room key and summoned a bellman with a knowing dip of the
head. Hoyle's overnight bag was whisked from him by a smiling porter
who said slyly, "Welcome back, Señor," and guided Hoyle to the elevator.

The rooms had been made ready, his and Maria's adjoining, numbers 405 and 406, with balconies facing out over the Calle Sagamaga.
Hoyle's reservations had been made in advance, and neither he nor
Maria had to undergo the ritual of checking in at the desk. All was
taken care of, Hoyle's bills settled generously in cash and more than
adequate gratuities set aside for the manager, the concierge, and the
bell captain. This ensured that Hoyle and Maria moved almost invisi-
bly into and out of their rooms, neat and inconspicuous.

As the elevator door opened on the fourth floor, the bellman handed
Hoyle his valise and accepted a small wad of Bolivianos. "The wine is
in your room, sir," the bellman said. He handed over Hoyle's room
key, smiled, and disappeared back into the elevator.

At the end of the hallway, Hoyle threaded the key into the lock and
pushed open the door. He had no idea if Maria would be inside, or if
she would even be able to join him. Their communication was by
means of notes left at the post office box, and Hoyle had last been able

to write her only that he had made accommodations for the weekend. He entered quietly and found the room undisturbed; noise from the street gave it a certain humming silence. He switched on the light to find bed and furniture just so and the fan slowly turning above. A bucket of champagne, a towel, and two glasses were placed on a tray on the table. The air held the faintest hint of perfume. The door to the adjoining room was opened a crack, and Hoyle tossed his valise on the bed and went to the door.

The room beyond was dark, and Maria was sitting by the window with her hands folded. Through the curtains, neon reflected up from the street upon her and gave an emerald cast to her shadow. She stood as Hoyle entered, and as she turned toward him, there was an expression of expectation and relief on her face. They embraced for a long moment and then kissed.

"Hello, friend," Hoyle said.

"I've missed you," she answered.

Hoyle kissed her neck and her throat and placed his hands on either side of her cheeks and kissed her again deeply. As they embraced, Maria felt the hard corners of a pistol tucked into a holster under Hoyle's left arm. Her hand pulled away from it. Hoyle at once sensed her uneasiness and understood the reason. There are people for whom guns are not objects or tools: They represent finite and dangerous things, like the edge of a cliff, or the open sea beyond a ship's railing.

"Let me get rid of this," he said.

Hoyle took off his jacket and threaded his arms through the shoulder holster. As he took off the weapon, Maria said nothing; she had not known until this moment that he normally carried a gun. He closed the pistol in a drawer of the nightstand, and Maria seemed a bit more calm. No more was said about it. The reasons that Hoyle might carry a gun, Maria had guessed weeks ago.

"I'm so glad you could come," Hoyle said.

"I almost couldn't."

He kissed her again. Drinking in her perfume, he closed his eyes. "Can you spend the night?"

"Yes. Tonight only," she answered. "We have one night."

They held each other, and in this moment having one night together was sufficient; the reasons for parting could be sorted out later.

"I'd like some wine."

Hoyle opened the bottle, making an apology that he did not have a sword handy to crack off the cork. At this, Maria smiled. Hoyle poured two glasses and pulled another chair up to where Maria had sat, just back from the balcony. Hoyle did not turn the light on, and they sat in the glow of neon filtered through the curtains. The champagne was good and smelled as it always did to Hoyle—like a woman. He drank his glass in two or three long drafts.

"Are you all right?"

"Yes," Hoyle said, "I think I am."

The business at the cemetery still troubled him. The pathetic state in which they'd found Tania, the tortures that Hoyle was certain she had endured, and the messy, deadly business that was ahead of her, all these things heaved up in his mind. Maria could not know what state of affairs distracted Hoyle, but she was his lover and was extremely prescient; she was certain he was troubled but did not think it best to ask him directly what it was that made him uneasy. She could hardly ask him, "So, how was your week?" She was certain that her lover was some kind of agent, and after all, what do you ask a spy if you don't expect to be lied to?

"You seem distracted," she said.

"I'm happy to be here—with you."

"Are you sure?"

He touched her face and kissed her lightly. "Yes, I'm sure of that." A moment passed as they sat bathed in the green light.

There rose in her some vague sense of guilt; this reflection danced with another, a sense of dishonesty, of immorality. It occurred to her that she was cheating against cheating. She had become a rare and wanton thing: a mistress who had taken a lover.

"Am I wrong to want to see you?" she asked.

"No," Hoyle said. "It isn't wrong. It feels right in my heart."

"And right in mine."

"You're beautiful," he said. Entirely true, and a perfect evasion, talk of Maria's singular beauty was better by far than talk of right and wrong.

"Do you want me?" she asked.

"Very much."

"I'm sorry, too, that we have to keep things hidden," she said.

"Maybe it's best that some things are just for us."

They kissed, a kiss that lengthened as it grew sensuous. Hoyle's arms moved around her shoulders and pulled her toward him. Maria put down her wineglass and turned herself to accept Hoyle's embrace. He ran his hands through her hair and pulled her close. Neither of them had thoughts anymore of the world. Or their troubles. Every care melted away, every duty, every plan, and they gave themselves and took for themselves; their world became their two rented rooms, a self-contained place without judgment or guilt.

HOURS LATER, THEY were still tangled together on the bed. Neither could sleep, so they held each other, listening to the sounds of the street below, quiet sounds now, for it was after midnight and curfew had put silence on La Paz.

Unlike Hoyle, who had only sketchy beliefs, Maria was still a Catholic. She closed her eyes as she held Hoyle and silently prayed the Act of Contrition in English. She had been told by the nuns at school that saying this prayer, even silently, would absolve her of all sin; she would be forgiven completely but would be diminished in grace for having sinned. Grace could be regained by many things, by good works, by taking communion, or by the blessing of a priest, or better, a bishop. Grace and forgiveness were more wholly attained by confession, but as a stopgap, the Act of Contrition would do. As a little girl, Maria had been told that grace was the spark that animated her body and gave it life. Humanity. Without grace, a human being was merely an animal.

Life had batted her about. Maria had seen much and lost nearly all that she'd seen or had. Saying the act was a small thing that she clung to, as she did her nightly prayers. The concepts of grace and forgiveness beckoned from a simple place far away from what had become an increasingly complex life.

The truth was, Maria no longer attended mass and felt very far from a state of grace. As she listened to Hoyle breathe, she prayed for forgiveness, not only for what she had done but for what she had dreamed.

"Are you awake?"

"Yes."

"I've had a nightmare," she said.

"I'm sorry," he said. "Of what?"

Maria closed her eyes. "I can just remember it. If I lie still. With my body in the same position. The dream will come to me."

"Because of the way you're positioned?"

Maria held herself still next to him. Her eyes were closed in concentration. "Yes. If I hold myself in the same way. With my arms and legs just as they were, the dream comes back."

In the slice of neon from the curtained windows, Hoyle could see a look of worry on her face.

"Doesn't that happen to you?" she asked. "Don't dreams come back to you when you lie a certain way?"

"No," he said.

"You must dream," she said.

"I do." The things Hoyle dreamed he did not often share. He touched her face. She turned her cheek against him, rising to his caresses, but he noticed that she did not open her eyes.

"What was the dream?"

"It was very upsetting. They said that I had killed a child. They said I was a murderess. That I'd killed a little girl and the authorities were after me."

"Was there a reason?"

"I didn't kill anyone. I could not. But I'd lied about where I was. I lied to my family, and I lied to the police, because I had seen the little girl just before she was taken and killed. I was the last to see her alive. At the beach in Verdan, where my family's home was. I woke just before they came for me. My mother realized that I'd lied about seeing the girl. It broke her heart, but she told the police that I hadn't told the truth. They thought I must be involved. It seems only a story to tell now, but it frightened me very much."

Hoyle kissed her on the forehead. He could feel the tension in her shoulders; she was trembling as she spoke.

"Who was the little girl?"

"My daughter." Maria breathed slowly. "But I don't have a daughter. In my dream, she was my little girl. It all came back to me when I moved my body. And when I stay in the position, I can see it all very clearly."

"You didn't harm the girl," Hoyle said, in judgment and exoneration.

"I could never."

"In your dream, who did it? Who murdered her?"

Maria remained in the same position under the sheets, her legs crossed, her arm across Hoyle's chest.

"I left her at the beach. I left her alone, and I should not have done that. And then I lied. I lied and said that she had run away—but it was me. I left her, thoughtlessly, alone at the beach. Someone, a man, someone I didn't know, took her and killed her."

Hoyle put his leg over Maria's thigh, then pulled her arm up around his neck. "Here," he said. "Move, so the dream won't cling to you."

"Do you think that I am insane?"

"Insane?"

"A bad person?"

"You've had a bad dream. That's a long way from being insane." Hoyle put his hand on her hair. "You are not insane. You're not even crazy."

"No one is perfectly sane."

"No."

Outside, the city lay still, but it gave off almost imperceptible sounds.

"I've told lies," she said.

"You're very hard on yourself," Hoyle said.

"I never think that I am. It's not right to lie."

"It was a dream, Maria. You did not hurt a little girl, and a lie told in a dream is not a lie."

Maria put her head on his chest. She heard his heart beat. How strong it was, she thought.

"Are you all right, little one?"

"Yes. I am now."

Hoyle looked at his watch on the nightstand. It was a very long time before morning. "Would you like some wine?"

"I would."

"Watch your eyes," he said.

Hoyle turned on the lamp, got out of bed, and walked to the table. Her eyes first pinched by the light, Maria watched him. His nude body seemed like a supple, hard machine to her, a thing that was powerful and well maintained. Like a weapon. There were shadows across the room where Hoyle opened the wine and found two glasses. He walked back to the bed without the least self-consciousness. Maria looked at all of him, his broad shoulders, the muscles of his arms and chest, his cock and balls. He was a specimen, she thought, and he was at ease with himself and with her. Hoyle handed her a glass and poured out a garnet-colored zinfandel. It smelled of oak and cinnamon. The bed smelled of them.

"Tell me about Alameda."

"He is vain."

"All men are vain. They're either obviously vain or secretly vain," Hoyle said.

"Which are you, then?"

Hoyle slipped back under the sheets and covered himself. "Secretly vain," he said.

"That is what I would expect you to say—something secret. Though I don't agree with you that all men are vain. And I don't think that you are vain."

"How do you know?" Hoyle smiled. "I think of myself as very handsome."

She had just watched him cross the room; naked, he'd moved with an unconscious, leonine grace. There were half a dozen mirrors around, but his eyes had not gone to one of them. Alameda would have stopped at each.

"You don't talk about yourself," Maria said. "And you rarely talk about what you do for a living. When you do talk about yourself, you say vague things."

"What do you think I do?"

"Do you want me to say, really?"

"Yes," Hoyle said.

"You've said you are a contractor, but you have a friend at the embassy."

"People have friends."

"And people have jobs, but your friend has the useless-sounding job of 'cultural attaché.' "

"That does sound useless," Hoyle admitted.

"And although this man is your friend, you have never told me his name."

"His name is Smith."

"Oh, this is really going somewhere," Maria said. "None of us has a real name."

"That is really his name."

"Are you sure?" Maria asked.

Hoyle was not. He shrugged.

"And although this man is your friend, you've never mentioned where he lives."

"In La Paz."

"Close to the embassy," Maria said flatly.

"You were telling me about Alameda." Hoyle smiled, and Maria gave one back.

"No. I was going to tell you what I thought you did for a living."

"Tell me."

"You are absolutely unclear when you want to be, and you are very, very good at turning a question and making people talk about themselves and not ask about you. I think that you are a spy."

"Do you think the United States has need of spies in Bolivia?"

"There is a war here."

"Not a war."

"Then almost one. You are a contractor, whatever that is, and you have been to Vietnam, and you were shot. And I think you have something to do with the war in Ñancahuazú. With the things that are going on there."

Her green eyes took him in sturdily. Hoyle was again struck by her, and he felt a shiver, a physical pop someplace behind his heart. Hoyle looked into her eyes, and it took every bit of his nerve to do so. She seemed to him so bright and perfect; it was almost as though he were afraid to touch her. Her face was not simply pretty, it had in it character, it communicated intelligence and wisdom; there was magic to this woman, and tragedy.

"You're a spy," she said to him.

"A contractor—for the government. And I work in the southeast."

"The guerrillas are in the southeast."

A moment passed. Long enough for Maria to shift her weight and hold him closer. Then he said, "We have secrets."

"We do," she said. "Why did you tell me your real name, Paul Hoyle, if you are a spy?"

"Please don't say 'spy.' "

"I'm sorry," she said. "I don't like the word 'whore,' either."

"Maria, don't say that."

"I am a mistress."

"You're not a whore, and I won't stand to hear it said about you. Even if you say it yourself. Don't think it. And please don't say it to me, because it is an ugly word."

Maria put down her wineglass and again put her head on his chest. She did not feel chastised. She had pushed him by saying something she had known would provoke him. She had hoped in a small way that it would. Not to fish for a rebuttal from him—she did not require her existence to be propped up. Maria was an exceptional thing: a beautiful woman who remained true to herself, true and blunt.

She kissed his neck, and for a moment Hoyle was glad that Maria could not see his face. He felt as though he were standing on a cliff edge a thousand feet above dark water. He did not like the word "whore," and he did not like the word "spy." The words might be closer together than he liked to think.

"Is Alameda corrupt?" Hoyle asked.

"This is Bolivia," Maria said. There was no judgment in her voice.

"Does he take money?"

"From where?"

"People. Political parties. The ministry's funds?"

"There's money from Presidente Barrientos, envelopes that come weekly. And he takes money from the PCB."

Money from the presidente was not a surprise; money from the Communist Party of Bolivia was.

"Are you sure?"

"Yes. He's met with Selizar Galán, maybe a dozen times. They meet at my apartment."

These get-togethers were not a complete surprise to Hoyle— Alameda was known to be an extremely venial man—but confirmation that a sitting minister was in contact with the head of the Communist Party: This was important.

"He sells press credentials and passports," Maria said.

"To whom?"

"Everyone, anyone. They're not peddled on the street. He's too clever for that. And what he sells is too valuable. The credentials are a ministry function. The passports are not."

"Where does he get the documents?"

"The minister of the interior."

Hoyle thought of a fat man with a pencil mustache, a colonel, one of Presidente Barrientos's coup partners from the air force. His name was Gallegos, and he was one of the few cabinet members who did not wear his military uniform daily to work. Clutching, materialist, and rapacious, he was the picture of a man who would take advantage of his situation.

"Is there a list?"

"Of what?"

"Of people he's sold passports to."

"Yes."

Maria knew by instinct where this was headed. Hoyle delayed; much was in the balance. He did not want to sully what they had with the business of the Ñancahuazú. He did not wish to put her in harm's way, but there were things that he had to do.

Hoyle drew a long, even breath and said, "It would help me if I got some blank press credentials."

He waited like a man who had tossed a stone down a well. Maria did not move but remained lying on his chest. A long moment passed, long enough for Hoyle to wish he could draw back his words.

"You have been to the office. Your friend seems to be on good terms with the minister . . . it wouldn't be a problem for you to apply."

"Do you know where the credential cards are kept?"

"In Señora Truillo's files."

"Could you get to them?"

Maria remembered Hoyle's friend dropping off the briefcase. "It seems to me that you've paid the minister—"

"We have," Hoyle said.

"Then he could give you credentials, all that you wanted."

Hoyle's voice was even. "We don't want to apply."

Maria drew the line that connected the dots. Hoyle and his friends wanted the accreditation of journalists, and they did not want Alameda to know. Maria knew that the Communists did not pay Alameda for nothing—any press credentials issued to a gringo, especially a gringo contractor, would be promptly reported to the Party. They would then be worthless as cover.

When Maria answered, her voice was without resentment or surprise. "Why should I do this for you?"

"You should not do it if it is dangerous."

"That isn't what I asked," she said.

"I'm working against people who are trying to start a war."

"Maybe they have their reasons," Maria said.

"I think they do. In Bolivia, the rich have too much, and the poor have nothing at all," Hoyle said, his words an honest mirror of his thoughts. "I despise poverty. And I despise greed. But of all things, most of all, I hate tyranny."

"Don't the Bolivians have that? Isn't there tyranny here?"

"I won't defend what the Bolivians have. There are greedy men everywhere."

"Then it's *Communist* tyrants you hate most," Maria said.

Hoyle propped himself on an elbow and looked at her. "I'm surprised you say that so casually."

"I'm not casual, Paul Hoyle. In Cuba the Communists killed my family. They took my home."

"Then help me."

She put her arm around him, and as she leaned forward, her hair fell across her forehead. She was not cold or distant, but she did not commit, either. She kissed him and then pulled back to look at him in the lamplight.

"I will think about it," she said.

37

T<small>ANIA WOKE AS</small> the sun was setting. She only vaguely remembered how she had come to this place, a comfortable bed in a large bedroom. Shreds of memories flickered in her mind, her arrest, a dozen different tortures and her own hoarse screams echoing, the incredible brightness of daylight and the two nameless Americans who had driven her to the cemetery and made demands before her release.

Tania turned her head slowly toward the window. Urban sounds came through the half-opened sash, the whirr of traffic and above that, the diffuse white noise of a city. The room about her came gradually into focus—twilight slanting; horizontal-striped wallpaper; furniture like you'd find in a family home: bedstead, night tables, and a dresser.

The room kept about it a sense of dread. As her senses coalesced, she was surprised to see a large man with ordinary features seated in a chair beside the window. Light through the curtain placed a gentle bar of light across his broad shoulders. The expression on his face was so bland as to put her at ease.

Tania did not know his name, but she recognized him as the same man who had accompanied Diminov to the cemetery. He looked at her for a moment, making sure her eyes remained open.

"Are you awake?" he asked her in Russian.

Sergev's voice was gruff but indicated a certain concern for her well-being. A professional interest, but authentic.

"Yes," she answered, also in Russian. "I'm awake now."

With a polite nod, Sergev left the room. Tania remained in the bed, not quite capable of movement. She heard a rustling outside the door. She lay completely still, her hands by her sides, and slowly became aware that she'd been dressed in a clean cotton nightgown. There was a bandage on her elbow and another on her knee, where the skin had been scraped off.

The man Tania knew as Robert entered, followed by the woman who had posed as her aunt. Since Tania had seen her last in Buenos Aires, the woman seemed to have aged a dozen years. Robert Diminov stood at the end of the bed. The aunt took Tania's hand in her own.

"How are you?" the woman asked, gravely solicitous.

"What day is it?"

"Monday."

In Tania's head, a slow arithmetic set itself in motion. She worked backward from the day of her arrest and then the surreal circumstances of her release. She guessed that she had slept in this bed for perhaps twenty-four hours. She still did not remember coming here.

"Where am I?"

"La Paz. A safe house," Diminov said.

The aunt checked Tania's pulse and listened to her heart with a stethoscope. She pronounced that Tania had come through her ordeal remarkably. Tania's thoughts darkened; if bones had been left unbroken and organs unruptured, it was more a compliment to her torturers than to Tania's constitutional strength. She had been beaten by experts.

The aunt put the stethoscope back into a drawer, and the man Tania knew as Robert pulled a chair close to the bed. His expression was manufactured but attempted to show great concern.

"Major Vünke," Diminov began. His use of her KGB rank brought to mind the charade in Buenos Aires when they had presented her with a personnel file and the decoration of the Order of the Red Star. Tania was too tired to say anything, so she just listened.

"You have made the greatest sacrifices that the revolution can ask. I want you to know that I have communicated directly with the center, and they are aware of the harrowing conditions under which you have served. Although you are exhausted, it is urgent that we establish what the enemy learned during the course of your questioning. The conduct of further operations depends on this information, as does the safety of other agents."

"What do you want?" Tania asked flatly.

Diminov and the aunt exchanged glances. The aunt, obviously, was the moderator of this discussion.

"Tell me what the police know," Diminov said.

"I told them you were a drug dealer, a Yugoslav I did not know very well, but that you paid me to smuggle one-kilo packages of cocaine out of the country. I said I had been doing this for you over the last three months."

"What did they ask you about the newspaper or the letter?"

"Nothing. The newspaper fell from my hand during the arrest."

"What did they ask you of Che Guevara or the operation in the Ñancahuazú?"

"They didn't ask about him."

"Did they know about the operation in Ñancahuazú?"

"They asked me about it vaguely. I said I knew nothing, that I guessed it was where they made the cocaine."

"Did they ask you about Sandoval or D'Esperey?"

"They did not." Tania paused, and her eyes assumed a distant gaze. "After the second or third night, the questioning pretty much stopped. What do the Americans have to do with my release?"

The aunt stiffened slightly; she would pick her words carefully and craft the answer. What Tania would be told would be true and not true, right and not right; Diminov and the aunt were tasked to solicit Tania's cooperation, her continued assistance, until the assignment was complete.

"The center approached the Americans. They were asked to intervene on your behalf," the aunt said blandly.

"Why?"

Tania knew, as did every player in the Game, that an individual was rarely of such value.

"You are an important operative who has served long in a critical position," Diminov said.

"Don't patronize me."

"Major Vünke," the aunt began, sounding very much like a grade-school teacher chastising a impertinent child, "a many-layered operation has been put into place to support you. Three regular KGB officers are in Bolivia on your behalf: Diminov, Sergev, and myself. We are all in-country under illegal cover. We are here to secure your release from Bolivian custody and to return you to the East. Much time, effort, and money have been spent, not to mention the lives placed at risk to get you out."

"Am I to be traded for someone else?"

"Our orders are to cooperate with the Americans to get you out of South America. To Vienna and then to a fraternal country. We have no embassy here in Bolivia. To exfiltrate you, we are, to a certain extent, dependent on the good graces of the Americans."

"In return for my release, what do they want?"

There was a pause. Diminov knew this to be the fulcrum point of the discussion, the aim and issue upon which the entire enterprise would turn. It was the aunt who spoke.

"The Americans want only one thing. They want you to guide Sandoval and D'Esperey to the guerrilla encampment in the Ñancahuazú. You are to tell Guevara the place of the supply drop, near the junction of the Iripiti and Ñancahuazú rivers. At a point following this, you will be extracted from the field by an American Special Forces team, given a clean set of documents, and allowed to depart to Vienna."

"Why don't you send me to Vienna now?"

"It is not that simple."

"You can't smuggle me out of the city and across the border?"

"No," Diminov said.

"You're lying." Tania's rising ire flickered in front of a blossoming and terrifying doubt. "I could leave on my own . . ." Her voice trailed into nothing.

"How?" Diminov asked.

Silence.

He went on, "Do you have papers?"

"No."

"Money?"

"Some," she answered.

"Major Vünke, let me review the operational situation for you. You have been in service, under deep cover, *illegal* cover, in one of the most repressive countries in Latin America. The Bolivian government is one of the most subservient and brutal tools America possesses in Latin America. Your cover has been blown, utterly. The National Police do not think you are a simple smuggler; nor do they think that I am involved in the narcotics trade. They know what you are—an officer in a foreign and hostile intelligence service. You were released only because a demand was made by American intelligence. Your release was granted contingent to our continued cooperation."

Tania again felt as though blows were being rained on her. Diminov continued to speak, but his words seemed delivered in handfuls, picked up and heaved at her, empty things with all the meaning wrung from them.

"They let you go because they know you have no means to escape the country. Your name and photograph are at every border crossing. If you did have enough money to bribe your way across the frontier, say, to Paraguay or to Chile, what would you do then? How would you secure papers to travel? And the countries through which you must pass—all of them are capitalist, all beholden to the United States, and then, of course, there is Interpol, another instrument that would be used against you. The entire international criminal apparatus would be brought to bear because you would be indicted as a drug smuggler by Bolivia." Diminov shook his head. "The Americans agreed to your release because they knew you could go nowhere. The price of letting you go is one more operational act on your behalf."

"I am to betray Guevara."

The aunt said, "This is an assignment. The orders come from the center."

"Why don't they simply say murder?"

"Who do you work for, Major Vünke?" Diminov said. There was no trace of menace in his voice.

"The Stasi," Tania answered.

"And for whom have you worked since you were assigned to Cuba?"

"KGB."

"It is through us that you hold your commission," Diminov said.

"The files and your ridiculous medals . . ."

The aunt crossed her arms. Diminov leaned back in his chair. His voice was even and reasonable. "The file is real enough. You are a commissioned officer in the Komitet Gosudarstvennoy Bezopasnosti and continue to be obligated as one."

Tania grunted. "What more can I do for proletarian internationalism?"

Diminov paused. "Is there reason for us to doubt your loyalty?"

"My loyalty to what?"

"The revolution."

"What will happen to Guevara?"

Diminov stood and fixed his gaze on Tania. "What happens to Guevara does not concern you or me. What happens to the men with him is also not our concern. I am ordered to get you out of the country, back to the East, and that I will accomplish. I cannot do that without the help of the Americans. In order for the exfiltration to go forward, you must direct Guevara to the supply drop."

He stood and walked toward the window. "Major Vünke," he said. "You have been through a terrible experience. The circumstances of your service have been difficult. You have shown dedication beyond the cause of duty, and the intelligence you have produced has been of the highest value—"

Tania stirred in a nausea of self-loathing. "I don't need to be cheered for."

"Do you want to go home?" the aunt asked flatly.

"Yes."

"Then there is one more thing you must do."

38

CHARLIE DROVE THE Impala up the *autopista* to El Alto, ten kilometers distant and almost five hundred meters above the center of La Paz. The traffic was light, and the day was sunny; in the passenger seat next to him, Hoyle seemed distracted, even melancholy, as the car drove up the long incline.

Charlie had picked him up at the safe house at Plaza España at noon. Rather, Hoyle had met him there, for Charlie had arrived early and parked down the block. Hoyle had arrived at the safe house by taxi, carrying an overnight bag. As he entered, Hoyle noticed Charlie parked down the block—he was an uncommonly observant man—and while Charlie waited, Hoyle had a beer and an orange and reemerged precisely at noon. Charlie knew Hoyle had spent the night someplace else, but he did not ask where. It did not concern him, even if it did interest him slightly; at any rate, Charlie did not wish his own comings and goings minutely examined, so he had no problem with Hoyle's private business.

Charlie recalled plainly the altercation between Smith and Hoyle at the casita: One component of their argument had involved a woman. Charlie felt no conflict over keeping Hoyle's secret. That argument had also been over Hoyle's beating of Major Placido. Charlie still bore a raw, ragged scar under his eye where Placido had clipped him with the pistol. Although Charlie did not feel completely avenged, he did take some happiness in the diminishment of Placido. Charlie had always liked Hoyle—to his mind, Hoyle was the most likable of all the gringos—and although he did not consider the man a friend (one is not often friends with gringos), Charlie was happy to help him, genuinely help him, and to keep his little secrets.

Hoyle sat quietly as Charlie drove off the *autopista* onto the Avenida Juan Pablo and then to the military airfield next to the airport. The grandly named Oficina de la Inteligencia del Aire was a rust-streaked Quonset hut at the south end of the runway. A captain was eventually located (he had forgotten the appointment), and given to Hoyle were several metal and plastic cylinders, each about the size of a beer can; film canisters from a Fairchild F-1 aerial camera.

The camera had been flown by helicopter over the lower reaches of the Ñancahuazú Valley. Reconnaissance cameras were usually considered spooky things, often the highest sorts of technology, but the F-1 was old, a surplus workhorse from World War II. Hoyle was not surprised to see it tossed into a corner with a dirty white sheet draped over the broad, stubby lens.

In this case, it was not the camera that was special but the film. The Bolivians had been asked to overfly and photograph the area around the recently captured farmhouse. They hadn't been told that the film they were using was of the latest type, a high-resolution infrared that would show heat sources under the tree canopy. The same type of film was being used in Vietnam. Charlie had given the pilots the canisters the week before and asked for routine photo coverage. The film would now be taken back to the safe house and processed secretly.

Hoyle seemed only slightly less distracted as they drove downhill and back into the city. Almost the entire trip passed without a word; Charlie was by nature quiet, and Hoyle was obviously in thought. As they drove into the basin containing La Paz, the sky seemed to yawn and tip open before them; the *autopista* continued down, curved and recurved, and the city sprouted on all sides, impossibly jumbled and dust-colored. Huayna Potosí loomed above everything; the mountain occupied a whole part of the sky and collected about its top a blue-gray ring of cloud. Charlie played the radio, pop music with English lyrics and rapid-fire commercials that blended together in Hoyle's mind. By degrees, he unplugged first the Spanish and then the English from comprehension, and as they turned off the highway, he barely attended the bewildering avalanche of syllables.

On Avenida Peru, they stopped and bought beer at a pushcart. Shadows were already cusping the shantytowns, and the air was slowly made purple. Hoyle gathered up twenty-four bottles of Taquiña to take back to the safe house; he also bought soft drinks for Charlie, delighting the cart's proprietor, a round-looking Paceña who opened her mouth into a cracked and uneven smile. As they loaded the beer into the back, a beggar tossed his sponge over two lanes of traffic, dodged across the busy avenue, and washed all the Impala's windows before Charlie could run him off. Hoyle gave him the change from the beer, and Charlie hissed at the boy, sputtering a curse at him in Guaraní.

They returned to the safe house to find a note from Smith. He'd been by at midafternoon and had taken an embassy car back to the military airfield. They'd probably passed each other along the *autopista*. Smith and Valdéz were taking a helicopter to Camp Esperanza to check on Major Sheldon and the training base at Santa Cruz. Santavanes was sleeping off a hangover in one of the bedrooms. Hoyle set to work with the film, and Charlie loaded the beer into the refrigerator, certain that Santavanes would seek relief when he woke up.

After about two hours, Hoyle laid out the negatives on a light table plugged into a socket in the kitchen. He scanned the illuminated negatives with a stereoscope before making individual prints. The photos were astounding.

The infrared film had seen "through" the canopy and revealed Camps 1 and 2 in incredible detail. Hoyle was astounded by their intricate layout. Each was surrounded by a series of camouflaged trenches and rifle pits. Camp 2, located on a steep mountainside, was practically unassailable. This confirmed the wisdom of trying to lure Guevara away from his bases. To assault such well-laid-out positions would be suicide.

Scanning the film, Hoyle was able to fix with certainty the main assembly areas and trails leading north, but he was puzzled that the infrared had detected only a handful of men on the ground.

"Anything?" Charlie asked.

"We found the camps," Hoyle said, "but not the people."

Charlie looked at one of the negatives on the light table. He could see plainly the zigzag lines of the rifle pits and the scattering of white dots that indicated human beings. There appeared to be fewer than a dozen men at Camp 2.

"Maybe they moved out."

Hoyle shook his head. "Look at the trench lines. They're still being extended. They're working on the camp." Where was the main column? Why would they continue working on a camp if it had been abandoned?

"I have to see Zeebus," Hoyle said. The film had been sent via diplomatic pouch, which meant that a favor was owed to Cosmo. Hoyle had made a dinner date with him for this evening.

Charlie shrugged. "Then it's Los Escudos. You'll eat well." Charlie considered Zeebus a gringo of the more common sort, meaning loud, ill-mannered, and stupid to the way of things. Charlie did not fault Zeebus for his appetite, however, and his favorite restaurant was one of Charlie's as well.

"Would you like to join us?" Hoyle asked.

Charlie smiled at the invitation. It would not have come from Zeebus or Smith, nor probably from Santavanes or Valdéz. Most Americans wished to avoid fraternization, as Charlie was considered "help," not management. The Cubans were a different matter. Though outwardly friendly, Santavanes and Valdéz were not without racial awareness. Charlie was unashamedly cholo, a Native American back a thousand generations; and there was a line, indelible and ancient, between cholo and Castilliano. This was not something Hoyle could solve; Charlie suspected that, like most gringos, Hoyle was aware of race only as it concerned blacks and whites, not Indians and those of Iberian descent. Los Escudos was owned by a chola, so Charlie would be welcomed there, and that may have been why the invitation was so ready. Charlie had never detected in Hoyle any trace of racism, but he did sense a small blind spot—Bolivia, like all Latin countries, had its conventions regarding *nativos*. Gringos like Hoyle always seemed unaware of the line that divided Indians and Europeans.

At any rate, Charlie had private business of his own tonight. He declined the invitation graciously and asked permission to check on his apartment, a small place behind the bus station. Hoyle knew he was not often there. They made arrangements to meet in the morning and drive back to the military airfield, where they'd catch an airplane back to Vallegrande.

Hoyle dutifully telephoned Zeebus at the embassy and confirmed the arrangements for dinner. On the way over, he checked his post office box, though, having seen Maria off at eleven that morning, he figured a note would be unlikely. There was none, and Hoyle tried not to be disappointed as he drove across the city to Los Escudos.

As usual, the meal was a spectacle. Magda, the owner, beamed and clucked as Zeebus put away plate after plate. Hoyle ate, and the food was quite good, especially if one's goal was to be stuffed to bursting and put into a digestive coma. Zeebus asked after Smith, hoping he had been stung by a scorpion, bitten by a rabid dog, or better, died of some slow, ghastly diarrhea that made him shit out his brains. Hoyle had to break the bad news that Smith was alive and well.

"How did your spooky film work out?" Zeebus asked.

"Okay."

Zeebus chewed. "How about the Igloo White stuff?" Igloo White was the code name of a program that used ground seismic intrusion detectors to monitor the Ho Chi Minh trail in Vietnam. Hoyle had ordered a dozen of the sensors to place in the Ñancahuazú Valley. The sensors, too, had come via diplomatic pouch.

"You opened the boxes," Hoyle said.

"Of course. You would, too. I don't know what's going on, but I deserve to have a suspicion."

Hoyle took a sip of beer.

"Come on, buddy," Zeebus said, "give me something."

"We found some trails."

"Hmm."

Hoyle sat, saying nothing more.

Scraping up some sauce, Zeebus went on: "We put down some of that stuff in Quang Nam, in I Corps—right off Red Route One. Really high-speed stuff. The things were supposed to smell human sweat. Detect humans by their odor. The sensors got dropped in by airplane, not hidden, you know, just parachuted into the trees, and the gooks found a couple of them. They had no idea what they were—they probably suspected they were some kind of listening devices. So they sent them to Moscow for analysis. The Russians figured out what they were and what they did. Next time we sent a team in for a recon of the trail, we found all these clay pots stuck up in the tree branches. The pots were full of shit and piss. Goddamn if that didn't set off the sensors. They signaled that there were hundreds of thousands of slopes out there in the jungle. They were picking up the piss and registering it as humans."

"We're not going to put in shit detectors," Hoyle said.

"That stuff is all shit," Zeebus said. "If you want to kill somebody, you've got to send people to do it. All this remote-control crap. Give me a cloak and dagger anytime."

"Well, we haven't found them yet," Hoyle said. "It's a big jungle."

"Too bad. Of course, being a contractor, like you are, the longer the job, the longer you get paid."

"What have you got going on in La Paz?" Hoyle asked.

"Shit, you don't tell me anything, why should I tell you?"

"Just because Smith torques you off, don't take it out on me."

"You're his buddy."

"I work for him."

Zeebus narrowed his eyes. "Well, that's your own fault, isn't it?"

"I wish I'd had you there for some career advice, Cosmo. You really are a genius."

Zeebus smiled. "I heard about the beef with Major Placido."

"A misunderstanding."

"You've got a temper."

If these assholes keep killing prisoners, this thing in the valley will get bigger."

"You think kicking their asses will teach them manners?"

"I don't want my job made harder."

"Just so you know, there's still major fucking heartburn over this at the embassy. Ambassador Hielman's just waiting for you two guys to step on your dicks out there. He sent a query to State when he heard you duked out Placido."

"I know you'll put in a good word for me."

"You're not helping yourself any."

Zeebus ate a flan. They talked of his coming transfer to Berlin; the paperwork seemed to be progressing slowly, but he was confident he'd soon be freed from La Paz. Zeebus seemed only slightly embarrassed when they were joined by a woman named Uta, a clerk from the Swiss delegation. She was jolly and big-boned and transparently in love with Zeebus, who, Hoyle noticed, wasn't wearing his wedding ring. Hoyle remained at the table only long enough to be introduced and to tell her that he was a petroleum geologist conducting surveys in the south, a friend of Cosmo's from college. Uta said she'd met Zeebus at a church picnic, and Hoyle wondered if the whole world was filled with liars. He excused himself, pleading another engagement.

On the way out, he paid Magda for their meals and for a few more rounds of drinks. Magda smiled an amazing mouthful of gold and said she thought Zeebus might be good for at least another gelato.

Hoyle left the Impala parked on the street and wandered a few blocks. It was full dark now; lights from the shops and signs were reflected up by wet sidewalks. It had rained quickly and silently while they'd eaten. Curfew had been lifted weeks ago, and La Paz seemed to have forgotten it. There were people about, and cafés and restaurants were doing business, spilling laughter and the clink of crockery out into the streets. Los Escudos was across town from the embassy, and the people Hoyle passed would not have recognized him. From afar, his height marked him as a foreigner, and closer, his complexion as a gringo; tonight that didn't matter very much.

Hoyle found a small place off Avenida Mariscal Santa Cruz, a neat, dark *wiskería*. He ordered a bourbon, and when the setup came, he asked the waiter for a pen and paper. He drank and began to compose a letter.

He wrote, *Darling*—. He thought to write *Dear Maria,* but he wished to leave her anonymous, as he would himself. Hoyle glanced at the time and wrote in the corner *11:30 P.M.* and *La Paz, Saturday.* He drank a bit, then went on, *I wanted to get a note to you before I left the city. I don't know exactly how long I'll be away, I think a week or so, but I'll make up some reason to come back.* Hoyle thought that it did not read well; it might be misunderstood. He wrote, *Some business reason, and I will try to give you as much notice as I can.*

The words flickered on the page, and they pinched him. He was reminded that he had to schedule his visits, as Maria had to make time to see him. Time for them both was purchased with lies.

I understand that you are taking a risk for me. I do not want to put you into difficulty. You mean more to me than you know. I miss you and I'll be back as soon as I can. A night with you is worth a hundred days. Please send a note to me when you can. And please tell me when you think we might be able to see each other.

The words disappointed him; that they applied to both their affair and the business he'd asked her to do also bothered him. Still, he put the pen into the small light from the candle and wrote, *I miss you and miss you every day.* He signed his initial, *P,* and folded the paper. He did not want to read it again. He thought it fell very short of the mark.

The bar and tables were filling up, and now that the letter did not occupy his attention, Hoyle was aware of sitting alone. He put the note in his pocket, placed some money on the table, and nodded to the waiter as he walked back into the night. *"Buenas, Señor,"* the waiter said in a deep and grave voice.

The evening was chill, and it occurred to Hoyle that he would have to drive to the safe house for an envelope, then out again to post the letter. He was maybe half a mile from Maria's apartment. He had walked from the restaurant toward her place; he knew that she had *una cita* that evening and that she was with Alameda. This tugged slightly at him, but he made the event a blank in his mind.

Though he knew better, he walked down the avenue toward Cochabamba and turned onto her street. The night spread overhead, and clouds wheeled about like stage scenery pushed around between acts. Hoyle walked slowly, having much time to weigh what he was doing. He thought that he would pass by for only a second, and if there was no one about, he would slip the note under her door.

The whiskey had warmed him against the high, thin air of the city. This was not the right thing to do—to drop off a note. It could be found by the wrong person; it might be mislaid. The correct thing to do was return to the safe house, get an envelope, and properly mail it. Maria could go to the post box when she had the time. When it was safe.

Hoyle kept walking. He put his hand in his pocket, and it fell on the paper. He looked ahead and saw Maria's apartment. He saw stairs leading up to the door, and a light on in the front window, her window. Hoyle crossed the street; there was no traffic, and there were no pedestrians near him, so he walked steadily on toward the light. It was her light among all the windows of the city, and when he came upon it, he looked up slightly from the street, and between the curtains, the light showed the color of her room.

Beyond the curtains, Hoyle saw Maria, and then he saw Alameda holding her. Alameda's arms were about her waist and his head inclined; they were kissing. For a moment Hoyle's brain refused to work, and he stopped dead on the sidewalk. It seemed as if the earth had avalanched under his feet, as if he'd been cast off it for an instant. At first there was no pain, and he took in the small view of the room; the couple entwined, and behind them the mirror on Maria's dressing stand, a hairbrush on it, cosmetics on a silver tray. Hanging across the mirror was a rosary of pearl and silver.

Seconds passed. For Hoyle, there was an expanding blank spot, disbelief and then empty shock, as in a man who looks down and finds a finger gone from his hand. Hoyle's eyes moved from the nightstand to Maria, and he watched as they kissed and continued to kiss. Maria's hands went up Alameda's back and to the back of his neck.

A shimmering malice blossomed around Hoyle's face, a burning as real as flame. His thoughts collapsed into equal parts hurt, fury, and humiliation. None of the feelings made sense. There was no rational way that he should be surprised or hurt by what he saw—Hoyle knew Maria was not his alone. But the sight of her in another man's arms stung him, vexed him, made him feel beaten and small. He could not help himself; a feeling of anger and duplicity condensed around him like little droplets of fog. He felt the letter under his fingertips and slowly closed his fist over it. He closed his eyes and opened them again, but the scene did not change: Maria was in the arms of Alameda.

They were making love.

Hoyle turned and staggered into the street, the city howling around him. He had watched, gripped by one agony, and now he walked away dragging another.

39

THE GLOOM WAS abiding. Above the canopy, there was no moon; occasionally, wind rustled through the treetops, and water came down from the leaves like a shower. Dinner in the evening had been the last of the rice and the meat of three sparrow hawks. The camp was very quiet, most of the men preferring sleep in their hammocks to shuffling about battling the rumbling of their guts and pangs of hunger. The fire was allowed to burn out, and Guevara wrote in his journal only briefly, a concisely worded entry noting that some of the men were quite demoralized. There had been no news from the runners he had sent south to Base Camp, and it was decided to send another courier. Marcos and three others were already heading south; it was estimated that they would reach Base Camp in two days. With luck, Marcos would cross with a return party heading north.

At night Guevara lay awake in his hammock and listened to Castro speak on the shortwave radio. Parts of the hours-long oration drifted in, clear and strong, and other parts were embroidered by static and an intermittent crackling, a sound like lightning striking. No one else crouched by the radio, and Guevara listened alone, the small sound of the speaker tittering through the darkened forest. The speech was interminable, Fidel rolling his "R"s, pausing in the middle of sentences, spellbinding himself if not his listeners. Guevara began to wonder why he'd bothered to listen. Fifo could talk!

He was about to get up to piss when, from the shortwave, came these words: "The imperialists have killed Che many times and in many places . . ."

Guevara turned his head. Castro droned on. "But we anticipate that any day now, where imperialism least expects it, Comandante Ernesto Guevara will rise from the ashes like a phoenix, seasoned by war, a guerrilla fighter, healthy. And that someday again we will have very concrete news of Che . . ."

There was a long, sustained burst of applause; on the radio, it sounded like the noise of a waterfall. The ovation continued, peppered with shouts of "Che *vive*." Guevara pushed his hand from under his mosquito netting and switched off the set. There was then only the sound of the river and the hum of insects. Hearing Castro's voice had made Guevara glum, and he was aware of a pain behind his heart. When sleep finally came, he surrendered without dreams.

The following morning he was up early, out and among Joaquin's troops toward the back side of the slope. He walked by himself, visiting each of the hammocks, trying to gauge morale, aware of the scant rations and hard miles over the last five days. He wanted to gain a sense of their feelings and instill in them the necessary spark to push these last two or three hard days back into camp. The men received him cheerfully.

Guevara could not help noticing that they were all looking harder, their eyes, especially. They had toiled mightily for the last four months, the march just one of many exertions. Their uniforms and boots were showing signs of heavy wear. Most of their trousers were out through at least one knee, and most uniform shirts were stained with sweat and white-gray around the collar. All had lost weight, some as much as ten kilos, and Guevara was but one of the three doctors among the column who could plainly see the early signs of malnutrition among the men. Some suffered from it patently—Inti and Miguel had begun to display swollen feet and hands—and all were increasingly gaunt.

For the most part, they were in good spirits, but a few were notably discouraged and did not pretend otherwise for their commander. Four of the Bolivian comrades—Chingolo, Eusebio, Paco, and the shifty-eyed Pepe—were of depressed manner and dampened enthusiasm. They were silently obstinate and disrespectful by turns, and already the others had taken to calling them *resacas*—the dregs. Guevara, too, knew that they were finished; these men were last on every march, straggling in as long as two hours behind the column. Selfish with exhaustion, they rarely assisted with the communal chores of making camp, gathering wood, hunting, or drawing water. Unless under orders, they sat moping, sometimes in a group, or worse, when they did get put to work (and always they had to be ordered), their griping, ass dragging, and dirty looks were spread around, as contagious as yawning.

This morning Guevara made no pronouncements. He simply talked to them as he talked to the others, calmly and firmly reminding all that thirty hard miles remained. He did not give a pep talk; for the dregs, it would be useless, and for the other comrades, it was unnecessary. Most of the men held their convictions as strongly as Guevara: They believed fervently in the cause, and they were confident in the idea that they would tear South America into pieces. *Resacas* on one end and the indomitable Joaquin on the other: The differences in morale were vast.

After his tour of the encampment, Guevara announced that they would eat one of the mules. Scarcely had he made the declaration than a shot rang out down the trail, and the haunches and loin of the pack animal were delivered to the campfire. Mule meat and mule ribs were roasted while a pair of rafts were built to cross the Rio Grande. The animal's burden (ammunition, supplies, and radio equipment) was distributed equally around the column and piled onto the remaining animals. As the bits and pieces were moved, the two remaining grizzled old mules stood picketed with their ears back, suspiciously sniffing the smoke that wafted down from the fires.

By late afternoon, cooking was done, and the first of the rafts was completed. Guevara ordered the center group to start a crossing. Piles of rucksacks and weapons and great masses of cooked mule flesh wrapped in sheets of tarpaulin were made fast, all was put aboard, and Guevara helped pole the raft out into the stream. The raft turned and lurched, tipping and flinching like a drunkard as the current carried it. Four of Guevara's group could not swim, and these men clung in a pile in the center of the craft, their teeth grinding and their knuckles white. At last the banks of the Ñancahuazú were reached, and the raft made fast to the bank. As the center group's supplies were put ashore, Guevara walked back up the riverbank to a spot across from the remaining group.

The animals were driven across by Pedro and Victor. Helped by an eddy and the remarkable steady swimming of the animals, all crossed and soon emerged dripping on the shore. Guevara watched as Joaquin's group piled aboard their craft, poling themselves toward the eddy. From the beginning, the crossing did not go well. The raft was spun into the middle of the river, and soon the water was too deep for the poles to touch bottom. Joaquin jumped in to hold on to the raft's side and provide propulsion by kicking. The eddy pulled them in the desired direction for a while, but the current proved irresistible. The raft was drawn downstream, and it was so heavily laden that twice it nearly capsized as it lurched over the tops of standing waves in the rapids. Within five minutes, Joaquin's party was swept around the bend and out of view.

Guevara cursed. As the raft disappeared downriver, he ordered Tuma after them. He scrambled down the bank quickly, mounted one of the mules, and rode off.

The sun was slipping below the ridgeline, and long shadows appeared gradually from the river bottom. Guevara made the decision to establish camp, feed his men, and wait for Joaquin to return. Nearly all of their clothing, equipment, and weapons had been waterlogged during the passage, and the men set about hanging clothing in the trees and disassembling and oiling weapons as another fire was built and the joints of the mule were reheated.

Guevara had lookouts posted up and down the river and ordered the men to eat. This they did eagerly, and the camp grew quiet with an enthusiastically conducted meal. Guevara sat apart as the others ate, picking at his food and scribbling an entry in his journal. He was less at ease than usual, as his forces now covered a wide area, and some were many miles distant. Taken together, the two detached groups—Pombo's and Marcos's—accounted for a little over a third of Guevara's total force.

Soon after nightfall, Tuma returned, reporting that he had ridden three miles downstream but had not found Joaquin. A thorough search of the riverbanks had not turned up bodies or equipment, so apparently, the raft had held together. Somewhere downriver, Joaquin had probably landed safely, but this unknown also contributed to Guevara's anxiety. Joaquin was capable, and Guevara knew that he would join the main body as soon as he was able. Guevara was careful not to show his disappointment, but he was frustrated and angry that the river crossing had gone badly. There was no target for his displeasure.

It was not Tuma's fault, and after all, it was Guevara who selected the crossing place. The responsibility, ultimately, was his.

Guevara thanked Tuma for his report and ordered him to his meal. The forest grew dark and was still.

Night was coming on, and there was nothing to be done. Wind blew in scented gusts from the river, and the rushing noise of the water over the rocks reminded him to set up the shortwave. He tossed the antenna wire up over a tree branch and tuned in to the frequencies listed in his codebook. He deciphered a brief message from Havana, blandly reminding him that Tania and the others could be expected at the main camp within a few days; it said also that a shipment of Glucantine would be forthcoming. The disease the medicine treated, leishmania, was a parasitical infection carried by sand flies. Leishmania was one of the few diseases the column had yet to face. Hunger for the men and asthma for their leader: Those had been problems. Mercifully, Guevara's affliction had abated in the last few days, though he, too, had symptoms of malnutrition, swelling in his legs and feet and a persistent tremor in his hands. The remedies for both, asthma and hunger, would be in good supply at the main camp. In this, he took some consolation. Even given a day or two to collect Joaquin's group from downriver, they could expect to be home within the week.

The entire column would be joined at the main camp, and D'Esperey and Sandoval would be there to exchange messages and to act as couriers. Guevara could suspect nothing out of the ordinary and had planned for no major reversals.

Soon he would have the column pulled together in the vicinity of Base Camp; he would again have connectivity with La Paz and Havana. In the last eight weeks, he had tested the men, and some, the dregs, had been found wanting. Of his forty-odd combatants, Guevara had perhaps twenty he felt were actualized into viable guerrilla leaders. Most of the rest would come. A few, the *resacas,* were done. Guevara decided that these four—Chingolo, Eusebio, Paco, and Pepe—would be expelled from the column and released from duty after the return to base.

It was possible to win the game with the cards dealt to him. The enemy was a balloon, bloated and vulnerable, and Guevara was a needle. The Bolivian army was stupid and corrupt, the Americans behind them decadent and gutless. Guevara expected the army to react with increasing brutality, to burn villages and displace people in their hunt for the guerrillas. Through propaganda, Guevara would turn this to his advantage. Truth was not handed down from heaven—it was made by human hands.

On his little hill, Guevara wrestled alone with the tribulations of command. He turned the facts over in his head and satisfied himself. With his forces dispersed, no single blow could take out the whole column. This half-truth gave some comfort but ignored a looming military fact: The occupation of a greater amount of territory brought with it the increased possibility of unplanned contact with the enemy. Marcos's element was out of touch somewhere to the east, and Joaquin's had landed at least three miles downriver. An enemy showing initiative could sweep up these three separated groups and crush them in detail.

Guevara should have worried more that this could happen, but he did not. Perhaps he knew the enemy well enough; he did know the Bolivian army to be timid and incompetent. Perhaps he was confident that the night and the jungle were vast, and his forces were small and kept safe within. And perhaps he was tired; he had done his best for the day, and it was too bad that his forces were split up and out of contact with one another. There was tomorrow, and tomorrow they would be brought together and back under command. In truth, and in a cold military assessment, Guevara was at this moment extremely vulnerable—his forces were scattered and in disarray, and no competent commander would suffer them long in this condition.

It was an error and a failing to camp and eat so calmly with three detachments out and their commander not knowing precisely where any of them were. But Joaquin was among those separated, and no one else dared say anything to the comandante. Those eating around the fire trusted in the man, who, after all, had written a book on guerrilla warfare.

In truth, the entire ascent of the Ñancahuazú had been a mistake. Training should be undertaken in the sanctity of home territory and not in the presence of the enemy. Under no circumstances should one conduct lengthy practice maneuvers while surrounded by an enemy force. Yet this was precisely what Guevara had done. He had deliberately sought out difficult terrain, such as crossing the San Marcos

Mountains, and this was done specifically to test men and strain resources. Eight weeks of hard marching had pushed his column to its limits. Men had suffered physically, and material had been lost. Now the column was scattered, its men were hungry, and several were sick with malnutrition. The crossing this afternoon had been a fiasco and half of the group swept away downriver. Throughout the column, clothing and equipment were in tatters. Guevara was playing hard and without a reserve. By the very nature of the conflict, the guerrilla operates against a superior force. Whether by insolence or the habits resulting from victory, Guevara was giving his adversaries little respect.

Now hammocks were hung by the banks of the rushing river and bellies filled with meat for the first time in a month. Sentries were posted, staring into the impenetrable night, and the men of the center group allowed themselves the confidence showed by their commander. If Che sleeps, the comrades thought, then we will sleep.

40

T HE NEXT DAY a number of things distracted Hoyle from the confusion in his heart. The first distraction came early; the usual daredevil flight from La Paz to the airfield at Vallegrande. The course was fraught with towering clouds, and even in places where the sky was blue, the plane shook and dipped violently. Perhaps the cause was meteorological, but the pilot, a swaggering twenty-two-year-old with mirrored sunglasses, did not inspire much confidence in his passengers, Hoyle, Charlie, and Santavanes. The flight ended with a spectacular set piece of a landing, a violent, dramatic event that threatened to punch the landing gear straight up through the wings. Remarkably, passengers and cargo were put off in one piece, and Santavanes, at least, was brought closer to true religion.

Back at the casita, Hoyle set to work in the radio tent. Since the night below Maria's window, a curious distraction had wafted after him. Occasionally, his thoughts were overwhelmed by a hollow ache, an emotion something like sorrow yet less pure, sullied by guilt and a certain expectation. It was almost as though Hoyle had anticipated being hurt. The relationship had fulfilled a subconsciously held prophecy.

Hoyle was a man who placed confidence in willpower. It was the rudder by which he steered his soul, and he tried now to *will* thoughts of Maria away. He tried to think of anything but the pang he'd suffered at Maria's window, and the widening hole jabbed in his heart. He had known from the beginning that Maria was being kept by someone else. He should feel nothing. For only the second time in his life, Hoyle was left to puzzle his own feelings and those he had placed in another. He cursed himself and shuffled the papers stacked on the rickety desk in front of him.

Overhead, the dark, hot cloth of the tent fluttered in the wind and called him to duty. Armed with the communication plan and the codes from Diminov, Hoyle drafted a series of counterfeit radio transmissions to be sent to the Ñancahuazú. The messages, purporting to be from Havana, promised a supply drop at the junction of the Ñancahuazú and the Iripiti in seventy-two hours—more than adequate time for Tania and her passengers to reach Guevara. The location was to be confirmed in person by Tania.

The promised supply drop was described in simple noun-verb-object sentences, the universal tone of operationalese, and although the bland third-person pitch was nearly the same across all languages, Hoyle carefully studied a dozen legitimate messages sent to Guevara from Havana, decoded and written out in Spanish and English. He concentrated on the originals, meticulously crafting his language to match as closely as possible the tone and diction of the previous communications. It was vital that his messages seem as authentic as possible, especially as they called for an extraordinary thing: the movement of a unit in the field.

Hoyle counted on several factors to sell his trap. The guerrillas were known to be short of supplies, and the raid on the farmhouse was certain to have been a blow to their logistics. The first transmission would offer boots, mosquito netting, ammo, and clothing. Hoyle did his best to make the shopping list irresistible, adding medicines, in particular medications for Guevara's asthma. The list offered practical items and a few small luxuries: canned milk and sardines. It might easily have been more modest. The circumstances in which the guerrillas found themselves were far worse than Hoyle could know. The promise of a supply drop, when it came, would be an attractive proposition indeed.

The last and most important part of the charade would be human. If the trap were to work, Tania would have to persuade Guevara to believe.

Hoyle worked through several drafts in plain language, writing in Spanish, as this was now the language in which he thought. As he worked on the text, the Green Berets put together an improvised directional antenna aimed into the center of the Ñancahuazú. The radio was tuned precisely to the frequency used by Havana, and the power of the closer transmitter ensured that the spurious messages would blot out any authentic traffic. The first transmission was scheduled for ten o'clock this evening.

As he finished the encode, the tent fluttered; it was three in the afternoon, the height of daylight, and Hoyle's eyes pained him as he walked past the tents and into the wavering heat of the afternoon. Wanting no company, he sat under a tree behind the casita, pulled his legs into the small patch of shade, and stared out over the red-dirt airfield. A cheerless wind came down from the hills; it was not enough to trouble the flies and barely enough to stir dust from the runway. Above the valley, a skein of interwoven clouds covered the dome of the sky, white on gray. From intermediate height, individual clouds put down patches of shadow across the hills, but the sun burned through most, giving the sky a milky glare.

The afternoon had made itself tedious, and Hoyle wished it were dark. He wished he were asleep and that his mind could be turned off. Now that his messages were done, there was little to do except try not to think of Maria. At this he failed with every beat of his pulse and felt miserable and stupid for it.

The wind gusted unconvincingly, and the sun surrendered a few more inches in the sky. Sunlight made the code numbers fall one by one from Hoyle's brain. There was nothing else to think of now that the numbers were gone, and the images of her came on in waves, fading, then waxing. Jesus, he thought, don't be so self-pitying. Hoyle tried consciously not to allow her name into his thoughts, but he remembered making love to her, drinking her in, becoming lost in her. Now his thoughts tumbled through what he knew of her life in Cuba and his life after first seeing her.

What was he to her? The answer had barbs in it. He could be only an irrelevant thing. It pained him to think that his part in Maria's life was so small. He wished he were drunk and then thought better. It would be worse to be heart-thumped *and* drunk: the twangy stuff of cowboy songs.

The clouds were rolling by, outrageously fast, and watching them, he was finally for a moment able to forget. Hoyle let his mind loose among the several shades of white and gray above the broken red ground at the end of the runway. A dozen shades of green mottled the hills beyond.

Guevara was there. Out there in the vastness, kept safe by it.

The guerrillas had struck three times and each time had come off victorious. By virtue of their stealth, the more timid of their enemies granted them ubiquity. They were everywhere because the army could not find them anywhere. But Hoyle knew better.

He walked toward the operations tent and could feel a peculiar tug, a flutter in his chest between his heart and stomach. He tried to ignore it, as he had for weeks ignored the gradually lessening pain from his ribs. The flip in his stomach was replaced by a grinding sensation, a buzzing in his head like static across a radio band.

Maria. And Maria again.

He sat down at a field desk, reading again the messages for Guevara, doing his best to ignore the pain behind his eyes. It was all simply heartache, made into physical symptoms because its victim was doing everything in his power to deny it.

41

UNDER THE CAVERNOUS roof of La Paz's main bus station, Rene D'Esperey and Carlos Sandoval sat at opposite ends of the platform and scrupulously ignored each other. Above them, finches and pigeons flitted among the girders and the afternoon sun slanted down through open spaces in the ceiling and the large half-circled ends of the building. Though the express bus from La Paz to the city of Sucre was scheduled to depart at three-thirty P.M., that hour approached and passed with no sign of the driver.

In dress and demeanor, D'Esperey and Sandoval stood out as foreigners. D'Esperey was twenty-seven years old and was of fair complexion and regular features. His sandy-blond hair was slightly shorter than shoulder-length, and he sported a drooping mustache. Wearing a turtleneck sweater and khakis, he might have been mistaken for a hippie gringo. His Spanish was good, rapid and idiomatic, but one could easily note in it a Gallic lilt; his French accent had been antidote to any bias against North Americans, and he was able to charm when he needed it.

Across the waiting crowd, Carlos Sandoval was much less conspicuous but still did not pass for Boliviano. He was also close to thirty, slightly built, with a high, bald forehead. Sandoval was Argentine and had about him the blank look of a department-store clerk. He was dressed in an open-collared shirt, jacket, and trousers. His hands were notable, his fingers long and tapered, betraying a sensitive, creative disposition. Sandoval was by training an artist, though an unvarying, circumspect temper prepared him well for clandestine work. Like all good agents, Sandoval shared with D'Esperey the ability to remain self-contained and outwardly calm. Both could chat readily with casual acquaintances; both had stories, immanently plausible reasons why they were visiting Sucre; and both had suitcases and backpacks and kept their luggage close about them.

A pair of soldiers walked down the platform, surveying the waiting passengers with rapacious stares. As they passed, D'Esperey ignored them, and Sandoval appeared to do some hard thinking. Both were relieved when the troopers began to question and then search passengers waiting for another bus; this task was sufficiently interesting to keep the soldiers occupied for half an hour.

During this time, the driver of the Sucre bus appeared, opened the locked door, and climbed aboard. He closed the door after himself, and the crowd watched as he conducted some unknown activity in the driver's seat. This went on for ten minutes, and then he threw open the doors, unbolted the baggage compartment, and began to take tickets. As the crowd moved forward, Sandoval caught D'Esperey's eye. They had expected to meet Tania on the platform; the trip to Sucre was just the first leg of the journey to Guevara's base camp in the Ñancahuazú.

D'Esperey sat on his luggage, watching the crowd load baggage and jostle onto the bus. As long as he remained still, Sandoval did, too. It was then almost 4:25, and D'Esperey sought out Sandoval with a glance. When their eyes met, the Frenchman shrugged almost imperceptibly. There was a decision to be made—whether to begin the journey or return to the safe house. D'Esperey watched the soldiers, happily unpacking suitcases and bundles on the next platform, and he knew that there were plainclothed policemen about.

Any of a dozen things might have delayed Tania. Some of them were minor, and some of them deadly serious. D'Esperey weighed the options: One of them was walking away with his luggage. He decided that it would be less conspicuous to board the bus, make the trip to Sucre, and try to find out what had happened from there.

He stood and lugged his pack and suitcase toward the rapidly filling luggage compartment. Sandoval waited a discreet amount of time and then followed. After stowing his luggage, Sandoval sought out a vacant seat at the rear of the coach. D'Esperey found a spot in the middle and opened a newspaper he'd found on the seat beside him.

After a few moments, the engine kicked over, the air brakes hissed, and the *flota* lurched out of the station. It turned off the Avenida Peru, then left, into the traffic streaming down Avenida Montes. As the bus lurched by the cathedral, a blue and white taxi overtook it, horn bleating loudly. D'Esperey paid little notice until the cab angled in front of the bus and slowed. The bus driver cursed and leaned on his horn, like any sane Bolivian, but the cab stopped. The bus halted behind it, both drivers gesticulating and punching at their horns.

D'Esperey, Sandoval, and all the passengers stared as a woman opened the taxi's back door and heaved two suitcases onto the pavement. At this act of impudence, the bus driver jerked the bus out of gear, and as the air brakes chuffed, he jumped down onto the street, cursing in a stream almost too rapid to comprehend.

D'Esperey craned his neck at the window, and what he saw puzzled and then startled him. The passenger alighting from the cab was Tania. Her dark hair hung close about her face, and it looked wet. Her strong jaw was set in an expression that was hard to read—determination, intense concentration, or perhaps unhappiness. Her gaze seemed fixed, and the muscles of her face were frozen like a mask. Traffic behind the bus immediately began to pile up, and the street became a symphony of car horns. Tania handed a folded wad of Bolivianos to the bus driver. From the window, D'Esperey could see the man's demeanor change in an instant; he smiled and nodded, took up both of Tania's suitcases, and heaved them up the stairs behind the folding doors. After Tania climbed the steps into the bus, the driver shooed a child from a seat and tossed her luggage onto the bundled possessions of a somber chola in a dark green bowler hat. The old Indian's goods were smashed flat beneath Tania's suitcases. The old woman did not protest, and the driver made no gesture of repentance. The people on the bus watched silently as the driver slipped back behind the wheel and pulled the lever to close the door.

Tania's eyes searched the passengers, finding first Sandoval and then D'Esperey. The two men drew and held breath. Her eyes passed over them; to D'Esperey, Tania seemed in this moment like a woman un-hinged. She had a wild, vacant look about her, an unknowable expres-sion that seemed equal parts ferocious and void.

D'Esperey was too stunned to react. Tania had materialized out of nowhere, halting the bus on a city street and audaciously snarling the busy afternoon traffic behind them.

D'Esperey was surprised, but Sandoval was livid. Slumped in the back of the bus, he averted his eyes in fury. The three of them were the only non-Bolivians among the passengers, a fact patently obvious to all, and as Tania found her seat and the bus drudged back into gear, Sandoval felt a burning sensation behind his ears. He was embarrassed and irate. Their journey was to be clandestine, and secrecy rested on discretion. What had made Tania so thoughtless? She was experienced enough to know what she had done. Her stunt had violated every rule of tradecraft and deportment.

Sandoval could see D'Esperey looking deliberately and intently out the window. His disbelief had given way to stunned resentment. Tania's stunt might have garnered the attention of the police. Sandoval had traveled from Buenos Aires under an alias, as had D'Esperey. Nei-ther wanted close scrutiny of their papers. It was incredible that the traffic police had not swarmed them.

Grievance stirred within Sandoval, anger and bewildered indigna-tion in D'Esperey. They both watched as Tania took out a shawl, wrapped it around herself, and settled into her seat to sleep. *Sleep!*

Lurching, bumping, the bus groped through the city, and as night fell, it rolled onto the dusty highway through brown scrub to Patacamaya and southeast, always southeast, toward Ouro. The road gradually de-scended toward the eastern desert, across several north-south mountain ranges and narrow valleys cut by rivers invariably running east. The city of Ouro passed, doused in the hours before dawn. At half a dozen *tran-cas* along the road, the bus would groan to a stop, and the highway po-lice would board and slash around with a flashlight. These stops passed without incident. In fifteen hours, not one word was spoken among D'Esperey, Sandoval, or Tania, and then the bus arrived in Sucre.

DAWN CAME IN red and gold, slanted from a torrid crimson sky. The bus passed down green hills and into the city of Sucre, a jumble of red-roofed whitewashed buildings. The former capital of Bolivia, Sucre clung stubbornly to a self-important colonial charm. At the bus terminal, passengers were disgorged, stiff and bleary-eyed. Sandoval, D'Esperey, and Tania kept ridiculously apart, separately dragging their luggage to the front of the terminal to the taxi ranks. No one from the bus seemed to cling to them, and they garnered no attention from the soldiers loitering by the ticket booths.

As they stood together on the curb, Sandoval spoke to Tania, keeping the tone of his voice pleasant but scarcely disguising his smoldering anger. "What the hell was that about?"

Tania blinked. "What?"

At this D'Esperey spoke up. "The taxi."

"Were you followed?" Tania asked blandly.

The men hesitated. Tania let the question rankle for a moment. "I wasn't, either," she said. "So don't worry about it."

Sandoval and D'Esperey shared a pointless look. Tania's attitude seemed blasé and above the mundane concerns of security. She stepped forward to the first taxi in the rank. The driver took her bags and then the bags of the others. Tania ordered him to drive to the Hostal Colonial, overlooking the Plaza 25 de Mayo. She paid for the trip and strode inside.

At the desk, there was some difficulty with the reservation, and the clerk announced that the rooms had yet to be made up. There was presently only one room vacant, a double. As it was only ten in the morning, he suggested they wait until the afternoon, when the hotel might have adjoining rooms. Tania said they were tired and would share the available room. The clerk suppressed a giggle, and neither D'Esperey nor Sandoval had the energy to object. The long trip had eroded resistance and whatever sense of propriety might have interfered. All signed the register. Tania was thought to be a prostitute from La Paz and was not troubled for identification. Sandoval and D'Esperey, more exotic in appearance, were asked to fill out tourist cards and did so, showing their forged papers. Beyond these formalities, the clerk paid very little attention.

In the room, a bellman wheeled in a cot, and Sandoval fumbled with a tip. As soon as the door closed, Tania astounded them by disrobing. She took off her jacket and skirt, bra and panties, and tossed them in a corner. D'Esperey blinked and then averted his gaze. Sandoval could not help but stare. His eyes took in the curve of her hips and the small dark triangle between her legs. He noticed that her arms were bruised, and there were several long welts across her back. Paying no heed, Tania swayed nude into the bathroom and closed the door.

D'Esperey shook his head, and Sandoval sat down in a chair by the window. The thought that Tania was insane crossed his mind. Both men felt abashed; Sandoval's machismo and D'Esperey's savoir faire were punctured. Her brazenness had fairly unmanned them.

In the bathroom, water splashed, and then the toilet rumbled. Tania padded back out into the room. D'Esperey did not look away. She drew the curtains all the way, then walked to one of the beds. Her breasts plunged as she bent to pull down the coverlet. D'Esperey watched her—he could not help himself—and she fixed him with a lucid, fierce gaze. Her head was inclined slightly; atop her high cheekbones, her dark eyes gave back no light. She looked at D'Esperey for several long seconds and did not give the impression of searching for words. Propped against the pillows, Tania seemed formal, and her thin mouth was set in a flat line. D'Esperey felt uncomfortably like Tania was looking through his skin at his bones. She slipped one leg and then another under the covers.

"Will you wake me?" she said.

"Of course."

The covers bunched around her waist and her breasts pushed visibly together as she rolled slowly onto her side. She closed her eyes and then said languidly, "Wake me up at six. We can all have dinner together."

IN A PLACE called El Verdugo, they were seated at a table beneath a leafy tree overlooking the plaza. Sandoval ate a plate of *pacumutu*, beef, rice, and cheese and D'Esperey a soup made of chicken and plantains. Tania did not eat but drank several Singanis, and as these went down, she became increasingly talkative, almost jovial. The change in her was marked.

Food and drink had calmed Sandoval a bit. After all, they had made it out of La Paz, they were halfway to their meeting with Guevara, and the evening was beautiful.

D'Esperey asked her, "How long is the trip tomorrow?"

Tania looked over her glass. "Ten hours. Including the walk from the road head to the Base Camp."

"How far into the forest?" D'Esperey asked. It took him a while to make up this sentence, for in public he could not make himself say the words "base camp."

"It's about a four-hour walk. But I'm going to bring us in the back way. It's a little shorter." Tania's voice trailed off, and she looked away from the table over the plaza. Around them, the whitewashed walls of the city were taking on the orange hue of dusk. She began to hum a tune—maybe it was Edith Piaf.

It again occurred to Sandoval, dejectedly, that Tania was totally insane. Without thinking, he said, "Are you all right?"

"Yes. I'm fine."

Her words were hollow, and when the waiter came by, she handed her glass up onto his tray and said, *"Más."*

"When did you first meet him?" she said to D'Esperey. "He" could be only one man. Che Guevara was the common axis of their turning worlds.

D'Esperey's eyes found Tania's across the table. Her gaze was not as intimidating as that of the nude woman sprawled on the bed; he pushed back in his chair. "In sixty-one. I went to the island as a graduate student."

"You know Barbaroja, of course."

Barbaroja was the code name of Manuel Piñeiro, the head of the "Liberation Department," the external operations division of the Cuban Dirección General de Inteligencia. As his name dropped, D'Esperey and Sandoval stiffened visibly.

"Relax," Tania said. "We can talk here."

The waiter came and placed another drink in front of Tania. When he left, she put her arm over the back of her chair. She seemed at ease, but there was much going on behind her eyes. D'Esperey was less inhibited than Sandoval; no one was in earshot, and it seemed safe to speak.

"Barbaroja arranged my first trip here in sixty-five," D'Esperey said. "I wrote a paper for the leadership about the selection of sites—locations for the venture."

D'Esperey was elliptical, but his meaning was clear. He had entered the country then and now as a journalist. This cover was close and solid; he was legitimately a writer of some moment in leftist circles. D'Esperey had first come to the attention of the Cuban intelligence service after the publication of his book, *Reigniting the Revolution,* a text heretical to orthodox Marxists. D'Esperey had evangelized the rural roots of the Cuban revolution, maintaining that the guerrilla fighter had a vital political role. He believed, like Guevara, that rural guerrilla nuclei could educate, inspire, and mobilize the peasantry. The conditions for revolution could be jump-started by this guerrilla nucleus; they did not have to evolve. The concept was essentially Maoist, and thus apostasy, but it was music to the ears of Fidel Castro and Che Guevara. During his stint as a lecturer at Havana University, D'Esperey had been approached by Barbaroja. Urbane, educated at the École Normale Supérieure, and from a wealthy, noted family, D'Esperey was no bomb thrower. And that is why he was courted. Swept up in the romance of the Idea, D'Esperey agreed readily, and over the next several years he served as an undercover courier for Cuban intelligence. He'd traveled widely in Latin America, ostensibly writing articles for Jean-Paul Sartre's *Le Temps Modernes,* but the most important part of his work was authoring studies for Havana on the ripeness of countries as revolutionary targets.

D'Esperey's report on the merits of a Bolivian revolution had recommended that a *foco* be established in the Alto Beni, a jungle region two hundred miles north of the Ñancahuazú. For a dozen different reasons, all of them bad, D'Esperey's advice had been ignored, first by Manuel Piñeiro and ultimately by Castro and Guevara. It could be said that the Ñancahuazú was chosen almost by default.

"I haven't gotten much help from Barbaroja," Tania said.

"You've done a lot here," Sandoval offered. If she *were* insane, he at least wanted to be in her good graces. He also knew, as did D'Esperey, that Tania was close to Guevara.

Tania did not acknowledge the compliment. "Barbaroja's a *conjo,*" she said. Her language was a bit rough: The epithet translated to a term somewhere roughly between "asshole" and "motherfucker." Tania continued to talk, about her travels, about her training in Cuba; she talked of dozens of things, maniacally, quickly, and always with her eyes darting about. She drank another Singani but did not speak a word of her arrest, nor of the torture that followed. She built a wall around herself with words, with facts and details that linked her to the two men at the table. She embroidered truths upon circumstances, immodestly claiming that the entire urban network was her creation, then understating an equally important achievement, brokering the transfer of arms to the farmhouse. She kept at it, and Sandoval became bored, then so did D'Esperey. They both thought her a bit of a revolutionary groupie, and the more she carried on, the less gallant her achievements seemed.

This was her intent.

Eventually, the recklessness and insanity of the taxi ride was forgotten, put off to exuberance or even a surplus of precaution—a bold move that, through its success, proved that the group had not been detected by the authorities.

D'Esperey knew himself to be a journeyman agent; for him, so far was so good. For the last six years, Sandoval had coordinated Guevara's efforts in Argentina, including arranging supplies and support for Masetti's and Atilio's failed efforts in Salta Province. Having survived the erasure of Masetti's network, Sandoval considered himself above simple betrayal. He'd long suspected that Guevara and Tania were lovers, and like many others, he was certain that Tania was devoted to Guevara.

Sandoval had hitched his star to Guevara, so if Tania was close to the comandante, Sandoval thought it best to remain cordial. D'Esperey and Sandoval could not imagine that any other threat existed—to them, to their enterprise, or to Guevara.

Above the plaza, the clouds were silver with moonlight. D'Esperey ordered a bottle of wine. Tania drank and even laughed and managed impressions as best she could. Somehow she kept the wires apart, kept her two secret lives away from each other, for if they ever touched, they would spark and explode.

Tania made these men believe, if not *in* her, then *about* her. She was ashamed at her success; she was ashamed of even herself, of the conceit that had made her loyal to a cause but to no one person. She was, despite herself, quite aware of the powers within her. She knew she was no friend, only an acquaintance, complete unto herself, always uncomfortable with others and as unknowable as the inside of a cloud. Feelings and illusions battled within her; was there nothing left that was human? Was her soul now nothing but ashes?

Couples walked by on the square, and Tania got a little drunk and felt a warm numbness rising about her cheeks. Her voice came to her sounding alien and distant, like her own words recalled—not heard, but filtered through recollection and prejudice. She seemed to have become a spectator, even to herself. She was smashed up inside, filled with self-pity and also dread. She had learned from so many performances, and now she was simply playing another part. Her masks were impenetrable, and her act masterful: Inside, defeated and alone, she felt like a person about to be hanged.

42

GUEVARA AGAIN HEARD the engine of an aircraft, though under the tree canopy, he could not see it. It had passed over them twice during the morning, each time continuing to the north and returning down the other side of the valley. Joaquin and Pombo agreed that it was definitely flying a search pattern. There was little chance that their party could be seen from the air, and no chance at all that they were leaving a discernible trail through the forest. Still, the aircraft was worrying. Guevara ordered the group to travel upslope and away from the river bottom, knowing that a lazy patrol of soldiers would follow the river. This he did as a precaution, though he knew it would slow the group by as much as two days. The aircraft was simply too persistent. Guevara had a nagging feeling trouble lay ahead.

For several hours, the main column had climbed away from the valley floor, cresting one ridge then another as the river was put behind them. The center group hacked through thick underbrush until they worked across a saddle and then turned sharply left, keeping close to a precipitous series of bluffs heading almost directly south. By midmorning the column was bunched, starting and stopping behind the trail cutters, with as much standing about as walking.

Guevara had decided to continue pushing south, though the night before, he'd received a message on the shortwave promising the delivery of supplies at the junction of the Iripiti and Ñancahuazú rivers in seventy-two hours. The message had come as an agreeable surprise. The resupply point was a hard day's march back downstream, and Guevara knew the terrain around the river junction fairly well. The radio transmitter had finally given up the ghost—its dunking in the river was only the latest of a string of hard knocks, so Guevara had not been able to acknowledge the message. He expected to fix the radio at base, or at least replace it with a backup, and anyway, he was eager to get his exhausted troops back to the relative comforts of the established camp. He had decided that he would continue toward Camp 2, and after the men had been fed and rearmed, he himself would lead a detachment to accept the supplies.

They stopped at noon, and Guevara allowed the group a few hours' rest. He intended to travel late into the evening, certain that then the airplane would not be flying and any Bolivian soldiers who weren't at their barracks would be standing around a blazing campfire. As the men rested, he studied the map and came to a disheartening conclusion. They were perhaps four miles north of Camp 2, and it was another seven miles or so to the Zinc House. They were at least three hours' hard march from base, more if they continued to travel off the river bottom.

But that was not what caused concern.

The aircraft passed over them again at a quarter to one. Guevara managed a peek as it flew over the trees; it was an old Piper, a high-wing single-engine Cub, the sort of plane used to spot artillery. He clearly saw the red, yellow, and green roundels painted on its wings. Despite a nonbelligerent appearance, it was a military aircraft.

Guevara took out a pencil and drew a long oval on the back of the map. He made an X at the bottom and assumed that this was where the Zinc House was located. He placed another X at the top of the oval; this was the position where the group now rested. He assumed they could not be seen from the air. Then why had they been overflown three times? He scribbled some numbers. It was approximately eleven miles to the Zinc House. An aircraft like a Piper Cub had a maximum speed of slightly better than a hundred miles an hour. They had first heard the sound of the engines at about ten o'clock and then heard them again at about a quarter to noon.

Was the aircraft flying a search pattern?

This was a simple problem of two-dimensional geometry, and Gue-

vara delighted in mathematics. Now a riddle of arithmetic might fore-
tell the future.

He stared at the oval. The aircraft wasn't searching randomly. It was
searching a pattern that corresponded to things on the ground. If the
soldiers had discovered the Zinc House, they would certainly search
around it. If they had an aircraft, it made sense that they would send it
to search the valley. That aircraft, ergo, would fly in an oval. Perhaps a
figure eight, but the calculations would be the same, or nearly the
same.

The sides of the oval were eleven miles long. Eleven miles down and
eleven miles back. Twenty-two miles. Thirteen minutes of flight time.

Added to that was the time it took to fly around the top of the oval.
What was the diameter of a broad, lazy turn? Guevara had piloted his
uncle's sailplane as a boy. He knew something about aircraft. The turn
would be about as far as the pilot could see on this partly cloudy day—
a radius of, say, ten miles. The circumference of a circle was the prod-
uct of π times the diameter. The diameter was twice the radius.

$$C = \pi(2r)$$

Mathematical simplicity. But was it truth? Or was this all the fantasy
of an exhausted mind? 3.145 multiplied by 20. Guevara scribbled,
squinted, cursed, and started over. The circumference of a circle
twenty miles in diameter was 62.9 miles. He sketched the oval again,
tracing over his lines and writing in the distances. His lips moved as he
wrote down the flight times. Six and a half minutes to fly eleven miles.
Times two. Half of 62.9 was 31.5. That distance would be flown twice,
so back again to 62.9. How long did it take an airplane to fly 62.9
miles at one hundred miles an hour?

Silence unreeled in his head. *Think.*

The edifice he had built of numbers shuddered and threatened to
collapse.

Think, conjo!

An airplane traveling a hundred miles an hour would take 37.68
minutes to fly 62.8 miles. Thirty-seven minutes and forty seconds.

That meant that total flight time around the oval was fifty minutes
and forty seconds. The plane had last passed over at a quarter to one.
That meant it would return at . . . Silence again, roaring silence.

The plane would return at 1:35, fifteen minutes from now.

Guevara stood up, intending to tell Joaquin, but stopped. The big man was sprawled under a tree, his weapon crossed in his arms, his head was tipped back, and his mouth was open. His breath escaped in a rattling grunt. He was dead asleep. There was no point in waking him with a prediction, especially if it foretold doom. Especially if it was wrong.

So Guevara waited, leaning back against a tree. He killed time, straining his ears, and five minutes passed like a week. Ten minutes passed like a month. Joaquin woke and stretched and got up to take a long piss. Still Guevara waited. Joaquin used his foot to nudge Pombo awake. *"Vamos,"* Joaquin said.

And then Guevara heard it, far away; closer, it became a popping sort of rattle. The hum of a single-engine plane. He looked at his watch. It was thirty-six minutes past one in the afternoon; the aircraft was on time almost exactly to the second.

"Joaquin," Guevara said flatly, "the army has found the Zinc House."

TANIA'S DRIVING HAD been manic, almost daredevil, and the men were quietly thankful when at last they heard the parking brake grind up and the vehicle's engine switch off. Begun well before dawn, the long jeep ride had taken them southeast from Sucre; from there they drove to the sad little pueblo of Tichucha, and then north on an increasingly sketchy road to El Meson. The jeep headed north up a slot of a valley to the place the telegraph wires ran out, a dusty clutch of stucco, tile, and thatch-roofed hovels called Yaquí. They left the jeep, and Tania paid the *corregador* ten American dollars to park behind his house. She told him she would be back within a week. The old man smiled, revealing black and diseased gums, and as he counted the five and five one-dollar bills, he could not have seemed less interested in Sandoval, D'Esperey, Tania, their backpacks, or the several pieces of luggage they'd left covered with a blanket in the backseat. They started their walk from the village at one in the afternoon.

Tania had promised them a four-hour hike, and it quickly proved to be all of that. On her previous visit, she had driven up the road from Lagunillas directly to the Zinc House. She did not think it prudent to come in again using the same route; ironically, she did not wish to draw attention now.

Her secrets bore down on her, and as they left the village, Tania became morose. Accompanying her on the trail were falsity and a twisted,
unfinished sense of mission. It came to her sadly how, seven years ago,
she had fallen in love; as all lovers do, she'd wanted possession of a
human soul. Guevara's soul had never been in her grasp, but his life
now was.

The walk started out easily enough, down into a wide, forested draw.
Tania led them across a creek that they managed to cross by leaping
from rock to rock. Neither D'Esperey nor Sandoval was an outdoors-
man. Their packs chafed, and by the time they began the climb up
from the Íquira, both were developing blisters and an attitude.

The forest about them was primordial, and the several changes of direction had left Sandoval and D'Esperey turned about. They did not
know the country, or the way, or even the final destination toward
which they labored. Subsumed by a thousand shades of green, they
heard only the sounds of the jungle, a tittering of birds, almost constant, and far off, the hooting of monkeys. Tania led them close to another small stream and then sat suddenly on a fallen tree to rest. She
said nothing to the men, not why she had stopped nor how far along
on their trek they were. They were left to gather from her expression
that they, too, should halt. Sandoval sat at once, struggled out of his
pack, and wiped the sweat from his bald head.

Leaning against his pack straps, D'Esperey remained on his feet and
looked downstream. The forest put in him a sense of awe. D'Esperey
was a man of cities and cafés, of salons and ideas—the wildness and im-
placability of the jungle cast all his thoughts about in heaps. D'Esperey,
the revolutionary, a genius who would remake mankind, stood dis-
mayed and humbled in a world that did not require men or their
dreams.

"How much farther?" he asked.

The buzz of insects answered; Tania had a map given to her by Guevara, but the positions of the camps were not marked on it. Tania had
made the hike up and back, but last time she had approached from the
southeast, via the Zinc House. She guessed that the camps were over
the next set of hills, perhaps the next. She was certain she was going in
the right direction, northeast, but until she could see into the Ñancahuazú Valley and sight the farmhouse, she could not tell them exactly how much farther.

This assessment set D'Esperey into a funk, and Sandoval asked pointedly if Tania knew exactly where they were.

"Maybe you want to navigate?" Tania sniped back.

Sandoval had received guerrilla training in Czechoslovakia and Algeria. He had been taught map and compass work but had retained only odds and ends. His mumbled answer made Tania frown. He looked down at his feet, and D'Esperey looked around. The tree canopy opened slightly above the watercourse, and sunlight came down in patches to the forest floor. Across the stream was a very large, dark snake sunning itself on a rock. Dark triangles lay across its back, edged with light gray scales. A shaft of sunlight came slanting through the trees, framing the creature as though it were the principal diadem in a museum of crowns. D'Esperey assumed, as novices always do, that it was poisonous. In this case, he was correct, abundantly so. The snake within his sight was pit viper, a fer-de-lance, and very, very deadly.

D'Esperey opened his mouth but did not speak.

Tania did not see the snake, or she ignored it. She stood and, without a word of encouragement or warning, continued with long strides up the next rise. Sandoval grunted as he put on his backpack and followed. D'Esperey backed after him, keeping his eye on the solemnly inert coil of reptile on the opposite bank. Two eyes, like shiny onyx beads, glimmered back at him. D'Esperey hoped fervently that the snake had never once mated and that it was as dead as last year's canary.

Up to the ridge and onto another, the two shining lights of the revolution panted after Tania and muttered curses. Finally, through the trees, scraps of sky were glimpsed close to the forest floor. Tania picked up her pace, and even Sandoval, who stared mostly at the trail, realized they were approaching an overlook.

At the edge of a sharp cliff, Tania halted. Below was the Ñancahuazú Valley, and to the north, skimmed over by clouds, were the promontories of Camps 1 and 2.

As D'Esperey stumbled up behind, Tania pulled him down and sought cover. Below in the valley was the Zinc House. Around it were a dozen olive-drab tents, and she could see soldiers, small flecks moving across the red dirt by the crook in the river. Neither D'Esperey nor Sandoval had been to the farmhouse; neither had any idea what they were looking at. They comprehended first the bend in the river, then a truck trailing a plume of dust up the valley floor. It meant nothing to them. Nor did the other trucks or the clutch of tents arced around the bend in the river. Tania made them understand that the army was at the farmhouse, obviously in force, and both men became sullen.

"Should we turn back?" D'Esperey asked.

The idea had not occurred to Tania that the army might prevent her from delivering her charges. Diminov had not told her that the Zinc House had been discovered. The Americans had not mentioned it. It came as a jarring shock that her mind had to overcome.

"How did they find the house?"

"Where—"

Tania held up her hand to silence them. She removed her pack and fished out a pair of binoculars. Lying prone next to a tree trunk, she pointed them down into the valley and watched the road and clearing around the house. She scanned up the tree line and around the bend in the river. She studied the army's positions, looking for assemblies of men, for mustering squads, for groups loading onto trucks. Any of these things would indicate that the army was preparing a patrol. She found nothing like this. The soldiers came and went as randomly as termites in a woodpile.

Tania guessed that there were three hours of daylight left. She did not know if this was sufficient time to cover the distance to the camps. The ridgelines between her and the camps were open in several places. If they continued on directly, they could be seen from the valley floor.

Continue or retreat; of their two alternatives, neither seemed attractive. The jeep and El Meson were three hours behind them. If they started at once, they would not reach the jeep until long after dark, and Tania doubted they could find their way up and over the several ridges and into the tiny village by moonlight. She felt certain she could navigate, keeping the Ñancahuazú in sight, but now, finding it in the hands of the army, she knew she had to keep out of sight from the valley floor. Before this, her task had been relatively simple. She had only to head northeast from El Meson. She'd counted on finding the farmhouse in the valley and then ascending to the camps by the usual trail. That would be impossible.

Crouched next to Tania, Sandoval and D'Esperey were faced with their first whiff of actual danger. It did not occur to her to ask what they thought—both were clearly out of their depth. As Tania put away the binoculars, her hands shook violently, and she was aware of their

eyes on her. The idiotic thought came to her to run down into the valley and surrender. She knew that the Bolivian soldiers would probably
murder them out of hand. She did not care. She had been sent to the
valley to betray and deliver destruction. Murder was around her at
every turn. She only slowly dismissed the idea of surrendering. She
looked on her death as the just deserts of her failure as a lover and
friend, as a daughter and true comrade. Shame at her mission, dis-
honor, and self-loathing uncoiled, and she felt herself dividing into
pieces.

Behind them, metal struck metal—the noise of a bolt plunging forward on a rifle. D'Esperey and Sandoval turned and gaped. Before
them were two men in olive drab; their hair was wild, and both had
dark beards. Their uniforms were dirty, patched, and mended with
large awkward stitches. Both carried automatic weapons, American-
made M2 carbines. The groups looked at each other, one armed, one
without weapons, one amazed, one in command. Sandoval did not
know whether to put up his hands. D'Esperey had sense enough to remain still, but it was several long seconds before Tania said to the
armed men, "Do you remember me?"

The closest of the two men said that he did.

The speaker was Arturo, and he recognized Tania as La Chiquita,
the woman who had visited the camp with Selizar Galán. The men Arturo did not recognize, so he did not do them the courtesy of deflect-
ing the muzzle of his rifle.

Tania came to her feet as though she were bearing an indescribable
weight. "Take us to the comandante," she said.

PART

III

Under Other

Skies

43

WHEN THE CENTER group at last came into the small clearing no one spoke and their footsteps were muffled on the forest floor. They had come at a forced march, an entire day and night, and now that they had reached their objective they staggered and placed their hands on the back of their necks, the way runners do after a race. To a man, they found shade against the bases of the trees, dropped their packs and rifles, and sprawled out.

Tania, Sandoval, and D'Esperey had been brought into camp and shunted to the corner next to the smaller fire pit. They sat silently and watched as the center group arrived. The guerrillas were dirty and skinny, slumped under the weight of packs; they looked to Tania like refugees. She was astounded by how bedraggled and exhausted they looked.

Guevara strode into camp like a compact tornado. He scanned the clearing and saw D'Esperey and Sandoval—last he saw Tania, and his expression laid waste to her. In his eyes was the smallest check, recognition only, not surprise, relief, happiness, or any emotion, good or bad. This was another hurt piled upon her.

"We found them on the ridge south of Camp One," Arturo said.

"You fucking idiot," Guevara shouted at him. "The army's swarming all around the place! I told you to stay away from the farmhouse—"

Arturo started to make some sound, perhaps the first two syllables of an explanation or defense, but Guevara came over the top of him.

"What the fuck? You kept back and forth—wearing out the fucking path! Now, thanks to you, they've gotten at the weapons. There's a company of soldiers in the valley because you are a stupid, lazy piece of shit."

The harangue went on, loudly, excruciatingly, and in several minutes Arturo's humiliation was complete. Guevara did not register the expressions of horror on the faces around him. He was congenitally unaware of the force his words had on others. He was angry and had a right to be. The farmhouse was compromised, captured by the army, and an enemy force was anchored there, at the very root of the insurgency. Guevara had never been one to mince words, and he did nothing to moderate his fury. He, too, was worn from the march, as tired as any of the men, for he had shared their burdens, and on top of that, the weight of command. This same man who had worked carefully to build up the strength and esprit of his men now ruthlessly disciplined them. He was no stranger to combat or to life under arms, but his experience was oddly skewed—he had spent most of his time in command, not in the ranks. In the six hundred days of the Cuban revolution, he had gone from being an anonymous guerrilla, a rifleman and medic, to the rank of comandante, a hero to the nation and much of the world. Those six hundred days were his only experience leading men in the field.

In truth, Guevara had never been spoken to as he rebuked his men; in the first place, he would not stand for it, and in the second place, no person except Fidel Castro had ever commanded him. In the end, Guevara had not submitted even to Castro—when he no longer felt inclined, they parted ways. Guevara demanded as much of the men who worked as much as he gave, which was all.

Reduced to an object of derision, Arturo couldn't even slink away. He sat, looking down, as mute as a scolded dog. Guevara then turned on Marcos, who got it doubly because he'd been in a position of authority and had disappointed on the march.

"And you," Guevara nearly spat, "fucking useless. You arrive three days before the main column—"

Marcos had a penchant for talking back. It did not serve him well. "I wasn't in charge of the camp," he said, snidely defiant.

Guevara's rage was incandescent. "You aren't fit to be put in charge of shit-eating monkeys! When did you arrive back at camp?"

"Five days ago."

"What time?"

"Midafternoon."

"Broad fucking daylight. You and the entire forward detachment. You walked right up to the fucking farmhouse? Guns, backpacks, radio? You don't give a shit. Do you wonder why the army's come? What the fuck, Marcos? Didn't I tell you—all of you—to stay the fuck away from the Zinc House? What do I give orders around here for?"

The camp was silent.

"Miguel will take your place as leader of the forward detachment. You are also relieved as third in command. You can go back to Cuba or serve as a rifleman in the rear detachment. It's up to you. You have no more responsibilities in the column."

The comandante's temper was famous, but this was the first time it had flashed in Bolivia. Mercilessly, Guevara stayed focused on Marcos. "What are you going to do? Go or stay?"

Marcos seemed as dumb as a scarecrow. It took him several seconds to answer quietly, "I'll stay." He licked his lips and said in a half-whisper, "I'm committed to what we're doing here."

"You don't act like it," Guevara shot back. He shouted over his shoulder, "Where is the goddamn food for the marching column?"

Pots were brought from the fires; rice and urina were dished out on banana leaves. All were served who had come off the trail. The men ate ravenously, the camp watchers made even more humble as the others shoveled down their meal. Guevara, too, was handed a banana leaf heaped with rice and stringy meat. The dressing-down continued as he shoved rice into his mouth.

"It's a fucking miracle the army hasn't captured Camp Two. A fucking miracle. You goddamn idiots. Isn't there any one of you that I can trust? Not one fucking one of you?"

Tania sat with the others, thunderstruck. Those who hadn't seen Guevara's temper were put into a trance; his words cut and his eyes smoldered. The objects of his rage were reduced to trembling wrecks—grown men, accomplished guerrillas, some known to him for years, were made mute and nearly distracted with humiliation. Guevara then turned on the *resacas*, the young Bolivians who had failed on the march. As he had been with the Cubans, he was uncompromising.

"And you assholes," he said. "Carrying a weapon is a privilege. It is an honor to fight for the liberation of the people. You have nothing to offer to your country, to the revolution, or to me. From this moment you are expelled from the column. Your weapons are to be given up. And likewise your equipment—it will be redistributed among the fighters. You are suspended from the cigarette ration. If you do not work, you will not eat. You are no longer combatants and will not be treated as such. You will remain at the camp, under the orders of your superiors, until we can find a place and time to discharge you."

Pepe, Chingolo, Paco, and Eusebio stood with their faces burning. They'd been tested and found wanting, they knew it, but this humiliation was unexpected and more so for being public.

Orders were given. Squads picked up their weapons and took to defensive positions downslope, between Camp 2 and the valley floor. The guerrillas assigned to ambush exited the camp quickly; it fairly could be said that they feared the enemy much less than they presently feared their commander. Guevara ate a portion of his meal and tossed the remainder back into the pot. Tania was gripped by the sight of him. He seemed simultaneously pathetic and heroic, greatness showing itself in him despite his tirade. He walked toward the second fire, and as he approached, Tania felt her legs start to go numb. He said nothing but bundled up Sandoval in an old comrade's *abrazo*, slapping him on the back. He then extended his hand to D'Esperey. "It's good to see you again."

He glared at Tania, and it astounded her that she somehow managed to rise from the log and stand in front of him. Her hands trembled, and there was a wringing pain in her abdomen. "I have to speak to you," she stammered.

"Talk here," he said curtly.

Sandoval and D'Esperey, already uncomfortable, positively squirmed. Neither wanted to be any part of what they thought was a private matter between Tania and Guevara.

Her knees trembled. "Alone, Che. I need—"

Guevara took her by the wrist, not gently, and led her ten or fifteen yards away from the fire. He spun her around impatiently. "I don't have time for this shit."

Tania's voice was strangled; she felt as though she were being suffocated. "The resupply at the river junction is an ambush," she said.

His eyes narrowed. The unexpected words crashed against his ears. He did not understand at first. "What are you talking about?"

"The supply drop in the valley. It's an ambush. The Americans are waiting there."

"You're insane."

"Listen to me. I have betrayed you. Since we first met. I have been working for the KGB. Informing on you. The Soviets now want you dead."

Guevara weighed Tania's pronouncement. It was incredulous; he tried to reconcile it to all that he knew of Tania over almost eight years, but his mind would not easily accept her words as fact. She described to him her arrest and the arrangement with the Americans that had set her free. She told him of her meetings in Buenos Aires with her Russian controllers and how she had begged the KGB to be taken out of service. She told him everything, and tears streamed down her face.

When it finally registered that she was telling the truth, Guevara's vision constricted to a shiny black tube. He struck her face with the back of his hand. The blow knocked Tania to her knees and the sound broke like a pistol shot over the clearing.

Joaquin dropped his food and came immediately to the comandante's side. The immense secret finally unburdened. Tania remained on the ground, great sobs breaking over her. Guevara took a step backward, panting as his asthma reached up from nowhere to choke the life out of him.

Joaquin stumbled when he saw the expression on Guevara's face. He had not heard Tania's words, no one in the camp had, but all had seen Guevara slap her down. In ten years Joaquin had never seen such a look on the comandante's face—rage, astonishment, and grief.

"What has happened?" Joaquin asked. He tried to lift the woman by the elbow. She remained limp. "What did you do?" he asked her. "What happened?"

Tania could only look down.

"Leave us please, Joaquin," Guevara said.

The big man retreated. All eyes were on Tania and Guevara; maybe twenty yards distant, they could be seen but not heard.

"How long?" he asked.

"Always."

"In Germany?"

She nodded.

"In Prague?"

"Since we met. Always since I have known you."

"Then I am a fool."

"I love you," she said.

Guevara glared at her. Their passion was a distant thing and he did not feign now to tell her that he had loved her. The wind stirred the trees and as the leaves murmured, it occurred to him to shoot her. This thought stayed with him for several minutes. He had long held the power of life and death in his hands—perhaps for the first time, he held the scales over someone he knew to the depths of his soul. He felt his throat tightening and the slow, sharpening pain unwinding in his chest.

"And them?" He jerked his head at Sandoval and D'Esperey.

"They know nothing. I informed on them, as I did on you."

"For money?"

At this Tania flinched. "No," she cried, "never."

"Why did you tell me now?" he asked. "Why didn't you just remain silent? Why didn't you let me walk into the ambush?"

"I couldn't do it," Tania said. "I could not be part of your murder."

"Why not?" Guevara asked flatly. "I'm only a fool, like other fools."

The full scope of Tania's duplicity evolved in his mind. There was almost nothing in his private or public life that he had not told her. He had confided everything, entrusted her with his most important plans; he'd talked to her about his failure in the Congo, of his troubled relationship with Fidel and Raúl. He stood reeling, struck stupid to think that everything he'd ever said to her was known by the Soviets—and now by the Americans.

Shame bawled around her, and Tania hung her head. She fully expected to be executed. What she did not expect was for Guevara to reach down and put his hand gently on her arm.

She lifted her face, and his dark eyes burned through her. His expression was without anger but was equally without gentleness. There are qualities that cannot stand alone. Mercy is one; it can exist only as an admixture of compassion, which is itself an alloy of many things—love, understanding, empathy.

"Get up," he said.

Tania came to her feet. She stood swaying with her arms wrapped around herself, a picture of abject misery.

"Go back to the others," Guevara said firmly. "Don't tell anyone what you have done."

. . .

HOYLE'S AMBUSH HAD been laid in tiers overlooking the junction of the Ñancahuazú and Iripiti. Both of the fire teams of Famous Lawyer had been camouflaged and arrayed on the hillsides, their automatic weapons and sniper rifles commanding the flat, broad field where the Ñancahuazú turned slightly north and the Iripiti entered steeply from the west.

The ambushers were decked in various patterns of camouflage, none of it U.S. issue. They paraded an assortment of weapons, Belgian FN rifles and Russian-made AK-47s. Also of foreign provenance were the small items they carried, knives large and small, cups and canteens, compasses, backpacks, belts and holsters. Pains had been taken to make sure each operator had equipment that was nonattributable—not overtly American.

Hoyle carried one of the team's Springfield sniper rifles, perhaps the only piece of certifiably American hardware that would be brought into the field. It was the weapon the Green Berets had christened "Cruel Jane," the long gun designated for night shooting. Bolted above its receiver was the bulky tube of a starlight scope. The night sight gave the rifle an awkward, top-heavy appearance, equal parts cumbersome and fierce, a thing of great power and menace.

Major Holland's entire team, as well as Santavanes and Valdéz, had been positioned in an inverted V facing the river. The ambushers had been hidden artfully, and the bait was displayed to maximum effect. At the edge of the clearing, several parachutes had been draped in the trees. The canopies billowed in the wind that came from the canyons, promising bounty.

The moon did not rise at all after dusk, and the stars were breathtaking; the Southern Cross rose over the bottom of the valley, and the Milky Way swayed through the entire sky, a turbid river of light. They waited in silence, not one man moving and no one speaking.

At three A.M. Hoyle switched on the starlight scope and pointed it at the clearing. For the period of his watch, he scanned through the nearly pitch black, the night scope rendering a world of light and dark green. Across the clearing, he could see the strange, billowing contours of the parachutes. He scanned carefully for upright shapes, and also for movement close to the ground—men walking or crawl-

ing. There was no motion other than the lazy blousing of the
canopies.

Hoyle strained to hear each sound in the night: the peep of frogs,
the rattle of insects, the small murmur of the breeze through the
leaves. He tuned in to the noise, placing the sounds in a sort of audio
perspective about him: tree frogs here, crickets there, in front of him
the steady hissing of the river. Hoyle knew that total silence often announced the presence of the enemy. These were little tricks learned in
Vietnam. All had served him well, like the plan for this two-sided ambush with its carefully laid fields of fire. The flat ground across the river
was a perfect killing field, as perfect as Hoyle could make it. All it
needed was victims.

But none came; dawn stole across the mountains, and it became
slowly and embarrassingly obvious that their bait had been ignored.
The forest around them was alive with the uninterrupted calls of a
hundred species of winged creatures. Hoyle stood in the foxhole and
stretched his legs. "We've been burned," he said quietly.

Santavanes flicked a large black scorpion off the hand guard of his
rifle. Hoyle watched as the arachnid went flailing through the air, pin-
cers waving and tail plunging about. It landed in the leaf clutter,
quickly righted itself, and scuttled from view.

Valdéz was sanguine. "Fuck this," he said.

Hoyle agreed. They were now faced with the delicate task of disen-
gaging. It was not as simple as walking away from the clearing. They
had announced the location to Guevara, even if he had not answered,
and it had to be assumed that he had not shown for a reason. It was unlikely that he just didn't want the supplies.

Everything pointed to the conclusion that Guevara had figured out it
was a trap. He had deduced this on his own, or he had been told. Tania,
whom no one, Russian or American, considered stable, may have
warned him. So advised, Guevara might himself lay a counterambush.
Hoyle knew that Guevara surely would send a reconnaissance team to
watch the clearing—Hoyle always attributed to his foe sound tactical
sense, and if he thought to do it, he figured Guevara would as well.

It was with the greatest caution that the Green Berets gathered together, keeping as much undercover as they could. It was not the time
to discuss what had gone wrong. It was time to get out and remain as
invisible as possible. Hoyle had gone into the field intending to engage

the enemy on terms that had not developed, and it fell to him to conduct the most difficult of all military maneuvers—withdrawal.

Hoyle's route took them north. The two fire teams walked as close as possible to their assigned bearings, scrambling sometimes up heavily vegetated slopes, kicking their feet into the damp earth and pulling themselves up by roots and branches. On the ridge above the river, both groups altered course to remain undercover.

At about noon Hoyle came upon a trail about two hundred feet above the river valley; running north and south, it had been hacked out of the underbrush, carefully leaving overhead cover in place. Hoyle halted the patrol and laid out a hasty ambush as he studied the tracks. Thirty men, give or take, had passed before the last rain. Some were heavily laden and a few were barefoot. Most of the traffic had gone south.

Hoyle did not wish to seek an extemporaneous engagement; nor did he have the manpower to pursue and locate Guevara's main force. Hoyle signaled to Santavanes, who removed a pointed cylinder from his pack. One of the Igloo White sensors, the contraption resembled an elongated and camouflaged funnel. Santavanes stepped about ten feet off the trail and pushed the end of the device into the soft ground. Using the heel of his boot, he sank it into the leaf clutter until only an inch or so remained above the dirt.

Santavanes bent over the gizmo, set the transmission ID code, the sensitivity of the sensor, and the number of days the device would be active. In the shade of a small bush, the device was almost impossible to see. If Guevara used the trail again—if even one man passed—the sensor would detect vibration through the earth and send a radio message indicating time, number of people, and direction of traffic. For the next thirty days, it would monitor the trail night and day, rain or shine.

In another three hours, the groups had laid a dozen more sensors and linked up on Hill 556. The helicopter appeared only twenty minutes late, and they were taken back to the casita.

Unknown to Hoyle, the pains he had taken in their extraction had been necessary. Guevara had sent Tuma and Begnino downriver to a promontory overlooking the Saladillo. They had taken a position just forward of the hillcrest, looking down on the river. They could not see the drop zone exactly, but their vantage commanded a view almost to the Palmarito, the place Hoyle had laid the first sensor. Hoyle had managed to retreat unobserved by only the barest of margins.

Tuma and Begnino had watched for an hour and then turned south toward the camps. As they started their return, they plainly heard a Bolivian helicopter pass down the other side of the valley. They could not know that this helicopter bore an ambush party. Nor could they have any idea where it landed, for the hilltop Hoyle picked as a landing zone was not visible from the river. Tuma and Begnino reported back to Guevara having seen nothing.

They had seen almost everything.

AN AIR OF TENSION hung around the camp. Guevara, oddly, seemed calm, even withdrawn. He sat on his hammock and smoked his pipe while working parties were arranged by Pombo and Joaquin to move upriver and recover the few remaining supplies. Moro had handed Guevara a vial of hydrocortisone from the medical cache. Moro told him there were only a dozen tablets. Guevara took this news with a composed indifference, though he did not know what he would do when these pills ran out.

Like Guevara, Tania had retreated to a corner of the clearing and sat blank-faced, staring out into the jungle. It was impossible for the men not to connect and compare the two individuals, Tania on one end of the camp, almost catatonic, and Guevara on the other, willfully composed. No one approached Tania, and she said nothing. This added, hour by hour, to a sense of anxiety felt by all.

At five in the afternoon, Guevara called for D'Esperey, who walked to the comandante's hammock and watched him lace his boots. He was again taken aback by Guevara's appearance; his clothing was filthy, and his eyes seemed sunken. It surprised D'Esperey that Guevara had not bothered to bathe or change clothes.

Puffing on his pipe, Guevara said, "Get out a notebook. This is what I want you to do." Soon D'Esperey was scribbling notes. "You have to get back to Havana as quickly as possible. We need more troops. Tell Fidel to send in another group. We need to take some pressure off the valley. Tell him, 'Do not fail to open a second front.'

"After Havana, I need you to return to France and organize a support network. I want it to have the broadest base possible—of course, it should be headed by the Party, but it should broadly include members of the left, whatever their persuasion. Journalists are to be specifically cultivated; activities of the Bolivian guerrillas should be made into news. If we win a thousand victories out here and no one knows, our work will be for nothing.

"I'll give you letters for Jean-Paul Sartre and Bertrand Russell, asking them both to organize an aid fund for the Bolivian liberation movement. These letters are to be published widely. Use your connections in the French Communist Party to organize channels for sending aid—money, electronics, and medicine."

He spoke also of recruiting a communications specialist and purchasing long-range radio equipment. D'Esperey earnestly ticked off his assignments, adding enthusiastic exclamations here and there. He was not aware that Guevara had watched him closely. Guevara was a good judge of men. He knew that D'Esperey could be of use, but not in the field. That was reserved for stouter hearts.

Next Guevara called for Sandoval, who came to the hammock without D'Esperey's sense of awe. Sandoval said that he was at Guevara's command but made no pretenses of serving as a guerrilla. Guevara had in mind for Sandoval a more specific task.

"My strategic objective is to seize political power in Argentina. What I want is to get together a group of dedicated countrymen, the best people available. I'll season them in combat for a year or two up here, form a column, and then enter the country, again in the north, but probably not in Salta."

Sandoval knew well the tribulation of Masetti and the failure of the armed group sent in with him. Sandoval had escaped both extermination and any share of the blame.

"You're going to head this up," Guevara said. "I want you to remain in Buenos Aires as long as possible before you have to join the forces in the mountains. You're going to be the principal coordinator, sending me people." Guevara paused and his eyes clicked over the camp. "I want a first-rate job. Not like this shit we have going on here."

Duty-bound, Sandoval told Guevara about Tania's shenanigans with the taxi in La Paz, though he did not mention the continuing oddness at the hotel in Sucre. Guevara shook his head. Sandoval was fishing for the reason the comandante has slapped her, but Guevara did not go into it. He continued to tell Sandoval of his plans. The column in Bolivia was to

be the mother column; he intended within a year to have gathered together five hundred fighters, Peruvians, Bolivians, Paraguayans, and Ar-
gentines. From this mother column, he would split off units and send
them into adjoining countries. Sandoval was to get in contact with specific members of the Argentine left, in particular Eduardo Jozami, and as
soon as possible send five men to begin training.

Sandoval's mind wandered. Guevara seemed unaware of the precar-
iousness of his position. Everything about the operation seemed ama-
teurish—Tania's waywardness, the compromise of the farmhouse, the
deplorable state of morale. The Zinc House had been intended to be
the central link of the logistical operation. Camps 1 and 2 were never
meant to be combat positions. Now, at a stroke, and before anyone was
really ready, the valley had exploded into war. Sandoval was also concerned that the Bolivian Party was not supporting the guerrillas in the
field. Many things worried Sandoval: how the guerrillas would stay
supplied, how they would recruit among the peasants, how he was to
communicate with them. None of this seemed to bother Guevara. He
put forward his plans, though they seemed occasionally fantastic. Sandoval was to coordinate with Pombo on the issues of transporting people and logistical support.

"How am I to coordinate with Pombo when he's in the field?"

Guevara waved his hand. "Work out a communications plan."

Sandoval frowned but did not say anything.

"Soon we're going to pull the army to us and bash in their brains,"
Guevara said.

Sandoval did not doubt him, but he could not help but wonder:
And what then?

44

HOYLE'S TEAM RETURNED to the casita, the mood notably somber. The ambush had not succeeded, but the patrol had been extracted without loss. The group had located a main trail above the river and put down sensors—this was itself no small triumph. If the guerrillas moved north, it was likely they would use that same trail; the path had been sturdily constructed and was concealed from the air. Guevara's back door was now alarmed, and the Bolivian army was camped out on his front lawn.

Still, there were several failures to report, and after Hoyle and Famous Lawyer had conducted their debriefings, Smith worked up a cable to Langley. He was careful to lace good news into his bad. Smith was a master at this. He knew that what counted most back at Langley were not results but the *perception* of results. The cable was pretty close to what they wanted, next to Guevara's head on a platter and his column shot and heaped into a ditch.

Guevara was in a battle for his dream and for his life. Smith's conflict was more accurately about his career—which amounted to pretty much the same things, a dream and a life—though in his case, hanging in the balance were not the aspirations and welfare of three hundred million South Americans.

Hoyle took his turn in a makeshift shower set up behind the tents.

The water was cold and so full of minerals that it barely allowed the soap to lather. Hoyle scrubbed himself as clean as he could, washing the dirt from his skin and the camouflage paint from his face and hands. As he washed away the dirt he felt a little better.

For the period of the mission, all of his humanity had been stuffed into a separate compartment. While he was "in," all the animal parts of his brain were switched on, his senses sharpened to the point of Zen, eyes and ears keen and the colors vivid and hot. It had taken all of his concentration to walk into the jungle hunting men, all of his wits and luck besides. Now that the animal centers of his brain were gradually switching off, emotion came rushing back in. The passion he felt for Maria stung like a handful of thorns. The first seeds of anger were sprouting, taking root in the black, shady dust of self-pity.

Hoyle dressed in dry khakis, and everyone assembled at the casita for dinner—arroz con pollo again, but this time it was made by Charlie and not laid down along Cuban lines. It was very good, and there was plenty of it and beer as well. Hoyle ate with Smith in the kitchen. After the meal, they walked out by the airfield and held a council of war.

"Are you all right?" Smith asked.

"Great," Hoyle said. He was off slightly—he'd downed two bourbons with his dinner—but Smith did not know if it had to do with the booze, the failed ambush, or something else.

"They do okay?" Smith asked, nodding back toward the casita, where the Green Berets still ate.

"They were solid," Hoyle answered. This was about as high as he praised fieldcraft. It was his first patrol since his wounding, and it might have been more on the mark for Smith to ask how Hoyle had done. The "failure" of the ambush was not as ruinous as a layperson might think. In spec ops, there was accomplishment in just getting in and out. The discovery of Guevara's main trail, though the result of simple good luck, was also something to sweeten the mission.

"I'm going to fly down tomorrow and see if I can get the Fourth Division off its ass. Major Placido's been transferred there as chief of staff."

"It wouldn't do much good to send me," Hoyle said.

"No, it wouldn't. I'm going to send you into La Paz. If I can get the Bolos to move up the valley, I expect they'll get their asses kicked."

Smith's pessimism was blandly professional. "What we need to do is stay ahead of the news story."

"Do you want me to talk to the minister?" Hoyle asked. He could not bring himself to say Alameda's name.

"No. Use the public affairs people at the embassy. No matter what the results are, have the U.S. press officer put out the straight dope—killed, wounded, and missing—and make sure it gets to Voice of America."

The goal was to make Presidente Barrientos face the music; if he wanted good news on the radio, he would have to make it in the jungle.

"Are you going to cut out the Ministry of Information?" Hoyle asked.

"No. What I need from Alameda are press credentials," Smith said. "Clean ones."

"Alameda's dirty," Hoyle said. "He's meeting regularly with Selizar Galán, the head of the PCB."

"How do you know this?"

"I know it."

"Tell me *how* you know it."

"The woman in his office. The Cuban woman."

Smith ignored the issue of the source for a second, and the fact that Hoyle had been warned away from Maria. "If Alameda's working both sides, how are you going to get press credentials out of his office?"

"I've got cooperation—I think."

"Think?"

"I'm pretty sure I can get a couple of blank credential sets."

"I told you I didn't want any sexual-cowboy shit."

Hoyle looked at his feet and then back at Smith. "You don't have to worry about that."

"How are you going to *make* the woman do it?"

"I've got leverage."

"I don't need this fucked up, Hoyle. I need Alameda in my pocket, singing our music when I want it. If you can't get blank creds out of his office—in the black—I don't need them. I'll do something else."

"Let me try."

"Don't fuck this up," Smith said.

He walked back to the casita. Hoyle stood out in the wide open. The long day was not over; the night was an hour or an eternity away.

Hoyle did not know what he would do when he saw Maria again. It occurred to him that the catastrophe in his heart was widening its grip on the entire world.

HOYLE FLEW INTO La Paz and first sent a note to the post office box. It was curt but said that he needed to see her, and instead of the hotel, he asked if she would meet him at a small café off the Avenida Camacho at seven P.M.

Hoyle went back to the safe house at the Plaza España and waited. He was not at all certain that she would be able to keep the appointment. He stalked around the apartment, restless and apprehensive. He thought to mix himself a drink and finally did so at five o'clock. Then he had another.

Hoyle drove across town toward the café, found a spot down the block, and waited in the car. At seven Maria appeared, looked around the tables on the sidewalk, and then stepped inside. Hoyle watched, knowing that she would ask for a table just inside so that they could meet and not be seen from the street. He knew also that she would be a bit nervous that he wasn't there, but he deliberately waited ten minutes before walking to the café.

Maria smiled as she saw him and Hoyle felt hot in the face. She was more beautiful than ever, and sitting down at the small table, he felt awkward and fretful.

"Hello," she said.

Hoyle did not say anything but smiled dimly, a false, meaningless expression.

"Should we go somewhere else?" she asked. "I have a couple of hours."

"We can stay here."

Maria looked about. The place was busy and was likely to fill completely. "Are you sure?"

"I don't have much time," Hoyle said.

The waiter came by, and Hoyle ordered coffee.

"Have you had time to think about what I asked you?" Hoyle asked.

An emotion more than disappointment showed in her voice. "I wanted to talk to you, not just stuff words in a mailbox."

Maria noticed that he looked her in the face but not in the eyes.

Someone in the crowd laughed loudly, and others joined in. It was remarkable that this happiness seemed to sputter out when it reached their table.

"Why did you ask to meet here? Why not the hotel?"

"You don't like it here?"

"It's not so private . . ." She paused.

Hoyle's coffee was placed in front of him, and the waiter turned away.

"Please, can we go someplace else?"

"I only have a little time," Hoyle said. "I have to ask you about the things we talked about."

Maria's eyes narrowed slightly. "The things you wanted from my office?"

"The press credentials."

"I put four blank sets in the post office box on the way over here," Maria answered. "I thought that would be safer than carrying them around town. Is that all you came for?"

"No," he said. He felt again a pinching in his chest.

Maria looked out at the crowd; she understood his behavior now. The fact that the credentials were in the post office box seemed to harden Hoyle's eyes. There was nothing to hold him back.

"I saw you on Saturday," Hoyle said.

Maria shifted unconsciously in her chair and put both her hands on the table. It seemed to Hoyle like a gesture of grief.

"We went to dinner. I didn't see you at—"

"At your apartment."

A few moments passed.

"I don't like to think of you peeking in on me."

"I didn't intend to."

Maria was unsure what Hoyle might have seen. She assembled as much dignity as she could. "You know that he pays the rent. He buys my clothing and food."

Hoyle started to say something, but it expired in a sound like a rattle.

"I am pretty much his possession," Maria said.

"You seemed willing enough."

"What do you want me to say to you? I am sorry that you watched me be a whore?"

Hoyle watched her expression become somber. He was expecting other words, but Maria said, "I am pregnant."

Hoyle's mind seemed to skip. He had mapped out what he wanted to say to her, but the words piled up in his head like a wrecked train, word upon word, sentence upon sentence. He sat rigidly in his chair, his jaw set. Maria saw in his eyes a coldness that she had never imagined.

"Who is the father?" Hoyle asked.

Maria averted her eyes and exhaled. She gathered herself and said in an even voice, "I'm not sure."

"How many of us are there?"

Maria bore this with as much poise as she could muster. "I don't think that you are trying to be cruel to me. Maybe you are."

"What have you told Alameda?"

"Nothing. Yet."

Hoyle imagined the sleek Alameda driven to rage. It would strain him, Hoyle thought. It must be all but impossible to keep it all straight, and now a pregnant mistress. Hoyle let this cruel thought evaporate in his mind; the force that made it disappear was a vestige of human sympathy.

"Now I wish I had not told you," Maria said quietly.

"Why would that matter? I would eventually know."

"I should have gone away. But I can't even do that."

Hoyle heard an American couple talking at another table. The man was in his twenties and had longish hair cut straight off about two inches above his shoulders. This made him look like a Saxon vassal. He was with a woman who had a pretty though unremarkable face and long, straight blond hair. They seemed to be lovers, perhaps they were on their honeymoon. Hoyle's gaze fell on them with envy and then a bland sort of derision. At their table, there were no problems, and at Hoyle's, there were many, piled up like dirty snow shoveled from a sidewalk.

"Do you love Alameda?"

"No," she said.

Hoyle surprised himself. "Do you love *me*?" he asked.

The words were let go from the middle of his brain out into the air. All at once, terribly, Hoyle felt like a buffoon, an idiot wandering without a village. The words could not be taken back, and Maria's expression was so pained it could not have been further from the word "yes."

In this silence, Hoyle looked away. To Maria, it was almost as though he had vanished. There was no expression on his face, or none that she could decipher, and he placed his napkin on the table. The gesture seemed conclusive, like a judge putting gavel to bench. Hoyle reached into his jacket pocket and put an envelope beside his cup.

"What is this?"

"A thousand dollars," Hoyle said.

Maria looked at the envelope as though it were a snake. She shook her head silently.

"Take it."

"I didn't come here to ask you for money."

"I brought it anyway."

Light from the street came in behind Hoyle, and beyond, a bus passed noisily. It sounded to Maria like a metallic thunderclap, as though all the machinery of the world were crashing to pieces. The noise overwhelmed her, and the envelope seemed to squirm before her eyes.

"Take it," Hoyle said. "It's what I would have paid anyone else."

The words pierced her, the way she had been pierced when she returned to Playa Baracoa from Lyon after the revolution. She felt as she had when the men from 26 de Julio told her that her father had been a swine and a murderer and that was why he was dead and that they had taken Consuela Madre and her brother to La Cabana. They'd shaved her head and hung a sign around her neck—PUTA Y PARÁSITA—and had denounced her before the entire town assembled at the *mercado*. Not one voice had been raised in her defense, not one person of the hundreds she knew had done anything but stand and stare at her. They had made her feel filthy, and she felt that again now. Maria looked again at the envelope, and the room about her turned darker. At the table across the café the American couple was laughing again; the sound seemed a long way off.

"I'd better go," Hoyle said.

"Don't do this to me," she said.

Her words came tragically up through the noise of the crowd. But something within Hoyle had broken, something hard and cruel had snapped off inside him, sharply and evenly, the way hard things break.

45

RENE D'ESPEREY HAD not slept well. When night closed over the encampment, he was awed by the complete and consuming darkness. It had taken him a long while to get used to the hammock; he was a restless sleeper anyway, and his movements were magnified by the hanging sheet of canvas. Twice he almost tipped out of it, and a few hours after sundown, he dared not even stir. He hung suspended between the black above and the black below, fully awake and listening to the sounds of the jungle—a grinding noise like a gigantic mill wheel. Finally, exhausted, he'd succumbed to a scrap of unconsciousness just before dawn.

Even in sleep, D'Esperey had been aware that around him spread a hostile place. The peril of armed conflict, that was something D'Esperey could grasp. In a small way, the danger posed by the army gave him comfort; he understood human conflicts, their roots, measures, and outcomes. What troubled him was the forest. The more he experienced it, the more the jungle was beyond his conception. It thwarted the senses, confused them with sight and sounds and smells. In places, the double canopy made it dark on the forest floor, even after sunrise, and last night it had been what the blind saw. He concealed his unease as much as he could, but he did not like being here.

Breakfast was coffee and *chankaka,* lumps of brown sugar. Bearing parties came and went from the camp all day. The bearers sneaked down into the valley to a number of hidden storage caves and brought supplies back to Camp 2, which was being configured as the main base of operations. Sandoval shared a tree with D'Esperey—their hammocks hung side by side—and Tania's hammock was across a small thicket by itself. She spent almost all of her time there, alone, and few of the comrades seemed to notice her. She was, as they all were, invisible at night, and when the sun came, she completely withdrew. She did not engage in the banter of the camp; she sat apart and joined only reluctantly for meals.

D'Esperey and Sandoval had been given their orders, and for the two urban revolutionaries, it would soon be time to go home. Scribbling notes in his hammock, D'Esperey was constantly reminded that in the jungle, a political philosopher was useless. He wrote earnestly in his notebook so the others would see him doing something. No one asked him to help carry supplies. He continued to look extremely engrossed as he copied out the list of contacts he would make and the things he would do for Guevara once he was delivered out of the jungle. The list was his ticket out. He wrote and rewrote, and overhead somewhere, an airplane droned. The men in camp ignored the sound of the aircraft, as they did D'Esperey.

They also ignored Sandoval. After rising, he spent the morning sitting on a fallen log, but he did not feel it necessary to compile notes for the comandante. Sandoval shared with D'Esperey the concern about how and when they would be delivered out of the combat zone. After breakfast, Joaquin had seemed impatient when Sandoval pulled him aside to discuss an escort party to lead them back to one of the main roads. The big man had been quite abrupt and Sandoval thought to mention it to Guevara.

In the late part of the morning, Coco came running into camp—the army had fallen into one of the ambushes set by the river. The initial reports were encouraging. Coco said that seven Bolivian soldiers had been killed, fourteen captured, including a captain and a major, and many arms taken, automatic weapons and three mortars. The news stirred the camp. Sentries were redoubled, and Guevara lifted himself out of his hammock and took up his rifle. Pombo and Inti went with him toward the scene of the action. It seemed incredible that there had been a firefight within a mile of the camp and not a single whisper of it had made it through the trees. D'Esperey asked to go along, but Guevara waved him back. Moro was put in charge of the camp guard, and for an hour or so, there was nothing to do but wait tensely and swat flies.

Guevara went along the path to the place in the steep canyon where the ambush had been laid. He reinforced the ambush party, and Pombo and the whole forward detachment swept the scene, gathering up Bolivian weapons and equipment scattered along the riverbanks and the forest floor. The entire action had taken less than six minutes. The number of weapons captured—sixteen Mauser rifles, three Uzis, one .30-caliber machine gun, two BZ rifles, three 60mm mortars (and sixty-four rounds)—indicated that the unit was probably company-sized. About half of the group had fled, carrying their weapons. The haul was still impressive. The ambush had been initiated by seven guerrillas. Seven men against forty.

The prisoners were herded into the jungle back to camp. The Bolivians were made to carry their wounded, and the officers were separated and placed under guard. As the prisoners were marshaled along, Guevara was careful to remain in the background, as low-profile as possible. He let Inti give all the commands, and Pombo supervised the counting of the weapons.

Back at camp, Inti acted as the guerrilla commander; he interrogated the two officers at length. Sandoval and D'Esperey were allowed to listen and take notes. Throughout the interrogation, the commanding officer, Major Baigorria, wept and sniffled embarrassingly. Kept in a group twenty feet away, his soldiers watched. Now and again a voice would come out of the group—"Shoot the fucker!" "He's mistreated us! Kill him!" This dirge went on most of the afternoon; it put the major into a depression. His nose red and his eyes puffy, he said to Inti that he planned to retire from the military. Separately, the captain commanding the infantry company claimed to have rejoined the army at the request of the Bolivian Communist Party. When this did not seem to impress, he gave the names of two other serving officers who, like him, would be willing to cooperate. It was obvious he was talking to save his life, and D'Esperey did not even bother to write down the proffered names.

As this happened, Tania sat in her hammock, staring out into the jungle; by and by, she curled up and began to shiver noticeably. Moro came by to check on her and discovered that she had a fever and was quite sick. He noticed the bruises on her arms and back. Her abdomen was rigid and extremely tender. Moro immediately suspected a bruised or ruptured spleen. It amazed him that she had been able to walk into camp. Her injury would only get worse unless she received proper treatment. Moro tended to her as best he could. There was little else to do but give her another blanket and some fresh water. As evening fell, he brought her some rice, but she would not eat. Moro saw that the comandante was studying, so he did not interrupt; he would tell him soon that he thought Tania needed to be taken to hospital.

Across camp, Guevara pored over the maps taken from the major. The typed orders found on the captain corroborated the story that two companies were based at the Zinc House. The major told Inti that an entire company was closing on Yaquí from across the valley, but it made no sense that the Bolivians would commit all their forces with no reserve. In this assessment, Guevara was correct, but he had vastly overestimated the tactical sense of the Bolivian army.

The prisoners could not be kept; there was no place to lock them up, and no food to feed them. Guevara would not stand to have them executed, so orders were given for them to be stripped of their pants and boots. The officers would be allowed to keep their uniforms, and the entire lot would be marched out of the canyon. They would be left to stumble back, defeated, to their base.

While this was done, their weapons were carried to the storage caves. There were so many guns and so much equipment that this took until past dark. Joaquin attended to the various working parties, making sure the last of the equipment was stowed away neatly and that the caves were camouflaged and the trails brushed over.

When Joaquin returned to the encampment, he found the comandante in his hammock, serenely writing in his journal.

"Do you have some time?" Joaquin asked.

Guevara closed the book on his finger but did not put it away.

"Last of the caves are seen to," Joaquin said.

"What about the prisoners?"

"Moro's group escorted them as far as the river bend. They're back, and the sentries have been rotated."

Guevara inclined his head and shifted the journal in his hand—he considered the conversation over—but Joaquin sat down on a log next to the hammock. There was a pause. Guevara's eyes fell on the big man as he laid his rifle across his lap.

"What's up?"

"A couple of things."

Guevara put the journal on the hammock. "Go on."

"What's with the woman?"

"What about her?"

In response, Joaquin simply raised his eyebrows.

"Our conversation is in confidence," Guevara said.

"Of course, Comandante."

"The resupply drop was an ambush set by the Americans."

The news hit Joaquin like a blow to the stomach. "How?"

"Our codes have been penetrated."

Joaquin shook his head. This at least explained Guevara's maddening indifference about the radios. Now, even if the transmitters were fixed, it was suicidal to use them.

"Are you sure the codes are blown?"

"Tania told me."

Joaquin looked steadily at his boss.

"She was arrested by the Bolivian National Police. The CIA brokered her release. In exchange for her life, she was to deliver Sandoval and D'Esperey into our camp, then guide us into an ambush."

"She told you this?"

"The CIA expected her to deliver our guests and move to the banks of the Masacuri to be extracted. The Americans were going to hit us when we showed at the drop site."

What Guevara did *not* say was that Tania had confessed to working for the Russians as well. He did not tell Joaquin that Tania had spied on him—on all of them—for the last seven years. The news of the blown codes was spectacular enough. The truth was too powerful to be delivered in a full dose. This small, bitter sip was enough for Joaquin. Guevara thought that the full story would make Joaquin want to abandon the whole endeavor. He watched as Joaquin sat absorbing, shaking his head and turning these revelations in his mind.

Guevara had a few long moments to weigh his deception. It had been a lie of omission. Not an untruth, technically; just part of the story. Guevara did not usually play fast and loose with the facts, but he knew, as did Castro, that truth was only a thing assembled from perceptions. No truth was absolute.

Joaquin flicked his head back at Sandoval and D'Esperey. "How come Tania knew the codes were blown and they didn't?"

"They're errand boys," Guevara said. "She didn't tell them because they didn't have a need to know."

"She's a fool. Or she is one dedicated comrade. All she had to do was drop off those clowns and run off into the weeds. If I had a free ride out of here . . ." Joaquin's voice trailed off.

"Where was she going to run to?" Guevara asked. "She doesn't know that the Americans won't just shoot her the minute she steps out of the jungle."

"How did she know that we wouldn't shoot her?"

"She didn't."

To Joaquin's mind, this explained why Guevara had slapped her. The things he knew assembled themselves into a plausible conclusion. "They're going to come back, Che, with more troops."

Guevara made a half-smile and shook his head; he was certain this was true, but he was just as certain that the army would always be defeated. "First they'll pull back."

"For now," Joaquin said. He looked squarely at Guevara. "They're idiots, this major and the children they sent out with him. They can't all be as stupid. We can't always expect them to wander into ambushes, throw down their guns, and run away. Look, the Americans know we're in the valley. All they have to do is squeeze. We have to pop out somewhere."

"The Bolivians don't know where we are," Guevara said. "Neither do the Americans. You heard the soldiers—they wanted us to kill their officers. They can't fight with a force like that. And you're right, they can't all be as stupid. The commanders will have to pull back and regroup. Then they'll begin to concentrate forces. That means we will disperse."

"We still have the rejects. They're not good to anyone. And Moro's told me that Moises is sick. Tania as well."

Guevara inclined his head at the mention of her name.

Joaquin continued, "Moro says she was beaten by the police. He thinks she has a ruptured spleen."

Guevara thought coldly of her betrayal. Feelings he could not con-

trol rose up. They turned themselves into words and were comprehended as thought: Perhaps she will die. Her death would make things
easier, but he would not kill her, nor would he let her die of compounded neglect.

"We need to get the guests out as quickly as possible," Guevara said.
"I've prepared messages for Havana."

Joaquin felt some relief. Havana would not abandon them. Help
would be sent. This is what he thought; he could not know any differently.

"Tomorrow I'll take the forward detachment and push toward
Samaipata," Guevara said. "I'll move as fast as I can. You take the sick
ones and the Bolivian rejects and fall back toward the Palmarito. I'll
drop off the guests on the Muyupampa Highway. Sandoval and D'Esperey can make their way back to La Paz."

"What about the woman? The Americans are going to know she
talked. How's she going to get out of the country?"

"I don't know," Guevara said. He looked around the camp but did
not see Tania's hammock. Darkness was already creeping up from the
ground. "Until she's well, she'll stay with your group. We'll rendezvous in ten days at the Iripiti."

"All right."

Joaquin stood. He was exhausted; his body hurt down to his bones.
He considered asking Guevara to reconsider the entire business.
Joaquin had not wanted to set today's ambush in the first place; he felt
that contact was too close to the guerrillas' base of operations. But
morale had been lifted by their triumph and Guevara was in a better
mood than he had been in weeks, so Joaquin could say nothing. Still,
he did not consider the conditions favorable. Too many things had
gone wrong. This business with Tania, the useless Bolivian recruits, the
broken radios, the captured base. A string of mishaps punctuated by
disaster. If they moved to disperse now, completely disband, they all
might still be able to get to the city. They could slip back to Cuba and
reorganize.

If it had been Joaquin's call, he would have cut and run. But he was
not in command, Guevara was.

"Get some sleep," Guevara said to the big man. "We'll get started at
midnight."

Willy came toward Guevara and Joaquin. The young man was out of breath and obviously elated. He'd come from one of the sentry posts overlooking the river.

"Comandante," Willy said, "the army is pulling back from the Zinc House. Trucks and troops—everything. They are leaving the valley. They're running away."

46

Hoyle was on the landing zone when the Huey set down at Vallegrande. Charlie was with him, and both turned their faces as the dust cloud swept around the settling helicopter. Smith jumped off the skid and Hoyle stood sideways when the helicopter lifted off, the dust again coming at him in a swirling sheet. As Smith approached, everything about Hoyle seemed tense and rigid. He had the expression of a man holding a heavy object over his head. The clatter of the departing helo abated, and they walked toward the casita, Charlie following a few steps behind. The sky was dappled with orange clouds, and beyond was powder blue—a strange, startling color for a sky.

Smith cast a lingering, sideways glance at Hoyle. "What happened to you?"

Christ, Hoyle thought, *do I look that bad?* "I got drunk in La Paz," he answered.

That was true enough, for after he'd left Maria, he had returned to the *wiskería* on Avenida Mariscal Santa Cruz and tied one on. He'd nearly wrecked the Impala, driving back to the safe house with one eye closed to combat a stunning case of double vision. It was as drunk as he'd been in a decade. The two nights since had been sleepless blurs. He'd drunk until he was sick the first night, and the second, back at the casita, he had worked all night to affix pictures to the press credentials, making up names and aliases to match the faces of Valdéz, Santavanes, Smith, and himself. His hands trembled as he did this—mostly from the booze—but it was not without gathered effort that he put away a dozen feelings, vague, hurting, self-devouring judgments about himself and everyone else.

"We heard about the ambush on the radio," Charlie said.

Smith shook his head in disgust. They walked on a few steps, Hoyle finally gathering his thoughts and pulling together words. "El Presidente said they killed fifteen guerrillas."

"In their fucking dreams," Smith spat. "They got waxed and ran all the way back down the valley. It's a miracle it didn't get uglier."

"Well, fifteen turns out to be the magic number," Hoyle said. "We got a hit on the trail sensors this morning."

Smith stopped and looked at Hoyle. His eyes narrowed behind the steel rims of his spectacles.

"Igloo White says fifteen bodies were headed north. They passed the southern pair of sensors at zero-eight-twenty-two this morning."

Smith stood for a moment, looking into intermediate distance. They both knew the sensors could be wrong; electronic things left in the jungle could malfunction easily. "We're gonna want to put some eyeballs on the trail," he said.

"I already sent in Holland and a four-man team," Hoyle answered. "They inserted on the west bank five clicks down from the oxbow. They should have eyes on the trail by sundown. They'll check the path and count the tracks."

Hoyle had anticipated confirmation and deployed a recon team within an hour of the signal. Smith thought Hoyle looked distracted, but he'd shown he was on top of the game.

"Forty less fifteen," Smith said, mostly to himself. "Where are the others?"

Valdéz and Santavanes sat on the porch, leaning back on a wooden bench. Valdéz looked up from his book and nodded as they passed into the house. Santavanes, as usual, was cleaning his pistols.

Smith hung his rifle from a nail and Hoyle sat at the table in the main room and thought about having a drink. He had felt wrung out at dawn but thought himself better now. He had made himself busy the last couple of days. It was too much for him to revisit what had happened in the café, though generalized thoughts of Maria surfaced almost continuously and had to be pushed back down. He had thought it would somehow make him feel better, tossing the envelope on the table, but it had not. Action and reaction. What he'd done had made him feel small and vicious; it had made him want to go out into the jungle and live on the edge that made him forget everything else.

The curtain pulled back, and Smith came over to the table carrying the old round felt-covered canteen in which he kept a quart of Kentucky bourbon. "You think Guevara sent a team north to check out the supply drop?" he asked.

Hoyle answered, "No. I think the woman tipped him."

Smith offered the canteen to Hoyle, who took a swig. As an afterthought, Smith waved it at Charlie, who sat next to the fireplace. Charlie didn't drink, so the gesture was superfluous.

Hoyle continued, "If Guevara knew it was a trap, I don't think he'd send just two squads to check it."

Smith took a sip from the canteen. "You think she walked up to Guevara and admitted it was a setup?"

"Yeah, I do."

Tania's choices had been unbearable. Hoyle tried to imagine the courage it had taken to admit to a personal betrayal.

"Then he probably blew her away."

"Probably," Hoyle allowed.

Valdéz came in and helped himself to some whiskey. He remained quite certain about all things Communist. "Fucking bitch," he said.

For some reason, Hoyle particularly remembered the passport, the one that Diminov had handed off to Tania in the newspaper. It was a standard Soviet escape document—Austrian, made out in the name Michel Nemick, a moniker that might belong to a man or a woman. It had been complete save for the picture. Hoyle remembered it, too, because he knew the street in Vienna: Wipplingerstrasse 23. It was nearly in the shadow of St. Stephen's Cathedral, in the oldest part of the city, an area bombed gratuitously by the Allies and then rebuilt almost with a sense of guilt. It all seemed fitting to Hoyle, a passport to nowhere filled out with an address wandered by ghosts. It didn't matter if Tania was dead, he thought, and the bitterness of this idea surprised him. He'd started to have flashes of cynicism, moments when he was tired of the whole nasty affair. Cynicism was the most dangerous emotion a man of his profession could harbor, for it would lead unvaryingly to brutality.

Smith announced that he would send Valdéz and Santavanes into the valley. They would travel unarmed and carry the press credentials obtained from the Ministry of Information. Santavanes would enter the valley in the south, taking the road to Pirirenda. He'd put about the story that they wanted to find the guerrilla leader and interview him. Valdéz would do the same thing, entering the valley from the north. It was not unusual for CIA operatives to use the press as cover, although it was increasingly avoided, since American journalists in Vietnam faced greater danger as a result. Smith had decided to send Valdéz and Santavanes because they were Cuban, and as a further false flag, they would carry Argentine passports and identity documents. Hoyle had reservations about sending anyone into the guerrilla zone armed with only a cover, but he did not voice them. Anyway, Santavanes could take care of himself, and Valdéz was willing, as always, to do anything that might kill Communists.

Smith expected no contact. All he wanted from their foray was reconnaissance and to put out the word that the "journalists" would pay one hundred Bolivianos to anyone with information about the location of the guerrillas. The army's reward program had yet to produce a single lead. Those unwilling to talk to the army might be willing to talk to writers, and the *"journalistas"* were offering twice as much. Guevara's first communiqué had been published only in the Santa Cruz paper. It had been pulled immediately by the military censors, and the editor had been jailed. Smith knew that publicity was vital to the guerrillas. He hoped that now it might prove irresistible.

47

S UNDAY WAS CALM in La Paz; the sky was a sapphire blank from the rim crowded with shanties by El Alto all the way to the white smudge of Huayna Potosí in the northern distance. Maria woke late, trying to outsleep the nausea that dogged her most after sunrise. Her tactic had worked this morning, and she rose a little past ten, pleased to be without the symptom. The cause was still there, she knew, and that was enough to make her thoughtful. She brewed a pot of tea and sat with it in the small kitchen. Loneliness joined her, sitting across the table, a companion who would not trouble her with words. The small apartment, otherwise quite pleasant, seemed like a place set a million miles apart from the rest of the world. Few sounds came from the street and the tolling of cathedral bells seemed to echo from an incredible distance. She heard them only after the tips of her fingers held a teacup, unsipped and gone cold.

Maria concentrated on the things that lay ahead. Sunday morning was nearly past, and in the afternoon Alameda would come. After he had taken his wife and young son to Mass, he would arrive, sometimes in sports clothing, occasionally still dressed for church. He would open the door to the apartment with his key and call for her. She had no idea how Alameda would react to her pregnancy.

She was conscious that there was another life inside her, though she hadn't yet felt any physical sensations beyond morning sickness. A pregnancy had seemed unreal to her, and when she first missed her period, she did everything to deny that it could be possible. Weeks passed, two months actually, before she saw a doctor and it was confirmed. Maria waited two weeks more before she even began to plan for it. She denied it to herself and told no one else. There was no one else to tell.

The evening she'd met Hoyle at the café, she was not sure that she would tell him, it had simply happened, and she wished now that she'd not said anything. She still had the thousand dollars, more money than she'd ever had at one time since she left Cuba, but the bills in the envelope gave her little comfort. Money did not give happiness unless it granted freedom, and Maria was not free. It was enough money to buy a plane ticket and to live modestly for a while. She could find work as a nurse, but she had no way to get out of the country. She had to tell Alameda this afternoon that she was pregnant, and as the moment approached, she grew increasingly fretful. Alameda could have no idea about Hoyle and would assume that the baby was his. It might be Hoyle's, Maria thought. It struck her how different these two men were: one brash and vain, one quiet and self-effacing, one a public man who sought always more attention, and the other a man who lived in shadow and shunned publicity as firmly as he avoided death. Both were powerful. Maria knew she was a toy to Alameda, a decoration. She did not know what she had been to Hoyle. It occurred to her that she had been alone too long and that her heart had been made too hard.

The electric clock in the kitchen made a low, rasping sound as it sawed through an hour and then another and Maria sat and thought about Hoyle. She wondered where he was and remembered his wounded expression as he'd handed over the envelope. He had seemed infuriated and shamed all at once, and as he had turned to leave, she'd seen in his eyes an immense and incalculable coldness. The look was frightening because she had not seen it in him before. His green eyes had been made into ice. He seemed to look on the world with a powerful, evenhanded malice, the way a tiger looks out through the bars of a cage. She did not think she would ever see him again. This fact, too, she had tried to ignore. It surprised her that the thought of never seeing Hoyle again made her feel strangely hollow. Her emotions were complex; there was uncertainty about her pregnancy and fear about her circumstances. She did not know what would happen, and already she

felt angst for the lies she knew she'd have to tell. But she did not con-
demn herself, not for her affair with Hoyle and not for what he had seen.
Life was complicated, bitterly so, and she did what she had to do to live.

Maria brushed her hair and put on the little makeup she normally
wore, eyeliner and a hint of eye shadow, a pale lipstick. She looked at
her face in the mirror and did not consider herself at all beautiful. She
saw complication and worry and half a dozen lies floating around her.
She thought, *I am a long way from the place I was raised*. There was so
much untruth around her, it seemed like the air that people breathed.

Alameda turned his key in the lock and came into the apartment at
a little past one in the afternoon. He was in good spirits and kissed her
and cooed some compliments. A look of interest, not quite sympathy,
came into his eyes. "What's the matter?"

Maria stood motionless, and Alameda took a step back, weighing
the expression on her face.

"I am pregnant."

Alameda's hand touched the buttons of his shirt, a gesture of slight
but genuine surprise. "Ahh," he said.

Maria's eyes did not release him. He walked to the couch and sat.
He gave her an odd look, half a smile.

"Well, this is a complication. How long?"

"Two months. Two and half."

Alameda crossed his legs and leaned his shoulder blades back against
the cushions. "Have you told anyone?"

Maria did not answer but gave a small shake of her head. She'd told
only Hoyle, and that could never be admitted. Alameda seemed to find
some relief in the fact that no one else knew. It occurred to Maria that
there were a hundred other things he might have asked—Have you
been sick, how are you feeling, are you happy?—instead, he wanted to
find out who else knew.

"I think that this will be the end of us," Maria said.

Alameda's head came forward unconsciously, almost a nod. "Non-
sense," he said. "This can be taken care of. In Bogotá, I can arrange
everything. It will be only a weekend away, and everything will be as it
was." He nodded, assenting to his own suggestion.

"I don't want it taken care of."

"Maria, don't be absurd."

"I have thought about it, and I want to have the baby."

"I care for you, but there are things that I cannot allow."

"I am not asking your permission."

Alameda could see Maria's reflection in the mirror over her dressing table. He saw also the rosary draped over the mirror. He looked at the floor for a moment. He made calculations. The basis of these reckonings was, of course, that he cared more for himself than he did for Maria or a child.

"Don't say foolish things. I'm not angry. Can't you see that I'm not angry? There is a proper way to handle this, and I can arrange it."

"I won't have an abortion."

She'd said a word that Alameda would have danced around for an hour.

"Not in La Paz, Maria. In Bogotá or Panama City."

"No."

Maria sat and drew in a breath. Alameda could not have expected this quiet and steely determination.

"I have had time to think about this," Maria said. "It would be easier and better for us both if I simply went away."

"You can't go anywhere. Not off by yourself."

"Please let me finish. I am merely an ornament to you."

"You are more than that."

"Not much more. You do not love me."

"The only words I have not said. That can't be what this is about. You can't be doing this to blackmail me into saying that I love you."

Her green eyes flashed. "You are a conceited man. Do you think I would do this to trap you? Do you think that's necessary for me?"

Alameda ignored the question. "Maria, I do care for you. Look around. Are you not provided for?"

"You have been generous," Maria said.

"I have. And in return, all I am asking you to do is think a little about the future."

"Your future or my own?"

"It can still be *our* future."

"I knew what I was doing when we started to see each other. I knew that this could happen. I did not know what I would do until a few days ago. I know that I cannot stay here. I know that you have a career and a family. I have always known that, and I have always put myself second." She paused, and her voice wavered slightly. "I'm going to have the baby," she said. "I am going to do it. All I am asking you to do is allow me to go away."

"Where would you go? You cannot go back to Cuba."

"I don't know. To France, perhaps back to Lyon."

"You are not thinking clearly. And then what? How would you live?"

"I can work."

"And raise a child alone?"

A few moments passed. She'd made the decision to keep the baby. She did not care now, really, who the father was; the child would be hers.

"You are not thinking clearly," he repeated.

"I didn't expect you to change your mind about my having the baby. I never thought to have the child here in Bolivia. I am prepared to go."

Alameda thought briefly of allowing Maria to go away, perhaps to Argentina or Spain. If she were provided for, there would be little shame in it for him. If the arrangement were discovered, there might be trouble with his wife and her family, definitely, but the political trouble, that he could weather. This was the private business of a public man. The president himself had a daughter in Chile. But Alameda did not wish Maria gone, at least not now.

"You need to think about this," he said. "It's only a small procedure. Then we can go back to the way we were before."

Maria was silent.

"Were you not happy the way that we have been?"

Had she been happy or in love, she would not have wandered into Hoyle's arms.

"*You* have been happy, Enrique."

"I will not stand for insolence. Not in the apartment that I pay for." Alameda slumped against the couch. "Where does this come from? Have you been talking to a priest?"

"It is my conviction." Her eyes showed this.

"An expensive one," Alameda answered. He did not conceal his opinion very well—he thought his mistress was beautiful, but it was entirely unnecessary that she be so willful.

"I am not asking you to pay for anything," Maria said. "I am only asking you to let me go."

Alameda stood and put his hands on Maria's face and swayed gently this way and that. He wore an expression of great affection. He ran his fingers through her hair and whispered against her ear, "You don't want to leave me. I know you don't."

Maria closed her eyes. It was as though her thoughts had given out altogether. She felt his arms move around her waist and pull her close.

"I will take care of you."

She wondered for an instant if he was telling the truth or spinning a more honorable sort of lie. Perhaps he did care for her, and that was the reason he had done all he had done—fed her, clothed her, given her a job and papers. Perhaps it was only that he pitied her.

He embraced her and kissed her neck, and Maria thought, *No one can sink lower than this—to be pitied by a liar.*

48

A T DAYBREAK HOYLE, Charlie, and Santavanes departed from the village of Pirirenda, following a ravine toward the Ñancahuazú River. Santavanes carried a complicated backpack on an aluminum frame. Deliberately and conspicuously nonmilitary, it was made of blue nylon and had two large pockets sewn on either side. Smith remarked that it was the sort of pack that hippies carried to Amsterdam. The backpack contained some food, two canteens, water purification tablets, a mosquito net, a hammock, and a rubberized poncho: things he would need to spend a few days in the valley. Hoyle carried an AK-47 rifle borrowed from Major Holland. This compensated for the fact that Santavanes was unarmed and Charlie had asked to be excused from carrying a weapon. The request had exasperated Santavanes, and Hoyle had calmly asked Charlie why.

The answer was delivered plainly: "I don't think that I could shoot anyone."

Hoyle granted Charlie's request, as he expected no trouble; all they meant to do was accompany Santavanes through the steepest terrain and deliver him onto the valley floor. Hoyle was fairly certain that Charlie's job description—whatever it was—did not include bearing arms during an insurgency, so he did not force the issue. Charlie nevertheless accompanied them, for reasons of prudence if nothing else, three being the minimum number of men who could go into a wild place and help themselves if one were somehow injured.

A trail led out of Pirirenda, following its eponymous creek, switching back a number of times and twice crossing the water at steep places where rocks and fallen logs made it possible to get over without getting wet. As the ravine opened, they abandoned the trail and kept close against the hillside until they reached a finger where the forest jutted into the valley.

The plan was for Santavanes to continue south along a hunter's trail that went down the valley floor. Two villages were along this route, Yaquí and El Meson, and Santavanes would offer money at each place to be guided to the guerrillas. This cover was his sole protection. The guerrillas had three times encountered the army and had each time released prisoners unharmed; it was assumed that they would not mistreat a journalist.

Hoyle checked his watch; it was eleven in the morning, and thirty kilometers upriver, Smith and Holland were preparing to set Valdéz on a similar journey. It was getting cooler, and even as the sun spread over the hills, Hoyle felt a chill once they stopped walking. As they rested, Santavanes went through his papers one last time. All were made out in the name George Andrew Roth, forming the legend of a freelance English-Argentine photojournalist. Santavanes passed his eye over the address on the documents, committing it to memory, as he did the particulars of the several visas stamped on the pages and the Buenos Aires phone number listed as an emergency contact.

"Almost time," Hoyle said.

Santavanes stood and pulled on his pack. They reviewed the procedures for rendezvous after the mission, evolutions of basic importance.

"Primary pickup will be the village of Yaquí in forty-eight hours," Hoyle said. "Secondary meeting place will be at El Meson in seventy-two hours. We'll check the roadside one kilometer south of town every twelve hours after that. You have your Coke can?" In Santavanes's pack was a can of Coca-Cola; it would be discarded at the side of the road as a signal that he was hiding nearby.

"I got it."

Santavanes had committed to memory the course of the river, the ravines and draws, and the locations of the crossings. He could draw the map from memory, a skill that, like the wearing of a cover, was vital to an agent in the field.

"You have any major deviations, it's your responsibility to get to a road or a telegraph. Contact the intelligence officer of the Fourth Division. We'll be monitoring there if you're overdue."

Charlie noticed that Santavanes's eyes were bright and that he looked eager.

"Okay," Hoyle said, "you're a go. Good luck."

Hoyle and Charlie remained in the tree line and watched as Santavanes passed down the trail. They were high enough on the hillside to watch him disappear and reemerge from the last stand of hardwood, and then monitor his progress as he worked his way down to the river and turned south. Hoyle stood cradling his rifle and leaning against a tree; he waited until Santavanes disappeared from view maybe eight hundred yards away, swallowed by the brush that crowded the riverbank.

"Is this going to work?" Charlie asked.

"He's pretty hard to kill."

Charlie smiled. It had been a good morning for him. He'd expected trouble when he'd asked not to carry a gun into the jungle. Hoyle had surprised him by shrugging and sticking the rifle back under the seat of the Land Cruiser. Charlie had meant it when he said he didn't think he could shoot anyone, and Hoyle silently agreed. Hoyle had shot people, several of them, and did not think it was for everyone.

IT WAS COLD at night, almost bitter under a sky without clouds, and Guevara's asthma gripped him so that he curled up in his hammock with his hands between his knees, drawing thin, shallow breaths between clenched teeth. He had given orders that the column was to continue south at three-thirty A.M., and when the time came to rise, his limbs were stiff. He imagined that the others could hear his bones creaking as he tried to rise and he felt as bad as he'd ever felt. Moro came to his hammock and shone a penlight into his throat, listened to his chest, and plainly heard the wheezing in it. There was no more Thomaquil, so he gave Guevara an injection of atrophine sulfate. It seemed to help, and Guevara was able to take down and roll up his hammock. Moro took the comandante's pack and carried it to the place the animals were being loaded.

"Hey, listen," he said to Coco. "The comandante is feeling like shit this morning."

"Who isn't?" Coco answered. His face was only a shadow, and the expression that framed this comment could not be seen.

"I want you not to load up the red mare," Moro said. "Have those comrades carry their own packs."

"Why?"

"Because the comandante is too sick to walk," Moro said.

The red mare was led into camp and the proposition put to Guevara. He resisted at first, but Moro prevailed, speaking to him privately and asking him frankly if he thought he was well enough to keep up with the column. Guevara knew he would hold the troops back—he had hardly been able to stagger to the fire to get coffee. Finally, he relented. Pombo helped him up into the saddle, patting the flank of the horse, a docile and placid animal. She had no name, and Guevara suggested Rocinante, perhaps the most famous nag in Spanish literature.

The column broke camp, and clouds lowered from the peaks in the hours before dawn, making the cold both damp and clinging. The night seemed to get darker, and as the moon had set to the west, Pombo led the mare by the bridle over the rougher parts of the trail. Where the column passed under tree cover, it was so dark that they had to keep together by holding on to the shoulder of the man ahead. Those on the point moved slowly by scuffing their feet forward like barefoot men crossing a strange, darkened bedroom.

In the blackness, occasionally there was a cough, or the creak of leather, and now and again came the sound of the mules snorting behind them. For the first part of the march, Guevara felt so bad that he was thankful of the dark. His breathing was labored, and his face was twisted by a nearly constant grimace; his ears were numb, and there was a hard, burning pain around his heart. He was embarrassed to be riding, but he was too ill to resist the consideration of his men. He calmed his indignity by telling himself that when the sun came up, he would dismount and walk. The asthma always came in waves, and this wave would pass, he was sure of that. But now his head drooped and his shoulders hunched forward as he surrendered to the easy swaying of the horse.

Dawn came slowly, and Guevara felt no better. If possible, he felt worse and twice had to dismount to vomit at the side of the trail. He let the men pass and waved away each concerned inquiry, saying sternly that he was okay and asking that he be allowed to puke in private like everybody else. Sandoval and D'Esperey witnessed one of these occasions and gave each other a long, serious look. Pombo urged them on with a few curse words and helped Guevara back into the saddle.

They made ten kilometers like this, stopping and starting, and at noon, under a low, drab sky, word came back that the forward detachment had surrounded a small farm owned by a Guaraní Indian couple. They blinked in terror and wonder as the guerrilla column came into their fields from the forest. The decision to rest at the farm was made by Miguel, who had replaced Marcos as head of the forward detachment. He knew that Guevara was sick and had deployed the men without asking advice from the center column. Guevara came into the first field on the red mare. He was draped in a poncho and had his rifle balanced across the pommel of his saddle. He rode right up to the small hovel and dismounted wearily.

The house was under a stand of trees, and a scruffy cornfield spread off to the east. Pigs rutted in a wallow fenced in by long split rails, and a mangy bitch circled the men, wagging her tail vigorously. As Guevara had directed, Inti had introduced himself to the man and woman as the guerrilla column's leader, but they saw through this and watched as Guevara's horse was led away and he was asked quietly about where to mount the guard. The farmer wore tan pants and a wool jacket, and the woman was dressed in a bell-shaped *pollera* skirt; they would have been fit for a postcard were it not for their poverty, which, up close, was dirty and aromatic. The man had a fedora pulled down on his head and pretended to speak very little Spanish. He was quite anxious for the guerrillas to move on, as he feared reprisal from the army.

Inti spoke Quechua and not much Guaraní, but he arranged to purchase some corn, pumpkins, and one of the pigs. The lure of money did not quite overcome the couple's fears, and the man seemed glum when it started to rain and Guevara announced that they would slaughter the pig and remain for the rest of the day.

Guevara sat on a log and had Willy bring him the transistor radio. He tuned to the local station in Santa Cruz and listened to music as he waited for the news. It was reported that up to twenty-five hundred Bolivian soldiers were encircling the Ñancahuazú, and that the guerrillas were digging in. The reports mentioned again the clash in the ravine and gave accurate facts reflecting the army's losses. The army claimed four confirmed guerrillas dead, "two of them foreigners," but gave no names or nationalities. The report also stated that U.S. Army advisers had established a training camp at Santa Cruz. Miguel was standing close when Guevara heard this and saw him smile. Guevara wanted more than anything to internationalize the Bolivian struggle. Now, in-country, there were Green Berets training Bolivian Rangers. He considered this an encouraging development. The facts increasingly supported his thesis, that the United States would prop up the thug regime of Barrientos, first with military advisers, and then, as the insurgency widened, with marines. This was good news, and with it, Guevara's mood lightened and his asthma lessened its grip. He was still exhausted. His legs were numb and his arms hurt. For the rest of the morning, he sat on the log and listened to the radio, and the comrades knew not to disturb him.

In the afternoon the sentries came in, and with them some children from El Meson. Prodded along in front of the sentries was a man with dark wavy hair and a full, drooping mustache. He had a strong jaw and cleft chin. He was dressed in sturdy hiking boots, chinos, and a white collared shirt rolled up to his elbows. Over his shoulder, he wore one strap of a large blue backpack. Guevara noticed him looking about and smiling when he saw the guerrillas. Guevara thought this odd, because the man was obviously under guard and seemed a bit too happy to be a prisoner. In any case, Guevara sized him up immediately as a city dweller, not a peasant. His boots and pack alone were worth several hundred dollars—a year's hard toil for a campesino.

Guevara watched as the man with the backpack was made to sit next to the pigsty. He lowered his pack and sat on it, and Willy leaned against a tree ten feet away and watched him.

"Who's this?" Guevara asked as Coco came on.

"A journalist." Coco smiled. He stopped short when he saw the look on Guevara's face.

Guevara was instantly furious. He held his tongue chiefly because he did not wish to reveal himself as the leader in front of this person, whoever he was. The men around him saw Guevara stiffen and clench a fist. He had been sitting on a log next to the house, and he came to his feet slowly. It was like watching a storm cloud billow up in a summer sky.

"Go get Miguel and Inti."

Coco stammered, "We checked his papers—he's legitimate."

"Get them. Now."

Coco scurried away. Guevara gestured to Pombo, who came over. D'Esperey followed him closely. "Find out who this guy is."

Pombo walked over to the pigsty, and D'Esperey put his hands in his pockets. "This might not be all bad," D'Esperey said.

Guevara ignored him and walked into the shack. He pulled up a chair and angled it at the corner of the table, the only other piece of furniture in the room. Coco came back with Inti and Miguel. Miguel had been sharp enough to talk to the sentries who'd brought in the man, and had taken up his papers and wallet. Miguel put the passport and wallet on the table. Guevara's head swam with exhaustion; his breathing was still labored, and the effort continued to wring him out.

"Fucking shit-eaters," he said quietly. "How did this person come here?"

"Kids from Bella Vista. He paid them to guide him to us," Miguel said. He waited for a tirade, but one did not come. Inti stood by the door and looked back at the man sitting by the pigsty.

"Did it occur to anyone on guard to send word or fucking ask before this clown was brought into the main camp?"

Miguel shifted on his feet. "I'll deal with that, Comandante."

Guevara opened the passport—Argentinean. It came to him that he had not been to his own country in almost eight years. He looked over the document, checking the photograph and looking for tampered seals. The man's name was unusual for an Argentine, George Andrew Roth, but the passport looked genuine, and it was without doubt the man's photograph. Anglo names were not unknown in Argentina; Guevara's own middle name was Lynch. There were other things in the wallet: an organizer's card from the Argentinean teachers' union, a checkbook from the Banco Rio de la Plata, SA. There was also a press credential issued from the Bolivian Ministry of Information, number 1397, dated three weeks earlier. George Andrew Roth was accredited to no newspaper or magazine but was listed as *independiente*.

"If you think he is a spy, we'll shoot him," Miguel said.

"I don't know what I think."

Pombo stepped into the shack, ducking under the main doorway. Sandoval followed him in, as did D'Esperey. It was getting a little crowded, and this, too, annoyed Guevara, but he kept his temper in check. It occurred to him again that he was worn out. As he exhaled, there was a low, whistling growl in his chest.

"Anything?" he asked Sandoval.

"Whoever he is, he's pretty well informed. He knows the disposition of the enemy between us and Vallegrande. He named the companies and battalions by number."

"He could know that from the radio," Miguel said.

"He knows Buenos Aires. And his papers look real," Sandoval said.

"What are the chances that a journalist just stumbles through a war zone and lands in our lap, looking for an interview?" Pombo asked.

"It happened to Fidel."

"Yeah, it did," Guevara said. He looked through the door at the pigsty. "Intrepid motherfucker."

D'Esperey spoke. "May I make a suggestion, Comandante?" Other men would have known to be silent, but D'Esperey continued. "Maybe we should grant him an interview—I mean with Inti, pretending to be you."

"Go on."

"You could release a statement. And this man could then guide Sandoval and me out of the combat zone to Samaipata or Muyupampa— we could catch a bus back to La Paz. I have press credentials. We could say we were traveling together."

Silence.

Miguel was not the only one who felt a twinge of embarrassment for D'Esperey, who nakedly wanted out of the valley the quickest way possible.

"We're trying to judge if this man is really a journalist," D'Esperey went on. "As a gesture of good faith, we could see if he would be willing to escort us out of the war zone."

"You seem eager to leave us, Monsieur D'Esperey."

"I am not a soldier, Comandante. I know that I slow the column," D'Esperey said. This was blunt and true enough. Though they had started the march with the forward detachment, Sandoval and D'Esperey had been among the last to reach the cornfield.

"I'll think about it." Guevara returned to the passport, and D'Esperey slumped out the door. Sandoval walked out with him.

"Maybe that's not a bad idea," Pombo said. "That guy leads them out, and we can turn north to join Joaquin. We'd reunite the column in half the time."

"I think that little *pato* just wants to go home," Miguel said.

"And we need to get them out." Guevara sat for a minute, not exactly in thought but distracted by his painful, shallow breathing. Then he gathered up the passport and wallet and walked out toward the pigsty.

Santavanes sat on the blue backpack and made his expression neutral. This was possible because he had an ability, a professional's attribute, to delay fear. This he did by separating cause from consequence; he was acutely aware that his papers were being examined and that the guerrillas would make a life-or-death decision based on their conclusions. Santavanes knew that if he was thought to be a spy, he would be shot immediately. He allowed his expression to betray only the amount of fear that would be felt by a normal journalist under the circumstances. He did not act like a man likely to be executed—he acted like a man waiting for an appointment. His act was impeccable.

Santavanes had seen Miguel carry his papers into the house, and as he waited judgment, he lit a cigarette and offered one to Willy. As they smoked, Santavanes looked around the farm. He avoided making small talk and counted the number of men, twenty-eight. He noted the number and type of their weapons, which were clean and in good repair. He was surprised that he did not see anyone carrying a radio—either a longer-range, high-frequency set, or smaller intersquad radios. He counted the number of pack animals and how they were loaded. That the men were gaunt and ate ravenously was also filed in his brain.

Inti granted an interview in his capacity as "commander" of the ELN, but Santavanes continued to note the deference paid to Guevara and wondered at a leader who kept hidden his office but not his authority.

As Inti continued his interview, Guevara put together a long letter to Castro, informing him of recent events. This was given to Arturo to encode and then write in invisible ink.

As Guevara assembled the messages, D'Esperey and Sandoval sauntered over. The Frenchman began a monologue about how useful he could be once he was back in Europe. Now that he had seen the guerrilla column in action, he could be an eloquent spokesman for the cause. Guevara listened, his mind roaming, sinking in and out of contempt. He had many factors to consider. It was vital that communication be reestablished with La Paz and Havana. He did not trust the journalist completely, and D'Esperey's plan to be smuggled out seemed a bit injudicious. It required that they place their faith in a man totally unknown. But Guevara was tired, and he'd had enough of this mincing and yapping.

"You want out?"

D'Esperey looked at Sandoval and started to speak slowly. "We both have things to do, Comandante. Important things. This might be the best opportunity—"

Guevara cut him off. "I'm washing my hands of it. You want this man to try to get you past the army? Go ahead and try." He got up and walked away.

D'Esperey looked about; all had seen Guevara's exasperation. D'Esperey felt a prickle of shame, but he did want out of the valley and out of combat. He consoled himself with the thought that there *were* things to do. Important things—for the revolution.

"We need to get back," Sandoval said.

"Che understands that," D'Esperey answered quietly. "He's just under pressure, that's all."

"Sure," Sandoval said. "That's all it is."

The words drifted away between the two, vain consolation, for they both knew that they had aggravated Guevara. D'Esperey had at least gotten what he desired—permission to leave, if not approval.

Across camp, Santavanes sat with Inti, close to the fire. He'd watched the two men speak to Guevara and had seen the comandante stand suddenly and stalk away from them. Santavanes poked at a notebook in his lap, scribbling down what Inti said, things about justice and equality. Under his brows, he watched the two men come toward him; he saw that besides him, they were the only men in the camp who did not wear olive green.

"Señor Roth," D'Esperey said, holding out his hand. "We have a proposition to make you."

49

OYLE AND CHARLIE drove first to El Meson, and then back-tracked to the flyblown pueblo of Tichucha. It did not unduly alarm them that Santavanes had missed the first two of his scheduled pickups. One more day passed without the signal of the empty Coke can at the side of the road. Valdéz had a similar arrangement on the north end of the valley. His signal was found by Smith and Major Holland, and his extraction was carried out by helicopter from a field between the Rio Grande and the highway town of Tatarenda. On the fourth morning, Hoyle and Charlie returned to the south of the valley and stopped the Land Cruiser on a rise two kilometers north of the Tichucha rendezvous.

Hoyle was not unduly worried but he was concerned. If this last extract window passed without a sign, Santavanes would be expected to communicate and get out on his own. Hoyle had inserted Santavanes; it was his business, and his duty, to extract him safely. An accident could not be ruled out, nor could something more sinister, but Santavanes was a resourceful and capable operator. Hoyle knew the man well and had worked with him on two continents. He'd turn up.

In midafternoon Hoyle caught sight of a blue fleck on top of a ridge. He swung his binoculars and zoomed them as much as he could; about a mile away, he saw a man carrying a blue backpack. With him were two others. Both these men also carried packs. Hoyle could see that one of Santavanes's companions was fair-headed and the other balding; both looked European. None carried weapons, and not one of them looked up the valley to the promontory where Charlie and Hoyle sat and watched.

Hoyle handed the glasses to Charlie, who followed with the binoculars as Santavanes again took the lead. The two other men trailed as they scuffed off through the brush and moved steadily downslope.

"Who's he with?"

"I don't know," Hoyle said. He remained on the hood, watching the slope below them with his bare eyes; the men were small dots moving down an undulating, grassy crest. Charlie handed back the field glasses and Hoyle watched as the men converged steadily on the road leading to Muyupampa. They slid down the embankment and traversed the dirt track in a place where a small spring had leached across the cut in the hillside. They crossed the road perpendicularly and then scrambled down the bank on the other side. Hoyle watched as Santavanes tossed a can back up onto the road, then went back downhill after the two men.

Hoyle considered what he had seen—Santavanes was no prisoner. He'd marked his extract and crossed the road in a conspicuous place. He knew that anyone checking on the extract signal would find the Coke can in the mud and also three sets of tracks. Santavanes surely knew that Hoyle was watching, yet he was leading the two men steadily away, down the valley toward the small town of Muyupampa. Obviously, he did not want to be taken from the field just yet.

Hoyle sat with the binoculars in his lap and thought. Tania had led two men into the guerrilla zone, and it now appeared that Santavanes was leading them out. Hoyle did not know why, but why didn't matter yet. Santavanes was alive and had declined to be extracted.

Charlie shifted against the bumper. "You want to go to the rendezvous site?"

"No. Not yet."

Still a mile distant, Hoyle and Charlie watched as Santavanes flagged down a truck belonging to the Bolivian National Oil Company. The three men climbed up into the back. The road was dry in the mouth of the valley, and a long tail of dust followed the vehicle as it rumbled ten miles through curve and hill into the small town of Muyupampa.

"Let's go," Hoyle said.

Entering town five or ten minutes behind the truck, Hoyle and Charlie passed down the narrow dirt streets under the eaves of red-tiled roofs. It had been market day, and the place was busy; oil tankers and *cammiones* passed mules and horses drawing carts of merchandise. Around the plaza, shopkeepers and vendors went in all directions, carrying goods and dismantling their stalls. Hoyle inched the Land Cruiser through the throng and passed close to where the oil truck had parked. Santavanes placed his left hand in the pocket of his chinos, their surveillance signal for "keep back," and Hoyle rolled slowly across the plaza toward the police station at the other end of the square.

Hoyle had now seen Santavanes's companions at close range. Both of his new friends seemed at ease, even happy. As they carried their packs to a small café off the plaza, they seemed to congratulate each other. Hoyle watched in the rearview mirror as Santavanes followed, his expression showing little. He kept his hand in his pocket until the group sat down at a table, lumping their packs beside them, then ordering beer and Salteñas.

Fifteen minutes later, they were arrested.

They had ample funds to pay a bribe, but Santavanes was careful to make sure the amount offered was insultingly low. A single sallow-faced police captain remained very courteous until he was sure there was nothing in this for him, and then he whistled for his men. Soon half a dozen armed officers stood around the table and the mood began to sour. Sandoval and D'Esperey became increasingly glum, but the encounter went exactly as Santavanes had intended. In a short while, they were handcuffed and led to the police station. When a major from the Departamento Investigacíon Criminal showed up, they were tossed into different cells with rice sacks over their heads. Though each of them had papers that were roughly in order, beatings commenced almost immediately. Foreigners were known to be operating with the guerrillas, and that was reason enough for a rigorous interrogation. In a very short while, their stories began to diverge. Sandoval and D'Esperey claimed to have come from the Ñancahuazú Valley, but neither told the same tale of the route they had taken, or whether they had spoken to the guerrillas. D'Esperey bravely insisted that he had talked to no one, while two rooms away, Santavanes provocatively revealed that they had been at a major encampment and spoken to the guerrilla commander. Sandoval was found to have a large quantity of cash sewn into the lining of his jacket, and the captain who'd arrested them in the plaza was left to wonder why they had not acquiesced to his modest request for a bribe. He could only hope that his career would be enriched, as his wallet had not been.

Two hours passed before Santavanes was dragged into a room behind the police station and the bag pulled off his head. He blinked back the gloom as he tried to make out who stood around him. Hoyle, Smith, and Charlie were gathered in a small, low-windowed room with a desk and roughly made wooden chairs. With them was a major from the DIC, who had assumed control of the prisoners from the locals.

"You okay?" Hoyle asked.

"Took you fucking long enough," Santavanes griped. There was a cut above his eye; it had bled gratifyingly and served as testimony to his treatment.

The major unlocked Santavanes's handcuffs and appeared contrite. "This was nothing personal," he said.

Santavanes rubbed his wrists. Already they were red and swollen from the handcuffs. He said, *"No es una problema."*

For Santavanes, the mock arrest and interrogation had been simply business. As they stood together in the back room, they could hear shouted questions echoing from inside the police station; for Sandoval and D'Esperey, the business was of a different sort. For them, a very real nightmare was just beginning. On the long walk to town, Santavanes had not even suggested that they rehearse a story. D'Esperey and Sandoval should have known better. They had counted too much on their documents and the kindness of a stranger.

"Did Valdéz get out?" Santavantes asked.

"He was extracted yesterday," Smith said. "You're the one who hit the jackpot."

"We don't have much time," Hoyle said.

Smith unrolled a topographic map on the desk. "Give us the locations first."

Hoyle handed Santavanes a pencil, and he peered down at the map, orienting himself and recalling the terrain, figuring it against the swirled lines of contour and elevation splashed across the map. He pointed and circled and drew arrows. "They found me here. At the second set of falls on the Tichucha River. The place I was held was here. A farmhouse about two clicks away."

Charlie handed him a wet cloth, and he pressed this against the cut on his forehead. He looked at the blood adhering to the cloth. "Fucking owie," he said.

"Have they established a new base camp?" Smith asked.

"No. I got the feeling this was just a rest stop. The farmers were scared shitless. An old man and woman—they tried to get rid of the G's as soon as they could."

"How many shooters?"

"They had patrols out, but I counted twenty-eight."

"Mortars?" Smith asked.

"Didn't see any. Just small arms. They had a thirty-cal machine gun. They were moving with a mule. They had about five pack animals." Santavanes stopped. His eyes flicked almost imperceptibly to the major, who sat sort of awestruck. It amazed him that the Americans had managed to put a man into the valley and count the guerrillas. Smith understood the significance of Santavanes's gesture.

"The major is written in," Smith said. At this attention, the officer from the DIC positively beamed, and Charlie noticed a thick gold tooth on the right side of his mouth. For some reason, this made Charlie think of cannibals.

"I saw Guevara," Santavanes said evenly.

"Are you sure?" Hoyle asked.

"Definitely. He let someone else give me an interview—a Bolivian pretending to be in command. But this guy was riding a horse, and everybody kissed his ass. I'm sure it was him."

"What about the woman?" Hoyle asked.

"I didn't see her. I heard them talking about rejoining the second column. North, somewhere, but no one ever said the location. I'm pretty sure the main column was headed back up the valley after they dropped us at the road."

"Tell us about your friends."

"The tall one's a Frenchman. Some sort of intellectual, an author or something. Wrote a book that sucks up to the Cuban's rural-based revolutionary shit. He's working as a courier."

"Not a journalist?"

"No way. He's a player. Guevara gave him letters to carry out."

"And the other guy?"

"Argentine. Some kind of Communist organizer. He seemed to

have pretty good access to Guevara. I'd say he's the cutout to operations back in Buenos Aires."

"Is he a journalist?"

"Neither of these guys is on the level. They were both already at the farmhouse when I was brought in. Both walked around without being under guard. It was the French guy's idea to come out with me. I agreed because I didn't know how long my cover would hold. He seemed to be in a goddamn hurry to get out. They both did."

Hoyle looked down at the map. "They released you here." His fingers touched a spot on the road to Tichucha.

"Around there. It was about three in the morning when they finally let us go. The guerrilla column turned north after they dropped us, I'm sure of that."

Hoyle looked at the map. He could not believe that Guevara had divided his forces. More astoundingly, he seemed to be moving along the water courses. It was almost lazy. The training of the Ranger battalion had been widely advertised on the radio. Did he just not think they really existed? Did he have that much contempt for the Bolivian army?

Charlie turned his wrist against the lantern on the desk and barely whispered, "It's time."

"Okay," Smith said to Santavanes. "We have to get you back into custody."

Santavanes stood, and the major tossed him the handcuffs. Santavanes blandly clicked them onto his wrists. "How long am I in for?" he asked.

"Sixty days," said Smith. "We have to sell your status as a legitimate correspondent. We used a journalist cover on you, and we have to make your treatment look equitable. That's going to require at least the impression that you're being processed along with the other captures."

"They haven't made me?"

"They don't have a goddamn clue," Hoyle said. He had been careful to make sure both Sandoval and D'Esperey had seen Santavanes being beaten.

"Now that you have confirmed that they are simpatico, their stays will not be pleasant." The major smiled.

Charlie was aware, if the major was not, that one of the reasons Santavanes was being so visibly played was to make sure the Bolivians did not murder Sandoval and D'Esperey. CIA wanted them interrogated thoroughly. That meant that they had to be kept alive. The conspicuous ruse had served two purposes.

"You're going to be transferred to the military prison in Camiri," Smith said to Santavanes. "You'll spend the first thirty days visible. But we'll keep you out of direct contact with the other prisoners. You'll be charged publicly, same as they are. Thirty days after that, you'll be moved to La Paz and quietly released."

"Per diem?"

Charlie was amazed at Santavanes's sangfroid. He faced two months in a Bolivian army jail. Even for a sham prisoner, this could not be easy, and all he seemed to be worried about was his pay.

"You'll be on full allowances for your entire visit. Station personnel will handle your exfil back to Langley."

"Money for nothing."

Hoyle shrugged. "Five grand for a rest cure."

The rice sack was placed back over his head, and Santavanes was led back into the police station. As the door opened to the small courtyard, Hoyle could hear questions being shouted, and a thumping noise like a hollow object being beaten on a wall.

50

AT THREE-THIRTY in the afternoon, promptly, Minister Alameda arrived at Colonel Arquero's office in the Palace of Justice. He was scrupulously on time, something of a reverse insult in a country that was very casual about appointments. Arquero's newly assigned aide-de-camp was a fresh-faced captain named Javier Pacheco; he had replaced Lieutenant Castañeda, who was transferred suddenly to the Paraguayan border. The captain clicked to attention as Alameda entered, but managed to seem inhospitable even as he offered coffee. Alameda declined, and the captain scurried into the inner office. Three or four minutes later—the interval seemed just long enough to snub—the captain emerged and held open the door.

Arquero stood and bowed slightly as Alameda came in. The men disliked each other but did so without rancor. They were like opposing parts in a complicated machine, one pushing, the other pulling. The spheres of their influence overlapped slightly. Alameda trafficked in varying shades of truth, propaganda, chiefly, but also in the remedy and suppression of facts contrary to the government's line. The facts Arquero dealt in were mostly outside the public eye—matters of military and police intelligence and the personal lives of the president's opponents. They were quite different physically. Arquero was a gangly scarecrow of a man, neat about his person but with a disaffected, almost priestly demeanor. Alameda was outgoing and charismatic, a dar-

ling of the press. These qualities contributed to Arquero's detestation
of the minister, as did a tinge of jealousy, though the colonel thought
himself quite above such base sentiments.

"Thank you for coming to see me, Minister," Arquero said. His
grating voice was a reminder that he had summoned Alameda.

The colonel gestured at a chair in front of his sarcophagus-sized
desk. "I thought it might be best if we spoke in my office. There is a
confidential matter, and I thought perhaps you might help me get to
the bottom of it."

The clock in the colonel's office clicked off the seconds it took for
Alameda to find a seat and say, "I'll do what I can."

Alameda sat and looked over Arquero's shoulder to the large American-made file safe behind him. The drawers were steel, and the cabinet itself was made of reinforced concrete. It had been a gift from the
American ambassador, a standard CIA office item used for the storage
of classified material. There was a large combination dial set in the center of the top drawer. Alameda suspected, correctly, that his own
dossier was kept among these files. The cabinet sat hugely in the otherwise Victorian office, out of place and yet organic to the man and his
occupation. The safe was the nexus of the colonel's empire—the documents within were the source of his power and the key to his survival.
Colonel Arquero remained very close to Presidente Barrientos despite
persistent rumors of private depravity. Arquero's services during the
1964 coup were still whispered about. Alameda, too, owed his career
to Presidente Barrientos, who'd personally elevated him from warrant
officer to major, then from major to minister. The colonel and the
minister served at the pleasure of the president; both men knew themselves to be safe in their appointments. There was only so far this discussion could go.

Arquero placed his hands on a stack of papers squared neatly on his
blotter. "May I be direct?"

"You may."

"I am aware of your contacts with members of the Bolivian Communist Party."

"And I am aware of the arms deal you brokered in Mexico City."

Arquero pursed his lips. They both had secrets to keep, and Arquero
could always do business with a man who had secrets. Arquero's arms
deal and Alameda's meetings with the PCB were just the tips of two

enormous, sordid icebergs. Their opening cards had been laid; both men held trumps.

"I'm sure you can appreciate that my dealings in Mexico were a matter of national security."

"And commerce."

"We both do business." Arquero smiled. "I meant to say that my business in no way relates to my personal politics."

"Of course not," Alameda said. The minister did not reveal that his own affairs were not strictly commercial.

"Then I may get quickly to the point," the colonel said. "As you are aware, the mercenaries who were captured in Muyupampa entered the country under alias. Their documents, I must say, were quite convincing."

"Sandoval and D'Esperey."

"And the third man as well."

Alameda tried not to show surprise. Most of the attention of the media and the interrogators had been focused on the others. "What about him?"

"The name on his documents is George Andrew Roth," Arquero said. "He claims to be Anglo-Argentine. He is actually a Cuban exile. His name is Felix Santavanes. Or rather, that is another alias. Santavanes is employed by the CIA. He entered the country illegally and is assigned to anti-guerrilla work with Mr. Hoyle and Mr. Smith."

"How do you know this?"

"I have a source within their group," Arquero said.

Alameda crossed his legs, doing his best not to seem impressed. "You are certain Santavanes is a CIA agent?"

Arquero nodded. "This is also confirmed by the fact that he has been segregated from the other prisoners. The Americans are overseeing the interrogations. This man Santavanes has been housed comfortably and is not being questioned."

"You've told this to the president?" Alameda asked.

"I've prepared a finding." Arquero caressed the papers on his blotter. "It might be better if *you* informed him."

It was unlikely that Arquero wanted to share credit for this information. Why didn't he tell the president himself? Alameda took a moment to consider the angles. "This man was traveling with two known collaborators? How did he gain their trust?" Alameda asked.

"That is the reason I wanted to speak to you before I reported to the president."

Alameda became impatient straightaway. "Let's not play games, Colonel."

"As you wish. Santavanes entered the Ñancahuazú Valley posing as a journalist."

Alameda frowned. "A journalist?"

"You did not know he carried press identification?"

"From whom?"

"From your office, Minister. Santavanes carried Bolivian press credentials."

"That's not possible. I issue those documents personally."

Arquero conjured a shiny paper from the stack on his desk. "This is a photocopy of his document: number 1397. The original was examined by my people in Muyupampa. It has since been destroyed by the Americans. Your signature was apparently forged, but the credential was real."

Alameda looked at the picture and did not conceal his bafflement. The face of the man was blurred slightly; it was a photograph of a photograph. Alameda did not recognize the individual.

"Did the Americans ask you to provide Santavanes with cover?" Arquero asked.

"No."

"Then how did an American agent receive a press credential from your office?"

Alameda handed back the paper. There could be only one answer. "It was stolen."

Arquero leaned back in his chair, grinning like a reptile. "Now, who might have done that?"

51

ON THE AIRSTRIP at Vallegrande, Hoyle received a note from Charlie, who appeared somber and even more inscrutable than usual. Charlie had just come from La Paz, and the airplane that had brought him stood on the runway, one engine feathered, one chugging. Charlie's expression was difficult to read, but he seemed worried when he shouted over the noise of the engine, "This is from Mr. Zeebus. He says that it is very urgent."

Hoyle opened the envelope and read:

YOUR PRESENCE IN LA PAZ (SOLO) REQUESTED IMMEDIATELY. COME AT ONCE NO. 172 AVE 16 DE JULIO.

The note was typed, which seemed odd for something urgent, and under Zeebus's scrawled signature was the alphanumeric N-357. This had been Hoyle's operator designator in Laos and was there by way of a bona fide. No one but Zeebus would have known it.

"Where did you run into Zeebus?"

"He came to the safe house at Plaza España," Charlie said.

Whatever the problem was, it had been important enough for Zeebus to commit a breach of security. The operations of La Paz station were supposed to be totally firewalled. It wasn't a surprise that Zeebus knew of the safe house at Plaza España—he didn't miss much—but it was highly irregular that he would actually go there looking for Hoyle.

"He didn't tell you what it was about?"

Charlie shook his head, looking even more serious.

Hoyle walked back to the casita and tried to figure what set of circumstances had combined to require his presence in La Paz. He anticipated a tirade from Zeebus. He returned to his small room and gathered up some clothing. He told Charlie that he would be reachable in the morning at Plaza España, and that he would be back as soon as possible.

"What should I tell Mr. Smith?" Charlie asked.

"Tell him it's politics," Hoyle said.

IT WAS AFTER midnight when Hoyle arrived at No. 172, a walk-up apartment off the Avenida 16 de Julio. Zeebus's note had not specified an apartment number. Hoyle scanned the mailboxes and rang the bell of a stranger on the third floor whose light was on. There was a buzz, and the door popped open. Hoyle unbuttoned his jacket and touched his pistol as he climbed the stairs to the third floor. There was silence behind the doors on each of the landings and only the whisper of passing taxis from the street. On the uppermost landing, a light shone from under the crack of a door; Hoyle looked down the stairs to make certain he had not been followed, then knocked softly.

The door opened, and Hoyle recognized the embassy doctor, the same man who'd treated him for his shattered ribs. The doctor had a drink in his hand. "Come in," he said.

Hoyle entered a small, neatly ordered living room. A couch, a pair of easy chairs, a lamp, and an open wardrobe crowded the space. The floor lamp next to the couch was putting down a murky pool of light. Hoyle could see a kitchen and a pair of bedrooms off a short hallway. It seemed a pretty standard safe house. Cosmo Zeebus sat on the couch with his arms crossed over his belly and his head back. His eyes were closed, and he seemed to be asleep. His tie was undone, and his jacket was laid over the back of the couch beside him. His shirtsleeves were turned up, and Hoyle noticed that there were small spatters of blood on his arms and the front of his shirt.

The doctor pulled the front door closed, and Zeebus opened his eyes and took a few seconds to regain consciousness. Hoyle noticed a physician's black leather bag sitting on the coffee table. It was open, and beside it were a few white squares of gauze and a pair of latex gloves turned inside out. Next to them were a scalpel, forceps, a curved surgical needle, and a tangle of catgut sutures.

"What's the matter?" Hoyle said.

Zeebus came to his feet by pulling his knees together, moving his legs to the side, and pushing heavily off the arm of the sofa. "I need you to ID somebody," he mumbled.

"Who?"

The doctor stood with his drink, looking down the hallway. Hoyle noticed for the first time that the doctor was dressed in duck trousers, sneakers, and a tennis sweater. There was blood spattered on him as well. He had obviously been called to duty from the tennis courts.

"What happened?"

Zeebus looked tired and a bit put out. "She's in the bedroom."

Hoyle pushed past Cosmo and opened one of the bedroom doors. The room was empty, which increased his sense of apprehension. He turned in the hallway. The doctor had placed himself in front of the other door. He said, "Be careful not to wake her, please."

Hoyle's mind pushed into fast-forward. He opened the door to find Maria lying on her back, blankets pulled up to her chest. A bottle of plasma hung from the bracket of the overhead light. A thin rubber tube spiraled down to an IV in her arm. A desk lamp was atop the bureau, with a handkerchief placed over it to cut the light. Long shadows went across the room. Hoyle noticed all of these things first because he did not want to look at Maria's face. It was lopsided. Her hair was pulled back, and there was a square of thick gauze taped to her forehead. Her eyes were closed, swollen and blackened. Her upper lip was split, and there was a livid purple bruise across her chin. Her throat was dappled with bruises—the brown-yellow blotches corresponded with the grip of a strangler.

Hoyle felt as though the floor was lurching under him. He held on to the door frame, looking at the woman in the bed. She was breathing, he could see that; her chest rose and fell steadily under the covers, and he noticed that she gripped at the blanket, the fabric knotted between her fingers as though she had clutched at the covers in a nightmare. Hoyle felt sorrow, agony; he wanted to embrace Maria and to cry like a child. He stood frozen, closed his eyes, and then opened them, but the scene stayed the same; behind him, Zeebus and the doctor said nothing. The apartment was still. He stood for a few long moments looking at Maria, the shadows across her face making her injuries seem even more disfiguring. The ugliness was like an arrow shot into Hoyle's guts.

"What happened?" he asked.

"A couple of goons kicked in the door to her apartment. I'm guessing they were Policía Nacional. They used a baton on her."

Hoyle was having difficulty focusing his thoughts, but words surfaced in his brain: The police were sent to do this.

"I've given her something to sleep," the doctor said. He wore the professionally concerned expression that was particular to the field of medicine.

Hoyle robotically stepped back, and the doctor closed the door. Hoyle staggered into the living room and lowered himself onto the couch. Something in him started to churn: fear and grief, then revulsion and anger.

"You know her." The inflection of Zeebus's voice was flat. The words had not been formed into a question.

Hoyle nodded. "I know her."

A few moments passed. Hoyle sat, just short of fury.

"Doctor, could you leave us for a few moments?" Zeebus asked.

The doctor put his empty glass in the sink. "Sure," he said. "I'm going to turn in." He walked down the hall into the empty bedroom and clicked the door shut. When they were alone, Zeebus poured out two bourbons and put one on the table in front of Hoyle.

"The neighbors heard the beating. They thought it was a robbery," Zeebus said.

Hoyle looked down the hallway to Maria's room. He had a bitter, fleeting memory of his own cruelty and the look on her face. He remembered the events that led to this moment, his own decisions, the things he had left undone. Now they were ordered neatly and in hindsight they pointed straight and inevitably to this calamity. He knew what had happened, and he mostly knew why. He did not know what would happen next. An emotion without a name welled up in his guts—just as quickly, it evaporated, leaving behind a residue of mockery and grief.

"How did you know to call me?"

"The French put Alameda under surveillance a couple of months ago. They found out about her, and then they found out about you. I got a call."

Hoyle said nothing and planned to say nothing. He stared at the floor.

"Look, pal. It took a lot of bullshit to get her here. She was left for dead. Whether or not she stays under protection depends on my getting the straight stuff from you. I don't give a shit about your operation up-country. But this impacts my little world, right here. You want a favor from me, then I get what's going on. Is she an asset?"

"She was working for me."

"That all?"

"No. That wasn't all."

Hoyle looked at the blood on Zeebus's shirt and realized that he must have helped carry her up the stairs.

"How did she get found out?"

"I don't know," Hoyle said. "I don't know how she got blown up."

"I don't normally get involved when things are personal. I try not to let them get personal."

"She was pregnant."

Zeebus shook his head. "She lost the baby."

Hoyle thought of murder. And then he thought carefully, as he did when he crafted an operation, and in his mind he began to put together an untraceable act of violence.

He stood, and Zeebus pushed himself out of the chair. His face looked gray in the way fat people look when they are tired. He stood between Hoyle and the door. "Don't do anything idiotic," he said.

Hoyle's words came slowly. "This was my fault."

Zeebus looked at him like a man who was owed a big favor.

"Alameda doesn't know where she is?"

"Nobody knows," Zeebus said.

"I owe you."

"Big-time."

Hoyle opened the door, and Zeebus said again after him, "Don't do anything idiotic."

.   .   .

THE BARBERSHOP OFF the lobby in the Hotel Cochabamba was a
three-seat affair, brightly lit, although a glass partition and venetian
blinds screened its patrons from the traffic in the lobby. There was a
mirror running the length of the interior wall, and above a trio of im-
maculate stainless-steel sinks, tiers of beveled glass held bottles of aftershave. His Excellency El Ministerio de Información sat in the chair
closest to the wall, draped in a crisp linen apron with his hair pinned up
in clips. The barber sat reading a newspaper by the door while a pretty
female assistant applied dye from a plastic bottle to the minister's scalp.
Alameda spent ten minutes looking at himself in the mirror, and after
assuring himself that he looked like Warren Beatty, he closed his eyes.
It was eleven in the morning; a sign on the door of the shop said
CERRADO, and the venetian blinds were drawn and lowered. The shop
would be closed to the public until after the minister's dye job.

    The door opened swiftly. The barber did not have time to look up
from his paper and could do nothing to stop the man who crossed the
shop in three large steps and yanked the minister's chair around. The
assistant stepped back with a squeaky shout of alarm. Alameda opened
his eyes and saw Hoyle standing over him. Alameda tried to stand, but
Hoyle kicked back the lever on the side of the chair, reclining it fully.
With one hand, he shoved the minister back. Alameda's windpipe was
nearly crushed, and his eyes bulged as Hoyle slammed him back
against the headrest.

    "Remember me?"

    Alameda struggled, but the angle of the reclined chair immobilized
him, and Hoyle struck him between the eyes with a clenched fist.
Alameda's head snapped back. The blow was terrific, and its shock was
magnified by the fact that he could not draw breath. Hoyle struck him
three more times, and Alameda's eyes rolled back in his head. He
slumped down, on the verge of unconsciousness, his legs sprawling off
the footrest. The force of the blows had knocked him out of one of his
shoes. Hoyle twisted a handful of apron tight around the minister's
throat and levered him out of the chair. The man's legs were rubber,
his body lopping about like a scarecrow, and Hoyle shoved him across
the room and slammed him into one of the sinks. Shelves against the
mirror shattered, and bottles and cans scattered across the floor. Talcum powder burst into clouds, and the piquant smell of aftershave
gushed into the room. Alameda's nose spurted blood, and hair dye ran

in rivulets down his face. Hoyle smashed him into the sink and then lifted him to within nose-biting distance.

"I guess the trouble with working for both sides is that you never know what shoulder to look over." He dabbed a finger into the hair dye running down Alameda's forehead. He wiped it under both of the man's eyes, then shoved him face-first into the mirror.

"See that? *See that?* That's what Maria looked like when they left her." Hoyle pushed Alameda down into the sink. Alameda stammered, choked. He could not form words. If he could, he would have begged for his life.

"You couldn't even do it yourself."

Alameda's senses were fleeing him; he was on the verge of blackout. "What?" he croaked. "What business of yours?"

Hoyle shook him like a terrier would a rat. "I ought to beat you to death. I ought to stomp out your heart." He jammed Alameda back down into the sink, pushed his head underwater, and held him there. After a moment he ripped him up by the hair. Alameda came up sputtering. Hoyle shoved him away, disgusted. Alameda sprawled on the floor, panting.

Hoyle drew his pistol and aimed it down.

"Jesus, no . . . No, please . . . I beg you . . ."

"This is what's going to happen. You are going to stay away from the woman. Forever. Nothing, nothing is ever going to happen to her. And here's why."

Hoyle fired a shot into the floor an inch from Alameda's head. The sound of the pistol exploded in the room. The report of the weapon rattled the glass, broken and unbroken. A grunt escaped Alameda's lips. The stunning, painfully loud noise of the shot echoed in his head.

"Pay attention," Hoyle said. "I'm going to tell your Communist friends that you've been keeping a list. All the passports you've sold them. I'm going to tell them that you've offered to sell this list to me. To the CIA."

"They'll know . . . I wouldn't . . ."

Hoyle fired another shot into the floor between Alameda's legs. He yelped like a little girl on a playground.

"It doesn't matter. I'll sell them my own list. You're as good as dead. Every day another Party member gets arrested. I'm going to put the word out that it's you providing the names. And then maybe I'll stop off at the DIC and tell them you're a Communist agent. Man, I'm gonna be busy, just trying to keep people informed of the shit you've been up to."

Alameda swallowed and choked. His lip was cut open, and his mouth was full of blood.

Hoyle put away his weapon. Alameda panted, trying to gather a lungful of air. His head pounded. The entire world he'd built and balanced so flawlessly was going to pieces. He had no idea what to say or do. A hundred half-thoughts flashed in his head. The Party would not take kindly to being informed upon. Even suspected informers were liquidated. But there was a deal to be made here. There was always a deal to be made.

"No," Alameda stammered, "wait, don't go. Don't go—" He tried to get up, but his legs wouldn't do as he asked. His hand came down on the shattered end of a bottle, and he added more of his blood to the wreckage.

"Good luck," Hoyle said.

Alameda heard the crunching of Hoyle's shoes on the broken glass and the oddly gay tinkling of the bell on the door as he left the shop.

52

AN HOUR AFTER dawn, the sky remained troubled and yellow; surly-looking clouds snatched at the hilltops as the column splashed across the Mosquera River and went into the forest again, men and pack animals alike made wide awake, then chilled and irritable, by the cold water. Guevara had been among the last to ford and did so with his feet dry on the back of the old red mare. Crossing dry-shod made him feel faintly guilty, and as the column reassembled on the far bank, he give his place in the saddle to Coco, who had an abscess behind his knee and was limping badly. Willy helped shove Coco up onto the back of the mare, and Guevara shambled along at the rear of the column.

An hour or so later the trail leveled and they came to the spot called Gálavez on the map. It had been marked by a small circle, the symbol for a village, but the place was only three huts on a hillside overlooking the river. As the army increased its presence in the valley, it spread rumors of Communist atrocities—lately peasants fled at the approach of the guerrillas. This was the case in Gálavez. The forward detachment found the first house abandoned. At the second, no one was home. At the third was a nervous peasant, his wife, and three children. The farmer said that the neighboring family had gone to Abapó to buy supplies, but he was obviously lying. In the first house, a fire was smoldering in the hearth, and chickens pecked at a bag of feed dropped in a doorway. When the scouts returned, they reported finding tire prints in the mud along the two-track road on the near side of the river. The peasant again said he knew nothing, though the tire tracks were fresh and the road was under half a mile away.

Guevara was certain the army was about. As a precaution, he ordered that the farmer's son, a gangling adolescent of fifteen, accompany the column until it reached the other side of the road leading to Abapó. The kid was named Tomás, and though his mother wept, he at first seemed flattered to be taken as a hostage. Guevara made certain he was treated well by the comrades. Tomás walked all morning, looking about the forest as though he had never seen it before. Guevara did not doubt that the father would inform the army that the guerrillas had passed; he could only hope that the man would not do so until his son was returned. If all went quietly, they would release the boy in the evening.

Guevara's guts rumbled, and these pains, in addition to his labored breath, made him melancholy and distracted. As they walked uphill from the river, the boy stayed close to him, following like a dog. Guevara had a premonition that there would soon be contact with the army. This was less clairvoyance than an assessment of warnings and indicators. There was the farmer's obvious nervousness and the tire tracks along the river road and something about the forest. The day was still, and the air hung between the trees like a thing pulled taut. Guevara sent Begnino up through the column to warn the forward detachment to be alert for ambush. This was done, and the remains of morning passed slowly, the column bunching up and spreading out as they negotiated some difficult terrain following the river north.

The boy became increasingly sad the farther they walked from his farm and by the middle of the afternoon, he skulked along with his hands in his pockets. As the trail climbed up past the headwaters of Suspiro Creek, the trees parted, and the column emerged at a shabby break in the forest. Stumps and ashes were scattered where brush had been burned and the clearing opened onto a series of neatly tended fields planted with corn and pumpkins. Clinging to the tree line, the column moved forward.

From down the valley came a growling sound, the noise of an aircraft engine, and without command, the column edged away from the open ground and took cover under the trees. The noise of the engine became louder and echoed off the hillside, a deep, throaty resonance. Guevara fished the binoculars out of his pack and pointed them up at the sky. The aircraft was not one of the slow spotter planes but a World War II–surplus Mustang fighter. The aircraft was sleek, and a shark's mouth had been painted on its nose. Slung under its wings were very modern bombs and canisters of napalm.

The column remained under the trees and watched the aircraft strafe and then napalm a hillside a mile away. Pillars of smoke blossomed up from the forest, and several seconds after the blasts, the sound rolled over them like stuttering thunder. The boy began to cry, and as the plane circled, the guerrillas watched their commander intently. He remained impassive. The burning hilltop was neither somewhere they had been nor a place they were going, and it did not matter if the Bolivians wanted to strafe empty jungle. When the aircraft at last flew off, Guevara ordered the column forward. Word was passed that they would stop in Piray, and the fact that the day's march now had an objective and an ending point lifted morale slightly. The comrades moved out with a purpose.

When they continued the march it took every bit of Guevara's strength to bear the weight of his pack. He stood panting and watched as the center group passed, and then he staggered a few paces after the mules and the horse. The trail was uneven, but once across the open space the cover was good overhead, and he did not worry any longer about the airplane. He walked about a mile, and his pack seemed to grow heavier. He had been without his regular medicine for days and he was nearly stupefied by the effort it took to draw breath. The column moved steadily, and he tottered under the pack, numbly placing one foot in front of the other. His lungs could not give him the air he needed, and his thoughts gradually began to come apart. What he sensed around him, the trail and the trees, the call of birds and the chatter of insects, all of it became a sort of hallucination, a perception close to what was happening but not reality. As he plodded along, his ideas reduced themselves to causes and remedies, to blacks and whites. Twice he nearly staggered off the trail and tumbled down the slope.

The column had moved on, and after a while, Guevara and Tomás found themselves alone on the trail. Only the boy noticed; Guevara was reeling and trembling, muttering gibberish and sweating profusely. An agony blossomed in his guts, a sharpening cramp that doubled him, and he lurched onto his knees at the side of the trail and vomited heavily. Light seemed to be going out everywhere after he'd puked, and when he tried to pull himself back up against a tree, his knees buckled. His rucksack pulled him over, and he was dragged onto his back.

Tomás watched indifferently as Guevara toppled over. Half-conscious, he tried to come to hands and knees. "Help me up," he gasped, but the boy did nothing. He looked up the trail. There was no one else in sight. The forest was silent, and there was only the sound of Guevara panting.

"Help me—"

Guevara vomited again, and Tomás took a step backward. He seemed astonished at himself, liberated by one small step toward his home. There was no one to stop him. As Guevara waved his arms for help, the boy ran away through the jungle as fast as he could.

Choking on puke and gasping for breath, Guevara sprawled on the trail and as he lost consciousness, the light came through the tops of the trees and rippled over him. This light became like the reflection of sun off the ocean, and a vastness bigger than the whole world seemed to yawn under him. He felt himself slipping off and down. The emptiness seemed to expand around him; his body had betrayed him cruelly, and these agonies propelled him deeper into empty space. Incredible shapes moved in front of his eyes, designs that could never be real, things he should have known were fantastic and absurd. For the rest, he remembered nothing, though his eyes remained open, and the sun shone into them and through them into his soul.

When Guevara failed to appear at the next halt, Willy came down the trail and found him curled into a ball, his rifle in the dirt at his feet. Around him, the leaf clutter was slick with vomit, and he continued to retch, bringing up small quantities of brown-yellow bile. As he vomited, his abdomen cramped, forcing his bowels to empty. Willy called up the trail for help, and Pombo and Moro jogged back. They looked on helplessly as Moro checked Guevara's respiration and called for his medical kit.

"Comandante? Comandante?" Moro shook him by the shirtfront.

Guevara groaned. His breath came in short puffs, his arms and legs were bent, and he trembled violently.

The satchel was brought back from the mule train and Moro used a pair of bandage scissors to cut an arm off Guevara's uniform shirt. He said to Willy, "Get his boots and pants off."

This was accomplished, though Guevara remained curled with his legs pulled up to his chest, groaning. He was covered in shit like an infant's, yellow and runny. Moro asked for some water to clean him, but Willy said there wasn't enough. The river was more than five miles behind them, and the village of Piray was an undetermined distance to the north. Moro scooped handfuls of dust from the trail and powdered Guevara's ass and the places where the shit had stuck to his thighs. Moro splashed his own canteen on his hands, wiped down Guevara's arm with iodine, found a vein, and started an IV. Willy held up the bottle of fluid.

"I'm going to give you some Demerol," Moro said. Guevara closed his eyes. "Demerol," Moro said again, but Guevara did not answer. Moro prepared the syringe. Belching and moaning, Guevara drifted in and out of consciousness. Every now and then, as he heaved to vomit, shit and liquid bubbled out between his buttocks.

Moro injected the syringe into Guevara's arm. For five minutes or so, he continued to writhe on the ground.

"What will it do?" Pombo asked.

"Kill the pain and maybe tighten up his bowels."

Finally, Guevara became quiet and passed into sleep. His arms and legs stretched out, and he was no longer trembling.

"Get his hammock off the horse," Moro said. "We'll make a litter and carry him. We'll make camp the first place we find water." He kicked Guevara's pants into the dust, scuffing dirt over them, then balled them up.

Others had joined and stood looking down at Guevara. No one noticed that the boy had run off. Guevara looked pathetic, smeared in his own filth, sprawled on the trail; every one of the comrades felt compassion and an equal measure of fear. Moro put away his instruments and carried his medical bag back to the mule.

"What's the matter with him?" someone asked.

"Dysentery," Moro said. "Maybe shigellosis."

"But you don't know for sure?"

Moro's eyes flashed. "No, goddammit, I don't know for fucking sure, but that's what I think it is. If it's something else, that would be bad, so let's get him into his hammock and carry him to where there's some fucking water."

Moro had never been heard to raise his voice, so the others quickly set about making a litter. The comandante was completely unconscious. His head rolled around, and his mouth dropped open as they put him into his hammock and carried him up the trail.

Moro followed the stretcher bearers, and Willy walked beside him down the trail. Miguel joined them, and when they were out of earshot of the stretcher bearers, Begnino's voice was solemn. "How bad is he?"

Moro scratched his beard. "You saw. It won't be so bad if I can keep fluids in him. If it's not shigellae, he'll make it."

Miguel shook his head. "This is all we need."

"I've been expecting this," Moro said. "Something like this. He's been close to physical collapse for almost a month."

Begnino touched his friend's arm. "What happens if he dies? Who takes over?"

"Joaquin," Miguel said.

"We can't find Joaquin."

"Then you take over," Moro said to Miguel.

They walked along, and the trees stretched over the path. The light that reached them was aqua.

"Moro, can I count on you?" Miguel asked.

"For what?"

"Somebody needs to talk to Che."

"Why would he listen to me?"

"You're his doctor."

"And you are second in command." Moro shook his head. "You think I don't know how fucked up this is?"

"We have to do something."

"We have no idea where Joaquin is. We've got the entire Fourth Division of the Bolivian army behind us. We're wandering around in circles," Coco said.

"That isn't news."

They walked for a while, Moro lagging a few steps behind. Exhaustion followed him like a shadow. He'd been sick, too, for days.

"I say we swing south back for the storage caves," Willy said. "We get the reserve radio and tell Havana to send help."

"The army's there," Miguel answered.

"We need to get a radio working," Begnino said.

"And what if the CIA monitors the radio?" Moro asked. "What if they send an airplane to drop napalm on the transmitter?"

"We need help," Willy said.

"You think Havana's going to send help after ten goddamn months? We're on our own." Moro said this so calmly that it astounded his listeners.

Coco did not believe that they were on their own, nor did Miguel. They believed that Havana would send help if only they knew how desperate the situation was. Willy also thought, though he did not say it, that Guevara was too sick to continue. The comandante was making wrong decisions. The decision to ambush the column so close to the base—that was a mistake. The decision to allow D'Esperey and Sandoval to leave at Muyupampa, another mistake.

"We've got to do something," Coco said.

"First thing I do is get him healthy. Then you can say to him whatever you want," Moro said.

"You agree with us? That we have to do something?"

"We have to do something," Miguel agreed.

"Don't count me in on anything," Moro said. "The comandante's in charge." He walked away from them down the trail.

Moro could not say it to anyone, but he wished he had never come to Bolivia. He was certain he would die in this place; perhaps not today or tomorrow, but he was convinced he would never see his family or Cuba again.

SUDDENLY, GUEVARA REALIZED he could see a face. Moro's face. There were voices around him and the sound of wood being chopped and the pack animals stamping at their pickets. He had lost track of time; it was late afternoon. He had forgotten that it would ever come, afternoon. The morning had been one prolonged agony and was a blur. Moro touched a stethoscope under Guevara's shirt and listened. Guevara turned in his hammock and saw Pombo and Willy sitting cross-legged nearby. They seemed anxious and grief-stricken. Both men smiled when they saw Guevara open his eyes. Guevara remem-

bered falling on the trail and being pulled over by the weight of his
pack. His tongue seemed coated in dirt and he was able to swallow
only with difficulty.

Moro held a canteen to Guevara's lips, and he drank. The water
seemed to bring him back. He realized that he had been moved and
that camp had been set up around him. He could see only forest, but he
heard the burbling of a creek and could smell the strong odor of shit.
With embarrassment, he rolled out of his hammock and apologized to
the others. Someone lent him a pair of pants and he was finally able to
wash himself in the creek. After he'd bathed, he felt enormously better,
and everyone was happy and relieved to see him up and about. None let
on how bad he looked, or how gravely they had been worried.

Guevara asked to be handed his map. Using a straw, Miguel pointed
out the location of the camp. Three hundred meters to the east was a
sketchy trail that led in tortuous switchbacks to a little village called La
Florida. Guevara made sure to walk about the camp, as much to show
himself to the comrades as to inspect the defenses. The encampment
was not well situated; it was too close to the trail, but it would do for
the night. He organized a four-man group to slip into the village and
purchase supplies. As the foragers departed he seemed much better,
and Miguel and Begnino did not think the time was right to speak to
him. Nothing was said about how sick the comandante had become or
the missed rendezvous.

Waiting for dinner, the comrades listened to the radio about details
of the trial of D'Esperey and Sandoval and then more glumly to the report of a battle between the army and a guerrilla detachment along the
Iquria River. The guerrilla unit had killed five soldiers and captured a
colonel and seven enlisted men. Following the clash, the prisoners
were stripped of their equipment, then released. This was definitely the
guerrillas' technique. Guevara knew this could only be Joaquin's column. The announcer crowed that one "antisocial" had been killed and
a corpse was being brought by helicopter to Lagunillas. The euphoria
about the report seemed to indicate some truth. Joaquin's column
would be hard pressed to fight, burdened as it was with both the sick
and the *resacas*. Morale slipped a bit at this news. The comrades shared
Guevara's frustration at having no communication with Joaquin and
no way to support him.

At full dark, the supply party returned. They'd managed to purchase a calf from one of the farms near the road, and brought back the news that fifty soldiers and *carabineros* were stationed in La Florida. Guevara thought it likely that the farmers would soon inform, but he did not worry that the troops would sally forth. They surely would not do so in darkness. He ordered the calf slaughtered, and the rest of the night was spent cooking beef and *locro*. Guevara ate his share but picked out the meat. Despite his careful eating, his asthma dogged him all night. Unable to sleep, he relieved Willy on sentry duty sometime in the small hours and sat listening to the steady hiss of the creek.

Guevara wondered what Joaquin would do after his contact with the army; if he had been hidden, he would now be forced to move, and this would not be easy, dragging the sick and guarding the *resacas*. Guevara cursed himself for bungling the rendezvous, and for a brief instant he imagined Joaquin's column and then his own surrounded and annihilated. No. That would not happen. The army continued to be hapless, though Guevara realized that they must inevitably get better.

What worried him was the way the peasants fled from the guerrillas. They were met with fear in most of the villages; those who did not run away stood with flinty indifference. It was a vicious cycle. To achieve more recruitment, they needed to carry out operations in populated territory. And to do that, they required more men. The actions thus far had all been successful, though Guevara knew that each time the guerrillas lost a man, it amounted to a serious defeat. Until they could recruit fighters to replace their losses, his men and his mission were in dire jeopardy. On the good side, the radio yammered constantly about the guerrillas and their legend was growing like wildfire. As far as Guevara could tell, the comrades' morale continued to be firm, though he understood that his illness was a concern to the men.

Guevara shivered, and the ache in his guts resumed like a belt pinched too tightly around his waist. The pain was like a nagging voice, chastising him for separating the column, panging him for innumerable failures. He did not doubt his leadership or his own sagacity; he could not imagine that anyone would question his ability to lead. Pride again, and pride compounded. Yet still the column was isolated, from Joaquin, from the network in La Paz, from the Party, and from Havana. The war that Che Guevara had made mirrored his own reality—it was a thing set apart from the entire world.

He decided that in the morning he would turn southeast and send out scouts again to try to locate Joaquin. Looking up at the sky, Guevara saw ten thousand stars and realized just how grand were his plans. He thought of Aleida and his family but pushed away memories of happiness and comfort; his responsibilities were to the world. Though he was unfailingly wary of self-centeredness when it existed in others, he did not see it in himself. He was proud, he knew, but did not comprehend that his pride was of the most dangerous sort, the sin by which the angels fell. It never once occurred to him to ask if his dreams were too grand to be made real.

53

THE DOG BARKED outside, half a dozen high, sharp yaps, and Honradez Rulon turned to look out the door. He could not see much beyond the small patch of light that spilled onto the mud of the front yard, but he heard the barking again, this time away and behind the house. Rulon's wife turned from the fireplace, and the children looked down from the loft as their father leaned toward the door. There was a stirring in the darkness, and he saw men, armed, bearded men standing in front of the house. Their clothes were caked with mud, and they were soaked through. Squatting by the fire, his wife picked up their infant, and her mouth opened to form some word, but Rulon lifted a hand to silence her and carried the lantern toward the door.

"*Hola,*" called a voice from the darkness, and Rulon made his face as cheerful as could be.

He stepped out the door, holding up the lantern, and saw four men with rifles. Two were close to the door, and another pair stood by the corner of the house. He could not see the faces of the two in shadow, but he could see the glinting outlines of their weapons. The tallest of the men moved forward into the light. Rulon slowly recognized the one his children had called *El Oso.* The big man stepped toward the door, his rifle hanging on a strap around his neck. Like the others, he was wet and dirty.

"Señor Rulon," Joaquin said. "Good evening." He pushed the rifle back over his shoulder and slowly put out his hand.

"Good evening to you, sir." Rulon held the lantern up with his right hand, and he awkwardly took Joaquin's hand with his left and pumped it. Rulon's lips pulled back into a counterfeit smile and his head bobbed up and down. Joaquin looked past the farmer into the dank light of the house. He saw the woman squatting barefoot by the fireplace. She clutched at the infant and looked out the door at Joaquin and her eyes seemed frozen in her head; her expression was somewhere between fear and annoyance.

"I hope not to trouble you," Joaquin said.

"How can I help you?" Rulon answered. Behind the house, the dog continued to bark.

"We'd like to buy a pig, if you have one to sell."

"Of course." Rulon grinned honestly this time, money being the thing dearest to him.

"Rice, too, if you have it."

Rulon tried not to look around obviously in the dark. "I do have rice and canned milk. Canned fish also." He stepped away from the door and waved the lantern around. He counted four armed men. The cagey peasant knew that there must be more outside the light of his lamp. "How many are you tonight?" he asked.

"Some," Joaquin said. He handed Rulon a small rolled bundle of Bolivianos. "That should get us enough," Joaquin said.

Rulon fingered the bills with his left hand. "Plenty, Señor," he said. "My biggest hog and more besides." He stuffed the bills into his pants and walked around the front of the house toward the pigsty, fairly dancing. When the farmer was out of earshot, Joaquin nodded to Braulio.

"Stay with the fucker," he said quietly.

In the house, the woman heard Joaquin and it made her heart tighten. She did not want to have anything to do with armed men, either the army or the guerrillas. Soldiers had been to the house just two days before, and she'd watched her husband perform in exactly the same manner—he'd smiled and made himself as helpful as possible. This was a dangerous business, and she feared that she would lose her life less than she feared that her husband would be killed or taken away and she would be left this hardscrabble farm and five hungry mouths to feed. She slumped, despairing, against the hearth, and when one of the children called to her, she hushed him sharply. She could no longer see anyone through the door. She strained her ears, sifting the night beyond the open windows, and after several long minutes, she was jarred by a gunshot and the long, screeching howl of the pig. There was another shot, muffled, a cracking sort of pop, and then silence.

She sat rigidly until Rulon poked his face in through the door and said quietly, "Don't worry, Mama."

She did not dare answer. In the time between the gunshots, her mind had taken her to terrible places and she started to shake and cry.

The hog was butchered, and a fire was built beside the house to cook the meat and rice. About midnight, roasted joints of pork were carried back to the camp in the ravine, and the comrades ate their first good meal since parting with Guevara. This had an immediate effect on morale, even on the invalids, Tania and Moises, who ate small portions of rice and drank boiled water. Overhead, the clouds broke apart, and stars spilled across the velvet-dark night. Joaquin and Marcos ate by the fire next to the house, banana leaves heaped with meat and rice, and after they had their fill, they wiped their greasy fingers on their trousers. There was food enough for all, even the *resacas*, and when the coals burned down, El Negro came from the camp and sat down next to Joaquin.

"How are they?"

"They both ate. We'll see if they keep it down."

El Negro watched Joaquin slump forward. For a long time, he sat with his forearms across his legs, preoccupied and silent. After a while Joaquin asked, "Are they going to make it?"

"Moises should be all right," El Negro answered. "I don't know about the woman. I'm pretty sure she's got internal injuries. I thought she was trying to kill herself this afternoon by walking."

The big man's clothing had dried where he was close to the fire. Elsewhere, across his back and the backs of his legs, it was still wet, and he shivered as he walked over to the house.

Joaquin gestured, and Rulon came out of the house toward him. "Do you know a place we can cross the river?" Joaquin asked.

Rulon nodded. "I do. At the regular crossing, the water is too high. But there is another place, farther north, where cattle can still be driven across." He added knowingly, "The army does not know about this place. Only I do."

"We'll want to cross tomorrow."

From inside the house, Rulon's wife sniffled. "I will have to check the ford," Rulon said.

"How long will it take?"

"It's only an hour to get there. Maybe a little longer. I can check it early in the morning and come back."

Joaquin did not trust the farmer entirely, though the meal had dulled his suspicion slightly. "How far up the river is this ford?"

"Three miles. Maybe less."

It was far enough away, Joaquin thought, but he would be careful.

"Then we will do this," he said. "Mark the crossing place with a piece of cloth hung from a branch. We'll wait near the ford. When it is safe for you to lead us across, all you need to do is show yourself near the spot. We'll find you."

"I'll start out in the morning," Rulon said, and he grinned as disarmingly as he could.

"It's worth fifty Bolivianos to you to get us across," Joaquin said.

"Thank you, Señor. The place I know is perfect. You will be safely across the river by nightfall."

He stood grinning, an expression without meaning, and Joaquin wished the river crossing were already accomplished. He wished that he had the river between him and the army and that he was miles away from this greedy, shifty son of a bitch. Joaquin was tired and cold down to his bones. Even in starlight, Rulon seemed to have a lying face, but Joaquin felt that the precaution of having him mark the crossing place would be sufficient. He would send scouts out soon after dawn, and they could watch the ford. Inside the house, the baby cried, and Rulon's wife whimpered for her pathetically.

"Tomorrow, then," Joaquin said.

"Until then," said the peasant, and he ducked into the house.

WHEN THEY HEARD the news that two prisoners had been taken, Hoyle and Charlie drove into the Ranger encampment at El Pincal at ten in the morning. Word had come first that the two had been captured after a fight, but the story gradually shed its more spectacular embellishments, and it was revealed that the two guerrillas had deserted and were not captured but had walked onto a stretch of the Camiri Highway, flagged down a truck, and asked to be driven to the nearest police station. They'd been handed over from the CID eventually to the army. Hoyle and Charlie had made the drive early in the morning as the treatment of the prisoners was still in some doubt. Hoyle did not want them murdered, especially if information could be had.

The site was neatly laid out. Sentries were posted in two places on the road. Hoyle parked the Land Cruiser, then walked with Charlie toward the small farmhouse that served as a headquarters. Gustavo Merán, Hoyle's comrade from the firefight at the river, called from a cluster of tents. He was now a *suboficial mayor*, sergeant major of the Ranger battalion. He looked sleek and fierce. When they met, Merán smiled slyly and said to Hoyle, "I see that you don't give up so easily."

Hoyle congratulated him on his promotion and his Ranger tab. For the compliment the old warhorse shook his head.

"Not much else for me to do," he said. Merán walked with them toward the farmhouse, exchanging a few words with Charlie in Guaraní.

Hoyle asked about the prisoners, and Merán became slightly less animated.

"Prisoner," he said. "There is now only one."

Charlie saw Hoyle draw a breath. Merán did not seem apologetic when he said, "The Fourth Division transported the men to the Ranger camp by helicopter. One of them tried to escape."

Hoyle's voice was a growl. "From a flying helicopter?"

Merán shrugged as they walked. Hoyle was furious but did his best to mask it. He calmed himself by bringing to mind that Merán had not committed the murder. The sergeant was unmoved about the death of an enemy.

"That man had information," Hoyle said.

"So does the other." The sergeant major had seen a lot of war in his life, all over the world, and prisoners sometimes fell from helicopters—in Algeria, in Vietnam, in other places. In Bolivia the death of a mercenary bandit would not even involve any paperwork. It occurred to Hoyle that the murder had been done deliberately to provoke him. Major Placido was on the staff of the Fourth Division. The trial of D'Esperey and Sandoval was under way and was proving to be an ongoing embarrassment to Barrientos's regime. The orders to reduce the number of live captures may have come from the top. In the eyes of the Bolivian army, this was not seen as criminal or even gratuitous murder;

it had been done for a purpose. The practice of disappearing captured guerrillas would probably be impossible to stop.

Merán went on, "In any event, it was not the Rangers who murdered him. It was the Fourth Division. The remaining prisoner has become extremely cooperative."

"Where is he now?"

"Here. In custody." Merán gestured toward the farmhouse. "The captain has prepared a briefing for you."

Hoyle found Captain Salinas sitting at a plank table in the small house. A pile of maps and an M2 carbine lay in front of him. Salinas was a tall man, lean of flesh; he had a sharp face and piercing eyes. He stood and smiled as Hoyle ducked through the blanket hung across the door. The captain's handshake was firm, and his gaze was direct. Salinas wore a field-green set of fatigues, and his paratroopers' boots were impressively shined. On his shoulder, he wore a shield-shaped patch emblazoned with the number 2, and above it, a yellow and black arc held the word RANGER.

Merán introduced Hoyle, and Charlie stayed outside. Salinas waved to a chair; Merán had coffee ready and poured out two cups.

"Can I send some coffee to your man outside?" the captain asked.

"I'd like it if he could speak to the prisoner," Hoyle answered.

"Of course," Salinas said. He nodded, and Merán brought Charlie into the house.

"I have prepared a thorough debriefing. As you have heard, the prisoner has been extremely cooperative."

"Has he been tortured?"

"That was not necessary." The captain smiled.

Hoyle turned to Charlie. "Talk to him."

Merán and Charlie went out, and the captain unrolled a topographic map and turned it around on the desk so Hoyle could see it.

"The prisoner revealed that he was part of a fifteen-man detachment split off from the main guerrilla column. The group contains four Bolivians who are disaffected and have been kicked out of the insurgent group. They were kept under guard. He said that within their column, morale was low, and that several guerrillas were sick and had to be carried."

"How many total?" Hoyle asked.

"One was killed by our forces last week. Two deserted. That leaves a total of twelve."

"Was there a woman among them?"

"Yes. He said she was German."

Hoyle did not say anything about Tania, though his question revealed to Salinas that he knew a great deal.

"The prisoner says that the detachment has been separated from the main column and has been searching for them."

This struck Hoyle as incredible. "They're lost?"

"Apparently so," Salinas said.

"We have placed sensors on one of the trails used by the guerrilla forces," Hoyle said.

"What do you mean, sensors?"

"Electronic devices camouflaged as vegetation. They detect vibration in the ground. They can detect the passing of troops."

The captain smiled wryly. That the Americans had such technology did not surprise him, though he did not necessarily trust electronic things left out in the jungle. "Who put down these sensors?"

"I did." Hoyle touched the map. "Here. On a trail axis we are certain is being used by the enemy." He explained briefly what the Igloo White devices could do. He continued, "Yesterday afternoon, the sensors indicated that twelve people had passed on the trail. Heading north."

Salinas had not yet taken measure of Hoyle, but the captain had been very impressed by Major Sheldon, the training officer in charge of Famous Traveler. Hoyle had revealed something; it was now Salinas's turn.

"This complements what we have learned from the prisoner. He says that his group tried to remain hidden, in encampments by the Iripiti River, and then by the Salado. They were moving north to avoid our patrols."

"They had to move after the desertion was discovered."

"That's likely," Salinas said. He lit a cigarette and continued, "We have had information from a patriotic farmer in the northern part of the valley. He claimed that the guerrillas will move across the Rio Grande at a certain place and that an ambush could be set up at the crossing point. The informant sent a relative to the village of Alto Seco.

The *corregidor* telegraphed the information to us. The farmer claimed through this relative that he could not make a report in person, as the guerrilla column was camped nearby and his family was at their mercy."

"Who commands this second group?" Hoyle asked.

"The prisoner said the leader's name was Joaquin. He is one of Guevara's lieutenants."

"A Cuban?"

Salinas nodded. "The general staff estimates Guevara's strength at three hundred men."

"We think his total numbers are around fifty. Total."

Salinas touched the map at the northern end of the valley, close to the Rio Grande. "Then this group being offered by the farmer—they are a detachment of some kind."

"Exactly," Hoyle said.

"Why has he split his force?"

Hoyle shook his head. "The detachment to the north may have been intended to carry out a diversionary attack. That might still happen. But they're isolated, and there is no radio communication. If we find them, we can step on them. This situation might not present itself again."

Salinas wanted to insert his troops as rapidly as possible. At his command were two platoons of freshly minted Rangers, eager and trained to a standard not common in a Latin army.

"I'd like to accompany your patrol, Captain," Hoyle said. "That is, with your permission."

"You are welcome, Mr. Hoyle. The sergeant major speaks very highly of you." Salinas nodded toward the door. "Will your man be coming as well?"

"No," Hoyle said. "He'll stay here."

Hoyle met with Charlie and confirmed that the prisoner was still alive. Barely. He had been beaten so badly that his body looked like a wrecked thing that clothing had been hung on. Charlie confirmed in general terms what the captain had said, that Joaquin's detachment was separated, that its morale was low, and that they were carrying sick or wounded. Hoyle attended the briefing of the troops, and Salinas again impressed Hoyle. The captain laid out the concept of operations using a standard American five-paragraph field order. The briefing covered scheme of maneuver, fire support, key teams and individuals, formation, and order for movement. There was a plan, and a plan if things went wrong. Famous Traveler had delivered on its promise to make soldiers.

As the briefing wound up, Hoyle stood and passed out a copy of Tania Vünke's photograph. "This person may be traveling with the guerrilla column. If she is, she's a live capture. Do not, I repeat, do not shoot this individual. She is to be taken alive."

The picture of Tania passed hand to hand; other than a few grunts, it elicited no comment. Provided the ambush took place in daylight, it was possible to spare this life.

"The engagement will require fire discipline," Salinas said. "In addition to the guerrillas, there may also be one additional noncombatant— the farmer who is to guide the guerrillas across the river. He, too, is to be a live capture."

Hoyle's fondness for Salinas was strengthened when he was named one of the three people authorized to initiate the ambush, along with Sergeant Major Merán and the captain himself.

With the briefing concluded, Captain Salinas called the troops to attention. He walked in front of them with his hands clasped behind his back.

"This will be the first test of Manchego Número Dos against the enemies of our nation," he said. "For the last twenty-six weeks, we have sweated and trained and watched as a mercenary gang of Communists has run riot in our motherland. We have watched our brother soldiers carried from the jungle, murdered. I am not asking of you, Rangers, that you give your nation your lives. You have already given your lives. Today I expect you to *take* the lives of the enemy. I expect you to crush them without mercy. I expect today that every Ranger will do his duty."

There were smiles and nods among the assembled Rangers. Then Salinas threw his head back and shouted, *"¡Victoria o muerte!"* The Rangers exploded in cheers, whistles, and raw animal howls.

As the group put on their packs and shouldered their weapons, Hoyle caught sight of Charlie. He was blessing himself with the sign of the cross.

54

JOAQUIN AND HIS column met their end this way:

Four Huey helicopters transported the Rangers to a landing zone five kilometers below the river. The troops quickly ordered themselves for movement, one platoon covered as the other advanced, and within four hours, Hoyle was settling in with the ambush party overlooking a broad, lazy bend of the Rio Grande. Thirty riflemen were arrayed in the brush and rocks overlooking the river. Through his binoculars, Hoyle surveyed the far bank; the crossing place had been marked with a white strip of cloth that appeared to be a kitchen apron. The river rolled past, and a light breeze muttered through the trees.

Hoyle positioned himself behind a fallen log ten or fifteen yards from the bank. Within sight were Captain Salinas and his radio operator. Between Hoyle and the captain were a machine gunner and two assistants. Hoyle watched as they silently set up their weapon and the loader positioned a one-hundred-round belt of ammunition.

Two other M60 machine guns were aimed on the crossing, and two dozen rifles besides. Each man of the thirty had an assigned field of fire, a space of river and bank to be swept with bullets, and the men of the second platoon deployed on the flanks had their orders as well. No one would fire until the ambush was opened by one of the officers authorized to begin the engagement.

The clouds drifted apart, and the sun spilled down in patches. Gradually, the afternoon opened, and the whole light of day came upon the riverbank. Hoyle lay with his weapon against his right shoulder, the muzzle and fore grip balanced on the log in front of him. The river moved past, brown and limpid, and as the sunlight became more defined, shadows came down sharply on the forest floor around him. The sun filtered through a double canopy and beyond the rocks and boulders that littered the river course; the tree line across the water glowed an almost incandescent green.

Hoyle's mind opened to the jungle around him. Sensation overcame and then displaced thought. His eyes scanned, and his ears filtered sound. An hour passed, then another. Hoyle smelled the forest, a scent of life and decay, and the river showed beautifully in the long afternoon. Leaves drifted by on the surface of the water, and now and again a whirlpool sucked past, spinning concave on the green-colored surface. On a branch next to Hoyle's face, a swordtail butterfly alighted, opening its wings, black and electric blue. Another joined the first, and they remained on the twig, brushing together black and white forelegs; the butterflies glimmered like jewels in a necklace. For a long while Hoyle did not look at the apron marking the ambush, as it seemed that nothing violent could ever happen on a day bright with butterflies.

The birds became quiet, and this slight change in the tone of the forest sent an electric current through the ambushers. Across the river, brush parted high up on the bank, and there was a small sound—the popping of branches. Leading a chestnut horse by its bridle, a short, dark-complected man appeared next to the apron. He wore pants made of homespun and a disreputable woolen jacket; on his head was a shabby fedora. The man peered out from the tree line at the rocks lining the bank. He held the horse's bridle and bent a knee, looking around at the stones, and then he gazed steadily across the river.

The distance across to the other bank was perhaps one hundred yards, and the lenses brought close the man's face. Hoyle recognized the brusque gestures and the dark hair and deep-set eyes. It was the farmer who had said he hated the Communists because they did not love the Virgin Mary. Hoyle remembered the man's name because it seemed so ill suited to him: Honradez.

Hoyle watched as the farmer flitted around the apron, looking up and down clumsily. Then he led his horse over the stones and a little way into the river and splashed handfuls of water up onto her flanks.

The old mare's sides twitched and shimmied. Rulon led the horse back up onto the bank and tied the reins to a branch. Hoyle diverted his eyes when Rulon turned his head and stared into the jungle close to where Hoyle was lying. I will not look at him again, Hoyle thought.

After a few minutes standing by the horse, Rulon walked back onto the bank and sat openly on a boulder in the sun. The afternoon was fading, and shadows were rising under the hills where the river turned north. Hoyle looked at his watch and thought that the guerrillas were close—they were probably watching the crossing. This was what Hoyle would have done, especially if he'd had to use a local guide. Hoyle did not think it likely the guerrillas would cross in full daylight. They might send across scouts; this, too, was what Hoyle would have done.

Hoyle lay still and watched the river. The apron waved in the air slowly, back and forth. Don't overthink this, Hoyle told himself. Let them come into the trap; they must come first, and then it would be decided how to open the engagement.

Across the river, Rulon walked from the cobbles and boulders at the river's edge and turned his attention toward the forest. It was obvious he'd heard something, though the noise did not carry across the water. The farmer took off his hat and waved it. Hoyle turned his head slightly; hidden a few feet away, Salinas had seen Rulon wave as well. The captain seemed to sink down slightly, flattening behind his rifle. Hoyle again looked across the river: He saw two men, and then a third, appear from the forest next to Rulon. They were dressed in muddy fatigue uniforms. Each carried a backpack and a rifle. Their clothing showed hard use and was stained with sweat and reddish dirt. One of the guerrillas stood under the apron and looked across the river. Hoyle could feel his heart beating steadily as he watched the men over the top of his rifle.

Hoyle tried not to focus on a single one of them but to watch them all equally. He marked out his field of fire, two trees between which his targets stood, and he looked about on the riverbank for places they would likely take cover when the ambush commenced. He would shoot first at the men who were visible and then spray the places of refuge. Thirty bullets were in the magazine of the weapon, and he carried five more magazines in his vest.

Hoyle could hear snatches of conversation over the murmur of the river. He could not discern any words, but he could hear plainly the clatter of human language. If these were the scouts, why didn't they cross?

The three guerrillas talked in a group, and Rulon stood slightly apart from them. Hoyle inched the front sight ramp slowly until it was centered under the three bearded men. Two more guerrillas came out of the forest, and then two men approached, carrying a poncho strung between long poles. Hoyle realized it was a stretcher. The guerrillas lowered it to the ground. They were carrying a man in a dirty shirt and dark green trousers. Hoyle counted the men visible across the river: six, then eight. He noticed that the stretcher bearers did not carry weapons.

It was a spellbinding thing to see the enemy this close. Most of Hoyle's business was conducted at night; it was the very first part of dusk, and he could see the men on the other bank clearly. He could make out their features. He could tell that some were tall and some were short, and then a large man came through the assembled group, and from the way he looked at the river, Hoyle guessed that this was the commander. He watched as the tall man shook hands with Honradez Rulon. Some of the men across the river took off their packs and knelt to scoop handfuls of water into their mouths. A few lit cigarettes, and others, having none, cadged puffs from their friends.

Hoyle felt sweat run off his temple and down the length of his cheek. His heartbeat had steadied, and he felt wet through his shirt where his elbows and chest rested on the damp earth. Across the river, the guerrillas stood indifferently, some looking upstream and others straight across the river. Not one of them seemed concerned to be standing about in the open, and Hoyle watched as the leader signaled back into the woods and another set of stretcher bearers trundled forward and lowered their load to the ground.

JOAQUIN STOOD IN the small patch of sun at the crossing place and looked across the river. The water was smooth and moved sluggishly, and he was pleased with the ford. They had not broken camp until after sunrise, and although he'd sent scouts forward, the crossing place had been under observation for only the last three hours. Joaquin himself had watched Rulon come and had seen him bathe his horse and wade in the river. As the stretcher cases were brought up, Joaquin thanked Rulon. The cover on both sides of the river was satisfactory, Joaquin thought.

Joaquin asked, "How deep is it?"

"As deep as my chest," Rulon said. "Your feet will be on the bottom the entire crossing. No one will have to swim."

"The crossing is straight?"

"Yes, straight across," Rulon answered. He looked at the other bank, where the rocks came down, and then he looked into the forest for a rather long time.

"You will lead us across," Joaquin said to the farmer.

The words struck Rulon like hailstones. The peasant was gripped by dread, but he made his face show nothing. Joaquin watched the farmer closely. Rulon knew that somewhere across the bank, the army was waiting; his life now depended on his ability to act like it was not.

"But sir, I do not swim well," Rulon said.

"You just told me it is not necessary to swim," Joaquin answered.

"It is shallow enough to walk," Rulon said.

"Then show us."

The guerrillas looked at Rulon without sympathy. The farmer swallowed hard and waded into the water directly. Around him, the jungle hummed expectantly, chirps and twitters and squeaks; Rulon heard them all keenly. The noise seemed like fire crackling in his ears. There was nothing else for him to do, so he walked out slowly, feeling along with his feet, and as the river came up around his waist, he felt it pulling at him, swirling colder than he had expected.

Joaquin watched from the shore, and the others lowered their packs, some unlacing their boots. Out in the river, Rulon waded steadily toward the other bank. Every step took him into a grasping sort of dread: *Jesus, don't let them shoot me. I am not armed. The soldiers must see that.* Rulon put his hands over his head as he waded toward the far bank, and he prayed as he raised his palms to the sky. *Please, God, protect me from the bullets.*

Rulon was most of the way across when Joaquin turned to Marcos. "Go on. I don't want him running away on the other side."

Marcos and three comrades waddled into the river, holding their backpacks in front of them and balancing their rifles on the floating packs. Rulon was in the middle of the stream now, moving in fits and starts, his hands still raised above his head like a priest rendering a blessing. The current swept around Marcos's chest, pushing him slightly to the left as he approached the far shore.

Now it was time to get the sick across. On the bank, Joaquin nodded down at the litters. "Help them up, and use the stretcher poles to put under their arms," he said.

The comrades helped Tania and Moises to their feet. The two remaining rejects, Chingolo and Eusebio, guided the invalids across the rocks and to the edge of the water. The stretcher poles were placed on either side of them like railings. Tania and Moises clutched them under their arms and stepped tentatively across the rocks and into the water.

Joaquin slung his weapon across his shoulders and waded in. When he was waist-deep, he unhitched his pack and floated it. Now that it was started, Joaquin wanted the crossing to go quickly, and he did not like it that the column was spread across the water. He watched the men trudging through the river, some pushing their packs, some dragging them; all the combatants held their rifles as high as they could, and it struck Joaquin as odd that Rulon kept his arms raised as he waded near the far bank.

It was as though he had a fear of getting his hands wet.

HOYLE WATCHED THE guerrillas come down to the river in a gaggle, mobbed together, with not one sent up- or downstream to provide cover. Hoyle had thought that scouts would be sent over before the main body attempted to cross, but several men entered the water at once. They were all in the river now, thirteen souls, counting the one who had betrayed. As they waded toward him, Hoyle saw Tania staggering into the current. He did not recognize her face at first; he did not even discern her as female. She stood out principally because she was so thin. A walking skeleton.

Hoyle pressed the fingers of his left hand against the safety lever. He could see the face of the farmer. Two guerrillas were drawing up to the bank, one of them directly in front of Hoyle.

What had made them forget the way rivers are crossed?

The guerrilla nearest to Hoyle came on, staring directly into the brush, with water sloshing off his shirt and trousers. He walked barefoot up the bank, his boots tied together and draped over his shoulders. Hoyle was under ten feet away.

Marcos took a quick step backward, and the rocks shifted under his feet. Hoyle kept the rifle steady over the top of the log, the muzzle laid so exactly that he did not have to move it. His mind had gone to that place where adrenaline stretches time. The seconds unfolded like hours passed in a dream, and Hoyle thought very calmly, *He's seen me.*

Hoyle pulled the trigger and held it back. The AK-47 bucked up, and Hoyle pushed his left hand down onto the hand guard in front of the receiver. In one second, the weapon barked five times. Marcos felt the pressure wave and the heat of the muzzle blast in his face. The concussion of the weapon was so close that it snapped his wet trousers back against the flesh of his thighs. Three bullets struck Marcos above his belt buckle, and two more hit him in the chest.

Hoyle watched as the guerrilla in front of him folded at the waist, his knees locked together. The first bullets smashed through his body and kicked up long splashes behind him in the river. A sixth bullet hit Marcos in his face, and he jerked as though he had been touched by an electric current. He staggered back into the water, and in that instant, the entire Ranger detachment opened fire.

The explosions of thirty rifles deafened Hoyle. The noise was too furious to be comprehended, and the rest of the ambush seemed to unfold without sound. Slender geysers were ripped from the surface of the water, and along the far shore, bullets could be seen chipping bark from the trees. Leaves spilled down from the canopy and fell quivering onto the surface of the water. Hoyle aimed at two men close to the far bank and pulled the trigger—a burst of fire exploded from the muzzle, and lead jabbed the men floundering with their packs. They were beaten down by Hoyle's bullets and a dozen others. Across the river, Rulon's horse reared and bucked. The old nag jerked its bridle free of the branch and reared as bullets cuffed into her flanks. Roaring and screaming, the horse went down. Hoyle could feel the banging of the rifles through his skin; the air quivered with lead. Tracers skipped off the water and wobbled off through the forest. Everywhere Hoyle looked was swept by gunfire, a perfect hurricane of lead.

JOAQUIN CAME ACROSS the rocks that hemmed in the river, and he held Tania's elbow as she took the stretcher poles under her arms. The *resacas* maneuvered the poles into the water awkwardly, as they did most of their assigned tasks, and the two sick people tottered cautiously over the rocks and then past the slippery stones underfoot at the edge of the water.

"Can you make it?" Joaquin said to Tania.

She did not answer but nodded and scuffed forward. He watched as the water came up around her and the *resacas* held on. As they advanced into the stream, Joaquin waded into the water to his knees. The river was greenish brown, and when he looked down, he could just see the tops of his boots blurred in tea-colored water. In this place, the river was about three hundred feet across, horizontal and smooth, deceptively so, because even standing in the shallows, Joaquin could feel the cool, steady pull of the current against his legs. The far bank was the mirror of the one on which he stood. Rocks and boulders were scattered close by the water. Slightly above, there was a band of red-yellow dirt and then a nearly vertical wall of jungle, verdant where the slanting sun fell and dark between the trees. He could see the comrades wading in an uneven line, pulling their rucksacks after them and holding aloft their rifles.

Joaquin noticed that Rulon had turned slightly in the center of the river. The farmer still held his hands overhead, but he also crouched down into the water. Joaquin saw that the farmer's eyes were screwed shut and that his face was twisted into a grimace.

Joaquin immediately sensed disaster.

A crashing sound broke over the surface of the water, *wham wham wham wham,* and Joaquin saw Marcos flinch backward, and then his head bowed and his legs went stiff. Joaquin heard a tearing sound, a sort of crashing; this second noise was louder and seemed to come from everywhere at once. He could not make sense of it for a moment, as its rhythm was complex and very rapid. Joaquin unconsciously lifted his rifle and sprayed bullets into the forest. He could see nothing through the jungle, not even the muzzle flashes of his attackers. Joaquin saw the water exploding around the comrades, and he saw the stretcher bearers dump the poles from their shoulders and then tumble into the shallows. Joaquin continued to shoot. His was now the only weapon returning fire, and his mind raced with the absurdity of it. In the river, the others were being flailed with bullets. Then Joaquin felt the rocks under his feet, and he turned and scrambled back onto the bank. The riverbank went white, as though struck by lightning. Joaquin stumbled and fell, then got up again. His sight became suddenly clear; he saw every stone laid flawlessly, every tree and branch, every leaf. He'd been hit, though he felt no pain, only a throbbing sort of numbness. Around his feet rocks shattered, and dust blossomed up from dry stones as bullets struck them, and just as he fell behind a boulder, he knew that every rifle on the far bank was tracking him. He felt a hot breath in his face, and he scrambled down behind the boulder. He could not believe that this was happening. *We have been ambushed, and this is how it will end, here behind this rock.*

Joaquin was sick at heart. He'd been betrayed, duped, but he had also failed as a commander. Behind the boulder, his hand automatically went to his ammunition belt for a fresh magazine, and his fingers closed over something warm and soft where there should have been metal. He realized that he was slick with blood. Bullets smashed into the front of the boulder, and the entire world seemed to vibrate. Shit, I will really die here, he thought. No one else was moving on the bank. A body lay in front of him, facedown on the gravel, and there was one behind, one of the cowards, the *resacas* who had run with the opening shots for the jungle. Again Joaquin's sight cleared. He felt no pain, and though he waited for fear to come upon him, it did not. He drew a breath and wondered, if he let it out, would he die at once? Then there was a scratching noise on either side of the stone, long bursts of machine-gun fire, and gravel spat up at him with a noise like rain makes falling on cobblestones; the small stones were being kicked up from the bank, and they were striking him, and Joaquin thought that he must not die cowering. He stood and fired at the jungle across the river.

He had been a singularly unlucky commander. They all had been unlucky. These were the last thoughts Joaquin registered. The rest was a howling, empty void.

HOYLE SCANNED THE river and kept firing, pointing his weapon unconsciously, aiming without thought at anything that moved, five-round bursts on full automatic. The AK-47 chugged in his hands; when it clicked empty, he rolled onto his back, peeled away the long black magazine, and inserted a new one. Hoyle came to his knees but did not fire. On the other side of the river, the tall man who looked like the leader fell into cover behind a boulder, and one of the machine guns trained on him. The gunner walked the fire in on the man behind the boulder, and a long burst tore sparks away from the rocks. Hoyle could see that this man was the last person moving. Every one of the Rangers' weapons was aimed now at him, and dust and sparks and tracers all kicked up around him. Consumed in a roiling cloud of dust and shattered rock, the big man stood defiantly, fired a dozen aimed shots, and then toppled on his back.

In a dying spasm, his rifle was held straight out above his chest. Lead, fire, and ricochets swarmed around, and the fusillade tore him to pieces.

Through this all the farmer, Rulon, stood trembling in waist-deep water, turned sideways with his eyes shut and his hands held high in the air. Not a single bullet came anywhere near him.

Salinas stood and blew a long blast on his whistle. *"Pare fuego,"* he yelled. The command was repeated down the line.

Ears ringing, Hoyle stood behind the log and tried to spit but found his mouth was like dirt. The barrel of his weapon had gone gray-white with heat, and he noticed that his hands were twitching. Hoyle stepped forward out of the brush and slid down the bank onto the rocks close to the river. The bend in the river was like a mirage. Everything seemed iridescent and out of focus. One of Salinas's platoon leaders had directed Rangers to either side of the ambush site and warned them to be ready to repulse a counterattack. None came.

Hoyle looked down onto the rocks in front of him and saw the bodies of Marcos and Braulio, their skulls ruptured by bullets and their faces made lopsided; the bridges of their noses had been smashed, and their eyes rolled right and left, like cubist portraits rendered in blood. Hoyle was struck by how silent the forest had become. The river glided silently, and the wind stirred the trees but did not murmur; it was as though the earth had been rendered mute.

Honradez Rulon stumbled out of the river and collapsed on his hands and knees. Ignoring him, Rangers dragged bodies from the river and laid them on the rocks. Rulon crawled forward and wrapped his arms around the waist of Captain Salinas and blubbered something. Hoyle could not hear it, and the captain simply pushed the man away.

Rulon lifted his eyes to Hoyle and cried out, "Excellency! Excellency! You remember me!"

Hoyle felt a jolt of disgust. Rulon sat half in the water and took off his hat and clutched it in his hands. Hoyle walked past him and said nothing. Rulon blinked around at the bodies and began to sob.

Hoyle waded to the far bank, and the sound of Rulon's bawling seemed to echo down a metal tube. In the middle of the stream, Hoyle passed by a body just underwater. Streaks of blood spun like rainbows on the surface, and a face showed yellow below it. The man's eyes were open, and his cheeks seemed puffed, as though he were holding his breath. A Ranger splashed in front of Hoyle, grabbed the corpse by the hair, and dragged it toward the shore.

On the far bank, Hoyle approached Joaquin's body. One leg was angled back under his thigh, and his fist was still closed upon his rifle. He had been shot through more than a dozen times, and his blood puddled the gravel around him. The corpse of another guerrilla lay facedown behind Joaquin, the back of his head lopped off. Directed by a lieutenant, a dozen Rangers dragged the bodies down to the river and laid them together in a line. The backpacks were piled together as well. Salinas and his men exultantly counted coup.

Gustavo Merán walked up to Hoyle and stood surveying the carnage. "They fucked up," he said.

Hoyle looked around at the bodies dragged up onto the rocks, and the rucksacks lumped in a row, both leaking water where they had been shot through. Hoyle did not see that Joaquin's holster was empty.

None of the men saw Tania lying at the edge of the jungle, not five yards away. She had been shot once through the back, the bullet exiting her abdomen, about an inch above her pubic bone. Her guts burned, her legs were becoming numb, and blood dripped into her pockets. In the brush, Tania lifted Joaquin's pistol and aimed it squarely at Hoyle's back. Her head swam with the agony of her wound and with the twin horrors of the ambush and her survival. She did not care if she lived or died, and she thumbed back the hammer and her eyes blurred with hatred. Tania leveled the weapon, and her hands shook, but still she held it evenly, and as she squeezed the trigger, there was an enormous explosion in front of her face.

In the same instant that the pistol discharged, Captain Salinas stepped forward and kicked Tania under the chin. The bullet slammed into the rocks at Hoyle's feet, and the ricochet screeched off into the trees. Merán and Hoyle both jerked toward the sound of the shot, their rifles aimed, before they saw the captain standing over Tania.

Hoyle watched Salinas kick Tania again in the chest; as she tumbled back, he stomped the pistol from her hand. He kicked her again, and she let out a sickening moan, more in defeat than in physical pain.

Hoyle walked over—it was only three steps—and realized gradually that the bullet she'd fired had been meant for him. Tania lay curled into a ball, her hands and abdomen covered in black-colored blood. She had her arms wrapped around her head, and she was sobbing, a low, muffled sound. Hoyle would remember to the end of his life the sight of Tania crumpled against the rocks. Her skin was pale, almost translucent; she looked like some sort of luminous child.

It was inexplicable that Hoyle had not been killed. Tania's shot had been point-blank.

Salinas bent down and recovered the pistol. He let the hammer go forward under his thumb and snapped the safety on. He handed the weapon to Hoyle. "You should shoot this fucking bitch," he said.

Hoyle looked at the weapon in his hand and then at Tania weeping. His skin crawled. The pistol shot had been so close that he'd heard the spent cartridge jingle onto the rocks. That sound was forever seared into memory, and now, oddly, Hoyle wished that Tania had not missed.

55

T O THE SURPRISE of everyone, Tania clung to life. She had been carried into an abandoned farmhouse about an hour from the river and spent the night covered in Hoyle's poncho on a pallet a few inches off the dirt floor. Hoyle and the Ranger medic did what they could for her, which was little. Tania was cleaned and her wound bandaged, but the medic was not well trained and, frankly, cared little about his patient. She needed the attentions of a surgeon, and it was obvious that without medical care, she would succumb to shock, blood loss, and eventually, sepsis. At midnight Hoyle prevailed on the medic to administer a dose of morphine. With this, Tania slept, and Hoyle took up a vigil.

The first light came in cold gray bands above the tops of the hills, and the dawn was astonishingly cold. When the sun came at last, creeping in dreary inches over the valley, Hoyle walked outside the farmhouse and stretched. The Rangers had moved for the landing zone, taking with them the guerrillas' dead, the corpses wrapped up in tarps and carried in triumph. Charlie appeared at midmorning, having driven to the end of the road from Vallegrande. He brought a note from Smith, congratulating Hoyle on the ambush and advising that he, Valdéz, and Famous Lawyer were now operating with a second company of Rangers in the northeasternmost quadrant of the valley. As

Hoyle read, Charlie looked in to see the woman on the pallet, barely breathing and perfectly, dreadfully still.

"What are we going to do?" Charlie asked.

"I'm not sure we can move her."

Hoyle folded the note and placed it in the pocket of his field vest. The words congratulating him on the ambush made him feel somehow dissolute and malicious, more like a criminal than a victor.

A small group of Indians passed the abandoned farm. They saw Hoyle and Charlie, so obviously people not of this place, and of course they knew that one of the wounded from the fight at the river was inside the house. Word of the ambush had spread almost the length of the valley. Hoyle watched as they passed, the men in shabby jackets and hats leading a pair of mules. No one spoke a greeting, or any other words, and as the grayness lifted from the ground, Hoyle and Charlie thought themselves a long way from the way things were supposed to go. Hoyle was at a loss, and Charlie wore a thin, indecipherable frown, the expression of a man who expects a bad thing to befall him at any moment.

"Everyone knows she is here," Charlie said. "What if the second guerrilla column appears? What if they try to rescue her?"

"If we move her, she'll die."

"Why do you care if she dies?"

Charlie's question surprised Hoyle with its candor. What did it matter if Tania died? She had broken their agreement, even if she had been only a party to it and not a principal in it. It was a flat miracle that she had survived the whirlwind of bullets. A muzzle aimed an inch to the left, a ricochet off the rocks, and she would be just another of the tarpaulin bundles being ferried back to the Ranger camp, her corpse a trophy for officers to preen around.

"I made a deal," Hoyle said, "to get her out."

"If we can't move her, how do we get her out?"

"I don't know."

Charlie had never seen Hoyle without a firm course of action, a plan, or a means to an end. He saw the lines in the corners of Hoyle's eyes, and for the first time, he noticed Hoyle's shoulders were stooped. Perhaps this was from the long time he had been without sleep. Charlie looked up into the hills. The sounds of birds and insects were just beginning. In the jungle around them, things warmed by the thin sun started to move and make noise.

"I have a cousin in Vallegrande," Charlie said, "he's a doctor. I can bring him here."

"You have a lot of cousins, Charlie."

"You need a lot of help, Mr. Hoyle."

"What kind of doctor is this cousin of yours?"

"Expensive," Charlie said.

Hoyle took the Rolex wristwatch off his arm and placed it in Charlie's hand. "Get him here."

MOVING WEST, TRAVELING alternately by day and short, arduous movements during the night, Guevara's column reached the village of Pujio, in a place where the departments of Santa Cruz, Chuquisaca, and Cochabamba come together. The previous day they had passed through the village of Loma Larga and had found it completely deserted. The inhabitants had scattered, afraid of both the guerrillas and army reprisal. In half a dozen places in the valley, civilians had been arrested on suspicion of selling provisions to the *insurgentes;* several men who'd been coopted to serve as guides had disappeared into police custody.

It was becoming common for the guerrillas to come upon deserted houses, though fires burned and pots bubbled within. As the column moved north and west, the people who did not flee became increasingly sullen. When the guerrillas did make contact, men and women seemed as uncomprehending and uncaring as clay. Rumor of the ambush on the river had spread from village to village, but none of the peasants encountered by the column spoke of it. Very few wanted to speak to them at all.

At dawn the column reached the town of Picacho and the highest altitude they had yet reached, almost seven thousand feet. Guevara had been in pain and had been vomiting. He slouched into the village on the back of the red mare, but as the sun got higher in the sky, the strength returned to his cramped limbs. The peasants of the village, a small place of about fifty houses, had been preparing for a wedding, and they turned out to stare at the guerrillas with a mixture of dread and fascination. It was learned quickly that the *corregidor* had left to warn the police that the guerrillas were nearby. As a reprisal, Guevara ordered that everything in his small grocery store be seized, though he had a lengthy receipt prepared and had Inti sign it as "commander" of the ELN.

Over a transistor radio came a broadcast in which Presidente Barrientos announced that Joaquin's column had been wiped out. Guevara did not believe this. There was another bulletin, this one describing a series of supply caves uncovered by the army, and the details were so precise as to leave no doubt that the story was true. It was obvious that someone had talked. The radio chattered on about documents and photographs but, more important, about medicines, food, and ammunition. Guevara and Inti were questioned about the broadcast by the village's schoolteacher, a thin man with eager, searching eyes. The teacher asked if news of the ambush was true, and both Inti and Guevara denied it. They thought it was impossible and reminded the teacher that the army had claimed to have wiped out the guerrillas many times over. The news of Joaquin's annihilation was dismissed as propaganda. The teacher had watched when the news of the supply caves was discussed, and he noted with a foxy sort of glee that it seemed to depress every one of the guerrillas who heard the news.

The way ahead to the village of La Higuera was open, and the hills and ridges looking down on Picacho were almost devoid of cover. Though it was daylight, and though they could be observed from the ridges above, Guevara ordered the column to continue moving. Miguel and Begnino exchanged glances but said nothing. Guevara had cursed when he heard of the discovery of the supply caves, and no one dared to further his wrath. Other factors also urged a quick departure; several of the comrades were sick, among them Moro, who also had to ride on a mule, and El Chino, who was nearly blind at night and was suffering from diarrhea and debilitating pain in his back. Tomorrow a decision was to be made about what to do with the invalids. It was thought best to move as far and fast as possible in daylight.

The forward detachment made slightly better time up the sketchy road, and the column strung out in a long line. The men of the center group moved slowly along with the pack animals, the comrades bent almost double under rucksacks filled with booty from the grocery store. Guevara dismounted and walked the final leg into the village of La Higuera, leading the red mare and carrying his rifle.

Mountains touched by cloud and blue loomed over the little town, a sad collection of a dozen or so adobe houses clustered around three dusty alleyways. Begnino, Miguel, and Inti were among the first to enter the village. They immediately sensed that something was wrong.

The men of La Higuera had all fled, and flitting between the houses was only a small number of women and children. Guevara ordered Coco to investigate the telegraph office. A search of the desk found a telegram dated a few days earlier; in it, the subprefect of Vallegrande had asked the *corregidor* to forward at once news about guerrilla presence in the region. The telegram reiterated the story of the ambush at Vado del Yeso, claiming that Joaquin's entire column had been liquidated. Guevara was shown the telegram and read it blandly.

The mayor's wife was located and brought forward, a small, stuttering woman in a faded yellow skirt. She trembled as she spoke and assured Inti that her husband had not answered the telegram about the guerrillas because there was a celebration in the town of Jagüey, and he had gone there to witness a baptism. A man was located in a cowshed behind the small school building. He claimed to know nothing about the movement of the army, where the mayor had gone, or even if it was actually daylight. His brown toes curled in the dirt as he spoke. Like the woman, the man was extremely nervous, but Guevara attributed his fear to propaganda spread by the army. He let the man go, despite the fact that he was obviously untrustworthy.

As the afternoon started, the heavens seemed to open and close; the sun rode occasionally in the blue parts of the sky and then was swallowed by gray. Though the wind blew, the air did not seem clean. The town had about it the smell of sweat and pig shit. Guevara had hoped to camp somewhere in the vicinity, but the mood of the place alerted a well-tuned sense of danger.

Guevara stood for a few moments by the doorway of the telegraph office. From inside he heard the sounds of sobs, and almost without thinking, he opened the door and stepped into the house. The office was a little dark room, with a crudely made two-level desk that held the telegraph. Twisted in helixes, old cloth-covered wires dipped from the ceiling and onto the desk. The telegraph itself was rusted, the key and sounder both made of tarnished bits of metal. It seemed a thing out of the previous century. In a corner of the office, an old woman rocked back and forth on the floor and cradled a little girl. The girl's arms and legs were bent and twisted, and her head seemed overlarge for her tiny body. As Guevara entered the room, the woman bowed her head like a dog expecting a blow, but the little girl's eyes held him; she did not blink or turn away. Constant pain had altered the child's face, making it grave and wise. The old woman held the girl tightly, and as he came closer, Guevara saw that the girl could not walk on her own. He knelt in front of the woman and tried to calm her as best he could.

"There," he said, "please, Señora, don't cry. There isn't any need."

The woman looked at him, her eyes were oily with tears. She was the telegraph operator's wife, and after the telegram had been found, she grew convinced that the guerrillas would return and murder her. She did not know anything but simple brutality, and her life had made good on her every dream of it.

"Please do not kill us," she managed to choke.

"Señora, we will not hurt you."

As Guevara squatted by the desk in front of them, a bitter perception came to him: *There is no need to harm these people. The world is killing them.* This thought crossed his mobile face, and again the woman began to sob. Words came pouring out through great waves of tears: "My husband only writes down what comes to him on the telegraph. You must understand that. We do not want any trouble with anyone."

"I do not blame you for trouble," Guevara said.

Beyond the open door of the office, he could hear the mules clomping by on the dirt streets; it was time to move out. He shifted off his rucksack and opened the top flap, then took out a small clutch of silver Bolivianos and pressed them into the woman's hand. It was hardly enough to feed her for even a couple of days, and some of the coins fell through her fingers and dropped silently onto the hard dirt floor.

"Will you take this money for me? In return, I ask only that you do me a small favor."

The woman's gaze was lowered; she did not look Guevara in the face, but the little dwarf girl stared at him, her eyes at once limpid and piercing.

"All I'd like you to do is promise me that you will ask your husband not to use the telegraph until the sun is down."

He repeated himself, slowly and gently; the woman kept sobbing, and he could not tell how much she heard.

"You don't need to be afraid of us," he said.

"But the army—" The word seemed to be the most terrible one she knew, and it came hesitantly off her lips, like an obscenity.

Guevara stood and pulled the telegraph wires from the wall. The porcelain insulators that held the wires came away from the ceiling in a brown dusting of stucco. He disconnected them from the rusty telegraph clacker and placed the device in the hands of the little girl.

"Tell them I destroyed the telegraph," he said. "You will be all right."

He pulled on his pack and lifted his rifle from the desk where he had placed it. At that moment the woman reached out and took Guevara's fingers in her own; her lips touched his hand, as she would have kissed the hand of a bishop, and the child's eyes opened and glared at him, the tiny body jerking with a wrench of pain. The woman let go of his hand and sobbed, *"Gracias, gracias."*

As Guevara ducked under the small door, he looked back into the room. The little girl was holding the disconnected telegraph and watching him with stony patience.

Willy and Pombo were outside the door, smoking cigarettes taken that morning from the grocery store. Guevara ordered the forward detachment to continue uphill and to take the rutted track toward Jagüey. For good measure, he reinforced the point, sending along an additional pair of riflemen.

At the edge of the village, the forward detachment passed a small adobe. As they did, a teenage girl and a young child ran from the back of the house; though called on to stop, they galloped quickly downhill and disappeared among the jumbled-together houses. The girl was shrieking something as she ran, her voice high and panicky.

Julio said, "Women love me," and Coco laughed. Miguel walked past a horse trough in front of the house and turned around for a moment to walk backward. "Check it," he said.

Closest to the door, Coco lifted the rude wooden bar that served as the latch. Julio went in first, holding his weapon in both hands, calling out, saying not to be afraid. He had expected to find the remainder of the family, and his eyes fell first on a chola woman standing at the back of the small room. She was shaking her head and lifting her hands to her face. Coco came in behind Julio, and his shadow fell into the small dark room, making it darker still. Julio saw the woman, and there was a quick, sharp movement in a doorway off the main room.

These things happened in half an instant:

Coco saw the muzzle of a gun, a rifle lifting up out of the shadows. He could see the front sights on the end of the barrel, three splayed pieces of metal swinging up in an arc. The weapon was an M2 carbine, the exact weapon he carried, and for that reason, he perceived no danger at first. The woman screamed, and Coco was amazed when a Ranger came out of the shadows in the back of the house. The man was tall and dressed in a green fatigue uniform. Around his arms and legs, pieces of black tape held bunches of grass and straw as camouflage. These gave the soldier the look of a malevolent, busted-open scarecrow. The Ranger's face was painted in black, green, and tan stripes, and as he lifted his rifle, it seemed to Coco that his eyes were yellow. The explosion of the weapon thudded in the small space of the adobe, and the noise was like a great series of thumps. An opaque white flash spilled out the end of the Ranger's weapon. His first two bullets struck the wall between Coco and Julio, and the third smashed through Coco's abdomen, square through the belt buckle. He was blown off his feet and fell through the door into the dusty alley in front of the house.

Julio was astounded by a ripping noise and then the banging flutter of point-blank automatic fire. He saw another Ranger, and another, all of them with their faces green and eyes like bogeymen. Julio managed to push forward the safety on his weapon, but not to fire. Two bullets struck him in the chest, and with a yelp, he turned, staggering for the door. Two more bullets found him, and he collapsed on the threshold, a geyser of blood spraying the wall from a wound to the side of his neck.

Outside the house, the noise of the first shots was muffled, a thudding series of bangs. Miguel turned in the street and saw Coco tumble backward through the doorway and into the dirt. He stepped toward his wounded friend, and their eyes met, but a bullet was fired through the front window of the house, and this struck Miguel in the center of his knee. He pitched forward; he had not yet seen a single enemy soldier. His leg crumpled beneath him, and he crawled forward to Coco, shouting. He could see Julio sprawled in the doorway, his body and the overburdened rucksack blocking the door, and he could see shadows moving in the house.

More gunfire came through the window, and the muzzle of a rifle poked through the door. As Miguel saw the rifle dip and fire two more bullets into Julio, he managed to drag Coco behind the horse trough. Bullets ripped through the wood, and the water went up in thin fingers. Miguel could now see Begnino pushing his way toward them. Begnino squeezed a long burst of automatic fire at the front of the house, and the shooting stopped within. He made it to the trough, slung his rifle over his shoulder, and grabbed Coco and Miguel by the back of their collars. He did not say a word, just pulled them off their asses and dragged them around the corner across the street. As they neared the corner of the buildings, shooting started again, and Begnino yelled down the street for covering fire.

Guevara ran across the small open space in front of the telegraph office and found shelter behind the steps of a small house. The sound of the ambush at first seemed to paralyze the comrades. The noise echoed through the several houses, and no one could see from where the shots were being fired or by whom. Guevara's mind became clear, as it always did when there was fighting, and the drab colors of the little town grew vivid in his eyes. The sky became like a vast jewel split open above him, the clouds and sunlight suddenly brilliant; he could smell the sharp tang of powder and hear a steady firing of bursts. Crouching, he moved forward against the wall, down two small houses, and toward the corner. A pulse of fire smashed through the adobe over his head, knocking him back and sending a cloud of powdered brick from the side of the building. There was shouting, and he bent around the corner and tried to figure out who was firing. He saw Begnino drag two men away from the horse trough and around the corner. It looked as though he'd done so out of exhaustion or because he had tripped, but then Guevara saw Begnino flinch and scramble back close up against the wall; he could see in his face a flash of confusion and pain. Begnino, too, had been shot—a bullet had grazed his shoulder—and he took cover against the wall, shaking his head and cursing.

The three wounded men were for the next several moments safe. The column surged through the village toward the sound of fire and took cover around Guevara. A steady barrage was put into the small adobe, and the front of the building was pocked thoroughly. The Rangers inside took cover, one of them sprawling flat behind the body of Julio, still wedged in the front door. Begnino and Coco were dragged back toward the telegraph office. As Guevara and Willy moved forward to bring Miguel to safety, a dozen bullets plunged out of the sky, knocking up dust around them. Miguel jerked and went limp between them, his rifle falling from his hands.

Guevara looked up. It was as though the bullets had rained out of thin air. On the ridge above the village, he saw a dozen more soldiers, moving and shooting; another group was across the road leading to Jagüey and taking cover in a horse corral on the other side. A deadly, plunging fire would soon envelop the entire town. Guevara dragged Willy away from Miguel's body, and they pulled Coco into the safety of the telegraph office.

Guevara slammed and barricaded the door. On the dirt floor, the wounded man twitched in a widening pool of blood, his breath wheezing out between pursed gray lips. Willy was opening a first-aid kit, fumbling with a bandage in a brown plastic package, but it was obvious to all that Coco's wound was mortal. In the corner of the room, the old woman and the dwarf girl cowered in terror.

"We have to move," Guevara said, "back down the road—downhill into cover."

Coco writhed on the floor, gushing blood. Begnino clutched him helplessly. Willy continued to unwrap the bandage, fixed on the idea of somehow fixing Coco.

Guevara said, "Begnino and I will take Coco. Get the others—"

"No," Coco gasped, "not me." He was wet from the waist down, soaked to the skin with gore.

"Hang on, friend," Guevara said, "we're going to take you back to the horses."

"It's over, Comandante," Coco said. His voice was choked; his throat was filling up with blood. "Forget me."

With astonishing deftness, Coco pulled the pistol from Guevara's holster, thumbed back the hammer, and shot himself in the head. Spattered by gore, Willy crabbed backward. The sound of the weapon was so crashing and unexpected that it was not immediately comprehended that Coco had taken his own life.

In the corner of the room, the old woman wailed, an inarticulate paroxysm of horror. Begnino's legs gave out under him; he slid down against the wall and swooned forward. Pistol smoke curled through the slanting light like the horrible evaporation of a nightmare.

For a few incomprehensible seconds, the shadows of the three men set on Coco's body. Just an instant before, he had been their friend and a comrade, and only five minutes ago, he had walked and laughed with all the world of life in him. His fingers gave a spasm and then he moved no more.

In the next instant, a burst of gunfire tore through the door, wood chips and dust roiled into the gloomy space, and bullets cracked everywhere against the walls. Everyone went to the floor, and it seemed almost as though the house were being shaken by a gigantic hand.

Guevara reloaded his carbine, and the others sat speechless in shock. Guevara alone seemed to remember that they were locked in battle.

"Get your squad. I'll cover you."

Begnino looked up, his face twisted into a grotesque blank.

"Head downslope for the ravine."

Guevara kicked at Begnino. When he did not look away from Coco's body, Guevara kicked him harder. *"Do what I say!"* he bellowed.

Guevara lifted the pistol from the dirt next to Coco's fingers and returned it to his holster. Across the street, he could see Pombo framed in a window. He whistled loudly and waved for him and the others to withdraw. Pombo nodded in response and pointed back into the village, toward the place the road came in from Picacho.

"Leave the dead," Guevara barked. "Take the ammunition from their packs."

Begnino and Willy did as they were told, their bloody fingers removing magazines and bandoliers from the two dead men. Carrying their weapons and this extra ammunition, they pushed through the office and climbed out a window in the back. Guevara leaped after them, his foot splashing in a black puddle of Coco's blood.

The old woman and the dwarf girl sat and rocked, sat and rocked; the woman muttered like an idiot, unhinged by violence.

Forever after in the village where she lived, the old woman would be called mad, and the little dwarf girl, the misshapen child with the luminous eyes, she would stay mute until the day she died.

THE SOUND OF gunfire drifted up to the ridge above the little town. The firefight surged and faded, rallied, and then finally sputtered out as the guerrillas took up their wounded and broke contact. Most of the village could be seen from the high ground—it was almost visible end to end—and Smith and Major Holland watched the Rangers move forward from their position at the horse corral and link up with the team that had hidden in the adobe at the edge of town.

Under a covering fire from a machine gun on the hill, a second squad of Rangers reached the center of the village and went from house to house. They signaled that the guerrillas were gone, having fled first down the Picacho road and then into the ravine that ran parallel to it, a place called Quebrada del Yuro, a densely vegetated, steep-sided draw that ran for about a mile north and south.

With their weapons slung in front of them, Smith and Major Holland made their way downhill and into the village. They watched Rangers turn over a body lying by the horse trough; others kicked open the doors of houses. Shouting, they moved women and children together into one of the dusty spaces between the houses, an alley near the center of the village. Three corpses were brought into the center place, guerrilla dead. The Ranger team from the adobe house was cheered by their compatriots.

The company commander was an unusually tall captain named Gerald Padero Cespedes. He had come with his radio operator from the road by the horse corral; his face was flushed, and he was euphoric. Like the other Rangers, he had black tape holding clutches of vegetation against his arms and legs for camouflage. It had been effective. Almost forty men had lain hidden in the short scrub on the hillsides above the village. The guerrillas had not seen a single Ranger until the men in the adobe opened fire.

Cespedes held the radio headset against his ear and listened; the radioman stood at the end of the cord and grinned.

"The guerrillas are withdrawing," the captain said. A highly professional demeanor did not contain his joy.

"You've done a superb job, Captain," Major Holland said.

"As long as they head downhill, I advise you not to pursue," Smith said to the captain. "Let them break contact."

Cespedes understood at once. The ridges around the Yuro ravine were devoid of cover. The guerrillas would be surrounded and sealed off. Holding the handset, he gave a few curt orders, and the crackle of radio receivers could be heard echoing from several places in the village.

Smith and Holland stood together and looked at the road twisting down and away from La Higuera.

"Who's on the other side of the ravine?" Smith asked.

"Sergeant Godshall. Lawyer Four."

Smith seemed to think for moment, looking at the terrain. "It's all over," he said.

Major Holland knelt by the body of Julio; the corpse had been dragged from the doorway and laid out in the street. In a dispassionate, clinical manner, Holland dropped the magazine from Julio's weapon and ejected a round from the chamber. He then went through the man's pockets and after that, the contents of his rucksack.

"Mr. Valdéz, stay with Captain Cespedes. I want all the other Lawyer units pulled back. The Bolivians will finish the operation."

Valdéz had just sauntered down off the hill. He'd been stationed next to the machine gunners concealed on the ridge and watched the engagement with barely constrained glee.

"What about the snipers?" he asked. "You want to keep them in?"

"Have Rangers take over the observation posts. This will be a Bolivian kill."

Holland returned from his search of Julio's body. He carried a thin spiral notepad and a map folded in squares and wrapped in wax paper. The map revealed the guerrillas' progress across the valley. On it, every camping spot was circled and dated. The penciled line ended at La Higuera.

"He's in a box, son," Holland said to Valdéz. "Houdini and a hard-on couldn't get out of that canyon. It's fucking over."

Valdéz removed three cigars from a case in his pocket. He handed one to Smith and one to Holland, and they lit them and smoked. No one said anything; it seemed a time for important words, and none came to tired men. The Rangers were now swarming over the place. They'd emerged from their hidden positions on the sides of hills, dozens and dozens more, and it once again seemed astounding to Smith that so many men had hidden, surrounding the village in plain sight. Every one of the Rangers knew that a victory had been won and that their enemy, so long successful, had been mauled and was at bay.

Valdéz walked toward the last house at the edge of the village. He looked off down the sloping road and into the canyon of Quebrada del Yuro. It was a bad, wild place.

That's where they belong, he thought. Fucking *putos*.

56

HOYLE'S NAP-DREAM was full of whispering shadows; the dreamscape around him gradually became blue, shot through with slanting rays of light, the fearsome hue of deep ocean water. In the dream, Hoyle was a victim of shipwreck and saw Maria floating among the wreckage. He swam to her as she sank, and he dived after her, deeper and deeper into blue desolation. Her hair bloomed around her face, that unmatched, beautiful face, and her eyes implored him to rescue her, but he was drawn away by some current. His hands briefly grappled her, held her, but she was pulled from his grasp and sank down into cobalt.

Hoyle felt a sorrow worse than he could have ever imagined. He had thought himself inoculated against grief, for he'd seen a thousand tragedies, but the dream imparted a suffocating sense of dread and then desolation and loss. Hoyle woke with his shoulder blades against the dank stucco of the abandoned farmhouse and sat completely still. It was late afternoon, and he'd been yanked from this dream by the repeated noise of a crow. His arms and legs were cramped, and a clammy sweat had soaked though his shirt and vest.

He pulled his legs under himself and stood. He'd slept barely an hour, he guessed, only long enough for his muscles to cramp and his head to be made foggy. Tania lay on the pallet with her eyes closed.

The yellow sunlight sloped through the doorway and gave her skin the cast of an alabaster saint. It was so still and quiet in the small farmhouse that it seemed to Hoyle all the earth had stopped spinning and nothing anywhere would ever move again.

Hoyle turned when he heard footfalls, and it took a few long seconds to register that the man standing framed in the doorway was not Charlie but Colonel Arquero. The colonel had a Mauser pistol in his hand, and next to him stood a plainclothed policeman who carried a short, jagged-looking machine pistol. Hoyle took a step backward. His own rifle leaned against the wall next to Tania, and it was a hopeless fantasy to even think he could reach it.

"Put your hands up," Arquero said.

There was an unaccountable note of civility in the colonel's voice. The policeman had stepped completely into the room and leveled his weapon at Hoyle. He was a mestizo with black eyes like voids; there was no doubt that he would shoot Hoyle down, and casually, so Hoyle lifted his hands.

Charlie appeared behind Arquero and stood self-possessed. He had the wan look of a betrayer but gazed steadily at Hoyle, not averting his eyes though watching haughtily, as if trying to make a judgment.

"You look surprised, Mr. Hoyle," Arquero said. "It's an expression I find amusing."

"Is this your cousin, Charlie?" Hoyle said.

Charlie's expression did not change, nor did he turn away. "I'm sorry, Mr. Hoyle. This was business." His voice was full and clear, as though he felt no shame for giving Hoyle to his enemy. Charlie acted as if what he had done was for the good of everyone.

Colonel Arquero handed a wad of green-yellow Bolivianos to Charlie and dismissed him with a feline tap of his wrist. Charlie slipped the money into his pocket and glided away through the door.

Hoyle could see the shiny faces of the weapons' muzzles and black down their barrels; it seemed as though the gun barrels held fast small chunks of night.

"We had quite a complicated ambush waiting for you on the road to Vallegrande," Arquero said. "You really would have approved." The colonel's eyes brushed to Tania. "But since you wouldn't come to us, we came to you." He aimed the pistol down at the woman's face.

"She's dead," Hoyle said. Death had come for Tania in the last hour before dawn. So gently had life slipped out of her that she had only once dreamed of paradise, and she was there.

The policeman nudged Hoyle back with the muzzle of the machine gun, and Arquero put his fingers to Tania's throat. She was cold and her skin was damp. A small exhalation came from Arquero, the noise of a suppressed grunt, and his eyes seemed to close slightly in thought. The expression on his face was strangely bored, though the corner of his lip bent in exactly one half of a smile.

"I'm sure you made every attempt to live up to your ridiculous bargain, Mr. Hoyle. You do impress me as a very earnest type." Arquero waved his pistol at the door. "Now," he said, "you will carry her body to the river, and then we will go for a ride."

THE ROAD TO Vallegrande got better the closer they drove to town, and eventually, it leveled out and became paved. Hoyle sat in the backseat, his hands bound in front of him. The policeman drove the familiar route, and Arquero leaned over the front seat, keeping the pistol trained at Hoyle's chest. They were driving toward the airfield and the casita. Hoyle's place of refuge would be no place of safety. All of the Green Berets of Famous Lawyer were with Smith in the field, and the house was empty.

"It occurs to me, Mr. Hoyle, that you were particularly unsuited for this assignment."

"You know, I guess I have been insufficiently ruthless."

"Don't flatter yourself." The colonel's arm draped over the car seat carelessly, but the ugly muzzle of the gun remained steady. Arquero had seen through the masked interrogation and correctly ascertained the parties behind his blackmail. He had done this shortly after his abduction by determining who had benefited from his coercion. His revenge on Hoyle had been long in gestation and meticulous in its preparation.

"Did you really think I'd be taken by your ridiculous masquerade?"

"Why not? This whole country's a goddamn Halloween party."

At Hoyle's condescension, the policeman's dark, blank eyes rose to the rearview mirror. The brutality in them was distinct.

"As much as I'd enjoy prolonging your end, it will be sufficient that your body be found at your headquarters in Vallegrande."

"Executed by the guerrillas, of course."

Arquero smiled. "A dozen witnesses will swear that your compound was set upon by a column of insurgents." He made an impudent, malicious gesture indicating impending murder. "The intrepid military adviser, killed in the service of his country. After the trouble you've been, at least you can be of some propaganda value to me."

The car drove on, its tires humming on the pavement. Now and again a rock cast itself up under the fenders with a bang.

"For that detestable bitch." Arquero shook his head. "How could this be worth it?"

Hoyle was silent, but he asked himself: For which woman had he given his life, Maria or Tania?

"You could have stayed on the right side of this."

"Which side was that, Arquero? The bloodthirsty bastards in the mountains or the bloodthirsty bastards in La Paz?"

"You are an ass." Arquero sniffed. "What great plans you must have had. How wonderful you must have felt to intend so much good."

At the side of the road, garbage blew into the air as the car sped past. When they came close to town, there were shanties on the right and left of the roadway, and people were about, the poorest people, who lived on the edges of civilization. The car slowed to take the oblique turn onto the road toward the airfield, and as the driver braked, a clutch of beggars moved toward the car. A boy of about fifteen stepped into the road that joined the highway, and the policeman leaned on the horn. Almost indifferently, two beggars lobbed their rags at the windshield.

It was a peculiar thing that Hoyle so closely watched the rags fly at the car. He noticed that they seemed heavy and sluggish in the air, and they smacked into the windshield, one at eye level with the driver and the second landing with a slap in the center of the hood. The rags were smeared heavily with axle grease. Wrapped in each bit of cloth was a single stick of dynamite, of the type miners used, a short red waxy cylinder. A lit section of time fuse sputtered from each of the explosive charges.

The first of the rags slid off the windshield and bounced onto the roadway behind the car. Hoyle saw the smoldering fuse tumble past the rear window. He watched the beggars flatten on the ground, and he saw the tallest one throw off a poncho to reveal the long crescent-shaped magazine of an assault rifle.

Fuse crackling, the second charge remained plastered to the hood of the car, less than a foot away from the driver. The policeman stood on the brakes, a gesture of instinctive futility, and Hoyle threw himself to the right, onto his shoulder. He curled onto the backseat and covered his face with his arms.

The first charge detonated behind the car, and the vehicle seemed to lurch up and to the right. A hot gust of noise surged against Hoyle, an overwhelming concussion, and in the millisecond it took to screw closed his eyes, the shock wave blew into the backseat and Hoyle perceived a jolt of starlight.

The second stick of dynamite then detonated against the hood of the car.

An orange ball of fire burst against the windshield, propelling a thousand cubes of shattered glass in front of it. The explosion tore off the hood, the roof buckled up, and the policeman was struck in the face by a piece of molten high-velocity metal. He was killed instantly.

Driverless, the burning car rolled back onto the highway and toward the median. It crossed the road, trailing white smoke, and came to rest upright in a ditch on the other side of the opposing lane.

His uniform jacket blown into ribbons, Arquero was thrown toward the steering wheel. He was knocked temporarily senseless by the blast, and his pistol skittered out of his hand and across the dashboard. In the backseat, Hoyle was whipped forward heavily as the car lurched to a halt. He pulled his bound wrists over the back of the seat and looped his wrists over Arquero's head. Pulling his bonds against the colonel's throat, Hoyle jerked back with all his might. Arquero's head snapped back, and his breath escaped in a sharp, guttural roar. Hoyle pulled tighter, strangling as best he could. Arquero struggled forward, and his outstretched fingers swung toward the dashboard. The pistol lay there, jammed under a layer of shattered glass. Fire now leaped from the engine; oil and fuel took light and spread across the entire front of the vehicle.

Arquero put his hand directly into the flames. The blood on his hands sputtered as his fingers closed over the weapon. Arquero whipped the pistol over his shoulder and cranked off a shot backward at Hoyle.

The muzzle blast engulfed Hoyle's face. The light was violent, unbearable, more astounding than any of the explosions or the fire. For the second time in fifteen seconds, he lost all sensation in his body. The bullet ripped past his face and tore through the roof above his head.

Hoyle lifted his bound hands, struggling with Arquero for control of the weapon—blood poured in a solid wave from a powder-burned gash in his face. Hoyle could see only in outlined smudges of light. The pistol pointed up, then to the right, and slowly, Arquero gained control of it. He turned in the seat and levered his arm down. Hoyle could still not see anything but a painful brilliance—in this aching glare, he felt Arquero wrenching his fingers backward. Arquero pushed down on Hoyle's wrists, and slowly, the muzzle of the pistol turned at Hoyle's chest.

Charlie then appeared at the passenger-side window. He jammed the barrel of a short revolver against Arquero's ear and fired a bullet point-blank into the colonel's head. Spitting blood, Arquero jerked forward, and his arms flailed wildly, like a machine out of control. He flapped onto the burning dashboard.

Hoyle fell backward onto the seat. The back doors of the car were pried open and Hoyle was dragged away from the flaming wreck.

Half-blind, half-conscious, Hoyle was not sure of what he saw. The beggars, all of them, carried pistols or rifles. They had thrown off their jackets, and red strips of cloth were tied around their arms above the elbow. Hoyle recognized their weapons as Russian and the armbands as the symbol and uniform of Communist militants. Hoyle saw Charlie waving his pistol. He heard shouts, and a joyous sort of growling came from the men surging around the burning car. Trembling, astonished, Hoyle could barely raise his arms and was unable to resist as he was jerked across the two-lane and onto the dirt road. He tried to bring his legs under him, but the men continued to pull him across the pavement.

Hoyle's ears buzzed, and it seemed like the light of the sun was being poured onto the road around him. The hands came off his body, and the men carrying guns stepped back and away from him. Light came from everywhere; it was as if he'd looked into the sun. He saw that Charlie was there. Again Hoyle could see an expression of restraint, almost of world-weariness, on his face. With his pistol, Charlie waved the others away, and then Hoyle remembered nothing more.

THE DOCTOR'S NAME was Anias. Long after dark, he came up to a small house perched on a steep hillside outside the village of Domasco. The door to the house was guarded by a thin man who held a pistol and a lantern, and when the door opened halfway, the physician scooted in like a burglar. Charlie had told him only that the patient was a gringo and that he had been in an accident. Anias came into the house and found Hoyle lying on a straw mat with his eyes closed. One arm was draped over his face, and when Anias gently moved it, Hoyle did not stir but remained unconscious. It could not readily be told if the patient was alive or dead, and Anias bent down and listened to hear the sound of Hoyle breathing. He could smell blood and cordite. Anias cleaned out gunpowder from a gash on Hoyle's face and bandaged one eye tightly. Dr. Anias was not at all certain that Hoyle would regain sight in his right eye. The burns on his face seemed to indicate that he had been struck by lightning, a man punished by God, and Anias did what small things he could for his patient.

Hoyle remained unconscious for most of the doctor's ministering. Outside, it began to rain, and the sound of it against the cobbles and tile roofs was first a whisper and then a steady drone. Hoyle licked the blood from his lips, and his unbandaged eye flicked open. He could not move at first, and he ached over his entire body. He could see no farther than a small blotch of lamplight, but he detected shadows shifting in the room around him, and he heard Charlie's voice, whispering the low tones all of mankind uses around the sick.

Hoyle heard someone say, "I closed the wound to his face. But there's damage to the retina. He's going to have to be kept still."

"How long?"

"A couple of days."

A door opened somewhere, and the sound of the rain surged into the room. Hoyle's knees bent in an attempt to roll over, but he gave up. Bit by bit, the things he could see with his left eye began to make sense: He saw a table and a chair and the pile of mats he was lying on. Hoyle touched his face and felt the bandage plastered over his right eye. A pain beat around his skull as though a bird were trapped inside.

Charlie sat across from the rack of mats. His legs were stretched out in front of him, and his ankles were crossed. There was a rifle across his lap, and his hands rested on it with seeming impatience. He was hardly recognizable now, tougher, self-assured, a man who'd done good. When Hoyle stirred, Charlie casually lit a cigarette. The match flared at

the end of his fist, and the red band of cloth wrapped around his coat
sleeve glowed. Hoyle realized that he had never seen Charlie smoke.

"You," Hoyle said, "you're Bolivian Communist Party, aren't you?"

The rain crackled outside the window. Charlie drew on his cigarette
and did not answer for a few seconds. A silver-gray wisp of smoke
curled up from his hand and hung in the room like the beginning of
hate.

"I always have been a member of the Communist Party. Since before
I came to work for the embassy."

"No one knew," Hoyle said.

"No one asked."

The smell of the dank room came to Hoyle, as though the mats
hadn't been dry in a hundred years.

"Tell me something, Mr. Hoyle. Why should rich people live on ha-
ciendas when poor children are dying because they don't even have
clean water to drink?"

"I can't answer that, Charlie."

"Why are you fighting people in my country who are trying to do
something about it?"

Behind Charlie, Hoyle could see two other men with rifles, the same
men who had dragged him from the car. They stood in various attitudes of deference, listening to Charlie. It was slowly obvious that he
commanded them.

"Why did you help me?" Hoyle asked.

"You are just one person. Killing you would not kill what you stand
for." Charlie placed the rifle against the wall. "I don't know why I
thought it could ever be different," he said. "My Party is like my country. The Party intended good things. But it is broken at the top. It is
spoiled. By greed. By the love of power. The Party betrayed Che Guevara because they were ordered to by Moscow."

"Charlie—"

"Do not speak, Mr. Hoyle, listen. I was ordered to liquidate you by
the Party. They ordered me to betray you. There is still a death sentence on your head."

"Why did you save my life?"

"What does it matter?"

Hoyle's fists clenched; maybe it did not matter. "What will happen
to you? When the Party finds out you let me live?"

"I am just another Guaraní. Just another Indian. I can walk away. They won't find me." Charlie stepped on his cigarette. "The end has come. The Fourth Army has cordoned off La Higuera. The Rangers have cut off Che Guevara and seventeen others in a place called the Yuro ravine."

"Is he still alive?"

"I don't know."

Hoyle got up from the pile of mats and staggered to his feet. Lightning flashed behind his eyes, and a numbness seemed to jolt through his body. "I have to get there," he said. "How far is it to La Higuera?"

"Sixty kilometers. You won't make it in time."

"I won't make it if I don't try."

There were police patrols in the streets, and no one could be certain which of them were loyal to Colonel Arquero and would shoot Hoyle on sight. Hoyle was taken by Charlie and the armed men to a house on the steep side of the village, and a rope was tossed out the back window of a place overlooking the highway. Charlie's cousin Barnabas waited below with a jeep. As Hoyle prepared to lower himself down the rope, Charlie handed him a shabby roll of paper Bolivianos and the Rolex watch.

"You'll need this. Getting around the roadblocks can be expensive."

Hoyle looked at the roll of bills—it was the same money Charlie had been given by Arquero.

"I thought you said this was strictly business."

"This is Bolivia, Mr. Hoyle. This is how we do business."

57

LIKE PHANTOMS, THE column glided through the forest at the bottom of the canyon. And they were very nearly phantoms. For the pursuing Ranger companies, it was as though the guerrillas had been swallowed whole into *la selva*. When Guevara realized that the army was mounting pursuit, he ordered that the pack animals be set loose and driven back uphill. The mules and the red mare galloped up the road and through the ranks of soldiers sent down from La Higuera. This confounded the trackers, and then a black night descended, and the rain washed away any trace of the column or its retreat south and downhill into the Yuro ravine.

The column groped down the canyon, then away from the cursed village. In places, the gorge was steep-sided and narrow; other parts were wider, perhaps five hundred meters across, and cover at the bottom ranged from scruffy patches of brush to thick stands of jungle. Moving slowly, the guerrillas made only two kilometers through the entire night. Begnino's shoulder began to trouble him, and he was the first to fall behind. Moro was too sick to walk, and El Chino was now nearly night-blind; they fell behind as well. The stragglers became separated from the main group at about midnight, and the entire column had to wait while the rear guard searched for them.

When they again took up the march, Guevara could not tell for certain how far they had traveled, and he dared not use a light to consult his map. He was sure the Rangers would continue the chase at first light. They would have called for reinforcements, and their superiority in numbers would be magnified by yesterday's victory. Guevara felt it was best to go to ground and wait. He halted the column in a thick copse of jungle, and the comrades spread out and took cover.

Little by little the rain lifted, and the clouds directly above the canyon began to pull apart. The sun pinched itself above the eastern rim of the canyon, but the clouds there remained in a thick, intractable layer, and the light came only as a vague shade of gray. Over the western slopes, the sky opened, and powder blue was lit by flecks of orange and gold. Although the sun was in the east, the light came from the west, creeping gradually down the steep sides of the ravine. It was a sky that seemed entirely wrong, reversed obstinately, and to compound this perception, a bright silver moon sank through the clouds of the broadening day.

As the light came down upon them, Guevara was able to consult the map and orient himself. Across the southern end of the canyon, a steep, mostly barren rise barred their way; there was no hope of crossing the hill in daylight. The column could not retreat back toward La Higuera—the army was there in force—nor could they move off to the west to ascend a pair of adjoining canyons, as these were nearly devoid of cover. If they tried to continue south or west, the soldiers on the overlooking ridges would see them clearly; and if aircraft came, they would be surely cut to ribbons. The column was bottled up, and soon it would be surrounded. Guevara grasped that he was in the worst tactical position of his life.

None of the comrades knew that as they'd passed down the canyon, a farmer had seen them, dark shapes lurching through rain. He'd seen their packs and weapons; the old man knew the canyon well, and he knew how far the guerrillas might go and the few places that they might find water or take shelter. He had sent his son pattering up the trail to La Higuera to warn the army, and the news reached Captain Salinas of the Rangers just as Guevara was making his morning arrangements.

At daybreak Guevara decided to break the column into three groups. Antonio and four others would be posted in a thicketed belt halfway up the western slope, and Pombo was to take his group to positions on the east side of the ravine. Guevara, Willy, and two others would stay with the sick in a stand of jungle at the bottom. Seventeen men altogether hidden in ragged insufficient cover.

The water and ammunition were divided up equally, and Guevara spoke to the comrades of their predicament. "I am not going to insult you with a pep talk. Our odds are not very good.

"Today we'll not seek to fight the enemy. Our positions will never hold. We'll lay up until dark, then try to slip out the bottom of the canyon."

A ring of anxious faces stared back at him.

"If we have contact, I will move toward the east ridge and hold them off as long as I can. We'll regroup on the other side of the hill to the south. Everyone who breaks the encirclement should find cover and wait there. Then we'll head northeast, toward Cochabamba and the border."

The noise of an airplane droned over them. They could not see it through the trees and the clouds, but it was an indication that the army knew where they were. The pink had gone out of the sky, and it would be full daylight soon. No one knew what to say, none of the comrades wanted to bring bad luck by wishing good luck or saying goodbye. Guevara looked around at the faces: How many times, in how many places, had he faced calamity with these same men? He had always before managed to smother defeat, and it was almost impossible for him to imagine anything but victory. In Oriente, in Santa Clara, in all of the Sierra Maestra, he had faced long odds. He had faced defeat in the Congo, and he had lived to write history. He still believed, that was obvious, and on this morning it was enough. One by one, the comrades each came up to him and shook his hand. Some embraced him. When they touched him, it was as though they were trying to capture some of the faith, the certainty, and the self-belief that had brought him so far. They did this, every one of them, even Begnino, who was wounded, and Moro, who could barely stand. They were all still the faithful, sharing a commitment to the Idea. Now, in silent affirmation, they dedicated themselves to Che Guevara and to what would come.

As the comrades dispersed into their hides, Guevara felt suddenly exhausted, and his chin drooped against the front of his fatigue shirt. As the comrades stole away, he did not watch them leave but sat in silence, weighing again the tactical situation. He thought if the column could evade contact until the afternoon, they stood a chance. They could fight until the light was gone, and in darkness the advantage was still theirs. But if they were discovered early, if the Rangers found them and began the battle in the morning, it would not be likely that they could hold out. Guevara wrapped his arms around his rifle, cradling it, and slumped against a tree. The last of the food had gone away when the mules were set loose, and his stomach grumbled. He contented himself with a slow pull of water from his canteen and tried to put out of mind the consequences of failure.

The morning passed quietly, and the damp cold went out of Guevara's bones a little. The sun came down almost vertically into the canyon, and the clouds scudded away from it. Huddled in a band of trees that offered concealment but little cover, Guevara listened to the wind rolling downslope and another airplane passing lazily overhead. When the wind shifted slightly to the south, all he could hear was a series of shouted commands coming from the ridges—the Rangers had arrived.

Willy and El Chino looked carefully at the comandante, but his face betrayed nothing. The comrades around him took some courage from this, and Guevara removed a notepad from his pack and wrote several dozen lines in black ink. He then tore the page from the notebook, rolled the paper into a tube, and inserted it into the frame of his pack.

They were under decent cover now, all of the column, and the Rangers did not seem eager to descend the ravine. Perhaps they would pass the day without being discovered. A hundred outcomes rolled through Guevara's head, and he looked up the slope to a long green belt of trees about halfway up the east side of the ravine. It was steepest just below the top of the ridge; there was a short, vertical section of cliff maybe five or six feet tall, and then the trees stretched all the way to the top of the ridge and over it. The rocks seemed to surround a small hollowed-out place overlooking the canyon. It looked like a bit of an abandoned castle. Guevara recognized this spot as a key position of defense, and he cursed himself for not placing some men there. The small band of cliffs could not be seen until after sunrise, and now there was too much light and not enough cover. The comrades would have to stay as they were.

Guevara got onto his elbows and stretched his legs out behind him, aiming his rifle up the canyon. On the ridges, the Rangers could be seen moving around in squad-sized groups. They moved quickly between bands of trees and did not spend much time in the open. The enemy had the high ground, and Guevara knew that if the Rangers showed initiative, combat would be opened.

As the morning widened, Inti went to replace Begnino in his observation spot on the western slope. The night had passed as an agony to Begnino; the wound in his shoulder had become infected and seared him with pain. It had not hurt badly when he was first shot, but now it ached greatly, and he decided not to move back with the other invalids by the listening place and lay down on the ground. Begnino did not think he would live the day, and if contact came, he was not sure even if he could move. In his mind, he made preparations to die. For an hour, there had been no sound from the ridges, no noise or movement, and Guevara thought it safe to relieve the sentries. He sent one of the most able Bolivian comrades, Inti, toward Pombo's position on the opposite slope. Inti and Aniceto tried to slip across an open space back down into the bottom of the canyon. They were seen by a squad of Rangers.

There was a crashing of gunfire, first a dozen then twenty rifles firing from the ridgeline and both sides of the ravine. Bullets smashed down into the bottom of the canyon, knocking the bark from trees, setting leaves spinning into the air, and raining down a shower of broken twigs and splintered branches. Bullets spanged off the rocks and kicked up spherical clouds of dust across the open places. Aniceto was cut down by a pair of bullets; one entered his back between his shoulder blades, and an instant later, another struck him under his breastbone as he pitched forward. He landed on his face, his carbine still clutched in his hands and his eyes pinned open in astonishment.

As Aniceto fell, there were shouts from the hillside, the Rangers exultant. A machine gun opened up from a position behind Guevara, the soldiers firing blindly, though effectively, into the brush at the bottom of the ravine. Tracers exploded off the rocks and caromed into the sky, and Guevara's group returned fire, spraying bullets back up the ridges. Their barrage did little—Guevara and the others were below their enemies, and what shots they managed to aim passed harmlessly over the Rangers' heads. The column was surrounded on three sides, west, east, and north, and the sun was showing hard on the wide barren hill that closed off the canyon.

Pombo and Urbano had gone to cover behind a boulder and were taken under nearly continuous fire. They could not retreat; they had watched Aniceto fall and knew that if they tried to cross the open space, they would be killed. A grenade was thrown down at them—it exploded first in a ball of orange and black shot through with sparks, then the concussion shook the slope and brought up a thick swirl of dust. Pombo and Urbano used the cloud to run from their obvious cover. Expecting any second to be shot down, they sprinted desperately toward the place Inti had found refuge. They made it. Urbano and then Pombo jumped into the small hollow, and for a few moments, the shooting on both sides lulled slightly.

In the bottom of the ravine, Guevara ordered the sick to fall back.

"We'll do better to stay together," Moro said.

"You're in charge," Guevara told him. "Head for the thickest part of the trees."

Moro hesitated, and Guevara's expression darkened. "Get going."

"I'll see you on the other side of the hill," Moro said. It sounded like a wish.

Moro and El Chino helped each other up and ran crouched back up the canyon. As they left, Guevara trained his binoculars again on the patch of wood halfway up the eastern slope. The short cliff below would allow him to fire straight across the ravine and command both slopes. It could not be fired upon even from directly above. Guevara slipped his arms out of the pack straps and filled his pockets with extra magazines. He did this without speaking.

Finally, he said, "I'm going to try to get to that cliff. You can stay here if you want."

"Fuck that," Willy said.

Guevara stood, and though Willy felt a whirling sensation in his stomach, he dropped his pack and took up the extra ammunition. They moved down the ravine and then started to climb. They moved upslope, crawling on hands and knees where the hillside was steep, and they scrambled through brush and under several squat, bushy trees. They made it undetected to a position slightly under the short cliff, and as they settled down behind some boulders, there came the sound of voices slightly below them and across the canyon. An officer was leading a group of peasant militia off the ridge and into the canyon. He had them arrayed in line, like beaters, and he was driving them toward the belt of trees where Moro had fallen back with the sick.

Guevara peered around one of the boulders, his head low and his face nearly pressed in the dirt. He was able to observe the movement of the troops without being seen, and as the officer ordered a second squad to form a line, Guevara and Willy opened fire. Their shots scattered the attackers and dropped the officer and two of the militiamen onto the dusty incline. The officer's corpse slid down the hill, rolling and sinking, all loose-boned, and a curl of dust smoldered up after it. The body wedged up against a rock, and the other militia scattered away as fast as they could run. A regular sergeant yelled for them to take cover, realizing that the fire was being directed at them from across the ravine. Shouting and cursing, he grouped the militiamen, and they opened a determined fire across the canyon.

Guevara felt a sensation of heat, then sudden numbness, and recognized that two bullets had struck the rock in front of his face. He flinched backward, and as he did, he lifted the muzzle of his weapon. A third bullet passed close to him; this time Guevara solidly felt an impact in his shoulder. He thought at first he had been shot. A red tracer bullet smashed into the barrel of his rifle, showering sparks, driving the butt stock into his arm and twisting the carbine violently from his hands. His weapon spun through the air and tumbled end over end away from him.

There was a moment of silence, and then a second burst of fire split the air. Guevara was back on his haunches and no longer under cover; the top half of his body was visible, and the militia availed themselves of this target. The reflex was now Willy's, and without a thought, he threw himself on top of the comandante. A bullet punched into Guevara's calf; a second round took the beret from his head, and in the spattering dust, the pair moved back, Willy dragging Guevara uphill and into the spreading shade of a wide thicket.

They collapsed into the cover of the small cliff bastion, and Guevara pulled his leg around with two hands to inspect the wound. A neat black hole had been put through the muscle above his heel, but he did not think the bone was broken. The wound was not excruciating, not yet, but he could not bear weight on it, and he sat cursing. They were in a small depression about six feet deep and ten feet across. Bullets snapped overhead and broke off pieces of rock and cast them up into the air. Guevara was soaked with sweat, and when he checked his pistol, he was astounded to find that the magazine had fallen from it. His rifle was fifty meters away somewhere downslope; he was without a functional weapon.

They were safe only temporarily. Above them, the trees were dense, and the cover was abundant. The other comrades were out of sight, below them in a strip of trees that ran along the watercourse at the extreme south end of the canyon. The rifles of the enemy commanded the open space; it would not be possible to link up with the rest of the column until nightfall. They needed to find cover.

"Shit," Guevara said, "I can still move. We should try for the ridge."

Willy again felt the swirling sensation; he knew it was fear, terror even, but he made himself stand. He slung his rifle and helped Guevara up by lifting him under the armpit. Guevara wrapped his arm around Willy's shoulder, and together they hobbled uphill, twice skittering and falling when the gravel below them gave way. But they made steady progress, staying under a few short trees, and the firing went on below them.

Guevara looked back down the rocky slope; he felt exhausted and hollow, and there was the taste of vomit in his mouth. He swallowed this down and looked at the ridge above, where he could see a skyline. Willy saw this place and started to guide the comandante toward it.

"We've gotten out of worse than this, Comandante."

"Really?" Guevara said. "When was that?" And they both laughed.

They were nearly to the stand of trees on the ridgeline, and the shade of the place beckoned to them. Guevara tumbled a third time, and Willy bore him up, lifting him by the shirtfront, holding on to him to keep his leg steady. They came finally under the trees, and Guevara could feel his heart pounding in his chest. The exertion of climbing had brought the wet pain to his lungs, and he gulped air through clenched teeth.

They shoved themselves up a small, rocky ledge just below the trees. When they were bringing their feet under them, a squad of soldiers burst out of the brush. A sergeant pointed a rifle at them and yelled, "Drop your weapons and raise your hands!"

For a moment time stopped like a broken clock, the troops aiming down on them and the two guerrillas standing at mercy. These soldiers were Rangers, the first Guevara had seen up close; their faces were painted, and their eyes were wild. They looked to him like carnival devils.

Time passed—twinklings, instants, not even whole seconds—time gaped open. All of them felt it, the Rangers, too, split seconds that poised somewhere between present and future. In this glimmering was the uncertainty of whether the sergeant would shoot, and the question of whether his men would fire if he did not. Willy still carried his rifle, though it was slung over his shoulder and not in his hands.

Guevara had never in his life been so close under the weapons of an enemy; he stood three feet from the muzzle of the sergeant's rifle and could see a feral sort of joy in the man's eyes. Death yawned in front of him, and he wondered why it did not take him into its maw. There was a flicker of blame—it was stupid to have climbed this ridge.

Then the expanding seconds became normal seconds. Guevara felt the wind blowing on him, and strangely, he heard the sergeant's heavy breath rattling. He separated slightly from Willy. Willy's fingers moved toward his rifle strap, but Guevara's hand met his and he pulled the sling off his companion's shoulder. The weapon clattered to the dirt. One of the Rangers stepped forward and grabbed Guevara by the shirt, jerking him off his wounded leg. Guevara pitched over, and Willy set about the soldier, shoving him away.

"Shit," Willy spat, "this is Comandante Guevara, and he deserves some respect."

The word "Guevara" seemed to electrify the soldiers. There was a struggle, Willy shoving, and a Ranger struck him with a rifle butt.

"Shoot the fuckers!" one of the Rangers shouted.

The sergeant regained possession of himself and kicked Willy's ankles out from under him. Guevara and Willy were both on their knees, looking like filthy communicants kneeling at the altar in a church.

The sergeant jabbed his rifle directly into Guevara's face. "Say your name."

Guevara looked at the sergeant and said very calmly, "We are worth more to you alive than dead."

A soldier came forward and snatched Guevara's pistol from his holster. One of the painted faces shouted again: "Kill them!"

"One last time, *capullo*," the sergeant bellowed. "What is your name?"

Guevara knew in this instant that his life was as cheap as a beast's, and the words in his mouth felt like ashes.

"I am Che Guevara."

58

LA HIGUERA HAD been transformed from nowhere to a place of military significance, as much as a desperate, shabby place can be made important for anything. Troops came and went from the open ridge above the town, and more than a hundred soldiers were in its streets, setting up tents, digging rifle pits, marching away into the ravine and back. Almost four hundred more had taken up positions around the ridges, and helicopters were landing on the tops of the lower hills, placing squads of soldiers between the Yuro ravine and the Mizque River.

Valdéz had spent a quiet night in the home of the *corregidor,* and after a breakfast of *api* and a cold empanada, he had reason to smoke another cigar. The mood of the troops was euphoric. The bodies of three guerrillas had been brought up the steep track from the ravine in the morning, and then three prisoners, one of them important.

Valdéz was asked by Captain Cespedes to identify the captured man called Guevara, and he came forward to take a look as the wounded prisoner was led into town on the back of a mule. The man's hair was dirty and matted and his beard unkempt. Guevara's hands were tied with thick rope, and there was a bloody wound on his calf. With an air of resigned gallantry, he sat on the mule and ignored the jeers of the soldiers. Valdéz had never in his life laid eyes on Che Guevara; he had seen only photographs of the man, but these he had studied with great attention and hatred. Valdéz told Captain Cespedes that he was quite sure the prisoner was Che Guevara. Both men transmitted coded messages to their superiors.

Guevara was pulled down from the back of the mule, and two Rangers hobbled him across the small dusty square to a lopsided adobe building that served as La Higuera's small school. Guevara was shoved through the door and down several small steps onto dirt. The floor was somewhat lower than the level of the street; the room was cold, and an unhealthy damp held about the place. One of the Rangers stood and put a boot down on Guevara's waist, pinning him into the corner while his legs were bound together.

Light came through the open door, and Guevara stirred against his fetters but did not struggle. The feeling had long ago gone out of his hands, and his leg pounded after the ride up from the ravine. After he was bound, soldiers dragged in two bodies; Guevara could not see the faces. Heads drooped at the end of languid, flaccid necks, and then the corpses were dumped like garbage on the floor next to him: Antonio and Arturo. They had been on the west side of the ravine, the slope opposite from where Guevara was captured, and he looked down at their motionless, blood-smeared faces and could only wonder how much more of the column would be brought up and delivered into this room. It did not bode well that Arturo's arms were tied behind his back. He had almost certainly been captured and then executed. Their uniforms were ripped and spattered with blood, sweat, and splashes of red mud. Both of their faces were turned toward him, with dark hair tousled across their eyes. It was loneliness he felt now; he was alone, completely so, and separated from his command, his comrades, and the desperate fight in the canyon.

Guevara's watch had been taken from him, and he tried to make himself remember how many hours had gone by since his capture. He could not hear shooting anymore; the ravine was several kilometers distant, and anyway, the wind blew down it and away from La Higuera. It was now up to Inti and Pombo. Unless they got out of the canyon and over the mountains in the next twelve hours, the trap would close on them, and it would be the end. Perhaps it was the end now.

Guevara thought, *It would have been better, quicker, if I had kept fighting down in the bottom of the ravine. So much less trouble.*

There was a shadow at the door, and then it opened. An officer, a captain, bent around and stared at Guevara. The man was in a dress uniform, jodhpurs and riding boots. He looked like a military buffoon. Guevara was stirred with a righteous sort of anger—the other soldiers had now and again opened the door to peer in at him, but this one did not disdain to gape. He stood in his peaked cap and his ridiculous buttons, smirked without shame, lifted a camera, and took a picture. He aimed and took three more photographs, then backed out the door and latched it shut.

Guevara's leg began to throb. He moved it slightly, but the effort was agonizing. When his calf scuffed across the dirt floor, pain flashed behind his eyes like a bolt of lightning. Some time passed, and he let his head drop. He sagged down against the wall and onto his side. He forced himself to ignore the squalor and death around him and imagined a map unfolded; on it, his journey was laid out, up the Ñancahuazú and then down, and the wandering course to find Joaquin. In his mind he flew over the desperate, rolling country, the jungle and steep-sided rivers. They might all be nameless places. Guevara had discovered unhappily that men barely lived here, and political consciousness did not exist. A shadow fell across the landscape, it crept over the place like a malignant vapor, and he thought, *That is where I am now, in the center of the darkness.*

It was no wonder the Indians and peasants had watched the column pass through with silent, uninterested faces. Guevara had been shown how totally unsuitable was the Ñancahuazú for his operations. It was not merely the topography or the terrain, which were brutal; it was the scarcity of the peasantry on the ground. And where they were found, they were more like settlers or colonists. They aspired to nothing beyond getting in a little corn or raising a few pigs or pumpkins; their lives were short and their children's lives shorter—they clung stubbornly to Inca beliefs made over in the guilt-embroidered vestments of Catholicism, the religion shoved on them by their conquerors. They had been kept so long without hope or truth that they did not want anything that could not be explained by a child. Theirs was a legacy of misery and filth, wretched with deprivation and exploitation. They understood nothing of politics and believed only half of what the priests told them of God. They lived as they had lived for a thousand years. In La Paz the generals and the exploiters danced around a circle of chairs. Coup and countercoup had never brought even a ray of light into the countryside.

Guevara had started out convinced of the way he had chosen. He'd been certain that the presence of the guerrillas in the countryside would lift the eyes and consciousness of the people. It would make them see that a better life was theirs to be taken. The sacrifices of the guerrillas living among them would educate by example.

None of this had happened. The theory of the guerrilla nucleus, the *foco,* had again failed. Che Guevara's grandest and best-laid plan had recoiled, crushed by indifference. Since the first ambush, he and his group had been on the run, fighting, always winning, but never gathering strength. Sickness, betrayal, and the apathy of the peasants had eroded his force. The guerrillas had moved through the countryside, holding out truth and justice, moving, always moving, and the peasants had ignored them. Few had cooperated, and not a single person had come forward to join the vanguard. Nothing had been more fatal to him than the barren climate of their minds.

Guevara had placed a lever under the great stone of ignorance and heaved; it had not budged. He shook his head to think that he had escaped starvation and drowning and the elements, the limitations of the human body and his own asthma. A willpower he had polished with an artist's skill had carried his weak legs and tired lungs.

Guevara had triumphed over nature, but not over the nature of men.

THE FOLLOWING MORNING a table was brought out into the dirt street in front of the schoolhouse. Valdéz set up a small stand and began to photograph the pages of Guevara's diary. The last entry was Saturday, October 7, 1967, two days before. As Valdéz turned pages and clicked the shutter, a jeep came heaving down the rutted track from Jagüey. Valdéz paid it little attention until it stopped close to the schoolhouse and Hoyle climbed out.

Hoyle's clothing seemed darkened by soot. His shirt was torn, and there was blood on it. A thick bandage stretched across his right eye; it was yellow with dust from the road. He looked as though he had passed through fire; his hair was singed on one side of his head, and there was a dark ferocity about him.

"Where's Smith?"

"Just took off for La Paz. The Green Berets, too." Valdéz shook his head. "Shit, man, what happened to you?"

"Where's Guevara? Is he alive?"

"Yeah." Valdéz jerked his head at the schoolhouse. "He's in there. They captured him wounded."

Hoyle looked over at the table heaped with Guevara's belongings. Valdéz's radio was set up next to it. Wires for the antenna had been thrown over the roof of a nearby house.

"Do you have communications?"

"There's nobody at the casita. They sent a C-130 for Famous Lawyer. All the Americans are pulling out." Valdéz seemed to twitch with enthusiasm. "They're gonna waste the prisoners. Smith said he wanted all of us out of here before that happened."

"Get on the shortwave. I want to notify Langley and Ambassador Hielman."

Valdéz looked at Hoyle in disbelief. "What for?"

"I want Guevara out of here alive."

"You're wasting your time."

"Notify the action officers by name. Tell them I want an immediate response."

"Nobody's going to stick their neck out."

"Guevara's alive. That makes him a prisoner of war."

"This isn't that kind of war, Mr. Hoyle."

Hoyle walked across the small dirt square and toward the schoolhouse. A pair of Rangers stood outside the door, their weapons held at port arms. Hoyle heard a spotter plane pass overhead, and its buzzing made him grind his teeth. Valdéz called from across the sun-beaten little square, "Don't get in front of something you can't stop."

Hoyle entered the small room and was struck at once by the smell of blood. He saw first the two bodies heaped in the corner, their arms and legs intertwined, lying flat and still as broken statuary. Guevara was lying in the corner farthest from the door. His hands were bound tightly, and his ankles were tied in awkward soldier's knots.

Hoyle asked the Rangers to take the bodies outside, and as the soldiers came down into the room, Guevara pushed himself up by an elbow. Hoyle was surprised by the depth of his voice and its calm.

"If you're going to dump them out on the street, I'd prefer for you to leave them here."

The bodies would have indeed been piled behind the schoolhouse. Hoyle nodded his assent, and the Rangers walked from the room, closing the door behind them. The coppery smell of blood came again strongly, and also the stink of piss and sweat.

Hoyle sat on a table against the wall. Guevara saw the soot on Hoyle's clothing and the bandage drooping across his eye. He wondered if this person had slept in a burning house.

"What happened to the man who was captured with me?"

"Three of your men have been captured," Hoyle said.

"Are they alive?"

Hoyle nodded. "I don't know for how much longer."

Guevara heard the accent and understood why Hoyle had been obeyed by the soldiers. "You are not Bolivian."

"No."

"I wondered when the CIA would show its face."

Guevara looked at Hoyle closely. After a few moments, he recognized the slope of his shoulders and his sandy hair. He looked at the boots and Hoyle's olive-drab trousers.

"You're the man from the riverbank. The one with the black rifle. The day Rolando was killed."

Hoyle did not answer. It seemed like a thousand years ago. He felt the strength evaporate from his chest and legs; a silence lengthened between them, and then a Ranger opened the door and looked in curiously. When the door closed again, Guevara put his head back against the stucco wall.

"They tell me this is the local schoolhouse. Look at it. Look at this place. It isn't fit for pigs."

"In Cuba it would be a prison," Hoyle said.

Guevara grunted and bent his knees. "I suppose I should have expected them to send someone like you. A true believer."

There was almost nothing Hoyle believed in now, and surely he did not believe in himself.

"Do you see those boys there? In Cuba they had everything they could have ever wanted. Yet they came here and were shot down like dogs." Guevara's voice seemed empty. "We came here to give hope."

"Perhaps that's what you did."

Guevara looked at Hoyle as though something bitter had gotten into his mouth. "There is no hope for this place."

"I'm trying to have you taken to Panama. In CIA custody—for debriefing."

"Panama? Are you going to put me in a cage, like a monkey, to show the world?"

"Bolivian command authority has made the decision to execute you."

Guevara shook his head. "They won't kill me. Not yet. Not without a show trial."

"They don't want a trial. They only want you gone. They want you to disappear."

Guevara remembered the frequent broadcasts about the trial of Sandoval and D'Esperey; though both had confessed all they knew about the guerrilla column, the spectacle had been an embarrassment for La Paz. He thought for a moment, and it occurred to him that even if he were set free this instant, there was really no place he could go.

"Why would you want to help me?"

"Maybe we both wanted the same things to happen here," Hoyle said.

"You don't strike me as the progressive type."

"I'm not." Hoyle leaned forward from the table. His hands gripped the edge of it, and he turned his face so that his good eye took in the man propped in the corner. "You were sacrificed," he said. "Your friends in Havana pulled the plug on you—Fidel, the DGI, the Russians, too. It was over before you ever got here. And you never knew."

"No . . . I don't believe that."

"Your communications. We monitored them."

Guevara shrugged.

"You told Fidel, 'Do not fail to open a second front.' "

"I won't discuss operational matters with you."

"He burned you, and then he handed over your entire operation to the Russians."

"That is not true," Guevara said. "We came to a place that was beyond help. I should have seen that. Before we were beyond help ourselves." He paused, looking at the bodies. "I never should have been captured."

"You shouldn't be murdered, either."

Guevara smiled sourly. "A moralist. On a battlefield. You must be a very lonely man."

. . .

HOYLE AND VALDÉZ stood next to the radio. Captain Cespedes sat against the wall, smoking a cigarette, quite satisfied that the ravine was surrounded and the bodies of four more bandits were being brought up by mule. Hoyle pressed one of the earphones against his head and listened to the interminable, empty static. Valdéz had sent the messages Hoyle had requested, but there was no answer. The static rolled on, a white empty hiss. It was slowly over this noise that Hoyle perceived the distant thump of rotor blades.

A helicopter landed on the flat place above the village, and two officers came directly toward the schoolhouse, a major walking a bit behind a colonel. The colonel wore a green tunic with gold shoulder braid, and there was a large silver-winged creature on the front of his cap.

The colonel pointed at Captain Cespedes. "You. What's your name?"

The captain tossed away his smoke and came to his feet. "Cespedes, sir. Machego Número Dos."

"Why haven't my orders been carried out?"

"I asked the captain to delay the execution," Hoyle said. "We're still photographing their papers, Colonel. Including Comandante Guevara's battle journal."

"That can be done when the criminals have been executed." The colonel started into the schoolhouse.

Hoyle reached out a hand in front of him. "Look, we're all just taking orders here, right? I'm trying to contact Washington. They might want him alive."

The colonel looked at Hoyle, and his expression was taut. "And then what? This isn't just some *compañero*. Some bandit. If Guevara were to be imprisoned in Bolivia, he would be a magnet for more mercenaries from Cuba."

"He won't be in Bolivian custody. I want to fly him to Panama for debriefing."

"It's too late," the colonel said. "Presidente Barrientos has announced our victory. He has informed the nation that Che Guevara was killed in action at the Yuro ravine."

. . .

IN THE DIRTY little square of La Higuera, Captain Cespedes held out five straws. The shortest was drawn by Sergeant Merán, who waved it in the air and said rather mildly, "I'll shoot the son of a bitch."

The second shortest straw was drawn by a corporal whose brother had been killed in the ravine. He seemed bitterly joyous as he unslung his rifle, peeled back the action, and checked that a bullet was lodged in the chamber. Hoyle looked across the street; three guerrillas had been brought up alive from the ravine and had been forced to sit in the sun against a low wall made of dust-colored brick. They had been questioned but would not even give their names, and Hoyle and Valdéz watched as Rangers came and prodded them toward an ambulance parked a slight way off.

The corporal who'd drawn the second shortest straw walked past, and his eyes were like droplets of metal. Somewhere a rooster crowed, and Hoyle watched as the prisoners were pushed down to their knees. The corporal walked toward them, carrying his rifle in one hand. As he came close, the other soldiers stood back. The wind blew like it does before a storm.

"Get to a land line. Try Zeebus at the embassy," Hoyle said.

"I did. There's nothing. They've all gone dark."

Hoyle could not avert his eyes from the men kneeling next to the ambulance. The corporal aimed, and three shots rolled out over the hills, long recurring thuds that echoed off the hillsides.

HOYLE OPENED THE door and stepped down into the room. Merán entered behind him. The door closed, and Guevara's eyes fell on Merán, who wore the obvious expression of an executioner.

Hoyle felt a sick sort of blankness; the thing that propelled him had evaporated. He felt without a purpose, and as Guevara turned against his fetters, he looked into Hoyle's face.

"Ah. The suspense is ended," Guevara said.

"I did what I could," Hoyle said.

"I wonder if you would do me the courtesy of helping me to stand."

Hoyle crossed to the corner of the room and helped Guevara to his feet. Leaning against the wall, he balanced on his wounded leg, finally placing his foot down on the ground so he could stand.

"Vanity is one of my many faults."

Hoyle took a step back toward Merán and was ashamed for it. Guevara heard sounds from outside the door: the crackle of radios, the noise of marching soldiers, then jeering again.

"There is a letter rolled into the frame of my pack. I assume you've found it."

"We found it," Hoyle said.

"I would appreciate it if you would see that it reaches my family."

"I'll do that," Hoyle said. The emotion in his voice did not have a name. "I'm sorry."

"Don't be. On another day, it might have been you standing against the wall."

By a great exertion, Hoyle moved toward the door; he felt as though the world would cave in. He had never in his life embraced the emotion of pity, but it pulled at him now, and a measure of futility made it bitter. Merán lifted his rifle and switched it from safe to automatic. Hoyle plainly heard the small click. Guevara gazed steadily at the man who would take his life.

The distance between Merán and Guevara was almost a dozen feet. Merán seemed unwilling to get closer; even bound and wounded, Guevara seemed to have in him the strength and wiles of a tiger.

Guevara's brown eyes shone brightly and his voice was even: "Go on, do your duty."

Merán fired in the middle of the last word, and Guevara's knees buckled as he fell back against the wall. As he toppled, he turned his face toward Hoyle. He lifted his wrist to his mouth, and his teeth bore down on his flesh as he tried not to cry out. His breath came from him in short, hard gasps, and his eyes blinked narrowly. His face became a mask of indomitable resolve.

Hoyle did not look away. Guevara gulped a breath and held it as Merán stepped forward and aimed a second time.

Guevara lifted his head from the dirt floor and looked Merán straight in the eyes. His teeth clenched together, and he said, "Today . . . you are shooting a man."

Merán fired again; the bullet struck Guevara in the heart, killing him instantly.

.   .   .

HOYLE LOOKED OUT into the sky. His eyes saw cloud and cobalt, but his mind did not register. He looked out of the moving helicopter, and the sky was a domain of pure and perfect silence, though the engine roared, and above him the rotors beat the air. At his feet, Che Guevara's body lay wrapped in a muddy poncho. The corpse was trussed up with rope and bound like a parcel: a dreadful gift for the republic.

Valdéz sat behind the pilots, his rifle held between his knees. Hoyle was seated in the open door, looking back and down. He had never been so tired in his life; his arms and legs seemed like ropes of clay, and it was only with great effort that he kept himself from pitching forward into a coma-like sleep. Hoyle lifted his face into the wind, and the sun blinked through the clouds. The light dazzled him, and for a split second, it was as though he had been consumed by fire, gulped into a smear of orange. He felt as if he'd been struck by some invisible force, a blow that had short-circuited his senses. Thought, emotion, memory—all were pried away from the coil of his body. The light was so abrupt and concentrated that he dissolved before it. Hoyle felt that he had been made into a vapor; he had become a ghost, no longer flesh, just a cloud of particles hurled over the land. The sensation lasted only a few seconds, then his mind clamped itself back under the dome of his skull, and his heart thumped in his chest. Compounding his bewilderment, he seemed to have returned to his body the second *before* the sun ray struck him. Hoyle blinked in wonder and fear; Valdéz shifted in his seat, moving his rifle from hand to hand, exactly as he had done the moment earlier. Hoyle told himself it was only déjà vu, a trick of memory, but this excuse gave no comfort. The time he had been cast from his body seemed like ten thousand years of banishment. Hoyle was left with the dread feeling that he was condemned to ride in this helicopter forever, sitting for eternity across from Valdéz, with blood on his hands and a corpse at his feet.

Hoyle looked down and saw the red dirt of the Vallegrande airfield heaving up under the skids; dust blew into the sky, and the helicopter settled. A panel truck rolled to a stop in front of the still-churning helicopter. The Huey's engine faded in a protracted whine. Hoyle slid from his seat and stood on the port skid as Guevara's body was pulled from the aluminum deck of the cabin and loaded into the truck.

As the corpse was handed over, a thick black trickle of blood oozed from a sag in the tarp and spilled into the gasping dirt. The doors of the van were held open, and a Bolivian officer gestured for Hoyle to come into the back of the vehicle with the body.

Hoyle lifted his fingers to the bandage across his eye and said to Valdéz, "You go with them."

Valdéz got into the van and pulled closed the doors. The truck rolled away toward the Señor de Malta Hospital, at the edge of town. There, Guevara's corpse would be washed by the sisters of the hospital and laid out on the sinks in the laundry. The face that had been haunted by frustration and passion was now calm; they sponged the thin, almost skeletal body and combed the hair out of his face. A hundred photographs would be taken of Che Guevara hauled out onto the cement sinks with his mouth ajar and his eyes open and bright. Townspeople, journalists, and military officers would all file past to make certain that the phantom of the Ñancahuazú had been after all only a man of flesh and blood.

In the night, after the pictures had all been taken, a fat-faced colonel came from La Paz to see that the body was buried in a secret place off the runway. Under a small moon, Guevara's hands were sawed off and placed in a jar of formaldehyde, a ghastly trophy for the generals. The bodies of Guevara and the others were tossed into a slit trench and bulldozed over. No marker or stone would be placed over their common grave. The story would be put about that Che Guevara had been cremated and his ashes dumped into the Rio Grande. To the killers in La Paz, deceit on top of murder did not seem a very great offense.

Hoyle walked half a mile from the helicopter to the casita at the far end of the airfield. He found the small house empty. The Green Berets were gone, their tents struck and their weapons and radios all scooped up and borne away. The place howled of abandonment.

Hoyle stumbled in. His head pounded, his limbs were stiff, and he collapsed on the cot and stared with one bleary eye at the ceiling beams. Somewhere a beetle crashed against the walls, flew in circles, and hit the stucco again and again.

After a few moments of gloomy silence, a flicker of self-loathing clutched at him; it took hold like a flame creeping over dried kindling. A cold, bitter light was put out by this flame of judgment. Hoyle imagined the serial failures of his life, his childhood, his marriage, his career in the agency. A succession of small and large calamities loomed behind his eyes; his life seemed to be a train of self-inflicted disasters instead of accomplishment. For his sins, he'd been sent to the end of the world and made an accomplice to shameful murder.

Why hadn't he done something? Why hadn't he taken Guevara away?

The men in the ravine and what they'd set out to do had been blown away, and there was nothing else to be done; no way for slaughter to be undone or for the dead to be made to walk upright and smile and go home to their families. Hoyle thought of the three prisoners marched behind the ambulance and of the corporal who'd calmly placed a muzzle against the back of their heads. Guevara had heard the shots before Hoyle came in with Merán; he had heard the shots that killed his companions, men loyal unto death, and then death came for Guevara, too. Hoyle had carried it in like an errand boy delivering a bill.

A useless idea of suicide came, and Hoyle remembered all at once the letter that had been found concealed in Guevara's backpack. His hand went to the pocket of his shirt, and he unrolled it.

The paper was jagged at the top, where it had been pulled from a spiral pad, and the handwriting ran across the lines in a fluid cursive. The ink was smeared on the edges where water had soaked through it, and stains worked along the folded creases. Hoyle held the paper up in the orange light that came through the open door, the last light of a day filled with dust and blood.

8 October 1967

My Aleida,

 If one day you read this letter, it will be because I have come to the end of my journey. I have tried to be a man who acted according to his beliefs. Many will call me an adventurer, and I am, but of a different type—of those who place their lives in the balance to demonstrate the truth.

 If my modest efforts have freed one person—saved one mind from enslavement—I will have succeeded. I depart a country and a people who received me as a son. And now I must leave you, the one perfect and beautiful thing in this world, and that wounds my spirit. Know always that I have loved you, only I have not known how to show my love. With you remains the purest of my hopes and the most precious part of my life.

If this final hour finds me under other skies, my last thoughts will be of you. Remember once in a while the tender lover who held you in moonlight. Remember the tears you have kissed from my eyes. My love to our precious children. I embrace you through eternity.

Che.

59

HOYLE STOOD ON the stairs and looked into the alcove of Maria's apartment. The door was off its hinges, and what he could see inside was the debris of looters. He felt that someone was watching him from the street and turned to see a pair of small, intense faces, with dark eyes and frowns, glinting up at him from the stairs. Two neighborhood kids stood with their hands on the metal banister. The silent children knew what Hoyle was just apprehending, that after Maria had been attacked, her neighbors had come into the apartment and taken what they wanted, furniture, plates and pots and pans, the curtains, even her clothing. The children had climbed the stairs behind him, and they turned and ran back down onto the sidewalk and away.

Hoyle stepped from the landing into the apartment. He'd never been inside, he'd only seen a glimpse of the place, a corner of it through the window on the night he'd seen Maria and Alameda. He could not imagine that neat, bright room now. It did not seem possible to even remember the bolt of emotion that had torn through him that night; his pain and humiliation seemed like an small, meaningless fact committed to memory.

Hoyle's shoes crunched shattered glass. The light through the broken windows came unevenly around him. The place was smashed up beyond the violence necessary for looting. Daubed in red paint on the wall were the words COMUNISTA, TRAIDORA, PUTA. He knelt and lifted a photograph from the floor; it was in a cracked wooden frame, and he poured the shards from the print and angled it into the light. What remained of the picture showed Maria standing on a beach, the sea the color of lapis lazuli. With her stood an older woman, her mother, definitely, for the lines of her face were the same, and the green eyes held the camera. In the photograph Maria was smiling, but her mother was not. She had about her an unsettled, anxious look, as though she had been troubled by a premonition. The photograph seemed like a mirror held up to a mirror of calamity.

"Hello?" he said into empty space.

A small sound came from the kitchen. It did not even at first seem to be a voice, merely the echo of wreckage.

"I'm here," Maria said.

Hoyle moved to the small room Maria used to prepare her meals. The cabinets hung open and had been swept empty; the stove had been pried away from the wall. Maria leaned against one of the counters by the water tap. Her lip was cut at the corner, and there were the yellow smudges of bruises on her throat and arms.

When he saw her, Hoyle felt as though he were a small scuttling creature, absurd and empty of anything. He did not try to escape by turning away his gaze. He looked directly at Maria, and she at him. There were a few long seconds when their silence was a curtain behind which anything could happen.

Maria saw the cuts and the bandage over his eye. Beyond his obvious injuries, there was something anxious and defeated about him. He seemed like a man who needed hope no longer: His end had come.

Maria remembered too well the things that had happened to her, the beating that had nearly killed her, her surreptitious convalescence, and the doctor from the embassy who'd helped her, but she had no idea what had happened to Hoyle. She inclined her head and started to form a question. Hoyle shook his head.

"I missed you at the safe house," he said. "The doctor said you left yesterday."

"I appreciate all they did for me. I couldn't stay there any longer."

"I'm sorry, Maria. I'm sorry this has happened."

Her eyes closed for moment, a gesture like surrender. She said, "Other people did this, not you."

Hoyle had dreamed of her so many times since the moment in the café; he'd wished ten thousand times that things were different, and until this moment, he had not specifically known what it was that he wanted. A thin strip of light came through one of the windows—it was ocher-colored, city light, and it lay like a discarded bit of crepe paper on the floor between them. With difficulty, Hoyle took a step toward her. His foot came down on a bit of broken glass, and it snapped under his shoe. Hoyle lifted up his arms, and Maria staggered into the space between them.

"I'm sorry. I'm so goddamn sorry," he said.

He held her tightly and pressed his face against her hair. Something seemed to break in her, and she began to weep. Her face was buried in his shoulder. She was saying something; he could not hear the words.

It had seemed so simple once, love and its opposite, and for a moment he pretended he understood, then he felt empty with the effort.

"I love you," he said.

Three simple words, and for the first time in his life, he expected nothing in return. His keenness to possess her had imploded. He did not expect her to say that she loved him, or even acknowledge his feelings. He said it because it was one true thing; he did not think she loved him, or had ever loved him.

It did not matter.

As he held her, his brain burned with the smell of her skin, and what he had in his heart for her he understood would not be given back. Hoyle knew that even if she did say the three words, they would be empty. He still loved her, more, much more, than he loved himself; the emotion inside him had come through everything—violence, jealousy, self-conscious grieving, and bitter hopelessness. He knew she did not love him. She had never pretended; she had affection for him, but it was not love. And it would not become love, not now.

How could it? Look at what had happened. He had caused this.

"What are you going to do? Where are you going to go?" he whispered. "You can't stay here, Maria."

"I was only a small part of this. Of things that were . . . bigger than my life. And now . . . I've lost everything."

Hoyle closed his eye and rocked her in his arms.

He felt the bandage on his eye press against her face, and he thought, *We are all lost.*

. . .

THE AIRPORT WAS a white cement building with a short glass-sided control tower perched in its middle. Its only ornamentation was a vaguely Incan frieze above the rectangular black-trimmed windows: masks with empty, pining expressions and grinning teeth. Hoyle pulled the Land Cruiser to the curb and slipped a few Bolivianos to a porter at the sidewalk.

"*Uno momento, Señor. Y entonces me piro,*" he said.

Hoyle opened the trunk and dragged out a small overnight bag and an attaché case. He placed these on the curb and helped Maria from the passenger seat. A pair of grim-faced military policemen watched him lead Maria into the terminal. The building inside was low-ceilinged, with a gray terra-cotta floor and fluorescent lights. The counter for Pan American Airways was a small three-agent affair, with one line reserved for first class. Hoyle walked to the head of this line and placed the overnight bag on the scales. "*Madrid y Vienna.*"

He waved the tickets at the agent, who looked vexed and started to say something about the flight's imminent departure. Hoyle's good eye rolled over the small, aggrieved woman, and she clammed up in midsyllable. There were tickets only for Maria, and the agent thought that both these people must have been in some kind of accident.

Holding Maria's hand, Hoyle took her toward a customs desk under a blue sign near the back of the building. A gray-suited immigration officer took the papers from Hoyle, opened the cover, and ran his eyes over the document. Maria's picture was affixed to an Austrian passport bearing the name Michel Nemick. The officer noticed at once that Maria was wearing the same dress as in the photograph and that her face was bruised in exactly the same manner. He noticed, too, that the passport was uncreased, though there were several visas stamped into it. As the officer examined her papers, Maria held her breath and heard a roaring in her ears. Two crisp fifty-dollar notes were tucked into the cover, and pretending to examine the visas, the customs officer placed the passport on the shelf under the counter. As he inked the stamp, his thumb glided the money from the pages. The bribe was not technically necessary. Maria's passport was of extremely high quality, the finest Soviet forgery, but the officer had already processed the flight's passengers and was not disposed to do anything else. Like everyone, the officer had a price, and exigency was factored into it. He handed the passport back to Maria.

"*Goce del vuelo.*" The officer gave a faint, insincere smile of complicity.

After the muted light of the terminal, the sky above the tarmac seemed astonishingly bright and the runway flat and vast. Outside the awning, a gaggle of passengers stood around the apron, waiting to be called forward by the stewardesses. As she stared about at the other passengers, Maria realized, slowly, that she really was going to leave Bolivia. She could not smile, even though she felt a great lightness of heart building in her. She could not trust the circumstances, she dared not, and thus she did her best to push down the emotion. She was still shaken from the brush with the customs man; she looked around and saw another policeman standing off to the side of the terminal. He carried a short, deadly-looking weapon—it frightened her like a broken promise.

Maria had experienced an odd sense of liberation when the officer handed back the passport—a snare that she had slipped through. And until this moment, none of the preparations or Hoyle's sincere reassurances during the long drive up from La Paz had meant anything to her. Now she saw the airplane, heard it, and she began timidly to hope again. Hoyle walked Maria out onto the tarmac and steered her toward the edge of the crowd. She listened to the whine of the engines starting one by one, and she smelled the sharp tang of kerosene as the plane began to make ready.

A woman in a plaid coat eyed them with the same wary disgust as the ticket agent. Hoyle's size and the gauze stuck over his eye gave him the menacing look of a pirate, something his intense demeanor did nothing to dispel. He waited until the plaid coat moved away, and he handed Maria the attaché case.

"There's five thousand dollars sewn into the lining. When you get to Vienna, contact the name in the address book. Tell her you're a friend of the organization. She'll get you new documents and an Austrian identity card. Pick a name and start a new life."

Maria held Hoyle and felt tenderness and gratitude, but also a building and gnawing sense of dread. Tears ran off her nose. She lifted her eyes toward the airplane, now humming and blowing and ready to fly, and fear clutched her. She felt like she was standing on the edge of a yawning, empty chasm.

"Please come with me."

"No. You deserve more than I can give."

Maria kissed him, and as she held him, she said again, "Please, Paul, please come with me."

Hoyle kept his arms about her, and though he'd been certain his heart was past being broken, he felt it divide inside him.

"I am afraid," Maria said. She could hardly see through her tears.

Hoyle held Maria and pictured her walking on a street in Vienna with snow falling around. He imagined a gray sky spread over her and snow clean and white and covering everything. He would no longer have the comfort of her; he said inwardly to himself that he must not even think of her any longer.

A stewardess descended the wheeled staircase placed against the plane. She waved a white glove at the crowd, and it edged forward, businessmen in jackets and ties and women in hats.

"Go. Make yourself a home, Maria. Give yourself a new life. Go and never think of this place again."

Hoyle embraced her one last time and then opened his arms to let her go, as he had let go of every other precious thing in his life. "Just go."

Maria reeled toward the airplane. As she climbed the stairs, she tried to remember what she had felt for Hoyle, but these recollections all seemed so distant that they cast no light into her mind. She knew he loved her; she'd heard him plainly when he said the words. She thought, *How wicked I must be.* She was leaving behind a man who loved her, and perhaps she was abandoning all love forever. Once she might have taken a different path, but it was too late now. She began to hate herself for accepting safety—hers was to be the unwavering guilt of a survivor. She was being allowed to go on living, though the wound in her heart was so great that it did not even occur to her to thank the man who'd delivered her from evil.

Hoyle stood alone on the tarmac and watched as the door of the airplane closed. As he turned, he saw Cosmo Zeebus walking toward him as fast as he could. "What's the hurry, Cosmo?"

The fat man seemed surprised to see Hoyle. "A warrant has been issued for her arrest."

"What for?"

"The murder of Colonel Arquero."

"She had nothing to do with that."

Zeebus shifted on his feet. He was looking about for the mechanics to put the stairs back against the airplane. "There's an Interpol red notice on her," Zeebus said, and he tried to brush past.

Hoyle lifted his arm to block him. "Let it slide."

"Not this time, Hoyle. The warrant came from the president's office."

"It's bullshit."

"It's real. She's a material witness in an assassination. You should have told me she was involved."

"She had nothing to do with it." This time Hoyle physically checked Zeebus from advancing.

Zeebus's eyes flashed. "Listen, Hoyle," he said. "You have no status here." "Status" meant diplomatic immunity. Hoyle was as open to police arrest as anyone else in Bolivia. Zeebus stepped past Hoyle and was brought to a halt by a distinct and fatal-sounding click.

He turned, they both did, and Smith stood close by. "Forget it, Cosmo," Smith said. "Just stand here and wave goodbye."

Smith had a newspaper in his hand, and sticking out from under it was the short barrel of a .38-caliber revolver. The weapon was aimed at Zeebus's belly.

"You're not going to shoot me, Smith. Not here. Not in front of a hundred people."

Smith's other hand dipped into his jacket. He pulled out a sheaf of paper. "This is a draft cable to the Directorate of Operations. A special addendum to the after-action report. You might be interested, Cosmo. It's all about you."

"What are you talking about?" Zeebus lifted his hand toward the paper. Hoyle watched as Smith lifted it up out of his reach.

"The guns you sold to Arquero?" Smith glanced over the paper. "Four hundred carbines and a hundred grease guns? Twenty-five thousand rounds of ammunition? Astounding."

Zeebus almost flinched at the words. "That was authorized," he stammered, "by Langley."

"But you lost control of the goods," Hoyle said. "Arquero turned around and sold your rifles to the guerrillas. That sounds like dereliction of duty. Now, how would that look in *The Washington Post*? 'CIA Sells Arms to Cuban Communists'?"

Zeebus started to go pink, then gray. "Arquero sold them, not me."

"*You* sold them to Arquero." Hoyle shook his head. "Face it, Cosmo.

KILLING CHE

Your contact single-handedly equipped the Bolivian insurgency. How's that going to look in your 201 file?"

The fat man clenched his jaw. The lights of Berlin flickered and went out.

On the runway, the engines were loud now, and the big plane turned about on one set of wheels and rolled unhurriedly down the taxiway.

"So here's the deal," Smith said. "We shred this—"

Zeebus grunted. "In exchange for what?"

"She travels. Zero interference from you," Hoyle said.

"What am I supposed to do about Interpol?"

"That's your problem. Make the red notice go away, or we cable Langley about your guns."

"You wouldn't do that."

"We might do it anyway, you asshole," Smith said.

Zeebus looked at the plane. "Give me the cable," he said, panting. "Deal?"

"Fuck you, Hoyle. Yes, deal." Zeebus's fat hand flapped. "Gimme the goddamn cable."

Smith placed the pistol in the pocket of his jacket and tossed the paper at Zeebus. Engines roared; the plane took a long roll and climbed slowly into the sky, pulling behind it a thin brown trail of soot.

Zeebus crumpled the paper and jammed it into a pocket. "No more favors. You're finished, Hoyle. You're little people from now on."

Smith and Hoyle walked to the terminal.

Zeebus called after Hoyle, "I hope she was worth it."

Hoyle did not look back. They walked through the glass doors and out into the parking lot. In the west, the sun was bright but very close to the horizon. It was the time for parting; the longer they stayed together, the greater the complications would be.

"I normally make it a point not to expect acts of valor from other people," Hoyle said.

Smith said nothing. His expression was impossible to read. He'd attended the press conference where Presidente Barrientos had claimed Che Guevara was killed in battle. Not murdered, but fallen on an honorable field of combat. Smith knew that the other guerrillas captured in the Yuro ravine had also been killed—martyrs for an idea and grist for the machine.

Hoyle stopped at the Land Cruiser and put his hand on the door. "You said this was just another shithole—"

"It still is," Smith said. There was no contempt in his voice. He, too, felt a sense of blame.

"Then why did you help me?"

"It took me a while to figure out that the questions are black and white, and all the answers are gray."

Smith had satisfied himself; he had done one thing for someone else. He might have done more, if possible, but he had made a small act of contrition. Smith had turned his back and let murder happen—Guevara's destruction had, after all, been his mission—but now he had made for himself a quiet conscience.

Smith looked back at the terminal. They both knew the sanctions that would be taken against them might not be merely administrative and professional. They might be physical.

"He was serious about little people. How are you going to get out of here?"

"Disappearing is the easy part," Hoyle said.

Smith put out his hand. "Good luck to you, Mr. Hoyle."

Hoyle had a feeling that he was jinxed and that luck, if it ever again attended to him, would not be good. Hoyle took Smith's hand and said, *"Buena suerte."*

Hoyle dipped behind the wheel of the Land Cruiser and pulled off into the traffic in front of the terminal.

He turned onto the dusty airport road, and then northwest, away from the city. The road dipped toward the sun, but Hoyle did not have a destination. It was a thousand kilometers of hard, unknown country to anyplace that might give refuge. To the northeast was Cochabamba, and west from there, Peru and jungle rivers twisting to the sea. It was the same distance south and east through the Chaco to Paraguay; and closer but more dangerous was the frontier to Chile. They would wait for him there; his face was known, this vehicle, too. Hoyle would head north.

The awful jumble of the last few months swirled in his brain, and he told himself that none of this would ever be his business again. An enterprise that had once been only mercenary had turned rotten. A hundred dishonorable facts were already growing walls like cells in a wasps' nest. Hoyle would exile them in a desert place in his brain. He knew, unhappily, he hadn't the strength of character to do otherwise.

There was an envelope in his pocket. Folded in half and half again was Guevara's letter to his wife. It would mean nothing to Zeebus, nor would it have figured into Smith's reports. Hoyle would post it to one of the addresses found among Tania's papers—one that would forward the letter on to Havana. Hoyle would do this once he was safe.

It was mostly dark behind him and the hulking mass of Huayna Potosí was drenched in orange light. Below it, the lesser peaks of the Cordillera Real clumped together like penitents wanting absolution. Hard shadows came up from the roadway. It seemed a forever distance to the place where the sun was touching the horizon—an insurmountable journey—but Hoyle drove on.

Acknowledgments

I have many people to thank, not just for help and encouragement while I wrote this novel, but for keeping me among the living. Love to Stacey, my wife, and to Paddy, my son, who reminded me that there is more in the world than the inside of other people's heads. I owe you.

Thanks to my father and mother, who have cheered me on, checked my homework, tucked me in, and patched me up long after I might have been expected to quit running into brick walls. I'm a singularly lucky man. Thanks to my dear friends Downs and Marianne Mathews, old hands in the writer's game who lent a keen eye and blue pencil to early drafts. This book is better because of you.

Gracias siempre to a friend and comrade who wishes to remain anonymous, Operator 143, who more than any other person advised on strategy, paid attention to the narrative, predicted the unpredictable, rallied the troops, and kept me on the trail through a long and arduous campaign.

Thanks also to readers of early drafts who put eyes on and told me where I was going: David Freed, Doug Stanton, Dr. Mac-Daddy Evans (himself a damn fine novelist), Karl and Nan Couyoumjian, Bob and Pam Currey, and photojournalist Steve Rowe. Liz Grenemyer, who told me of boarding school in Germany, and again my pop, whose own experiences added to the descriptions of war in the jungle. I had help with clandestine work from a trio who wish to remain anonymous, old Company hands who have moved behind the curtain on the stages of history: Thanks to the Count, Fuzzy, and Mr. BPA.

My agents—not secret but literary—Julia Lord and Joel Milliner, need to be mentioned as friends and wiser souls. Special thanks to my editor, Bob Loomis, at Random House, who patiently helped me through the underbrush and who again took a chance on me. *Tu etes el Jefe*. Thanks also to Dennis Ambrose and Beth Thomas for diligent copyediting and preparation of the manuscript.

Thanks to David Lindroth for the maps that accompany this book. The originals were drawn by my own somewhat shaky hand and bore only grudging resemblances to facts on the ground in Bolivia. Apologies also for the spellings of place-names; many are words taken from the Quecha language and are inconsistently rendered in the source material. Again, any irregularities or mistakes are my own. Thanks a million to Lance Moody and Mike Kirton, two comrades who never stopped believing.

If this book seems realistic in historical detail it is because of the scholarship of the biographers of Che Guevara, among them Henry Butterfield Ryan (*The Fall of Che Guevara: A Story of Soldiers, Spies, and Diplomats*), Jorge Castañeda (*Compañero: The Life and Death of Che Guevara*), and Jon Lee Anderson (*Che Guevara: A Revolutionary Life*).

My work was informed by hundreds of other sources, including Che Guevara's own writing and those of his comrades in the Ñancahuazú, the survivors, and those who sacrificed all. A list of historical and biographical material, as well as a brief epilogue, can be found on my website at www.killingche.com.

CHUCK PFARRER is the author of *Warrior Soul: The Memoir of a Navy SEAL*. A counterterrorism consultant to the U.S. and foreign governments, he is also a screenwriter whose credits include *The Jackal, Darkman, Red Planet, Hard Target, Virus,* and *Navy SEALs*. He lives in Michigan.

ABOUT THE TYPE

This book was set in Galliard, a typeface designed by Matthew Carter for the Merganthaler Linotype Company in 1978. Galliard is based on the sixteenth-century typefaces of Robert Granjon.